RECALL

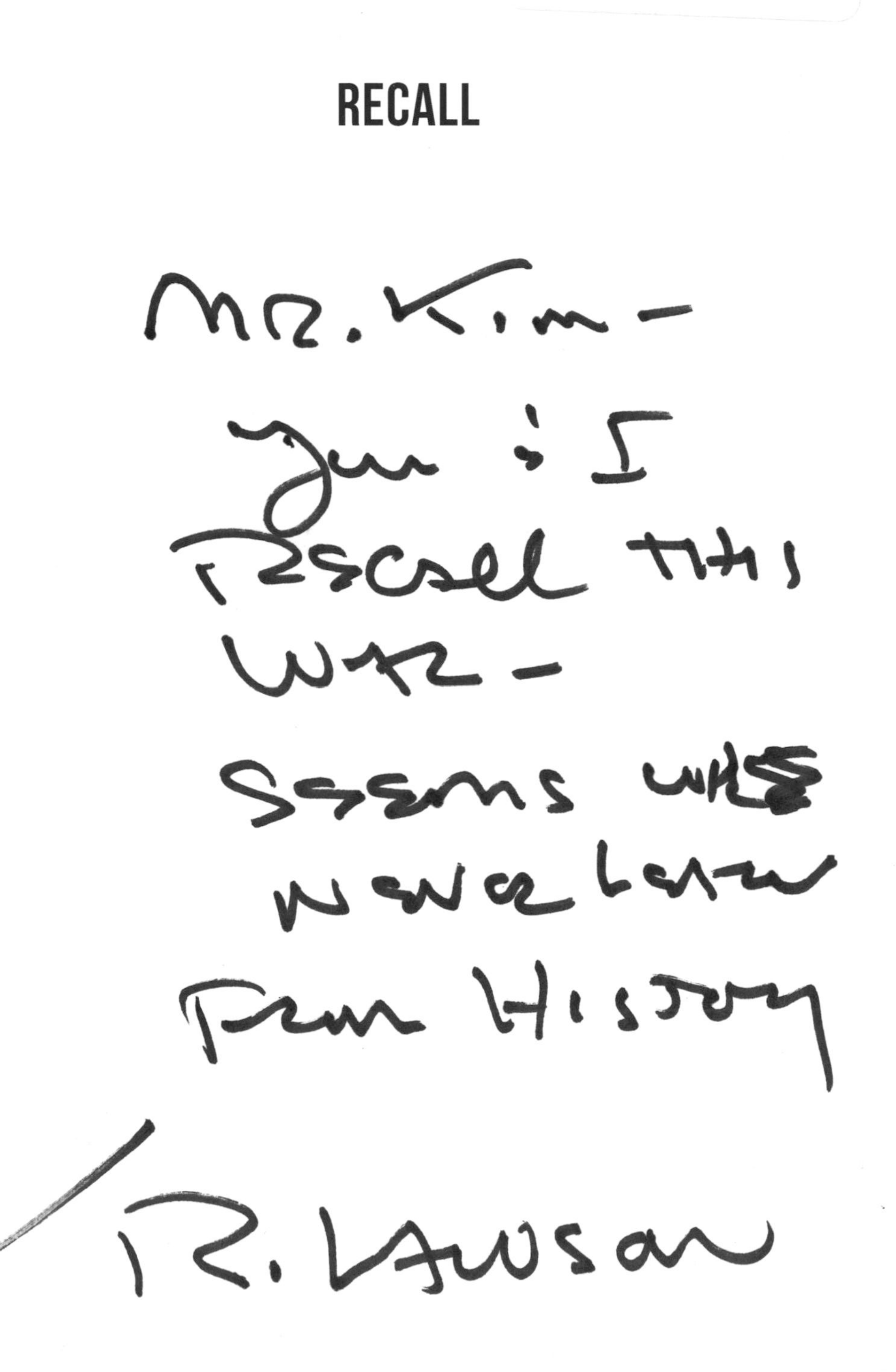
Mr. Kim –
You & I
recall this
war –
seems like
never learn
from History
R. Lawson

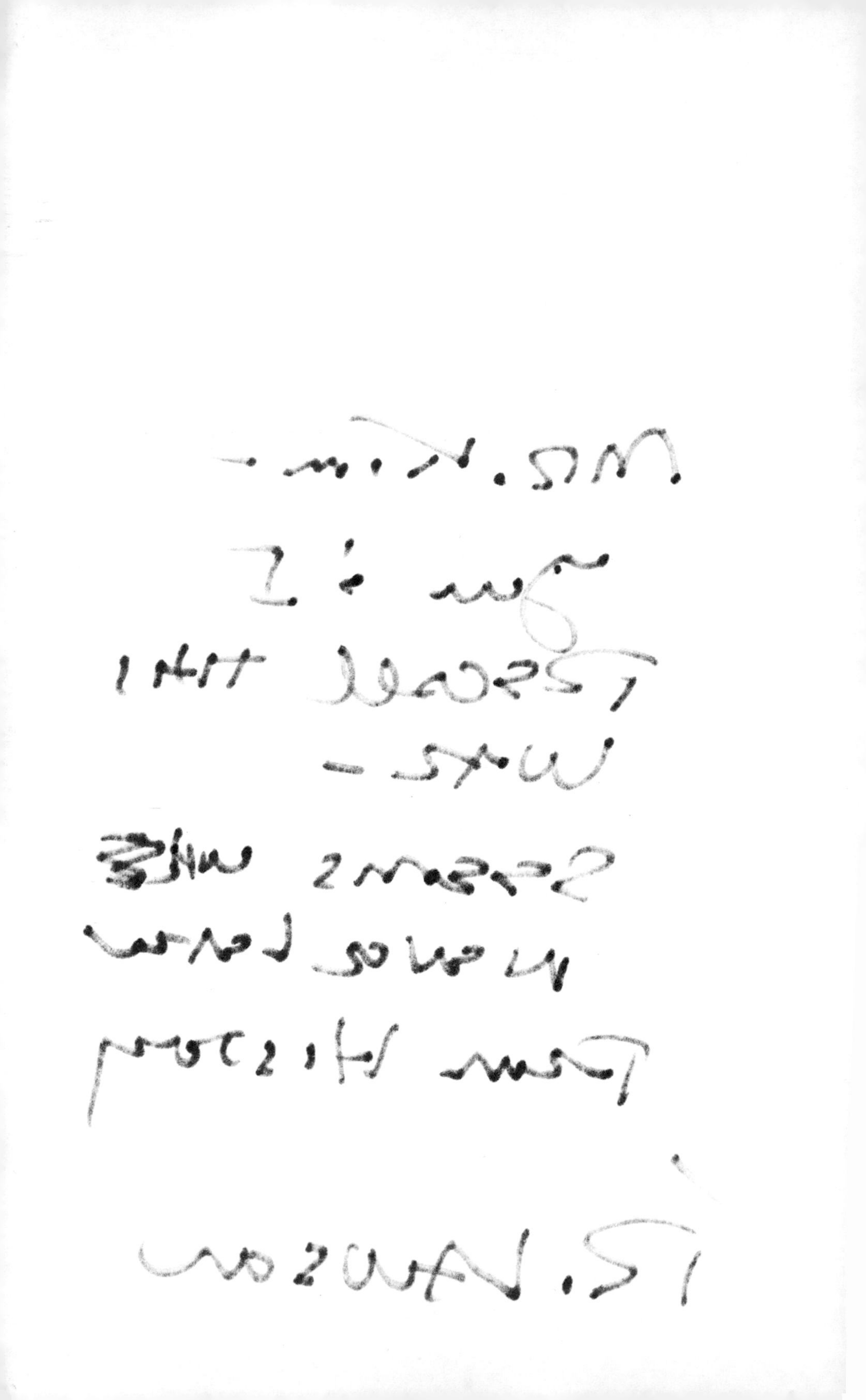

RECALL

A FICTIONAL ACCOUNT BASED ON FOUR TRUE-LIFE HEROES IN THE VIETNAM CONFLICT

R. LAWSON

Editor/Book Shepherd: Ann Narcisian Videan, ANVidean.com

"Turning and turning in the widening gyro the falcon cannot hear the falconer; things fall apart, the center cannot hold, mere anarchy is loosened upon the world."

—W. B. Yeats, *The Second Coming*

To the more than nine million who served honorably in Vietnam and the covert wars in Southeast Asia, Laos and Cambodia. Of those, several were personal friends dating back to my high school days in the 1950s and the years afterward. These buddies deserve special recognition, as I have an idea of what they went through. By coincidence, we all showed up in Vietnam in some military capacity during the mid- and late-1960s. All saw combat action and were decorated. Some paid a serious price.

TABLE OF CONTENTS

INTRODUCTION

This particular account of Vietnam and its aftermath is viewed through the personal experience of four young men who grew up together on the Eastern Shore of Maryland in the fifties. Ten years or so later, in the mid-1960s, they found themselves thrust into a foreign battle on an Asian continent nine thousand miles away.

Their firsthand point of view may be enlightening to curious younger generations, not even born then, who are interested in military and political history, particularly Vietnam. The main characters' impressions may possibly appeal to those who've heard or read conflicting stories about Vietnam—some accurate, some not, and some simply war stories embellished or modified to fit a certain personal or media bias.

Academic scholars may dismiss this account as just another war story. Well, it may be to some, but probably not to others who served tours of duty in Vietnam. The story should resonate with most veterans. They may identify with this version. In fact, this story could easily be a variation of their stories or one of their comrades'.

Vietnam is a kaleidoscope of tales, some grim and a few humorous, but most share the frustration of that nebulous war effort. In any case, this account should provoke thought, that's the prime intention of relating it so many years after the fact, not so much as a diatribe, but as a word of warning.

The basic message: we need to learn the lessons of Vietnam. Its history offers a valuable central theme with political, social, and moral importance.

The narrative lends a different perspective to this stormy period in American history. As the author, my intention is not to be authoritative, but simply to recount the characters' personal journeys—how four young men experienced Vietnam and observed its impact on American society in the following decade.

The reader is free to make the call to agree or disagree with the viewpoints expressed. That reaction is only natural to expect with all the existing controversy regarding Vietnam.

I have no axe to grind other than those opinions, observations, and reservations expressed in the prologue, introduction, and epilogue. The main characters, however, relate some strong viewpoints for the reader to consider. They make assertive statements that might stir you up, offer perspectives to challenge your preconceived notions, or just jar your memory to recall the unending news reports pounding the nation's daily consciousness at that time.

As a country, we really need an honest self-assessment of why and how we engage in war. We should critically evaluate how we elect and judge our leaders' moral compass to engage in, lead, and conduct a war. We should also look closely at how to end a war, defining victory on terms that anyone can easily understand, rather than relying on "nuanced" doublespeak.

Morality is not relative, as some would have you believe. The president has constitutional war powers. Give some serious thought as to how much we should entrust that person with that enormous power. Vietnam has some important lessons about the integrity of the nation's highest office and its inner circle. Right and wrong should be moral absolutes without shades of gray, especially when committing to war.

***

For the historical record, well over nine million people served tours for our country in Vietnam over that extended fourteen-year period, starting with the introduction of military advisors in 1961 and ending with our complete 1975 withdrawal. That represents 9.7 percent of their generation, in contrast to the one percent serving in the military in 2016. Two-thirds were volunteers and one-third drafted... quite a disparity from today's professional military. Out of that large number, I'm sure a lot of opinions were formed based on their personal experiences, but no one had a forum to express them.

There's room for disagreement about Vietnam, especially when factually based. The officially documented facts in the declassified CIA records I referenced illustrate the discord and disagreements of that era. I reviewed them, not without some remorse at the lessons missed or ignored during the war. The French, fighting in inhospitable terrain, suffered 70,000 losses in Vietnam before we became involved. How could that morbid lesson escape recognition? Why did *we* expect a better outcome? Why should it have been different for us in an asymmetrical war? I came away with the impression Vietnam did not have to turn out the way it did, with two countries torn apart—theirs and ours.

I thought about Vietnam periodically for almost fifty years before deciding to write my characters' story. I wanted to try to figure it all out while I had time to conduct some basic research, and still recall most of the details. I served over there as a flight surgeon, but experienced only a fraction of what the real fighters did. I could "see the tree, but not the rainforest." I served, they fought.

This story is about them, not me. I never had to wade through the rice paddies, tangled vines, or elephant grass to fight in thick rainforests. I never encountered giant anthills taller than a man in the triple canopy jungles they fought in, or slept out in the monsoons, like most of our troops and my protagonists. I never got shot down, never went out on platoon missions, or experienced close-quarter combat, ambushes, or surprise artillery attacks. My USAF experience was limited mostly to air evacuations, not the down-and-dirty stuff they encountered. I flew in and out of the battleground above the fray. Therefore, I rely on their experience and my research to fill in the big picture, and to find a message in it all somewhere.

Later, in the following decades upon my return, I witnessed the war's detrimental sociologic fallout in San Francisco, up close and personally. The protagonists' story is well worth telling, and I chose to relate it in a fictional narrative for personal reasons to protect privacy rights. It's a legal thing, let's be realistic.

As the Mark Twain quotation goes, "truth is stranger than fiction, but it is because fiction is obliged to stick to possibilities; Truth isn't." I couldn't make all this up … that would require too vast an imagination. I left graphic parts out. War is nasty and, believe me, there is no need to go there. I'll leave it for you decide what is fiction and what is fact. I won't go there either. That's my disclaimer, let the chips fall where they may. Believe what you will. There's room for other interpretations of the Vietnam experience. This is theirs and mine.

Why bother to write about a war that brings up negative connotations fifty years later? Because there are so many misconceptions, so many lessons unlearned from the Vietnam experience. Hopefully, the younger generations can learn from my generation's mistakes, rather than repeat them. That's the take-home message and my purpose in relating my characters' saga.

As a final sad reflection, many of those who served over there forty to fifty years ago still consider Vietnam a military victory, but acknowledge it as a political loss, a defining foreign-policy failure. At the height of the war, North Vietnam regulars (NVR), and the Viet Cong (VC), launched one of the largest military campaigns of the war. Named after "Tet"—the Vietnamese New Year—the 1968 Tet Offensive resulted in the loss of almost 4,000 Americans, but more than 58,000 of the enemy. Think about that statistic a moment. The enemy suffered as many killed in one year of warfare than the U.S. did in ten years. Furthermore, no major cities were lost in South Vietnam during Tet. Sound like a successful campaign?

Most would define these impressive statistics as a victory. Nevertheless, regardless of the overwhelming superiority of the numbers in our military's favor, the '68 Tet Offensive was the pivotal political and social turning point against America's involvement in Vietnam. Our body-bag tally and the public's negative perception of the war became more important than the staggering sixteen-times-greater, enemy body-counts in the ultimate test of conflict resolution—war.

In retrospect, American public opinion actually was the first domino to fall in 1968, not Vietnam.

Things got real ugly at home, fanned by the media after Tet. Our troops' superior "kill numbers" became meaningless as an anti-war herd mentality emerged, gained momentum, and dominated the discussion of Vietnam over the next decade. The topic became the cause célèbre for the disenchanted anti-establishment crowd and the anti-war protesters in the streets.

Returning home, vets would not discuss the subject with anyone other than family, close friends, and comrades for many years. They felt maligned by much of secular society, not respected. Some harbored resentment. Others felt unappreciated, lost. Rightly so, they received shabby treatment, disrespect, even the humility of being spit on in public.

History repeated itself. French troops had received similar disrespect and humiliation returning home to France from Vietnam decades earlier, after their 1954 defeat at Dien Bien Phu, which forced them to withdraw from Indochina.

Our vets were scorned, even slandered in some political quarters, including Congressional hearings by a shameless officer, who wrote his own after-action reports. He sustained three minor injuries, one from fragging himself, and managed to obtain three Purple Hearts, which granted him leave from the theater after a short four-month tour of duty. Recall that sorry episode? You may know to whom I'm referring. If you don't, look it up.

Meanwhile, the liberal media at home pounded a drumbeat of negativity. Few vets received the hero treatment most deserved for their service. They laid it on the line for our country and received little or no gratitude in return.

Their contentious homecoming reception stands in stark contrast to the warm welcome and empathy for those returning from the Middle East wars recently, the wounded warriors. Has there been an epiphany resulting in a serious change of heart, an awakening of America's human spirit?

Perhaps America has experienced a renaissance of values, I hope so. Most would agree Vietnam was a muddled mess, no matter what side of the difference of opinion they are on. But, in the final analysis, it never was the fighting man's fault. Never. Certainly, with no reason or justification to denigrate him, he deserved our respect, not scorn. After all, there are no noble wars, just noble warriors.

It remains argumentative and difficult to figure out what went wrong, starting from the decision to commit to that war, and moving through three administrations' nebulous strategies—two Democratic, one Republican—to conduct it: JFK, LBJ, and Nixon. And lastly, the humbling terms of our withdrawal from the theater in helicopters from Saigon rooftops left many wondering if it was really worth it in retrospect. Does this episode accurately represent our America, the home of the free and the brave? Did Vietnam trigger the beginning of decades of cynicism? Distrust of our government? Did it exacerbate the polarization of the political spectrum? Pithy considerations to ponder. Think about it and draw your own conclusions.

***

So, how did four young men—who played on the same high school championship football team on the Eastern Shore of Maryland in the mid-fifties—wind up nine thousand miles away in the war-torn cities and jungles of Vietnam? How did they find themselves emerged in a virtual alternate universe, and forced to cope? Now, that's a long story involving improbable odds. Is it attributable to mere coincidence, or dramatic irony?

Biff Roberts and his three teammates' homespun back-stories and subsequent Vietnam experience will give you a different perspective of that difficult and confusing period in American history.

Three other characters play a significant role in this convoluted saga with their personal involvement influencing the main characters' life paths. Their uncanny interplay compels one to consider the validity of the six degrees of separation theory. Their opportune interaction and coincidental connectivity to the main characters' adventures are the reason I also present their interesting backgrounds. They later sway critical outcomes as the odyssey unfolds.

Let me share with you the long story of these characters. How I recall it, a fictional historical narrative chronicling the ups and downs of their personal journey through a turbulent time: Vietnam and its aftermath.

PROLOGUE

The Viet Cong surprise attack on Pleiku in February, 1965 changed the complexion of the war. Since 1961 American troops acted only as advisors to the South Vietnam's AVRN. The attack forced LBJ to authorize offensive military reactions, no longer able to vacillate in the face of mixed reactions in the homeland.

Two weeks later American planes started bombing North Vietnam. Front page news in the *New York Times* extolled "Operation Rolling Thunder." F-105 "Thuds" and F-4 Phantoms started flying missions out of three airbases in Thailand, and later from Danang, striking North Vietnam targets. Carriers in Yankee Station launched F-4s off the deck for target suppression of North Vietnam's surface-to-air missiles, or SAMs, and conventional anti-aircraft fire. "First in, last out" characterized their dangerous mission to protect the fighter-bombers.

A second major escalation occurred one month later in March 1965 as the 9th Marine Expeditionary Brigade landed at Danang. Five thousand Marines under Brigadier General Karch supplemented those Marines landing earlier at Chu Lai. They were assigned a significant new mission: U.S. combat troops became authorized to carry out "search and destroy" (S&D) missions. They pursued an aggressive military stance and, in taking this action, the U.S. no longer served just as advisors to the ARVN, they now had authorization to conduct offensive operations.

This new policy represented a seminal policy change. It essentially transformed Vietnam into an American offensive war four years after JFK accelerated the Truman/Eisenhower program, in 1961, by introducing more American military advisors into the "conflict" in the Mekong Delta.

JFK justified taking this action ostensibly to prevent the spread of monolithic communism as envisioned in the "Domino Theory." This premise, threatening America's intervention in Southeast Asia, theorized if Vietnam falls, all of Southeast Asia follows, as one nation topples one after the other, succumbing to communist control.

Vietnam represented an intrinsic part of the predominant "Cold War" global psyche at the time, becoming integral to the strategy of containing communism universally. In this sense, Vietnam became a proxy for the Cold War.

LBJ took the war one huge step further with the 1965 escalation following the Pleiku attack by allowing America to go on the offense. LBJ and his advisors thought this show of force intensifying America's commitment would send a powerful message to NVN. They hoped it would solve the problem of the dwindling support for the war at home and soon end the war by bringing North Vietnam to the negotiating table.

The policy was designed not to win the war, but to end it.

***

That would not be the case, however. The controversial policy objective proved to be folly, and doomed to failure. The fighting in Southeast Asia would last for ten years, costing our nation more than 58,000 casualties, and almost ten wounded for every military mortality since President Kennedy introduced the first Vietnam military advisors in 1961.

JFK's patriotic exhortation, "Pay any price, bear any burden…" begs the question: "Was the price too high, the burden too onerous?"

To put those harsh statistics in current perspective, consider that America's Vietnam War casualty statistics were almost fifteen times greater than the combined Iraq/Afghanistan losses over their similar ten-year periods. Those two, decade-long wars amounted to approximately 4,000 casualties. Yet, DC politicians at that time still referred to the fighting in Vietnam as a "conflict," not a war.

Doublespeak and spin for public consumption, rather than transparency, characterized LBJ's administration. They never really leveled with the nation. Rhetoric rarely matched reality. The public and Congress were intentionally deluded in some cases, and our military betrayed in other instances.

Vietnam is not a heartwarming story. Almost half the U.S. population born following the war has no direct recollection or knowledge of the war. For many of the other half, the war has faded from their consciousness, or they have passed away. This narrative should refresh recall of the major events. However, for those who served, Vietnam is not a distant memory. It has a way of staying with you, popping into consciousness from time to time. There is no blocking it out. Some still suffer disturbing flashbacks.

During the Vietnam War, truth became the first casualty, which presents one powerful reason to reevaluate its history. Eventually, the administration's disingenuous behavior resulted in a serious backlash with dramatic unintended consequences. As people caught on, disillusionment crept in, cynicism gathered, and support for the war waned in the mid-1960s. Many young people strongly disapproved, dodged the draft, and took anti-war protests to the streets, burning their draft cards. Some crowds became unruly as peaceful protests turned into nasty confrontations with the police that escalated into riots.

As this novel's epigraph metaphorically expresses, "The falconer lost control of the falcon as things spun out of control, fell apart, and anarchy loosened ..."

Abraham Lincoln observed, "You can fool all of the people some of the time and some of the people all of the time, but you cannot fool all of the people all of the time."

The societal repercussion from the war's backlash represented another significant price paid by America. The magnitude of the cost to our unique American culture is not easily quantified, much less foreseen. In retrospect, there are too few tangible benefits to measure against that particular cost. Vietnam became a war too painful to consider in the social context of risk/benefit calculations. Analytics will never explain Vietnam.

The collective hostile fallout and cynical political reaction to the Southeast Asian military venture swept over America, beginning with the San Francisco Bay area's vigorous anti-war demonstrations, soon intensifying into a national anti-war activist movement.

Simultaneously, an extraordinary countercultural revolution occurred in the sixties involving a wider scope of issues, which exacerbated the anti-war debate. Further social conflicts arose, sharply dividing the country. Worldviews clashed as the country veered on a collision course. The angry division festered and burst in the later phases of the Vietnam War with widespread public protests and swelling disorder, resulting in a level of anarchy. It's a sad, but interesting epoch of history... if you are willing to wade through the background, sort through its complexity, and attempt to decipher its lessons.

Noteworthy CIA intelligence estimates from that era, for the most part, became declassified during the 1980s. The critical knowledge contained in these reports offers some interesting and cogent insight into that controversial and divisive time. I reviewed them for months with some dismay.

Case in point, Vietnam presents a classic study of teachable moments and unintended consequences resulting from inept action or inaction, false narratives, disingenuous motives, and conflicting rigid mindsets. Hallmarked by strategies complicated by generals fighting the last war rather than the next, and politicians meddling in military affairs. This fictional historical narrative gives the reader an ample overview of examples. Some will shock you.

In retrospect, it's difficult to understand why historical lessons were not learned in Vietnam's context before we became involved. Many fine analytical and authoritative historical accounts have been written but, to some, Vietnam still remains a puzzle in some respects. To countless others, it's become a collection of buzzwords, or reduced to sound bites such as "a quagmire," and "body counts." It is also still a source of nightmares to many survivors.

To the abandoned South Vietnamese, it became a "killing field" or, after we left, "reeducation camps." Only the "boat people" escaped the chaos after the last of our non-combatant personnel abruptly departed. Many left from rooftops by helicopters in April of 1975 as enemy troops closed in on Saigon, two years after our fighting troops left. After Congress cut off funding for South Vietnam, no hope for the inhabitants' survival remained.

As North Vietnamese tanks rolled down tree-lined Dong Khoi Boulevard within the ravaged capitol city of Saigon, citizens fled in terror. Many climbed over the U.S. Embassy walls and the Pittman apartments, praying to catch a ride on a departing chopper. The scene of the last American CIA officers, LaGueux and Polgar climbing into a helicopter with Ambassador Martin captured the pathos, the final humiliation.

Operation "Frequent Wind" evacuated 5,000 Americans, and 60,000 Vietnamese assets and refugees by helicopters to offshore ships in two days. The enemy had closed the airport at Tan Son Nhut, cutting off that escape route. Not a pretty sight then, or forty years later, as I recall the episode.

THE FOUR COMBATANTS: IN MEDIA RES CAPTAIN CODY JOHANSSON

Pleiku, Vietnam
Corps Tactical Zone (CTZ) II
7 February, 1965–0450 Hours

"Incoming!"

The startled sentry rushed to sound the general alarm, ducked, and jumped over the sandbagged berm into the nearest revetment. Others on night patrol quickly scurried to the safety of nearby bunkers as a barrage of 81mm mortars, rockets, and artillery rounds quickly followed.

The surprise predawn attack ignited massive explosions inside the vital central highlands military installation. The concussions shook the ground, flames and smoke enveloped sections of the base burning uncontrolled. The inescapable smells of war punctuated by the acrid, metallic odor of gunpowder, sulfur, and pungent munitions propellants quickly filled the air as an intense battle ensued. Scattered shouts from the wounded resounded, calling, "Medic! Over here!"

The blaring alarm combined with explosions stirred the base into defensive action. Soldiers immediately responded, trained for combat. They rushed to counter the enemy's blitz after a brief moment of confusion, astounded by the magnitude of the surprise attack by the Viet Cong (VC), launched from a nearby rainforest.

"Charlie's" stunning offensive created a breach at the base's northwest perimeter secured by concertina wire, magnesium trip flares, and lethal claymore and trip-wired Bouncing Betty mines. Nevertheless, the enemy engaged in suicidal attempts to overrun the base, capitalizing on the element of surprise. Large numbers of daring VC guerillas reinforced with North Vietnam Regulars (NVRs), charged through the breach.

The brazen enemy advanced in reckless waves, attempting to cross the barbed-wire rift and mines planted outside. This foolhardy effort tripped the mines and flares, resulting in a massive munitions display. Blown ten feet into the air, their bodies silhouetted eerily against the flashing light of the explosions in the dark night sky. Nevertheless, a secondary enemy wave ignored the threat and renewed the assault. Some slipped through, hopping over dead comrades to miss remaining mines. Crazed, they charged with total disregard of the lethal hazards in their impassioned effort to penetrate the perimeter minefield and overrun the base.

Rallying his company, Captain Cody Johansson led his men against the swarming attackers head on. Deploying his three platoons, a mix of American Special Force advisors and the Army of the Republic of Vietnam (ARVN), they thwarted the enemy's invasion through the penetrated outer boundary with military precision. Despite suffering serious fragmentation wounds, Cody courageously led his men in intense combat, often in close quarters. He'd trained them well. They prevailed.

His distinguished performance that early morning would earn him a Purple Heart and award of a Silver Star following the after-action report (AAR).

COLONEL AL RUEY

Chu Lai Air Base (AB) Flight Line
Marine TAC Base
CTZ I, 0500 Hours

"Colonel Ruey, emergency call for you!"

The anxious flight line Sergeant handed the field phone to the squadron commander of SATS/MAG-12. The NCO's grim expression forewarned him of trouble brewing.

"This is Colonel Pettyjohn, base commander at Pleiku. We're under siege, request immediate close air support. We're in big trouble, VC attempting to overrun the base through a breach in our northwest perimeter as we speak. Attack being staged from the rainforest about six klicks north of our position."

"Can you provide adequate FAC for us, Colonel Pettyjohn?"

"We'll try to get forward air control out there to spot for you. They hit our runway, but I think we can still get a few of our Bird Dogs up in the air to locate enemy positions for you."

***

In 1965, GPS coordinates were not the primary navaids. The USAF/GPS project began in 1974, utilizing twenty-four global satellites, not becoming fully operational until 1995. So, for combat operations in Vietnam, pilots flying close air support used forward air control (FAC) rather than GPS coordinates to mark or direct the fighter planes to the enemy targets' location. To ensure the safety of friendly forces in close proximity during the battle, no drops were authorized until obtaining FAC clearance. There were no smart bombs, and no laser guidance at that time. FAC cleared each and every drop to avoid friendly fire. That required the pilot to attack using his fixed gun sight to track the target until the pipper was on the target at precisely the correct drop altitude, airspeed, and dive angle. Flying close air support in the Vietnam era required exceptional pilot skill and coordination with FAC, and a special breed of men who could multitask under duress.

In a typical close combat support situation, FAC—flying in low, slow, fixed-wing aircraft—would communicate with ground troops on Fox Mike (VHF/FM radio) to assess the situation, then relay the critical target vector information to the fighter pilots on the AN/ARC-34 airborne UHF channel, known as "uniform" in brevity code. Spotter recon aircraft—"Bird Dogs," like an O-1E Cessna—then released a marker rocket on the target and gave the okay for the fighter pilots to release ordinance on the target, by then clearly identified by smoke. Flyers called this white phosphorous smoke "Willey Pete." in military phonetic parlance.

Communication was critical and a bit complex. The pilot had five radio control heads and could listen to the two FAC channels simultaneously, but could talk only on one at a time. The emergency Guard Channel (243.0), intercom, and squadron communication channels operated on UHF. They added to the pilot's tasks while engaged in battle, avoiding anti-aircraft fire, and attacking the target flying at three to four hundred knots.

This rundown gives you an appreciation of the skill set required to fly close air support.

***

"I read you, the Bird Dogs will facilitate our targeting, but some additional ground FAC would help us avoid friendly fire."

"We'll try to provide some ground FAC, but we're taking heavy incoming. So much shelling, I deferred going through our chain of command and decided to contact your squadron directly for this mission request. I'll take some heavy flack for not going through channels,

Colonel Ruey, but that's how bad the situation is over here. I didn't want to waste time. They can reprimand me if I'm still alive. We're in dire straits, need your help, Colonel."

His sense of urgency was not lost on the Marine squadron commander.

"I picked up on your shortcut. I agree, not wise to waste time on chain of command at this early hour, considering your present circumstance. We'll get all over it, Colonel. Hold the fort. My squadron maintains a dozen A-4s on our hot pad ready to scramble for contingencies like this. We'll be in the air in less than ten minutes. You're only a short hop southwest of Chu Lai, so hang in there, we'll soon be on our way."

He handed the field phone back to his sergeant, turned, and addressed his fighter pilots grouped for a flight training session.

"Okay, fellows, cancel our early morning exercise."

They'd come to expect the unexpected in Vietnam, and sensed such an event had come up as they read their commander's demeanor: no time to waste.

"Change of plans, we're going live over Pleiku, guys. The base is under siege. They'll provide some FAC, but we may have to improvise. It will test your skills not to kill any of our boys with friendly fire. Arm your missiles. We'll go max ordinance and arrange to refuel in the air on the way back."

The pilots knew the Pleiku area well from prior reconnaissance exercises over the South Vietnam highlands. Previously, Ruey's squadron of MAG-12 fighter jets flew from carriers in the South China Sea to respond to emergencies like this. Recently, though, Marine squadrons became land based on short Seabee-constructed runways closer to the action. Chu Lai was one of the first, located in CTZ I on the coast of the northern sector of South Vietnam, fifty miles south of Danang.

Repositioned from carrier-based Yankee Station in the South China Sea to Vietnam's east coast helped protect bases like Pleiku in CTZ II near the Laos border. In fact, the Marine A-4Es would quickly cover the ninety miles southwest and, once in the air, reach the besieged central highlands base in about seven or eight minutes at 600mph. Confidence ran high that they'd keep the enemy from overrunning the important base once they unleashed their superior firepower.

Pleiku bordered the Ho Chi Minh trail winding south through Laos's triple canopy rainforests and jungles to Cambodia. Both were designated "over the fence" in military jargon. The base provided Military Advisory Command Vietnam (MACV) reconnaissance and strategic information on the trail's traffic, which included intelligence vital to the conduct of the war.

Delivering close air support on short notice worked for the Marines. That's what they did—tactical support from short airfields, designated "SATS," at Chu Lai.

"Let's shoot for wheels in the well at o-five-fifteen, ten minutes from now. Hustle up, Charlie's doing a number on our guys. Green 'em up."

That statement, which they knew meant to turn on armament switches, created a buzz of animation. The squadron commander sensed the wave of excitement sweeping through his fighter pilots as they scrambled to their planes, ready for action.

"Beats the hell out of training drills. This is what it's all about, guys. Live fire in a hot zone, the real deal. FAC will be limited, as I said, so be real careful of friendly fire. This will be a major encounter. Control your altitude, speed, and attack angle. Don't want anyone stitched by ground fire, fragging themselves, or auguring in. Got it?"

All wing and squadron commanders have three ambitions: achieving Ace status, which is five or more kills; making his star, aka brigadier general; and protecting his pilots. The last ambition distinguished Colonel Ruey. His sincere concern for their safety was not lost on them. Flying close air support at 400 knots with someone shooting at you while monitoring multiple channels of communications required remarkable skill . . . a professional exercise not for the lighthearted.

"Yes sir," came the collective response. This standard operation procedure had been drilled into them. Marines believed in repetition until SOPs became ingrained, discipline reigned paramount in the Corps.

Colonel Ruey smiled with anticipation. "Let's show 'em what we got, fly boys."

They picked up on the subtle Marine swagger in his carriage as he hastened to the hot pad. Ruey's confident attitude pumped up his squadron. His calm leadership dispelled any fear they might harbor regarding the danger of a combat sortie.

Ruey climbed into his lead A-4 fighter jet as if no hazard existed, just like he was going out on another routine flying day.

No "oo rahs" necessary, his cool manner said it all, inspiring them to do their thing—close air support.

"You got it, Colonel!" his hotshot wingman shouted, definitely jacked up at the prospect of a major engagement. He flashed a thumbs-up as he hustled to his aircraft, a sleek Skyhawk with nose art: "Scooter" painted colorfully on the A-4 fuselage.

Josh Neelson had already distinguished himself in sixteen combat missions since he arrived a month prior from carrier duty aboard the USS Constitution, operating off the coast in Yankee Station. The kid could fly.

The fighter jock hoped for a MIG kill, but would be disappointed. There would be only one A-4 kill during the ten years of war in South Vietnam, while F-4s claimed 164 MiG kills over Laos and North Vietnam later in the war. MiG-21s or 17s rarely ventured into South Vietnam airspace.

Quintessential fighter jocks are always primed for missions. And, they loved to fly into battle with this commander, proven to be one of the best. You wouldn't hear it from him, though. Readily acknowledged the top gun, Ruey could fly circles around anyone. The squadron would chase the enemy into Laos, if necessary, to make this sortie a success, despite the restrictive rules of engagement.

Minutes later, JATO tanks propelled the aircraft into flight off Chu Lai's short aluminum plank runway, each fighter hit the afterburners as the jet took off loaded with 8,500 pounds of ordinance: iron and cluster bombs, Zuni missiles, napalm, plus two 20mm cannons on each fighter jet. In combat pilot jargon, "Twenty mike-mike, nape, and CBU."

CAPTAIN ROE MACDONALD

Tan Son Nhut (TSN) AB Flight Line
MACV Command Post, 7th Air Force HQ
CTZ III, 0540 Hours

With the rising sun, the stifling humidity picked up at the strategic airbase four miles north of Saigon. Steam rose from the Tan Son Nhut (TSN) tarmac. Soon, it would be like a sauna on the flight line. It was already ninety-two degrees with eighty-eight percent humidity.

The ever-present smell of freshly burnt JP-4 aircraft diesel permeated the mugginess with a smell of kerosene. The pungent odor competed with the strong smell of mosquito repellant recently sprayed near Papa San's flight line café. Neither smell encouraged an appetite. Fortunately, pleasant whiffs of breakfast cooking on Papa San's grill made it tolerable for the flyers short respite.

It made Captain Roe MacDonald long for a breath the fresh salt air, the aroma of the Chesapeake Bay where he'd grown up. Though humid in August, it never got this uncomfortable back home. Not even close. He fought back a brief wave of nostalgia. Reverie must wait.

The captain had a job to do, with no time to reminisce. He wiped the sweat from his brow. His olive-drab nylon 86th MAC flight suit was already damp from perspiration, and salt stains caked the armpits. The flight surgeon had just joined his crew for breakfast at Papa San's small flight-line café… nothing fancy, but suitable for a quick bite for those on a tight schedule. No time to be picky on short breaks between missions. He'd be back in the air in an hour or so. Time to chow down.

Loud Beatles music blared from Papa Sans' radio tuned to his favorite station. The AFVN "Goooood Morning Vietnam" station pumped out GI favorites. He tried daily to drown out the sound of ramp compressors. They continuously pumped air to assist the APU's cranking up the engines of large United States Air Force (USAF) transport planes parked nearby. The rotary-prop *whomp-whomp* of choppers coming and going overhead added to the constant noise. TSN was a busy 24/7 operation, and the racket on the ramp drove Papa San crazy.

Roe's squadron's C-130 aircraft had landed forty minutes before, arriving from the Philippines' Clark AB loaded with ammo and 81mm mortars. The loadmaster and his airmen busily reconfigured the cargo turbo jet for air evacuation missions after unloading the munitions. A normal routine for the military airlift command (MAC) crews: flying back and forth to the war zone, ammo in, wounded out, a day-after-day grind encountering just enough VC ground fire to break the tedium. Vietnam was a lot of things, but never boring.

Making that case, the sudden squawk of the café's walky-talky intercom suddenly interrupted their meal and animated chatter.

"Attention all crew members, Pleiku is under siege. Hundreds wounded. Half of base hospital blown up. Your new 86th MAC orders are to proceed immediately to Pleiku with as many medics and medical supplies as possible. Assault-landing precautions advisable. Stay above fifteen hundred feet on approach to avoid small arms fire. No known enemy anti-aircraft capability. Pleiku's runway intact, but many aircraft disabled and on fire. Take due caution. Out."

"Jesus! No fucking let-up in this Godforsaken place," one pilot bitched.

"Let's roll guys. Move it out," another said as he took a last gulp of coffee, crushed his cigarette, and rushed to file the new flight plan at base ops.

After drafting anyone around the flight line with a modicum of medical experience available on such short notice, the crew was airborne in less than thirty minutes.

They did not request F-100 Super Sabers from the 531st Squadron stationed at the nearby Bien Hoa AB's Third TAC Fighter Wing to escort their C-130 Hercules turbojets full of medical supplies and personnel. They were assured of a safe arrival at the besieged recon base in the northern highlands. The nearest MiG was 500 miles away in North Vietnam, and there were no VC anti-aircraft guns reported en route. They would face no danger until descending under fifteen hundred feet on approach to land at Pleiku, then ground fire might get dicey.

CIA DEPUTY STATION MANAGER BIFF ROBERTS

U.S. Embassy Saigon
Later the same morning, 0600 hours

Biff Roberts' secure line rang loudly, jarring him half awake. Bushed, he'd fallen asleep well past midnight slumped over his desk littered with official paperwork, mostly highly classified documents.

Biff was the CIA's new deputy station manager under diplomatic cover at the Saigon Embassy. His posting involved coordinating a vast network of clandestine ops for the "Company," the CIA's affectionate nickname in intelligence circles, and his demands could become mind-boggling at times.

In Vietnam, he directed the agency's Special Activity Division—an elite paramilitary unit, little-known except to those with a need to know. "Covert" hardly described the SAD. They could go deep dark, and did on many occasions. They spread disinformation, performed psychology operations (psyops), and undertook clandestine tasks... some distasteful behind enemy lines, some unmentionable, and some never forgotten. The latter included dark missions involving targeted and political assassinations. Basically, the SAD conducted a secret war within a war, sometimes referred to as a "shadow war."

Based on his exceptional talents and performance at "The Farm"—the CIA's training center in Virginia—Langley posted Biff to Saigon. He had become the youngest operative ever to assume such an influential position, which was especially noteworthy in wartime. The Director of

Central Intelligence, or DCI, conferred this unusual accolade despite Biff's youth and limited field experience. Recruited only a little more than a year out of Yale, his trainers at the Farm praised him as a "once-in-a-decade graduate with an uncanny talent for operating in the clandestine world. A 'natural-born spook,' they dubbed him."

That last reference was all the DCI had to hear, "Natural-born spook." That rare designation had never failed him or the CIA in assigning exceptionally challenging tasks to prospective undercover field officers.

Few possessed his coveted trait: combining an inborn proclivity to endure with an innate tenacity to stay alive in the dark shadows of the clandestine world. Only the fittest survived the Darwinian challenge.

CIA tapped Biff Roberts for their operative position in Saigon, covering him with a diplomatic post at the U.S. Embassy. They deemed him a perfect fit.

Given the awesome responsibility, Biff was dancing as fast as he could to adjust to an ever-changing drumbeat in this new role. There appeared to be no rhyme or reason for many orders coming down from MACV. No amount of training at the Farm could have prepared him for the unknown challenges. He wondered if the assignment was an honor, or the ultimate test of his survival skills in a war zone. He strove to master the tasks, pushing himself to the limit, often forced to wing it in an uncomfortable on-the-job training role requiring weighty decisions, many on the spur of the moment.

Vietnam—a hotbed of undercover activity, stealth, intrigue, and bureaucratic nightmares complicating a nasty war—demanded extraordinary resilience. Less than three months into his assignment, the young operative often toiled late into the night trying to get the job done in the complex environment.

Already a particularly rough week, with never enough hours in the day to accomplish his mission, he was dog-tired. When the phone rang, he dreaded to pick it up, anticipating the message would simply pile on more responsibility and make his tension headache worse. He hoped they'd call back and give him time to collect himself. He stalled. Maybe they'd give up and try again later.

Most of the time he functioned on overload, often feeling like a dog chasing its tail. Though frustrated, he fought not to form a negative attitude regarding his Vietnam mission like the inept senior operative he'd recently replaced. The task presented too many Whiskey Tango Foxtrot propositions, no-win situations, and circumstances out of control. How could he succeed at this assignment where others had failed? What had he gotten himself into? Had the Directorate of Operations, the DO, set him up? Perpetrated some kind of cruel joke? He didn't recall pissing anyone off. Why subject him or anyone to this bedlam?

The phone continued to ring. He checked his watch: 0600, with dawn breaking. Yet he was still not fully awake... still collecting his wits.

His predecessor burned out in record time. He never really got to know the cynical old honcho, since he wasn't much help in the acclimation of a newcomer to the challenge. Rather than serve as a mentor, he was anxious to return to the States to retire. In fact, he couldn't wait to get out the door.

Following his brief last handshake, he had sardonically remarked, "FIGMO, I'm outta this fucking boondoggle. Good luck, Biff. You'll need it."

Quite obviously, he didn't give a rat's ass about giving a heads up to the newbie, and Biff soon learned the acronym's meaning. "Fuck it, got my orders."

So much for the buddy system. Pretty much on his own, he'd reconciled to suck it up as a "FNG." He'd discovered that acronyms and slang were common military forms of expression in Vietnam, another language in fact. That's the way they talked over there, like in some kind of code. FNG meant "friggin' new guy." This new military language would require him to develop a whole new vocabulary. His Yale education seemed a century ago. Vietnam presented a whole new learning experience in more ways than one.

What the hell, he resolved to adapt. This FNG was wired differently, dedicated to persevere and make things happen. He strove to avoid a jaded FIGMO mindset. Not into pissing and moaning, he resigned to tough it out, deal with it... starting with answering the damn annoying phone. He rubbed his sleepy eyes, recognizing the caller would not give up. No fucking way. The persistent bastard was determined.

Vietnam presented a stream of emergent situations. He'd learned that nothing remained constant in Vietnam's dynamics, except the ever-changing circumstances. You could count on unexpected situations cropping up at inopportune moments. Exigency seemed an ironic "given" of sorts in Vietnam, an observation fellow field officers joked validated Murphy's Law.

At this hour, it had to mean an emergency call. Maybe SAD had run into another snag in their new Phoenix program, a tactical plan plagued by fits and starts. They called him day and night for advice.

On top of all his major responsibilities, Biff integrated intelligence among the various agencies and the military in South Vietnam involved in this complicated program. In fact, he'd passed out at his desk late last night studying current intelligence reports from the local field of battle. He'd also decoded cables from Langley and Commander in Chief, Pacific Command (CINCPAC) designed to establish the Phoenix program. That was an intelligence-based program designed to eliminate VC infrastructure in the vital Saigon sector.

The first thing he saw though his bleary eyes as he decided to answer the phone was a large white board on the wall opposite his desk posting current, known, VC threat locations in MR IV, the Saigon region in South Vietnam. Startled and disoriented at first, the board reminded him he was safe in his Saigon Embassy's office. Still groggy, he got his bearings and groped to find his phone across his littered desk in the dimly lit room. It also jogged his memory to get a stronger watt bulb for the old gooseneck lamp he inherited from his predecessor.

In the past three months out on SAD missions, he'd awakened in some strange locations, disoriented and tense: nasty places without walls or roofs, weird places with annoying insects and creepy, crawly creatures. The threatening Southeast Asian jungles didn't leave a light on for you, much less a comfy bed. It seemed the enemy always lurked behind the next vine-entangled rock or stand of bamboo ... not conducive to a good night's sleep. Vietnam had a tendency to make you jumpy. He welcomed the sight of the white board, confident the VC couldn't get to him here.

Keeping track of VC guerilla activity was nerve wracking. The National Liberation Front, or NLF—the official name of the Viet Cong—kept on the move with their hit-and-run tactics, and put his SAD recon missions at risk. The white-board positions changed a dozen times a day.

Changing conditions kept his staff hopping and analyzing intel reports from assets in the field. This human intelligence, or HUMINT, involved daily tracking of the enemy in the Phoenix tactical area of responsibility.

Still not fully awake, he reached to pick up the Embassy red phone. It sat at the far end of his large desk, next to his EE-8 field phone, satellite phone, AN/URC-10 survival radio, and his PRC-FM radio. Communication devises in Vietnam were vital. He was well stocked for every eventuality but an atomic bomb attack. Finally, he answered on the twelfth ring, and inadvertently knocked over a vial of his "daily-daily" anti-malarial pills.

"Shit," he muttered as the pale blue capsules scattered across the desk. "Hello, Roberts here." He wished for a cup of coffee.

"Brace yourself, pal."

Biff recognized apprehension in his fellow field officer's voice. A call from the night operations desk downstairs was usually never a good sign, especially from a persistent caller. His headache was about to get worse.

"How's that, Jim? What's up? I'm braced."

Now fully awake, he expected bad news.

"Bad sit-rep, Pleiku is getting pounded big time by the Viet Cong. Not just the usual boonie-rat skirmish. VC launched a massive predawn attack in battalion strength including heavy arty 105mm Howitzers, they think. They staged the attack from the rainforest just six klicks north of the base over an hour ago, can you believe that?"

He successfully deciphered Jim's jargon … the new language. "No fucking way, battalion strength, including heavy artillery from a position so close by the base?"

"They probably captured the arty from the ARVN, my guess," Jim ventured.

"That's really a bad situation report, Jim. Got any further details? Zulu?"

"Yep, reports say an estimated fifteen hundred VC reinforced with North Vietnam Army regulars launched the assault from a position right in the airbase' own backyard. Bastards inflicted a lot of serious damage. Zulu high, estimated a hundred or so casualties, planes on fire, base hospital partially demolished by mortars and artillery. Fortunately, they missed the ammo dump. Reports keep piling in as we speak. Let me tell ya, this is a BFD!"

"Holy shit. Heavy losses, tell me more. We've got a major frontal offensive on our hands, a huge departure from the routine VC hit-and-run skirmishes."

"Right on, got that right, boss. Fortunately, Colonel Ruey's A-4s scrambled from Chu Lai and the sortie's currently bombing and rocketing the hell out of the VC, kicking some serious ass, FAC reports."

"Good to know Pleiku's getting close air support. Thank God."

"Roger that. Word is a ranger captain by the name of Johansson saved the ground fight by swiftly leading his company into the battle, manning the perimeter breach to prevent a rout. Report says he got wounded pretty bad in the firefight, but kept on gunning VC down. Almost singlehandedly prevented the VC from overrunning the camp. Brown bar's action report says this captain created his own killing zone. The battle's winding down, lasting less than an hour, now entering the mop-up phase."

Biff's interest soared. Could Johannson be his high school buddy? "How's that, Jim? Did the lieutenant give any further details on this encounter … this ranger's action?"

"Early reports say this captain kept rapid-firing his M-16, mowing VC down despite bleeding like a stuck pig. His company lieutenant estimates this guy Johansson must have lit up over thirty bad guys with his sharp shooting. In the after-action report, the lieutenant said it was a fucking unbelievable display of marksmanship, like an out-of-body experience. This guy kept popping one VC after another."

"Really? Tell me more about it."

"The company lieutenant claims he's never seen anything like it in his two combat tours in 'Nam. He likened Johansson's display to something out of a shooting arcade, an unreal exhibit of sharpshooting, with this ranger swinging his M-16 in wide arcs, only seconds between getting off shots. He said the guy followed the bust caps with brief full auto bursts spraying the attackers' onslaught. He never saw anyone go through so many clips with such accuracy, called the guy a friggin' Rambo."

"Impressive, must have been quite a scene with him rocking 'n rolling."

"Report said this guy, Johansson, never missed!"

"Good for him," Biff interjected. "Sounds like Cody."

"Cody? You telling me you know this marksman Johansson on a first-name basis?"

"Sure do. He's always been a crack shot, shooting squirrels hopping through treetops at age twelve. Tops in skeet competition in Maryland at age sixteen. That performance doesn't surprise me a bit. Cody obviously was in a zone. I imagine it was a lot easier mowing down VCs than shooting clays for him."

"You're talking a small world."

"Seems it is, Jim."

"Other reports coming in from Pleiku go on to say that we've got flight surgeons and triage medics flying in from Tan Son Nhut led by Captain MacDonald. Wouldn't surprise me if you knew of him, too. Everyone's heard about his heroics. He's established himself as an accomplished trauma surgeon, got quite an impressive record in 'Nam. Doc fast-ropes out of 'dust off' choppers and zigzags through minefields under enemy fire to rescue wounded men with his medics ... that kind of gung-ho stuff everyone is raving about."

"You bet I know him, another fine fellow ... excellent air-evac surgeon. In fact, before you ask, I also know the Marine A-4 squadron commander quite well, Colonel Ruey."

"How do you happen to know all three of those guys involved in this battle, boss?'

"It's a long story, Jim, goes way back to all four of us playing high school football together."

"No way, are you putting me on?"

"Nope. Crazy how we all ended up here, huh? It's a quirk of fate, hard to believe, in fact. Interesting twist, tell you the story later, okay? Let's concentrate on this VC problem for now."

"Okay, it can wait, but promise to tell me the connection later on. It's a fascinating string of coincidences."

"You got it. A never-ending string, it seems. I promise to tell you the whole story over a beer."

"It's a deal. I'll even buy. What's our plan now, Biff? What course of action do you want me to initiate?"

"Right now, let's get our unit to investigate the breakdown in our intel coordination up there in the highlands. How in the hell did a recon base like Pleiku allow an enemy battalion to bivouac that close? Bring in heavy artillery? Six klicks, you said? That's only a little over three and a half miles. It had to be a breakdown in the system somewhere. Or, maybe some spy set it up. Pleiku is a reconnaissance base keeping an eye on the Ho chi Minh trail, for Christ's sake. Not a good show by our recon boys. Somebody fucked up big time."

"No argument there, Biff."

"Look at it like this, Pleiku is a vital link in our defense of the highlands, especially protecting highway 19. I'm sure we'll get a load of flack from MACV over this. They'll want to lay the blame on someone else to cover their sorry conduct of this friggin' war. They'll concoct a typical CYA story. They don't want to face LBJ's criticism back in DC."

"You nailed it, boss. So, what do you think is gonna happen now? This is the third serious attack on U.S. military installations in Vietnam in less than six months, with zero response from us. Recall last Christmas? Sappers bombed the Brinks base officers' quarters (BOQs) in Saigon. Before that, the VCs hit Bien Hoa with a sneak mortar attack from the local rice paddies. We're taking casualties right and left, and putting up with all the Saigon government's BS. The friggin' South Vietnam army can't get their act together. This is a pathetic show, boss. This is no fucking way to fight a war."

Biff opted to try for diplomacy and to rationalize the situation. "I agree, the ARVN is often ineffectual, and Washington's mixed signals further complicate matters. Indecision is a terrible state of affairs, Jim."

Obviously, one of his best field operatives needed to vent his pent-up frustrations triggered by the tense Pleiku situation. Biff shared his frustration.

"It's South Vietnam's war. We're just advisors" he reminded Jim. "Seems nobody's on the same page. If I'd seen this movie before I'd know what to tell you, pal."

The CIA coped with a difficult position. DC ignored most of their intelligence estimates. The vacillation and lack of a coherent policy by LBJ's administration compounded the messy military situation. Frankly it lacked direction in many cases. It was becoming increasingly difficult for him to manage the CIA's covert war in Vietnam behind this backdrop of ineptitude. Mixed messages regarding an overall strategy, which lacked definition in the first place, further complicated his job. He tried to figure out why so much muddle? It made no sense to him.

Well-reasoned CIA intelligence estimates and recommendations were often overlooked for political considerations, expediency, or lack of focused commitment to win the war in the shortest period of time. DC typically waffled and constrained the military effort by restrictive policies on rules of engagement, which dictated that Laos and Cambodia remain off limits to counterattacks. That self-imposed course of action provided sanctuaries for the Viet Cong to escape pursuit and regroup. Not a sound prescription for victory. They also prohibited bombing North Vietnam strategic supply depots in populated areas of Hanoi, or blockading their critical Haiphong Harbor. To top it off, they turned down CIA propositions to bomb dams on the NVN border next to China to flood much of the north and critically disrupt hydroelectric power. All three recommended actions may have assured a speedy victory, according to the CIA's calculations. It seemed so clear to him, why did the strategy elude them?

Biff's exasperation finally got the best of him. "What the fuck are they thinking back there in DC?"

In his role as deputy station manager, he usually reserved his private thoughts. He typically tried to play it close to the vest, observe protocol, and avoid criticizing superiors or delve into messy politics, let alone blurt obscenities about them. He scrubbed at his eye with the heel of his hand. Apparently, his exhaustion had begun to take its toll.

"Beats the shit outta me, boss. They ignore most of our recommendations."

Jim knew this. Biff knew this. The CIA's recommendations generally fell on deaf ears back in D.C. The chain of command channels often ignored.

If that problem was not enough to cope with, ongoing conflicts between America's MACV and the corrupt Saigon government and its inept army bred another steady stream of frustrations. It was typically, "situation normal, all fucked up." One SNAFU after another resulted from lack of proper leadership and command structure. Most of all, though, the problem rested on the deficiency of a sound, coordinated strategy to confront the VC's guerrilla warfare.

Biff had to deal with this annoying bureaucratic BS, the political intrigues and jealousies, and bickering on a regular basis. He'd been in Saigon just over three months and it was already getting old ... very old. When things got fucked up beyond all recognition, FUBAR, it had a way of sapping one's enthusiasm for the task at hand. But, he plodded on. It didn't fit his nature to give up.

Biff surely understood Jim's feelings. In fact, he shared many of them. Vietnam was a dysfunctional military environment. No other way to describe it. A war without proper direction fought with irrational binding, self-imposed restrictions, and characterized by infighting among decision makers. This resulted in a war of attrition without a strategy conducive to winning a swift victory.

Jim called it spot on. This was no fucking way to fight a war.

Biff reflected. *War is the ultimate zero-sum contest—you win or you lose. What don't they understand about that axiom? How fucking complicated is that? We can never win with the present strategy, if you can even call it that.*

Nevertheless, he attempted some encouragement.

"Hang in there, partner. I anticipate an escalation of the 'conflict,' as they call this friggin' war. LBJ can't afford to lose what little popular support his administration has in the States. I predict they will up the ante. This sneak attack at Pleiku will force their hand."

CHAPTER ONE
THE ROAR OF THE CROWD

Eastern Shore of Maryland 1954

The deafening roar of the crowd fills the stadium. Thirty seconds to go—championship football game on the line, everyone on their feet. The tight spiral of Biff Roberts' perfectly thrown pass appears to be right on the mark to Roe MacDonald cutting into the end zone...

It doesn't get any better than this. Excitement has been building for weeks. This memorable Friday night welcomes autumn to the Eastern Shore of Maryland with a championship game, the first in memory. The humid summer's swelter—with its annoying insects and unpredictable, barbeque-ruining thunderstorms—fades into memory. The focus changes to football. Tonight's game represents the season's pinnacle with the Delmarva title at stake. The captivated crowd jumps up and down, roaring with expectation as the ball travels to the end zone.

The ball moved almost in slow motion against the backdrop of delightful autumn foliage surrounding the stadium. Oaks, sycamores, and maples capture a parade of color matched only by the spectacular sunsets across the Chesapeake Bay's marshlands and inlets. Life is good on the Eastern Shore, with a nip in the crisp air, and a huge flock of migratory Canada geese above, flying artistically in a V-shaped formation. Hunting and the fall harvest are huge attractions around these parts, but this contest is bigger, much bigger. Finally, Wicomico high school has a serious contender for the Delmarva high school football championship.

Friday night football, with all its hoopla, is about to reach its climax. Wicomico faces the opposing team from Laurel, boasting multiple championships led by a pro halfback prospect, Ron Wallen. The chances for an upset have never been better for the local team. The outstanding play by the home team's quarterback Biff Roberts and halfback Roe MacDonald is complimented by the team's two gifted ends: Al Ruey and Cody Johansson. All four players have earned All-State Maryland. The stadium is packed, with standing room only.

Wisps of ground fog frame the beams of the arc lights illuminating the field as the ball sails towards the end zone. The crowd's rapt attention focuses on the tight spiral as the ball sails toward the end zone...

Wallen closes in fast on MacDonald... Will he be the spoiler?"

CHAPTER TWO
THE BACKSTORY

Step back for a moment. Life evolves in curious ways. Twists of fate, irony—call it serendipity—often lead to unpredictable, unexpected events and outcomes. The story of these four young men, following their last high-school football game, is remarkable. Their interaction over the next two decades tests the uncanny nature of coincidence. This championship game represents only a prelude to their colorful careers and life paths.

Their backgrounds lend perspective to their future developments and inexplicable interaction. While many high school boys wander aimlessly through the maze of adolescence, a choice few will follow a circuitous, but certain, path to the center of life's labyrinth. They will achieve the status and distinction of manhood much earlier in life. This big game represents the apex of their adolescence and the beginning of their adult lives that will enigmatically converge over the next twenty years.

To understand the maturation and development of these four young men, it is necessary to understand the context of the mid-fifties on the Eastern Shore of Maryland, and the background that shaped their character. Why is this important? You will see as the story unfolds. The mark of a man is how he handles adversity. This environment shaped their personalities, their perception of the world, and sustained their will to persevere against the odds.

At the mid-twentieth century mark, the cultural fabric on the Delmarva Peninsula was religious, conservative, and industrious.

Welfare was practically nonexistent. Charity was strictly for the sick, lame, or destitute. Contracts were sealed by a handshake. A man's word was his bond, integrity the byword. Friendships were genuine, loyal, and enduring. And, all doors need not be locked at night. Basically, Eastern Shore men valued centuries-old, traditional societal beliefs.

World War II and the Korean conflict were over. Eisenhower was the universally respected POTUS. FDR was still a hero. Life on the Eastern Shore was tranquil. The credo "God, Country, Mother and Apple Pie" was not a cliché, but a defining characteristic at that time in Chesapeake Bay country.

This society served as a foundation in which the four Wicomico stars were raised. The quarterback, Buford Cavendish Roberts V, a very likeable lad with a pretentious name, always wore a smile or grin on his face, sort of like he'd just heard a good joke or was about to tell one. Not the least bit affected, he simply disliked the name Buford, and insisted everyone call him Biff. His father shared this same disdain, and went by his first initials B.C. The names Biff and B.C. worked for them.

"Better than Billie Bob or something like that," Biff joked.

His best friend, Roe MacDonald, the team's star halfback, often wondered out loud, "Why in the hell would someone name their son Buford for five generations if they really didn't like the name? And, why keep putting Roman numerals after it? What's that all about? They're not royalty."

Good question...

The Roberts were not considered rich, just "very well-to-do," the polite society term for the privileged class. Biff's dad and grandfather attended Yale. Both played baseball there. Biff was an outstanding high school pitcher, but an even better high school quarterback. His sturdy six-foot-four-inch frame was imposing. He could toss a football "forty yards into a peach basket," as the expression goes around the Eastern Shore. As the big man on campus, handsome—with blonde hair and blue eyes—of course, all the pretty young girls loved him. His peers admired him too. Besides being BMOC, Biff was also an excellent student who mentored younger athletes who strove to follow in his footsteps. He had not one ounce of conceit in him. The Wicomico County newspaper played up his key role in the upcoming football contest with Laurel. To all, Biff was a "hail fellow, well met," an appellation appearing in the high school's 1954 yearbook.

Roe MacDonald was also a fifth-generation product of the Eastern Shore, raised in an upper-middle-class family. His ancestors emigrated from Scotland in the early 1800s during the famous potato famine. They settled on the Choptank River, which feeds into the Chesapeake Bay. The first generations were shoremen, sailing their two skipjacks, named "Nancy" and the "Four Brothers," for nearly a century. They were accomplished sailors who always seemed to find the best part of the bay to harvest oysters. Their business flourished selling the catch to Crisfield shucking houses.

Roe's dad, Malcolm, departed the seafaring life. He graduated from the University Pennsylvania Medical School up in Philadelphia and became a general practitioner. During the Great Depression, he essentially practiced pro bono for two years. He was occasionally paid in chickens, seafood, corn, or some work around the house or yard. Fortunately, the family was frugal and had saved enough to weather the economic downturn of the early thirties. Roe made good note of his family's resilience.

Of Wicomico's four, star football players, Roe was the most exciting to watch, with his zigzag running style and breakaway speed. Fearless for a smaller player, he showed remarkable skill at catching passes, and converting them into long gains and touchdowns.

Biff joked that Roe ran like a rabbit, fast and unpredictable. Roe was well built on a stocky five-foot-ten frame, and always stayed in excellent condition. He had twinkly hazel eyes, short brownish-blonde hair, and a ready, friendly smile. He was generally a quiet sort, analytical and quite scholarly. In fact, he was awarded "Outstanding Student Athlete" by his peers and teachers.

Everyone considered Roe "cool," not so much in the hip sense, but in the collected sense. He possessed remarkable self-control. The guys on the team noted Roe always had his "stuff" together, although they used a profane word.

It was a toss-up between Roe and Biff when it came to leadership qualities. Both were outstanding and destined for successful careers that would cross paths over the coming years in unpredictable, fascinating ways.

The team's tight end, Al Ruey, is best described as strong, affable, and unassuming. His dad had a large soybean farm outside of town where he worked long hours while growing up. He loved to run, and became a cross-country champ. His friends joked that his demeanor reminded them of the old adage, "Strong, silent type," Even the school's 1954 yearbook ascribed this moniker to him. Al would go on to serve three tours in Vietnam, destined to greatness as a decorated fighter pilot. He would also earn a promotion to a brigadier general in the Marine Corps.

The fourth player, Cody Johansson, the right end, was something of an enigma to local folks. His family came over from Sweden in the late 1700s, settling in Lewis, Delaware. The early colony enjoyed amicable relationships with the local native Shawnee Indians. In fact, in generations past, one of Cody's paternal great-great-great grandfathers consorted with a Shawnee who bore him a son raised by the Johansson family as one of Cody's genetic ancestors. About six generations later, the suppressed Native American gene was partially expressed in Cody's darker skin, high cheekbones, and thick black hair. Cody looked different from the other boys. His pale blue eyes were inconsistent with features usually associated with Native Americans'. Cody's incongruous appearance baffled and confused the town folk below the Mason-Dixon Line. He wasn't really "colored," but his skin certainly wasn't white either. Some suggested he spent every hour of the entire summer on the beach at Ocean City obtaining a perpetual tan mixed with a sunburn.

Cody was definitely a different breed to the locals. The fact that he wore his black hair pulled back in a thick ponytail further confounded people during a time when a crew cut served as the predominant fifties' hairstyle for young men. Some wondered if Cody was making some kind of flaky fashion statement. But, most recognized Cody as anything but a flake. His model behavior engendered respect, even though his appearance remained a contradiction. Folks adopted the attitude, "Don't judge a book by its cover."

The tight end was a lanky, wiry kid with sinew attained from working hard on the family farm, just like Ruey. He loved to run. He was the Delmarva champ miler, typically beating Ruey by two strides in the shorter distances.

The'54 Wicomico yearbook described him with "Still water runs deep." Socially a bit of a loner, he preferred to hunt and fish. He spent more time with his Chesapeake Bay retriever "Schooner" than with his high school teammates. The town folk admired Cody most for his shooting skills. He won many skeet and trapshooting contests, a champ at sixteen. During bird season, he was without peer in marksmanship. Cody became an Eastern Shore icon: a chance to hunt with Cody and Schooner represented a lifetime experience, something to brag about.

For some reason, there was always a hint of a dark side to Cody, though he disguised it well. Perhaps he subliminally sensed that is ancestry and appearance somehow impaired his social acceptance by others in the southern community. Racial relations were good, but far from perfect. This drove him to achieve in every endeavor he undertook. Unrelenting, he succeeded.

His self-perception was unnecessary, though. The vast majority of the locals admired his achievements and grew accustomed to his different appearance. They were certain he wasn't colored, or he wouldn't be able to attend their segregated all-white school. So they assumed somebody must have checked that out.

In the early 1950s, schools in Maryland were "separate and equal." Prejudice took a back seat when it came to Cody. No racial tension existed locally, even though most small towns below the Mason-Dixon Line were predisposed to bias at that time in history. In the absence of ethnic rancor, everyone respected each other in this rural mid-Atlantic region.

***

The week before the big game, fervor and a crescendo of enthusiasm built toward the momentous event. The Thursday evening before the big game, the four young men decided to go to the Roundhouse for burgers, fries, and colas after football practice. The cheerleaders heard about it and met them there. Word got around town. Soon the shiny silver-domed Roundhouse was packed with fans.

The Roundhouse was a classic fifties burger joint with red vinyl booths, black-and-white tiled floors, and counters with red vinyl stools.

The fans admired the team, bought the boys' and the cheerleaders' dinners. They plugged nickels into the Wurlitzer jukebox playing rock and roll songs by Chubby Checker and Wild Bill Haley. The music blared until nine o'clock as everyone enjoyed a good time. Just before they left, a song came on by a new voice from Nashville, a relatively unknown singer by the name of "Elvis."

Looking back over the years, it was amazing everyone could have that much fun without beer, and be home and in bed by nine-thirty. But, those experiences represented the times more than sixty years ago on the Shore. If you were not around to experience them back then, the basic down-home lifestyles weren't very complicated, which may be difficult for current generations to understand.

Game day finally arrived. From the opening kickoff it was apparent this would be a hard-fought contest between two well-matched and talented teams. The competition became intense, and excitement mounted as the scores went back and forth with outstanding plays on both sides of the ball. The crowd went nuts, the roar deafening.

With less than a minute to go, Wicomico had possession of the ball on Laurel's thirty yard-line, with the score tied twenty-eight all. The home team, Wicomico, huddled…

Biff looked at Roe confidently and called, "Wing right halfback flare on three. Left end runs a post pattern, right end cuts short over the middle. Got it, Al? Cody? Let's bring it home, guys. This is what it's all about!"

"Yeah, man," Roe grunted. "Just hang it up there. I'll pull it in, Biff."

"Okay, pal. It's up to you. Let's go!"

They lined up for the final play in Wicomico's signature wing-T pass formation. The opposition knew the play, the crowd knew it, and Roe knew it was his time to shine. Biff's deft touch had mastered the delivery of the ball on this play, resulting in many touchdowns by Roe during the season.

Wallen, Laurel's star back, an awesome tackler as well as a runner, recognized the formation and hoped for an interception as time ran out, forcing overtime. He anticipated what was coming and, moments later, closed in on Roe with a burst of speed as Biff passed the ball in a tight spiral as Roe made a tight cut to the end zone.

The crowd roared another decibel as Biff's perfectly thrown pass looked to be right on the mark in the end zone. Out of his peripheral vision, Roe saw Wallen closing in fast. The halfback added an extra sprint of speed to deftly cradle the football.

Almost simultaneous with the reception, Wallen crashed into Roe. The impact of the collision could be heard in the stands, and the crowd gasped in unison as the clock ran out. Somehow, Roe managed to come down in the end zone in time, still holding the ball.

As the stands erupted, Roe sank into unconsciousness, lying in the end zone clutching the winning championship touchdown ball close to his chest.

The roar of the crowd quickly died. For a moment you could hear a pin drop.

CHAPTER THREE
CONCUSSION

St. Mary's Hospital: Salisbury, Maryland

Dr. Lon James appeared at the ER waiting-room door. His expression gave no hint as to what he was about to report to Roe's parents, Dr. & Mrs. Malcolm MacDonald. Dr. James was a colleague and longtime family friend of the MacDonald's. They tensed until he spoke.

"Good news. No skull fracture, and Roe's vital signs are stable. Neurologically, he is semiconscious with some waxing and waning symptoms suggesting a moderate concussion. He soon should be fully awake. I plan to keep him in the hospital for observation for forty-eight hours. No visitors until I give the word, okay? I am very optimistic he will make a full recovery without any neurologic complications."

Tears pooled in Roe's mother's eyes and Malcolm put an arm around his wife. "Thanks, Lon. We appreciate your good care and judgment. We'll get the word out."

Dr. James put his hand on his friend's shoulder in a friendly fashion. "I understand your son was able to hold onto the winning touchdown pass despite the hard hit by Wallen."

"He's a tough kid, Lon. It was a fair, but hard, hit by Wallen. If the shoe had been on the other foot, I'm sure Roe would have dished out the same … a clean hit, but powerful, trying to force a fumble with the game on the line."

"Well, it looks like Wicomico will finally have a Delmarva football championship after all these years. Can you believe it?"

"It's great for the town and county. Laurel has dominated football on the peninsula for too long. I think you'll see some good competitive college players come out of this game."

***

Wallen later became an All-American halfback at University of Maryland and an All-Star pro for the LA Rams. He was runner-up to Allan Ameche for Rookie of the Year for the National Football League.

But, the four Wicomico boys followed different pathways and never played football again.

After high school graduation, they enjoyed a great summer of partying together on Ocean City's beaches, but rarely saw each other beyond that. They went off to college, pursuing their separate careers and other interests. They returned to the Eastern Shore for short holiday visits, but family time and commitments to studying for exams after the holidays occupied most of their time.

Cody remained more interested in hunting and field time with his retriever Schooner than his buddies. Biff was busy introducing his new college sweetheart, Mary Beth, to his family, while Al spent time out on the farm with his aging folks, with his dad in ill health. Roe occupied most of his time hitting the books for pre-med tests.

They continued, though, to share a genuine affection for one another as they became men, ready to accept lifetime commitments and responsibilities.

On the few occasions they did get together, the boys always talked about the "Big Game." The down-homers never stopped talking about that game, and insisted Wicomico would never be the same without them.

The four teammates had no foreknowledge of what the future held for them. Much less an inkling how the evolving Vietnam conflict half a world away would interrupt their careers in the next decade and have a profound influence on their lives. They had no idea that, by a series of strange coincidences, their paths would converge in a series of fateful episodes over the next two decades or so.

CHAPTER FOUR
THE INTERVENING YEARS

Roe recovered without complications from his concussion and went on to attend the University of Pennsylvania. On Dr. James recommendation, he never played football again as a precaution. Scholastic achievements earned him early acceptance to Penn Med School where his dad had trained. He excelled clinically. Roe decided to pursue surgery as a specialty. He had outstanding MAT scores, which allowed him to match with top programs. He narrowed his choices to the University of Pennsylvania, Stanford, and the University of California, San Francisco.

However, the Vietnam War interrupted his best-laid plans. Roe enlisted in the USAF, attended the school of Aerospace Medicine in San Antonio, Texas, and earned his wings as a flight surgeon. Within the year, he was assigned to the 86th MAC at Travis airbase in California, but soon stationed on temporary duty (TDY) to Clark airbase in the Philippine Islands. From there, his duties took him to Tan Son Nhut in 1964, a strategic airbase outside of Saigon, and in 1965 to Danang, 380 miles north. As an Air Evacuation Officer, Captain MacDonald was now on a challenging career path in the Viet Nam conflict.

***

Meanwhile, Biff matriculated at Yale, the third of the Roberts family to do so. He disliked the town of New Haven, but loved the campus. Both the baseball and football teams recruited him. Unfortunately, he blew out his anterior cruciate ligament (ACL) in the first fall scrimmage, effectively ending his football career.

After that, he pursued baseball with a new intensity. The pitching coach refined his curve ball and change-up to go with his awesome fastball, clocked at more than ninety miles per hour. Biff was Yale's ace for three years, winning the Ivy League baseball championship in his senior year with his team. He graduated in three years by taking advanced courses during the summer.

Biff joined the ROTC as Vietnam started to heat up. However, unbeknownst, other career paths lay in wait. He was "tapped" to join the secretive "Skull and Crossbones Society" at Yale. There his life took a life altering turn.

Maybe this was the beginning of his penchant for secret activities. Shortly thereafter, the CIA recruited him. He attended Langley's "Farm" and graduated at the top of his class. The Farm's training facility is located at Camp Perry, Virginia. The rigorous course lasts about one year, including special instruction in cryptography, paramilitary activities, surveillance, and counter-surveillance. The training is conducted by senior CIA officers, some dating back to the agency's World War II predecessor of the CIA, the OSS. Biff excelled at the Farm, loving every minute of it.

Original OSS evaluation techniques from the days of "Wild Bill" Donovan were still employed at the Farm. For example, if a trainee had a special aptitude for computers and cryptography they transferred him over to the National Security Agency, a separate government branch in Fort Meade, Maryland. The NSA specializes in foreign government communication and intelligence analysis, (SIGINT).

SIGINT was not Biff's inclination or skill set. The CIA selected him for the national clandestine service. The Directorate of Operations, DO, had big plans for him. He aspired to become a spy, an operative, designated as a field officer in the CIA. In the FBI these officers are called "agents." This service is responsible for collection of foreign intelligence using covert action and recruiting human intelligence sources (HUMINT) referred to as "assets." His veteran superiors praised him not only as "a once in a decade candidate", but deemed him "a natural-born spook." Unusual accolades for such a young man, twenty years old just out of college.

With his training complete, Biff then had two choices. One was with the special activities division (SAD), involving high-risk covert paramilitary operations and collecting HUMINT in hostile territory. This involved highly classified activities, dark ops in areas where, if the field officer was caught, the government would deny his very existence and hang him out to dry, not attempting to rescue him.

Biff's second option was to become a CIA case officer posted to an overseas U.S. Embassy with undercover identity to recruit assets and compile HUMINT. Usually this entailed a diplomatic post conferring immunity to foreign prosecution, if discovered.

Biff chose the second option at this stage of his career, but got an unexpected add-on task. The "company," as the CIA is known, posted him as the case officer to the U.S. Embassy in Saigon. His talents were so admired by the training staff, they made him Deputy Station Manager, another accolade for such a young operative—in fact, unprecedented. In addition, his covert talents were so impressive the CIA assigned him as an adjunct to the special activities division known simply as "The Staff." In that capacity, another unprecedented appointment for a young man, his star would shine the brightest and lead him to direct the SAD operations in Vietnam.

The Staff was an ultra-secretive unit, an outfit of operatives with special paramilitary skillsets, but no diplomatic security (DIPSEC) if captured or exposed. His existence would be denied. He'd be on his own to survive.

However, just before he was about to depart to Saigon, the agency assigned him a short stint to coordinate operative intelligence for the associate director for military support (AD/MS) in Vietnam. This unit provides joint-force commanders with national intelligence estimates and operative intelligence for the military.

Jumping right into the unpredictable life of a covert operative, Biff became involved in "predict the future" scenarios to aid precise planning of covert operations. His first CIA job appeared promising in the beginning, but ended in an inauspicious manner.

In 1960, General Eisenhower authorized the CIA to train a brigade of exiled Cubans, about 1,500 men in Guatemala, for a Cuban invasion to overthrow Castro. In April of 1961, JFK authorized this "Army of Liberation" to invade Cuba at the Bay of Pigs. JFK desired "plausible deniability," so unmarked planes and ships were employed. The CIA was to coordinate the attack through Covert Ops at the Havana station and Santiago base. The operative details fell to Branch 4 Cuba under the Deputy Director of Plans for the Western Hemisphere. But, failure to coordinate plans with the NSC Division Chief, and the Deputy Director of CIA led to a major SNAFU. Air Ops were a separate division from covert support, paramilitary Ops, or both. This critical factor somehow fell through the cracks.

The failure to adequately communicate and coordinate air cover and landing of ships close to shore, as well as maintain covert security, resulted in one of the greatest military fiascos in U.S. history. Thirteen hundred exiles were captured and 200 killed by Castro's forces.

The JFK Administration was severely embarrassed. Allen Dulles, the CIA director, was fired over the fiasco. JFK was infuriated and vowed to overthrow Castro. The president decided to double down and instituted a backup plan through the CIA, "Operation Mongoose," under a legendary officer, General Edward Lansdale, who had extensive covert OSS experience dating to World War II in Burma, China, and Indochina. The OSS was the precursor to the CIA. Unfortunately, this CIA operation to topple Castro's regime also turned out to be a dismal failure. JFK fumed.

Biff, dismayed, wondered how he ever got involved in two such fiascos. Not an auspicious beginning, he worried his career would be besmirched, possibly ruined even before it got started.

Biff's original Vietnam assignment, turned out to be more propitious. He seemed destined to excel as Deputy Station Manager under diplomatic cover in Saigon. His duty involved a separate, influential assignment to Hickam AFB to serve as Vice-Chairman of a CINCPAC Intelligence Committee in Hawaii set up to evaluate multi-service intelligence data and manage covert operations in Southeast Asia. His job, to advise the Commander in Chief, Pacific Command, would test his intellectual abilities, and allow him to show his true mettle and intellect.

***

After graduation from Wicomico, Biff's teammate, Al Ruey, attended the University of Virginia in Charlottesville on a full-ride scholarship. Al, a science major, busted his butt to maintain a 3.8 grade point average. Later, he pursued a Master's Degree in Aeronautical Engineering at the University of Texas. In grad school, he joined ROTC.

It became evident that a national draft would be necessary as the conflict in Southeast Asia escalated. Al enlisted in the Marines, attained the rank of lieutenant and attended boot camp at Camp Lejeune, North Carolina. His athleticism and intelligence made him a standout candidate to move up in the ranks.

Al elected to become a Marine fighter pilot and was assigned to the Miramar Naval Air Station outside of San Diego. He trained with the same intensity and ability that made him a standout at Lejeune. His outstanding performance did not go unnoticed by his superior officers, who assigned him as a member of an elite fighter squadron flying A-4 Skyhawks. This squadron was destined for future duty assignment in Vietnam. Al was thrilled at the prospect.

***

The fourth star of the championship football team, Cody Johansson, went to the University of Maryland on a full athletic scholarship, planning to play on the same football team as the star runner Ron Wallen. But, Cody dislocated his shoulder in the first scrimmage, so he decided to stick to cross-country competition. He excelled in distance running, and lettered in the sport.

Cody remained a loner, diffident by nature, and the large campus gave him plenty of room for his private life. He had a few friends, but didn't require them, self-reliant as they come. He wasn't depressed, but despondent, missing his family and his Labrador retriever, Schooner. He often daydreamed about hunting with Schooner in the fields and back bays of the Eastern Shore. He thought about going back after college and running the family farm, as his dad's health failed. His mom had her hands filled caring for his father and the farm.

These plans were interrupted by the escalation of the Vietnam conflict. Over beer one evening in a local pub, one of his teammates told him he was joining ROTC to avoid the draft and ending up as a frontline grunt. Sounded like a good idea to Cody, who signed up the next day on campus.

Cody took his basic Ranger training at Ft. Benning, Georgia, attaining the rank of second lieutenant in the U.S. Army. The training officer suggested Cody train for the Special Forces Ranger unit. His sharpshooting skills and superior condition would benefit him and fast-track his career. It sounded like a logical progression … his skill with an M-16 rifle made his veteran trainers at Benning envious.

Again, it was no surprise that Cody excelled in the Special Forces. Assigned as a platoon commander his leadership shined. He was promised early promotion to first lieutenant and, soon after, to company commander with a rank of captain if he volunteered for Vietnam duty entailing a one-year tour of duty.

Ready to do something different, Cody elected the military option, though he had no idea how different life would be halfway around the world. Soon thereafter, Cody received his orders to fly to Saigon where he would be assigned to the Mekong Delta, serving under Colonel Vann's military advisory unit in Corps Tactical Zone (CTZ) IV.

The war with the Viet Cong was already raging in the Mekong Delta, the rice bowl region south of Saigon. Cody would see action that his young mind would never have imagined in his wildest dreams in early 1963.

***

So, essentially, that's how the four young men wound up in Vietnam about the same time.

Except for some weird twists of fate involving their interaction, this was probably not a whole lot different story than that of many others who were destined for duty in Southeast Asia. Jobs, careers, and education halted; families and loved ones left behind; not knowing if or when one would return from an unfamiliar and dangerous journey. That was a common theme, but these four young men come to make different thematic statements based on their experience and their perception of the war's reality. They sought answers to the confusion of the Vietnam War.

Life is stranger than fiction, which is a mere imitation, especially when it involves a complex, faraway war that few if anyone really understood then, or even now. Answers are elusive.

CHAPTER FIVE
COMING OF AGE: MURRAY ROBESON

Brooklyn, New York 1950

"Car! Look out."

Kids scattered from the narrow street to let the slow-moving car pass, only a brief interruption of their stickball game. This popular game is played with a broomstick handle and a tennis ball. The rules are the same as baseball, and you play 'til dark... or Mom calls.

This game was the default favorite in New York City, as the legitimate baseball diamonds in the park were always occupied by big kids who never let littler kids play. Stickball became the next best thing. The kids loved every minute of the game, a NYC tradition, a rite of city youth passage.

The neighborhood drivers were aware of the games and drove with caution through the narrow streets of Brooklyn. They knew most of the players. Many had played as kids on these very same streets and respected the game's limited space.

Murray Robeson was big for sixteen years old, a bit chubby. His long dark curly, hair and steel-rimmed glasses gave him a look of a youthful symphony conductor, not a stickballer. Murray had a ready smile, and bubbled over with enthusiasm in all his endeavors. Murray wasn't a natural athlete, but competitive in stickball, always one of the first selected in pre-game choose-ups.

His dad taught mathematics at NYU and his mother instructed music protégés at Julliard. Murray's parents immigrated to the USA from Vienna in 1938, just before the Nazi invasion with fellow Jews, the Kantors.

Thanks to the violin coaching of their friend, Mrs. Kantor, Murray performed at Madison Square Garden at the age of fourteen. One of the Kantor's two sons, Eric, was a brilliant scientific mind and musician. He became a role model for Murray, who graduated with honors at Yeshiva of Flatbush, Erasmus Hall High School, and Harvard College. Eric, who achieved his Medical Degree at NYU and a neurology fellowship under the renowned Harry Grundfrest at Columbia. Eric became a leading authority on cognitive function, eventually mentoring Murray in neuroscience.

Murray's fascination centered on memory. Influenced by his mentor, he studied extensively on the subject and became an authority in his own merits. Under Eric's tutelage Murray focused on the theoretical reconstruction of memory through "cognitive enhancers."

This was an unexplored field at the time. Murray demonstrated rare foresight in pursuing the emerging science of the brain. His scientific writings on "Memory: scientific basis and clinical implications for cognitive restoration" were widely accepted in his field, especially with Doctor Eric Kantor's endorsement.

In the sixties, he attained a level of fame as Vietnam vets returned, many suffering a range of post-traumatic stress disorders hindering them from smoothly assimilating back into society.

Remember the name Murray Robeson. He plays a vital role later in this story's saga with one of our Eastern-Shore boys.

CHAPTER SIX
AVOIDING THE RUSSIANS

Prague, Czechoslovakia December 1956

In the ninth century, Prague was a small, hillside village on the banks of the Moldavia River, where Hradcany Castle now stands. By the twelfth century, Prague was the center of the Bohemian Kingdom. Charles IV, King of the Sacred Roman Empire, expanded Prague by building the new city and establishing the prestigious University of Prague. The former bohemian city became a cultural center after the Hapsburgs conquered Charles IV's entire bohemian region in 1526. The Hapsburgs ruled for a long period until 1918.

Prague became the capital of the Czech Republic shortly after 1918. Its reputation as a cultural center flourished. Noted artists, writers, and intelligentsia congregated there. Some compared Prague to Paris. This city was known as the inspiration of Mozart's Don Giovanni, the Marxist literature of Franz Kafka, and Goethe's Dr. Faust.

But, three decades or so later, Prague became known for something more plebian, and problematic—a crucible for communism. In the late forties and fifties, it became the birthplace of the "human socialism experiment."

The city attracted radicals, activists, and communists from all over the world. Russia had brutally occupied Hungary just a month before November 1956, when it launched a fearsome tank assault against civilian insurgents. The Czech soil loomed a fertile target, and the residents recognized the imminent threat. Who could escape it?

A dark cloud gathered over a Czech Republic fearing the same fate. The citizens divided into card-carrying communists and those who resisted Stalinist repression. A politically polarized society existed, foreshadowing events that would occur elsewhere in coming years.

While beer gardens, pubs, and bars never closed, the mood in Prague definitely lacked vitality. Life was not good. In fact, it became increasingly oppressive. People were overtly depressed, and their attire reflected their mood. They dressed in dull, drab olive-green garments, or teplaki tracksuits, and kedsky basketball shoes. Once a vibrant, attractive society, the citizens became morose, declining physically and emotionally, their characters mere shadows of their former animation.

A cohort of intelligentsia, however, refused to fold. Resolutely, they took steps to resist communist totalitarian domination, vowing not to buckle under.

***

The Marcocek family found themselves among the resisting stalwarts. Ivan, a well-educated mathematician and engineer who graduated from the University with honors, conspired with the clique of resisters. He took a fellowship with Atonin Spacek, a renowned scientist in math and technology.

Ivan's wife Sabrina, born in the Ukraine, moved with her family to Prague during her childhood. A charming, small woman of high intellect, she maintained a keen, devoted interest in the arts: theater, music, literature, and painting. Sabrina was a member of the Prague Black Light Theater, and numerous other small theaters: the Drama Club, the Gate, and the Balustrade. Totally immersed in Prague culture, she associated with other intelligentsia committed to Czech liberty.

Through her associations, the Marcoceks became close friends with Jiri Anderie, a laureate graduate of the Academy of Fine Arts whose art later exhibited worldwide. Jiri persuaded them to move to his neighborhood in Hanspaulka near the famous St. Matthews Church.

He lured them with stories of a much more pleasant and peaceful neighborhood, filled with like-minded, well-educated people, actors, and artists, many known to Sabrina. It seemed an ideal environment to raise their gifted daughter, Natasha.

Jiri traveled often for art exhibits, bringing home stories of life in liberated countries. The concept of liberal democracy influenced him and his crowd of dissidents who feared domination by Soviet-style communism.

Their conversations prompted Ivan to recall one of Anderie's famous statements, "The one who loves jazz cannot become a member of the communist party." Quoted from a man whose surrealistic art was often compared to Chagall, it revealed another dimension to his friend's vibrant personality, and influenced Ivan's worldview.

Ivan subsequently held many discussions with his mentor, Atonin Spacek, regarding the bleak future for Prague. He observed that Russia's invasion and occupation of Hungary as an ominous prelude to tanks invading Prague. Ivan had a troubling premonition about this unthinkable event occurring sooner rather than later.

Actually, the invasion would not arrive until twelve years later in 1968, when Russia brought "winter to Prague in springtime."

Long before then, the Marcocek family had safely settled in Palo Alto, California and Prague had become a distant memory.

Jiri had been correct. "You must have freedom." Palo Alto brimmed with the freedom of opportunity. They'd found a new home.

Ivan held a position as a top engineer at Hewlett Packard. Sabrina became involved in the San Francisco art and music scene. Natasha blossomed at Palo Alto's top prep school, Castilleja. At age twenty-one, she graduated from UCSF Nursing School and accepted a job offer at San Francisco General Hospital's ER. She had grown into a charming, mature young woman with beautiful facial features accompanied by a pleasant smile. Her engaging personality reflected her inner self-confidence, born of academic and social success. In an interesting twist, Natasha's evolution will later unravel a key mystery in this story.

CHAPTER SEVEN
THE SUMMERVILLES

Sacramento, California 1955

The Summervilles left Missouri in 1933 during the third year of the Great Depression. President Hoover's ill-fated economic policies exacerbated an already sad state of fiscal affairs. The 1929 Stock Market crash, followed by bank runs and failures, perpetuated a national disaster. Raising federal taxes placed the final nail in the coffin of government fiscal irresponsibility. Unemployment reached twenty-five percent. Credit was nonexistent. They had no choice but to head west like many others.

They migrated to California in storybook fashion, arrived in Sacramento during the harvest, and secured labor jobs. The family worked hard in the great American tradition, and within a year could afford their own home.

Jeff, the patriarch and a workaholic, climbed the ladder in the classic American tradition. He got a job at McClellan AFB, west of Sacramento, and eventually rose to the level of GS-18, a pay grade equivalent to a colonel. This enabled him to educate his three children: two boys and a girl.

They were particularly proud of Ann, their daughter, a brilliant child. Jeff emphasized to his children that they should take every opportunity offered for educational advancement. Ann took that to heart.

The small, attractive, studious young woman became a scholar at UC Berkeley, graduating with honors with a double major in poly-sci and history. She received her master's degree, then a PhD in 1962 at Berkeley.

Her thesis, "Southeast Asia—Geopolitical Considerations" soon caught the attention of policymakers in DC.

With JFK's limited intervention in Saigon politics and the commitment of military advisors at the time, Vietnam was just reaching national consciousness. Guerilla warfare was a relatively unfamiliar concept to the U.S. military. The prevailing opinion regarding communism's threat in Southeast Asia was the Domino Theory, the basis of America's intervention in Vietnam.

In Sacramento and most places outside Washington, D.C., this premise was an esoteric topic. Ann, though, understood the theory's ramifications, expounding on this concept in her thesis regarding the origin of the Vietnam conflict, detailing its complexities and pitfalls.

On Cal's Bay Area campus, Ann was a conservative academic existing within Berkeley's radical, left-wing, progressive, activist environment. Describing her worldview as unwelcome would be euphemistic. She stirred a rumpus on campus. The Students for Democratic Action attempted to trash her thesis.

Ann considered the SDA nothing more than a communist front organization, and ignored their protests as limiting free speech. Yet, they didn't back down in their criticism, or stop trying to curb her free expression of a contrarian ideology.

In the late '60s, the SDA engendered the radical splinter group called the "Weather Underground," an anarchist group dedicated to the overthrow of the U.S. Government, They used bombing of government buildings as their signature expression of revolt.

None of this distracted conservatives and moderates in many national think tanks who became aware of Ann Summerville's thesis and recognized her brilliance. She quickly attained the academic equivalent of rock star status in DC, and her thesis became a hot topic in national newspapers and on black-and-white TV.

Her ideas caught the attention of several influential members of the State Department and National Security Council (NSC) in Washington DC. They flew Ann to Washington, interviewed her, and hired her on the spot as a consultant to the CINCPAC Intelligence Service at Hickam AFB, Hawaii. The newly formed committee consisted of representatives from top-ranking intelligence services, military, CIA, the NSC, and other consultant security advisors. Their task: collect and correlate the best-case intelligence estimates to conduct the war in Vietnam.

Ann's position was lofty for someone of her young age, but she measured up to the task, mature and well qualified. Some considered her a conservative policy wonk, but she was actually quite open-minded. She had a great capacity for pragmatism, and visualizing the big picture became her strength. Her aptitudes ranged widely. Based on extensive research, she had the ability to process complex information into workable programs. She presented fairly the conflicting pro and con options to the committees, and listened well.

These characteristics were in high demand in late 1962, as conflicting views and recommendations on Vietnam were rampant. Mass confusion reigned in some quarters searching for a consensus program on how best to manage the escalating Vietnam problem.

Over analysis and contentious disputes paralyzed policy decisions in many cases at the top levels of command. Ann had the ability to cut through all of this rigmarole and present a venture's odds of success or failure like a Las Vegas bookmaker.

Though highly intelligent and well read, she never came across as imperious or imposing.

But, she could also sound very convincing, arguing her case like a trial lawyer. Woe to the one who challenged her without substantial factual data to win his argument. He was in for a long day.

***

Vietnam in 1963 was an enigma to most. Proper approaches and solutions were hotly debated, though sound solutions to pithy problems remained elusive. No one could convincingly argue how big a threat Vietnam's fall to communism would represent to Southeast Asia. Was the Domino Theory correct? If Vietnam fell, would the other regional Southeast Asian countries topple, one after another? What would this mean to the United States' image and reputation? What was the national interest in becoming deeply involved? It was a particularly tense time in Vietnam and the

States. Diem, the President of South Vietnam, had been assassinated in early November 1963—some thought with CIA sanction and complicity.

Three weeks later, President John F. Kennedy was shot dead in his motorcade in Dallas, Texas, Washington surged with turmoil and the nation reeled with confusion following those back-to-back events.

Lyndon B. Johnson then became president, and inherited the Vietnam War LBJ required accord, a solid game-plan to solve the Vietnam problem. Though his primary vision focused on establishing "Great Society" goals, LBJ did not want to be bogged down in Southeast Asia. LBJ sought direction in Vietnam, but conflicting opinions confused the impatient man. Just how much was at stake in Saigon? How much U.S. involvement was indicated?

***

Ann took her new position on the committee only two weeks after Diem's assassination, and walked right into this political storm.

One of her first activities related to the new job involved attendance at the first joint CINCPAC intelligence committee meeting, where she delivered a thought-provoking lecture on the history of Vietnam and its geopolitical considerations. This information and the committee's recommendation would soon arrive on LBJ's desk in Washington D.C.

LBJ's close advisors and staff remained split on Vietnam involvement. He could sense the public's unrest heading in the same direction if he made the wrong choices, so awaited the CINCPAC-Saigon intelligence committee's recommendations with great anticipation.

CHAPTER EIGHT
MEKONG DELTA, VIETNAM

January 1963

Cody Johansson completed his ranger training at Ft. Benning, Georgia, in late 1962. Awarded the rank of second lieutenant, he received a certificate signifying "Top Graduate" by winning all the small-arms competitions, and for excelling in the jungle survival school in Guatemala. Basically, Cody had become a snake eater, a master of all the combat techniques necessary to fight a war halfway around the world in another jungle.

He was the first of the four high-school buddies to arrive in Vietnam. He flew to Saigon with other Special Forces troops on a MAC C-135, bringing the total of America's expeditionary force to 11,000 advisors in early '63. A crusty old staff sergeant met them at Tan Son Nhut Air Base. Not the gregarious sort, he saluted and, without fanfare, transported Cody and four other Rangers on a bumpy hundred-mile trip over the potholed Trung Luong road, a narrow thoroughfare congested with every conceivable form of traffic. Cody calculated, at their slow speed, it would take four to five hours to reach My Tho, a port city south of Saigon.

The sergeant rarely engaged them in conversation as the Jeep wined through the scenic wetlands and rice fields separated by coconut grove jungles and rustic villages. Normal life appeared to carry on despite the war. It reminded Cody of the humid backwaters of the Chesapeake Bay, though without the jungle atmosphere. His comments and questions to their driver went unanswered, so he gave up. Obviously, his rank did not confer the privilege of a casual conversation in a war zone. A briefing of any sort appeared out of question, so he didn't go there.

Not a happy camper, Cody observed. He'd soon meet other unhappy campers.

My Tho—located in the upper Mekong Delta, where the Mekong River empties into the delta—served as a hub for exporting rice to Southeast Asia. Besides being a major commercial link, the city housed the command post for ARVN, South Vietnam's army, at the time engaged in fighting the Vietcong to maintain control of the vast Mekong Delta. Tactical operations took place here to protect a marshland of rivers known as the "Rice Bowl of Indochina."

Cody was about to become one of many advisors for MACV in the Corps Tactical Zone (CTZ) IV. His job: assist and advise the ARVN in battle ops.

Upon arrival, Cody looked fit for his new combat role. A military crew cut replaced his ponytail. His pressed camouflage uniform with its ranger logo, shiny paratrooper boots, and black beret identified him as an elite commando. Rigorous training had buffed the well-delineated sinews of his muscles, and he projected the image of readiness to spring into action at a moment's notice. He holstered a .45 caliber service pistol at his side, and an M-16 rifle equipped with a full auto switch swung casually over his shoulder. A gun belt reinforced the "don't mess with me" image, not unlike photos of Che Guevara.

Cody's first assignment posted him as an expeditionary special force advisor under Colonel John Vann's impressive command. The colonel had a distinguished team of 200 officers and commandos assigned here. They said he was a hardened soldier, but if he liked you, he'd give you the shirt off his back.

Cody had studied the maps in the stateside briefings handout, and learned multiple Mekong Delta rivers empty into the South China Sea at My Tho, a key city in the warzone. As they drove through the city to their headquarters, he took it all in.

Nothing like this on the Chesapeake Bay, he mused.

The city still showed much of the French Colonial influence in architecture and maritime activities. Boats and ships of every size and description clustered the harbor, with barges and sampans tied up on the shorelines where piers were not available. The bustle of a mass of humanity indicated that the My Tho remained a center of commerce for the many peasant villages and hamlets scattered throughout the northern Mekong Delta.

Breaking his prolonged silence, the sergeant stated that many peasants reached the city by boat and that My Tho remained a pivotal city during the course of the war. Without warning he slammed on the brakes to avoid hitting a horse cart darting across an intersection, and, with a "sorry," resumed his quiet state negotiating the clogged roadway.

***

Cody arrived in late December at the end of the southern monsoon season. It lasted from May to December in the southern part of Vietnam. In contrast, up the coast to the central highlands and North Vietnam, the monsoon season was just the opposite, January until May. A third monsoon season occurred along the Vietnam border with Laos and Cambodia more than 400 miles north of the delta. It was always raining somewhere in Vietnam.

MACV quartered Cody in the expeditionary force compound of old French Colonial buildings sporting white stucco structures with brick foundations, capped by orange terracotta tile roofs. He soon learned these buildings had a quaint, interesting non-military history.

MACV leased the former Catholic Seminary from the Roman Catholic Church. Priests had trained here while in exile from North Vietnam. After the 1954 Geneva Agreement ended the war with the French, a mass exodus of ethnic Chinese and Catholics from North Vietnam sought refuge in nationalist South Vietnam. Ho Chi Minh persecuted Catholics and ethnic Chinese in the North, hastening their exodus by the thousands. Many settled in My Tho and studied at the seminary before the military took over the premises. The expeditionary force still referred to the two-story, L-shaped building as the "Seminary," but it was no longer reverent. It bustled with military activity.

Colonel Vann had built an impressive reputation as a pre-eminent soldier and logistic commander, directing the upper Mekong Delta operations from the Seminary headquarters. The colonel's group had been beating up the Viet Cong for the past year with surprise helicopter assaults involving one- to three companies. A company consists of 120 to 150 men in three platoons. This tactic required multiple helicopters to carry out multiple drops. It also necessitated considerable preplanning and coordination among American advisors and the ARVN. Large Huey helicopters could carry a platoon of approximately thirty men.

Cody would soon learn the chopper tactic conferred a huge advantage. Most of the roads in the delta were rudimentary, one-lane, rutted, and pot-holed beyond imagination. Multiple single-lane bridges with old French Guard posts hampered traffic flows. Cars, jeeps, and scooters all competed with water-buffalo-drawn carts and pedestrians for passage.

Further complicating transportation, the Viet Cong often mined the roads. Helicopters naturally became a prudent alternative to these obstacles. Their surprise attacks kept the enemy off guard and eliminated safe havens in the northern delta.

Farther south and to the west, close to the Cambodian border, the Viet Cong had secured most of the delta up to the Parrots Beak area, a safe haven in Cambodia territory sixty-five kilometers northwest of Saigon where the VC and NVA recouped. Rules of engagement forbade chasing them there, until someone stumbled onto the efficacy of covert ops.

When war did not intrude, the delta presented a tranquil setting of century-old customs. A typical postcard sight would be a young boy in his pajama outfit and conical straw hat, riding the back of a water buffalo with a white egret perched beside him. Peasants would till the rice paddies from sunup to sundown, while chickens, ducks, and dogs roamed freely throughout their hamlets.

The peasants ate well. There were so many rivers, canals, streams, and dikes in the Mekong Delta that the rice paddies were flooded year-round regardless of the dry season beginning in January. Vegetation flourished in the Delta, framing a checkerboard pattern of rice paddies, irrigation canals, and dikes. Occasional wide rivers of the delta intersected the paddies. Twenty-foot-high water palms, bamboo, and coconut palms grew along the edges. These trees were accompanied by groves of papaya, bananas, mangos, limes, oranges, grapefruit, and assorted tropical flowering plants. The rivers yielded bountiful fish, eel, shrimp, and crabs. During the monsoon flooding, the rice paddies became fish ponds.

This rural scene appealed immensely to Cody, an Eastern Shore outdoorsman. He took it all in, and reflected to his fellow advisors, "What a shame to disturb this pastoral serenity with a war. These poor peasants don't give a damn about it. They are just trying to survive."

***

Cody immediately took a liking to Colonel Vann's no BS attitude and military carriage that implied authority and control. The natural leader of men was fast becoming a Vietnam military legend. The colonel was the genuine article, not a "ring knocker," an academy grad without combat experience.

Cody didn't know it, but Colonel Vann had selected him on the recommendation of his training officers at Ft. Benning. They had informed him that Lt. Johansson could predictably lead a company of ARVN commandos and actually get them to do their job. Not an easy task considering their lack of discipline and tactical aggression.

That was all Colonel Vann needed to hear. He decided to mentor Cody and bring him up through the ranks swiftly if his performance in battle matched his training achievements and recommendations. Colonel Vann recognized there was a world of difference in how men behaved under fire with their lives and others' on the line. He anticipated Cody would have the right stuff to prevail in combat. He was a good judge of men.

Cody didn't disappoint the colonel. In his first performance of duty on 2 January 1963, in the battle of Ap Bac, Cody confirmed the colonel's confidence in him, despite the fact that the overall battle plan did not go as designed. Unfortunately, the attack fell into the "all the best-laid plans went south" category.

Here's how those plans turned into "an absolute cluster fuck," as one of Cody's NCO's stated later using the acronym, "Charlie Foxtrot" military phonetic.

Colonel Vann was a favorite commander of Colonel Porter, the III Corps commander of expeditionary advisory officers. Colonel Porter gave Vann free reign in planning assaults. Colonel Porter had under his command three of the nine South Vietnam Army Divisions—comprised of ten to fifteen-thousand men per division—to defeat the Viet Cong in the northern Mekong Delta. Colonel Vann's performance in the past year had been so far superior to any other battalion officers that, when he presented a proposal, Colonel Porter simply cut the orders.

Colonel Vann had an outstanding operations officer in Captain Ziegler, a West Pointer with an uncanny ability to evaluate intelligence reports and organize surprise chopper assaults. Captain Ziegler and his intelligence officer Drummond had been monitoring reports by L-19 spotter planes indicating a Viet Cong buildup in Tan Thoe and Bac. The two hamlets were located on the eastern edge of the Plain of Reeds. A captured VC radio had been monitored, confirming the spotter's reconnaissance. Captain Ziegler presented Colonel Vann with his assault plan.

"Ap" means hamlet in Vietnamese, lending to the mission code: "Ap Bac." The mission was planned for dawn of the 2nd of January. Although the dry season had begun, the assault teams and ten choppers unexpectedly encountered heavy ground fog, hampering the swiftness and coordination of the attack. The expeditionary force expected to encounter a VC Company of 120–150 men. The intelligence estimate was, unfortunately, off by half.

More than three hundred VC, well armed with captured U.S. weaponry, were dug in. The VC somehow anticipated the helicopter assault after a two-and-a-half-month lull in large-scale action. They suspected an attack to coincide with the end of the delta's monsoon season. The VC were well fortified and camouflaged in fox holes, trenches, and machine gun nests along the dikes and ridge lines of Ap Bac and Tan Thoe. They were veteran fighters, some dating to the conflicts with the French a decade earlier. The assault would not be a cakewalk.

These two hamlets were connected by a small river on the eastern edge of the Plain of Reeds. Seasoned VC guerillas in their forties with ample war experience had dug in a tactical position to provide crossfire on attacking ARVN troops with their American advisors. The 600 or so peasants and families wisely fled their hamlets to avoid the expected battle, sensing the danger of staying. The ARVN failed to sense the danger, however.

Drops of ARVN troops were intermittent because of the early dawn ground fog. Vann had specifically instructed the H-21 transport choppers to stay in LZs at least 300 yards away from the ridge lines, emphasizing that at this range .30 caliber fire is minimally effective. At 200 yard's distance accuracy greatly improves, defining a hit or a miss.

Several South Vietnamese chopper pilots unwisely disregarded Vann's instructions, approached too close, and were promptly shot down. Escort Huey gunships fired their machine guns and rockets at the entrenched VC on the bank, providing cover for the troops who became effectively pinned down in the rice paddies well short of their objective. Not an auspicious onset of the operation.

A company of ARVN M-113 armored carriers progressed slowly up the road to rescue them and to launch a retaliatory attack. They were late in arriving, which compromised their rescue mission.

Colonel Vann in his recon aircraft above the fray, monitoring the action below, became dismayed with the lack of coordinated maneuvers and adherence to the battle plans. A SNAFU developed right before his eyes because the South Vietnamese failed to follow straightforward orders. Though not unprecedented, it was disheartening nevertheless, and becoming a trend.

They just don't get it, he thought.

Command relationships between the American and South Vietnamese officers were not firmly established in 1963. The U.S. served only in an advisory capacity. This created enormous tension among the American expeditionary officers who rebuked the ARVN for lack of discipline and fighting spirit. All of Vann's well-laid plans were failing because of ARVN dysfunction, poor communication, and failure to follow the basic assault plans.

The one bright spot in the operation was the performance of Cody's company. While attacking the flank of Bac, his men encountered heavy machine-gun fire. In the fog it became difficult to make out the exact location of the incoming fusillade of .50 caliber bullets.

The ARVN Company balked and stopped in its tracks. This behavior astounded Cody. He spoke no Vietnamese, and his ARVN lieutenant's English was limited. Cody instructed Lt. Chu that the machine gun nest must be disabled before an assault could be safely mounted.

No response.

What's with this dude? Cody thought.

He had no tolerance for indecision and inaction. He grabbed an RPG, rocket propelled grenade launcher, from an ARVN Sergeant and cautiously proceeded with his M-16 up the hill, while his company watched a safe distance away.

He stealthily progressed to the flank of the enemy gunners nest. The machine gun loader's head popped up at intervals above the revetment and sandbags. Cody patiently waited, timing his appearances. He surveyed the machine gun nest through his polarized field binoculars and formulated a plan.

The VC's head appeared. Cody's M-16 accurate aim dropped the loader with one head shot. In the brief moment of confusion that ensued, Cody swiftly advanced to a higher vantage point, giving him a clear view of the gunner's nest. Before the VC could react, he launched a grenade from the RPG into the nest, destroying it.

The ARVN Company observed Cody's courageous actions. Impressed, they responded immediately by advancing up the flank of Bac to join up with Cody. They recognized that this American was a leader they could safely follow. This American knew what he was doing.

Lt. Chu, embarrassed, tried to jump aboard this spontaneous bandwagon of "Esprit de Corp." Without recrimination, Cody welcomed him back into the fold, taking care not to cause further loss of face to the Vietnamese lieutenant.

Cody's company swiftly occupied Bac, out-gunning and securing the outpost. He established Fox Mike (FM) radio communication both with the troops trapped in the rice paddies to his south, and with Colonel Vann up in his spotter plane on VHF. The colonel instructed Cody to hold his position until the SNAFU in the southern sector was resolved.

He congratulated Cody on achieving his objective of occupying Bac, swiftly and with few casualties. But the mishaps did not end there.

To further complicate matters, a series of ARVN miscommunications and lack of follow-through then ensued, resulting in "a military debacle," to use Colonel Vann's description in his after-action report (AAR), later that day.

In a few hours of battle, the ARVN had botched the entire operation on the southern flank. It became apparent to Colonel Vann that he must withdraw the troops, which made him livid. To minimize further casualties, the colonel advised ARVN to rescue the wounded and dead and withdraw. A frustrating, but necessary decision, but he was bound to the conditions of engagement dictated by higher command.

This was Cody's introduction to warfare in Vietnam, and the paradox of contradictions was not lost on him.

The Fort Bragg Special Warfare Center advised "tact and diplomacy when dealing with the Vietnamese." The basic problem in early 1963 in Vietnam was that the ARVN refused to take orders from the Americans, and the Americans lacked the proper authority to issue orders and conduct the battle—a classic "Catch 22" situation.

Back at the Seminary, when Colonel Vann wrote his seething AAR on Ap Bac, he excoriated the ARVN performance as "a military fiasco."

MACV Commander Harkins wanted to fire Vann, but was dissuaded by Colonel Porter and other commanders. Colonel Vann's exemplary record of performance spoke for itself. It would be a grave mistake to dismiss him for what other senior officers perceived as his candid assessment of South Vietnamese shortcomings effectively hampering the war effort.

"Someone had to say it," Cody confided to his comrades. "FUBAR best describes the operation."

Colonel Vann told Cody that he admired such courage and conviction, but could not decorate him with the Bronze Star he deserved. The JFK Administration had not authorized military decorations for South Vietnamese Expeditionary Forces at that time, 1963, explaining how he dealt with a lot of ring knockers. Instead, the colonel promised to promote him to full lieutenant at the next staff meeting. Vann further promised Cody that he personally would move his military career along.

Cody had recognized he'd witnessed a 'cluster fuck' in that failed operation, but offered no opinion to his CO. Not his place. He thanked the colonel for his promised promotion. As the colonel looked him in the eye, he sensed the colonel's disillusionment, and that he was about to take him into his confidence.

The colonel allegedly put his hand on Cody's shoulder and patted it lightly. "Cody, as you go through life, you'll find out there are more horse's asses, than horses."

That concisely summed up Cody's first military action in Vietnam.

CHAPTER NINE
MISSION EMERGENCY ROOM, SAN FRANCISCO

November 1963

"Dr. MacDonald ... ER ... Dr. Roe MacDonald ... ER," the overhead paging system blared.

Roe McDonald heard his page and rushed to the emergency room. Nothing unusual...as a busy surgical resident from UCSF rotating through the Mission ER at San Francisco General Hospital, he was used to emergency calls.

It was eleven o'clock Friday night, and the "Gun and Knife Club" was just warming up. The auto accidents' victims and LSD jumpers, predictably, would come in later that night and keep the operating rooms hopping.

Mrs. Fogler, the head ER nurse, greeted his arrival. She was an elderly, crusty, no-nonsense RN with incredible experience. If she got mad, she could make a sailor blush with her profanities. Many a drunk cringed under her rebukes. Some of the residents joked that they built the Mission ER around her.

"Hello, Dr. Mac," she said. "There's a bar fight victim over in cubicle number four ... hit with a broken bottle. You won't need much lidocaine anesthesia to sew his wounds up, he's wasted."

She gave Roe a pleasant smile, seldom seen on her face. She liked him. Roe was one of Dr. Blaiser's up-and-coming "hot shot' residents.

"Natasha will give you a hand. She's setting up a local anesthetic and suture set right now."

"Who's Natasha?" Roe asked.

"Recent grad from the UCSF nursing school. From Prague originally... a lovely young woman, well trained. You'll have no problems."

"Okay, thanks, Mrs. Fogler," Roe replied politely. "Looks like I'll be down here in the ER a lot tonight. No need to stay upstairs in the residents' quarters... the famous room 210." He winked.

Mrs. Fogler laughed, catching the innuendo. "Sure, Dr. Mac."

Room 210 was notorious for late-night escapades. "I'll see that a resident's room is reserved for you down the corridor."

***

Roe pulled the curtain back on the number four cubicle. Mrs. Fogler was right. The guy reeked of alcohol and appeared really zonked.

She sure got that lidocaine idea right.

Shortly after assessing the patient's status, Roe caught a pleasant scent and the presence of someone beside him. He looked around and met Natasha's beautiful blue eyes. With her blonde hair pulled back in a ponytail, she was very attractive. Simply lovely, actually. In fact, stunning. *Wow!* He restrained from vocalizing the thought.

"Hi, I'm Dr. MacDonald."

"Nice to meet you, doctor, I'm Natasha Marcocek."

"I see you've got everything ready for me. If you'll give me a hand, I'll debride the wound. The usual cleanup and sew-'em-up routine. I'll use a 4/0 nylon suture on a C-1 needle. Okay?"

Natasha appreciated how quickly he assessed the situation, ready to address the problem. She had heard a lot about Roe from other RNs, some who had a crush on him. Natasha thought him even more handsome than described. He came across as the quiet, strong type. She found herself attracted to him instantly... infatuated.

He had earned accolades early in his career from "Blaiser," as the residents affectionately called the chief of surgery. And, so far, Roe had lived up to his reputation as a budding trauma surgeon.

This doctor certainly acted cool in a crisis.

Roe instilled half-percent lidocaine into the wound and cleaned it with hydrogen peroxide and diluted betadine solution. He debrided all the devitalized tissue and was ready to suture the wound, closing it primarily.

"Natasha, would you be kind enough to open the 4.0 nylon suture and hand it to me?"

Natasha wore a surgical scrub suit with a loosely fitting blouse. As she leaned over to hand Roe the suture, Roe couldn't prevent himself from peering down her V-necked blouse. The gape revealed lovely, bra-less breasts.

She caught him gazing at her. When their eyes met, she smiled mis-chievously. It was if she could read his mind.

Roe returned the smile. "I've always been a student of anatomy. Yours looks fine."

Natasha laughed. "Thank you, doctor."

Roe set a new world record suturing the wounds, covering a tinge of embarrassment over the incident, though Natasha acted completely unabashed.

Briefly, he wondered about asking her for a date. No, that would be too impulsive.

Relax, fella, don't hit on the nurse, he instructed himself. *Not cool.*

"Natasha, thank you for your help. It's almost midnight. I'll have to check on a few patients upstairs, then I'll sack out in one of the ER rooms Mrs. Fogler reserved for me. If you need me, I'll be there."

Natasha thought to herself, *Is this an open invitation?*

Resident Sleep Room 2 a.m.

The door opened quietly. In the slit of light from the hall, Natasha peeked in on Roe. He was sound asleep, dead to the world in his scrub suit. Natasha entered the dark room and quietly closed the door behind her. Only the dim fluorescent light from the bedside radio clock lit the room.

After a moment, her eyes accommodated to the room's darkness. She approached Roe's bed. He was passed out on top of the sheets. Boldly, she tugged at the drawstring to his scrub pants.

Roe awoke, somewhat groggy. “Who’s there?”

“Natasha,” she warmly replied.

Roe sat up. He could barely make out her silhouette.

“You seem to have more than a passing clinical interest in my anatomy, doctor.”

“Yes, as a matter of fact. I’m a great admirer of human anatomy, especially when it’s well endowed.”

“Do you believe in the Garden of Eden?” she murmured seductively, still tugging suggestively at his drawstring.

“I could become an ardent believer.” His own anatomy already showed his ardent belief.

Natasha pulled her scrub blouse over her head, revealing her lovely upper torso. She bent over and kissed him softly, and her breasts brushed his chest.

Was one of his wildest sexual fantasies about to become true?

It was.

CHAPTER TEN
INTEL MEETING I

Hickam AFB, Hawaii November 1963

The Vietnam conflict appeared to be spinning out of control. It soon became apparent that this war would lead to increased American commitment. CINCPAC commanders had formed a joint intelligence committee to coordinate actions and recommendations of the various intelligence services involved in Indochina and the Pacific Theater.

Timely, clear, and concise intelligence estimates were required for Washington DC policy makers. The Joint Chiefs of Staff (JCS) and the National Security Council (NSC) distilled this information and offered their recommendations to JFK's administration following the normal chain of command.

Kennedy's administration and the NSC wavered in their stance toward the South Vietnamese government of Diem, and remained conflicted regarding a sound strategy to deal with multiple-faceted problems. Viet Cong insurgents were making significant inroads in the Mekong Delta. Diem's national army was losing control of the countryside. Buddhists were protesting in the streets of Saigon and Hue. Some burned themselves in self-immolation. Horrifying photos appeared in the daily newspapers. Saigon was on the verge of coming apart at the seams.

Captain Richard Noreika, a former nuclear submariner, co-chaired the conference with Biff Roberts, CIA's new deputy station manager in Saigon. Noreika was one of Admiral Rickover's boys, a hardnosed, no nonsense officer. A graduate of the Naval Academy, Noreika's service obligations were heavily ingrained. He knew a lot about communism, especially the Soviet version. His nuclear submarine spent a lot of time under the North Sea playing war games with them. But, he acknowledged that he was not as well informed regarding the Southeast Asia situation and the intent of the communist brand in that region of the world. He sought outside council rather than rely solely on military advisors—someone to offer a fresh look at the challenge.

On the other hand, Roberts was new to war games, but on a fast tract in his new role. He offered a fresh perspective based on CIA intelligence.

The committee consisted of senior intelligence officers from the various services. Colonel David Turner, a former SAC B-52 pilot and a West Point graduate represented the Army. He was a scholar in the history of conventional warfare, but still learning about asymmetric conflicts like Vietnam that required different tactics and strategies.

Colonel Andres Rodriguez spoke for the Marines. A seasoned officer, he was a protégé of Colonel Brute Krulak, and firmly grasped the situation in Indochina. He was outspoken—some said "opinionated." He shared Biff Roberts's conviction that intelligence of the human kind (HUMINT) was the most valuable source. This officer was not reluctant to buck the trend, or butt heads with other intelligence services. He shared this additional characteristic with Roberts. In fact, he had joined the CIA field officer in authorizing several "Reclamas" of Vietnam policy.

A "Reclama" expressed a contrarian view, one different from the committee's consensus recommendation submitted to Command. In general, Colonel Rodriquez was convinced the CIA provided the most accurate field estimates of the situation in Vietnam. It drove Andres and Biff up the wall when Washington D.C. failed to take their reasoned and well-researched recommendations. Who knew the Vietnam situation better than experienced field officers with reliable assets and resources, and actionable HUMINT?

The United States Air Force's representative was a Korean ace fighter pilot who had quickly moved up the ranks. His record of six MiG kills certainly helped his promotions. But, nothing assisted his swift climb through the ranks more than the active support of General Curtis LeMay. Colonel Josh Havenmeyer was a quiet, pensive officer who listened intently, never speaking unless the situation demanded. On these occasions, he spoke with authority, straight to the point, commanding close attention.

The group included all the various service intelligence staff and attaches, but Captain Noreika recruited a knowledgeable civilian consultant: Ann Summerville from San Francisco. She would give the committee a historical overview as well as an objective non-military viewpoint of the current situation in Southeast Asia. The State department offered her a five-year contract, plus an attractive stipend including a living allowance for private quarters off base.

Some officers expressed reservations at inviting a civilian to attend this conference, despite the fact that she had top-security clearance. At any time there could be a knockdown, drag-out incident with this high-pressured group of Type-A personalities.

The general sentiment of most committee members: Ms. Summerville had been intensely vetted, but could she take the heat?

Captain Noreika made the customary introductions, particularly laudatory in respect to Ann. The captain referred to her role on the committee as the "Devil's Advocate," tasked to challenge preconceived notions and in-bred bias among the various intelligence communities.

"Listen up, gentlemen. You just might learn something," he challenged the officers.

Ann approached the lectern, poised and totally in command. For such a young woman, she showed not a hint of nervousness. The audience was impressed with her attractive, well-dressed appearance, and her academic resume' placed on the desk before them. But, could she walk the talk?

She smiled politely and thanked the captain for his kind introduction. She began her dissertation with a quote from George Santayana from the *Life of Reason*. 'Those who cannot remember the past are condemned to repeat it.'

"I'm quite sure you are familiar with this oft-quoted axiom. It is especially appropriate to Vietnam, and well worth emphasizing. Allow me to briefly summarize its long history. I intend to lend a different perspective to the situation we face. What you can anticipate with our involvement in a military intervention in this country. It might deflate your expectations despite our enormous technological advantages in a military encounter with a third-world country. I fear Vietnam won't be a cakewalk."

"The history of Vietnam is one of repulsing invaders periodically over millennia. Their victorious resistance to foreign domination became ingrained as a signature trait. The Vietnamese culture worships Mandarin warriors. These icons maintained their will to prevail and persevere against greater odds. Their doctrine's keystone is to wear down the more powerful enemy by protracted warfare in inhospitable terrain."

Ann paused for effect, "Sound familiar? Sound like the asymmetric, guerilla warfare occurring in Vietnam? The warfare that defeated the French?"

The conference audience shuffled in their seats and murmured among themselves.

"She doesn't beat about the bush, comes right to the point," Noreika said to Biff in a hushed voice. "Good analogy."

"And she's just getting started," Biff responded.

"Gentlemen, Vietnamese resolve and determination won independence from China in 938 A.D. after a millennium of revolt and sacrifice. Unfortunately, every new Chinese dynasty from then until the French Colonial era in 1850 tried to invade Vietnam. This incessant warfare only increased the Vietnamese resiliency. They developed a concept that a weaker force can defeat a stronger one through a war of attrition."

She had captured their full attention with this historical perspective. Everyone recalled the disastrous French defeat at Dien Bein Phu in 1954, almost ten years before. They nodded their heads in agreement, listening intently.

"For generations, this concept became indoctrinated in their national psyche. The enemy was lured into inhospitable terrain, rainforests, jungles and mountains, and worn down with hit and run ambushes and delaying tactics. Famously, ancient warrior Dao used this tactic to defeat the Mongols when they invaded Vietnam in 1284 and 1287."

A few more murmurs…

"Now, surely you remember Genghis Khan? His grandson, Kublai Khan, the famous Mongol warrior, led the invasion and was defeated by

Vietnamese General Dao. Dao's military manual is still the classic reference source for training Vietnamese officers"

She went on to explain how, one hundred fifty years later, General LeLoi used General Dao's tactics to defeat the Ming dynasty invaders.

"The Vietnamese have long memories and infinite patience, gentlemen. That's a take-home message.

Ann detailed how the third-famous Viet General Nguyen Hue defeated an invasion of the Chinese Manchus with a surprise attack using swift tactics overpowering the enemy. General Hue attacked at midnight on the fifth day of Tet, the Chinese New Year lunar holiday. He caught a superior force off guard and annihilated them. The victory is still celebrated on the fifth day of Tet every year in Vietnam.

"Why this history lesson?" she asked. "The lesson is not a trivial observation. This Vietnamese tradition of resistance to outside aggression supports my contention that this resiliency has become ingrained in national folklore and the heritage of their Mandarin Warrior class. This historical mindset is what you are up against currently in Vietnam."

Coronel Turner, representing the Army, turned his gaze on his compatriots and back to Ann. "Interesting thoughts…" The others nodded in agreement.

Ann paused to double-check her paperwork. "Let me continue to trace Vietnamese history; its centuries-long lessons beg for our understanding. From the beginning of the fourteenth to the late eighteenth century, the Nam Tien advanced southward, as the Mandarin warriors of the north moved through the central highlands to the Mekong Delta, all gradually occurring over a period of 450 years. The peasantry, as well as the Mandarin class, worshipped ancestor Mandarin warriors on par with animism and Buddhism. Temples dedicated to historic heroes are still found in most villages in Vietnam. These national heroes attained cult status. Never underestimate the value Vietnamese culture places on physical courage and bravery, from the Mandarin warrior to the peasant cultivating his rice paddy today. It's intrinsic to their psyche."

She glanced around at the small group of officers and staff to gauge their level of interest. Seeing all eyes riveted on her, she continued. "In the nineteenth century, French military superiority and organization, plus modern technology and weaponry, allowed the French to colonize Vietnam and Indochina. Nevertheless, rebellion after rebellion over the next one hundred years provided evidence that the Vietnamese will was not broken. The French occupation could not erase the long rebellious history of this resolute country.

"The Vietnamese were awaiting new leadership. On the horizon arose Ho Chi Minh and the Viet Minh to remind the country of their proud history of rebellion. After over a hundred years of occupation they finally repulsed the French at Dien Bien Phu in 1954. The French lost 70,000 men in that war, a fact either not widely known or ignored."

She reordered her papers, tapping their bottom edge on the lectern several times, gauging their response. "I doubt you have forgotten that ten years before that event, the Japanese were unsuccessful in their endeavor to dominate Vietnam during World War II. Why am I recounting this history? Because this long, illustrious history documents that the Vietnamese are fiercely independent, resolute people. Above all considerations, they want liberty to pursue their lives without foreign interference. This is the primary lesson of their history. They are steadfast and will persevere under any circumstances, no matter how long it takes. This is a critical lesson we must learn to avoid repeating the history of prior invaders, gentlemen."

The officers stirred. The Marine's Colonel Rodriquez looked at his cohorts and sensed similar impatience on their faces. He was eager to test her argumentative mettle, her patriotism, and commitment to the war cause.

"Mind if we ask a few questions now, Ms. Summerville?'

She held up one hand. "Bear with me to make a few more points of interest you need to consider first, gentlemen." Without skipping a beat or showing any sign of discomposure, she dove back into her dissertation. "Consider the *modern* history of Vietnam. After their defeat of the French in 1954, the Geneva agreement partitioned Vietnam along the 17th parallel. This arbitrary division resulted in a mass migration of over two million people, many ethnic Chinese, from the north to the south of Vietnam, accompanied by thousands of Catholics. The exodus resulted from Ho Chi Minh's intolerance, not without some factual basis of persecution."

"Following the defeat of the French at Dien Bien Phu, the Viet Minh and their leader Ho Chi Minh became national heroes. Ho accumulated a lot of political capital with this victory. His group set up camp north of the parallel. Unfortunately for us, he is an avowed communist. But, I ask you to consider the following considerations in that context.

She raised one finger. "Is Ho a puppet of the communist block?"

She raised another finger. Is Ho controlled by the Soviets and the Chinese?

Another joined the first two. "Can you equate Ho with the totalitarian, brutal suppression of Stalin? Or, the cruel intolerance of Mao?"

She waited while they took in her three questions which made them uncomfortable.

"Those are disturbing, but important questions for us to consider in this conference. There is absolutely no question that Ho Chi Minh believes and pursues a Marxist doctrine. There is also no question that Ho is capable of brutality, but he prefers political means. Basically, Ho is a nationalist who accepts communism in his philosophy, distribution according to need. Ho has dedicated his life to this doctrine, but much more importantly to the reunification of Vietnam as one nation. That's his primary focus, one unified Vietnam."

Ann had correctly predicted the conference response. These indeed were disturbing questions challenging the conservative military audience. She observed that some officers were straining to maintain self-control and discipline, to remain polite. She simply smiled at them pleasantly and continued as they squirmed.

"In South Vietnam, gentlemen, there's another form of nationalism in Ngo Dinh Diem's government. He favors capitalism and democracy in theory. In practice, though, Diem falls well short of these lofty goals that we associate with our American ideals. In fact, in recent years, Diem's government has become part of the problem rather than a solution. Especially noteworthy is his insensitivity to the peasants' and Buddhists' concerns. He's failed to gain their support, a critical shortcoming in leadership.

"Nevertheless, we chose sides and supported Diem. Eisenhower granted $100 million in 1954 to Diem's government."

She put down her lecture notes. "Let's pause for a moment" Ann began to walk the perimeter of the room, so the officers had to turn to watch her.

"Try to examine or imagine Eisenhower's mindset in that time frame... why he took that action. Eisenhower believed in a monolithic form of communism. In his view, communism had a universal, geopolitical goal of global domination enforcing Marxist doctrine. The cold war followed, resulting in a standoff. As a result of the threat of mutual nuclear annihilation, no détente was ever reached. The Cold War mindset has persisted and is coming into play with Vietnam."

Back at the lectern, she leaned forward on it. "Now this statement may shock you. I propose that this committee challenge the accepted dictum that Vietnam is part of a massive communist conspiracy dominated by the Sino-Soviet Block whose aim is to conquer and control Vietnam and all of Southeast Asia."

Audible gasps and exclamations erupted, some profane.

Captain Noreika tapped his glass, signaling they needed to maintain self-control. "Easy, fellows! Listen up."

Ann simply smiled again, not the least bit ruffled.

"From my study and observation, Vietnam is a civil war between the communist north and the nominal democratic south, not part of a massive global conspiracy. From my perspective, both are dedicated Vietnamese Nationalists, which may be the overriding issue among them, rather than establishing a global concept of communism. The latter is not the driving force in my opinion."

"Ho may accept Soviet and Chinese aid, but nothing is further from his objectives than to have foreigners, especially Chinese, occupying and controlling Vietnam. Can Ho be violent? Ruthless in pursuing his goal? Yes, unequivocally."

She frowned, but didn't skip a beat. "Consider this contrarian ideology for a moment. In a basically agrarian society, is communism an unacceptable form of government? Perhaps not. Does the end justify the means? Perhaps. We may all come to different conclusions to these questions. Our judgment is colored by the personal bias that communism is inherently a bad and unacceptable concept. Does a third world, agrarian society without hostile international intentions pose a threat to our national security? Is communism a priori, an inappropriate concept for them? Are all forms of communism equal? Can we equate Vietnam's threat with that of China and Russia? Is Vietnam an existential threat? Put plainly, what's our dog in this fight?"

Colonel Havenmeyer from the Air Force tightened his lips. The others glared at her with visible outrage. Some bit their tongue. Colonel Rodriquez shook his head and opened his mouth to speak, but Captain Noreika tapped his glass again,

"Gentlemen!" he admonished.

Unabashed, even in the potentially volatile environment she had created, Ann continued her controversial dissertation challenging their collective mindset, pressing her points.

"Ho redistributed rich owners' land to peasants in North Vietnam. The methods may be flawed, but is the object or concept unacceptable in this particular somewhat primitive, third-world society? Is that symbolic communist issue worth our getting involved in a war over there? How is that in our national interest? Why is that action an imminent threat?"

That statement raised a few eyebrows and caused a few more grumbles among the group.

Colonel Turner whispered to Rodriquez, "Where the hell did Noreika find this pinko?"

If she overheard the comment, Ann didn't react. "In other words, are all forms of communism equivalent? Or, are some more egregious, oppressive and harsh? That's not to say I am promoting any form of communism, only questioning how judgmental we should be toward third-world countries indulging in this form of government. Should we impose our standards on them? Get involved in nation-building projects? Just what is America's vital interest at stake in Vietnam? I doubt they are conspiring to attack us. How great a threat are they to us? Ask yourself, is Vietnam a worthwhile endeavor on which to impose our will?"

A pregnant pause followed.

"Ideas have consequences. Some consequences have unintended results. Consider the present-day Vietnam situation for instance. Take an objective reckoning of the current circumstances. Following ten years of support, monetarily and militarily, to train their army and prop up their government, South Vietnam is in shambles. Diem and his brother Ngo were assassinated just last week. The CIA has been implicated. Since when did the U.S. government sanction and facilitate assassination of elected leaders of a sovereign foreign government that is supposedly our ally? I don't want this accusation to turn into an orgy of recrimination, but these assassinations are overtly a prime example of an idea that resulted in horrible unintended consequences."

Biff squirmed at this comment. Only he, among this elite intelligence group, knew the true backstory of that escapade.

Ann's unabashed statement set off more grumbling, prompting Noreika to tap his glass loudly to restore order again. The mood was souring, straining to remain polite, but it did not dissuade Ann from continuing her challenging perspective in her Devil's Advocate role, castigating the rumor of America's alleged involvement in the Diem coup d état.

"I'm here to make you rethink entrenched positions, gentleman, and question accepted dictums. So let's do that. Is this assassination act the compendium of our involvement in South Vietnam? Our primary idea was to support a democratic government and train the South Viet troops to fight the communist liberation front represented by a proxy, the Viet Cong. How did the unintended consequence of ten years of incremental increase of U.S. support end up in our complicity in a coup d état? What did we gain? The fallout has resulted in a military junta government both dysfunctional and corrupt, certainly not an improvement by any stretch of imagination over the Diems. Furthermore, despite our strong support, one-half of the Mekong Delta rice bowl is now controlled by the Viet Cong. Did anyone in Washington do a cost-benefit analysis of our investment in Vietnam? Shouldn't we expect a better return on our investment? Would you personally engage in such a risky undertaking? A truly objective observer might consider our venture in Vietnam a folly, gentlemen."

Ann could see her remarks inflicted her intended objective: to get this group to critically assess America's role in Southeast Asia. Their expressions and body language indicated clearly that they were hostile to the confrontation of accepted ideas, the status quo. She continued to challenge their rigid mindsets.

"The peasants have been relocated into government hamlets. This has caused a total disruption of their daily lives. They miss their villages and rice paddies, to which they are forced to walk every day, some at great distances. The peasants are intimidated by the Viet Cong, and frustrated by the ARVN's inability to provide security. All they want is to pursue their way of life. The hearts and minds of the countryside are not with Hanoi or Saigon. They have no political persuasions or inclinations. They just want liberty to conduct their lives without interference.

"As Edmund Burke wrote in 1791: 'Liberty is no mere abstraction; it succeeds only where the climate of social and political responsibility is universally accepted and respected.' This is hardly the case in Vietnam in November 1963, gentlemen. Without the support of its citizens, urban and rural, South Vietnam cannot and will not win this war. It's as much a political as a military reality. No amount of military advice or monetary support can negate the prodigal conduct and impact of this civil war in Vietnam.

"Ask yourself, honestly, how involved should the U.S. become in Vietnam? Consider this bottom line. Is our homeland at risk? Is the war really vital to our national interest? If so, please define the military and political objectives for me. Would congress and the American public support commitment of U.S. combat troops in the future, if put to a vote?"

The military found this shocking, one whispering, "This woman is bonkers."

"My comments are intended to shock you into thinking from a different perspective. Prompt you to reappraise the situation and adopt a fresh approach to achieve a pragmatic solution. These are vital questions this committee should address in the current context of its intelligence data and estimates. Hopefully, sound recommendations will influence Washington policymakers. Although I concede that may be a pipedream with their preconceived notions and priorities.

Biff flattened his hands on the table. "Got that right." Loud enough for her to hear.

She acknowledged him with a tilt of her head and a smile. "Finally, consider the Domino Theory, the justification, the pretext for our presence in Vietnam. We may be seeking an answer to this critical question for a long time to come. Our allies in SEATO think we should take a stand in Vietnam against communist aggression. They have a vested interest in seeing us succeed in Vietnam. SEATO also wants the British to succeed in Malaysia against the insurgents there. These are critical geopolitical considerations for us to deliberate and debate."

She observed the officers' shifting eyes, readjusting their seats, tapping toes, and drumming fingers, all signs of anxiety at these challenging thoughts. She had provoked some uncomfortably serious second thoughts and misgivings about unanswered questions plaguing Vietnam, but she could not stop now.

"What about Laos? Should I go there? The covert war has been going on in Laos for almost fifteen years, involving CIA paramilitary forces enlisting tribal warriors. The conflict's outcome is still in question. Presently, U.S. Special Forces and the CIA are supporting Loyalist troops with the enlistment of Meo and Hmong tribal mercenaries against the Pathet Lao and the North Vietnamese army. Is Laos expendable? Or should we take a strong stand in Laos as well as Vietnam?"

Captain Noreika observed the officers growing tension and reactions reflecting their displeasure as Ann continued her forceful arguments.

"She's really laying it on," he whispered to Biff.

Ann moved to the side of the podium and leaned in towards the group. "Consider Cambodia. A situation is brewing there. Where does it all end? How many commitments can we manage or afford? Where do we take our stand?

"My personal viewpoint is that President Kennedy bought into the Domino Theory, thus committed to Vietnam. After the Bay of Pigs fiasco in Cuba in April 1961, followed by his faceoff with Nikita Khruschev in Vienna in June of 1961, JFK wants to make a show of force in Vietnam. I don't think the president is nuanced regarding the different forms of communism. In my opinion, JFK views communism as a 'monolithic world threat,' just as Eisenhower did. I think he truly believes that Vietnam is a vital key to prevent the loss of Indochina to communism and won't allow it to happen on his watch. The very fact that he has increased the number of military advisors allowed to strike back defensively indicates to me he's decided to make a sincere, dramatic stand in Vietnam. He has drawn the proverbial line in the sand.

She sighed and placed her hands on the side of the lectern for emphasis. "Here's my honest assessment. Currently, we have 15,000 military advisors in South Vietnam and things are still a mess. JFK recently granted another $500 million in aid to an ineffectual Saigon government. Henry Cabot Lodge has replaced Nolting as ambassador in Saigon. It reminds me of a Bobby Dylan lyric, 'The times they are a changing.' Where does the escalation end? Are we condemned to repeat the mistakes of the French? Critically ask yourself, do we really want or need this war? Will it get worse before it gets better? Past is prologue, gentlemen," her somber expression reflected her earnestness.

The room fell silent, apparently with the weight of stunned thought and puzzlement. Satisfied with her job as the "Devil's Advocate," Ann gathered up her reference papers and returned to her seat.

The officers were just now beginning to understand the significance of her position in that role, and how out-of-the-box ideas might require them to radically readjust their military mindsets.

She didn't care if the disgruntled officers thought she might be a "Communist mole," or just another Berkeley "whacko" stirring up trouble. Or, that her presentation represented an outrageous Whiskey Tango Foxtrot moment.

The expression on Biff Roberts' face told her he thought she might actually be the right dose of medicine for this committee to jar their consciousness to the realities of protracted war in Southeast Asia, and an impetus to consider the downside of America's commitment. Exactly why Captain Noreika had made the right choice in choosing her as a consultant to shake up this committee. They needed fresh ideas, a new perspective. Saigon was a mess.

The Navy Captain's expression looked hopeful, whether due to her presentation, or his trust the war situation would soon improve, she could not discern.

None of them could anticipate that in two days' time, on November 22, 1963, JFK would be assassinated in Dallas. Or, that then Lyndon B. Johnson would become President of the United States, and the U.S. military would go on DEFCON 2 alert with B-52s armed with nuclear bombs taking to the air and awaiting orders to strike.

CHAPTER ELEVEN
JOIN THE CARTEL

Tijuana, Baja Mexico 1964

Tijuana is a grubby tourist town just across the border from San Diego on the Baja Peninsula. Impoverished, the town spawns all kinds of criminal elements: pickpockets, con men, prostitutes, petty thieves, and hard-core drug syndicates. While bars, nightclubs, brothels, and tourist shops flourish with American dollars, the general populace remains poor and greatly uneducated. If that's not bad enough, they are continually taken advantage of by the criminal element, especially the cartels. Only their Catholic faith and family values sustain them.

Many Mexicans aspire to get to America legally or illegally to seek a better life. They dream of leaving the rundown town with poorly maintained buildings, shanties, and ticky-tacky shops. At times, it's difficult to determine whether an edifice is half-built or half-demolished. Trash often goes uncollected. Paper, cans and debris litter many of the streets and sidewalks. Corruption is rampant, even among some police officers. Across the border, San Diego looms as a mirage beyond the Baja desert landscape.

Ricardo Sandoval and his partner in crime, Jorge Gomez, saw an opportunity to expand their marijuana trade to this northern haven. The border enforcement was relatively relaxed in the early '60s, which made it easy to transport their drugs. The competition in Tijuana was increasing with other local drug lords, so they considered it a good time to move on. So, they did.

Experiencing prosperity in San Diego within months, their drug cartel operation expanded to Los Angeles, and up to San Francisco. Occasionally, lower-ranked dealers would get busted, jailed, or deported but, in general, business was good. Prospects brightened with the oncoming Cultural Revolution on the campuses and cities of the west coast in the mid '60s. Opportunity knocked . . . they answered.

Mid-Ocean Golf Club, Bermuda 1964

Bermuda, an enclave for the avid golfer and a prime vacation spot, is located just a short flight from the east coast. What started out as a joke, ended up in an unusual twist of fate.

Randy the Rastafarian reigned as the premiere caddy at the Mid-Ocean Club. If he had a last name, no one knew it, except the starter who paid him. Everybody requested Randy. He knew every blade of grass, and every distance to the pin. Once he observed your swing he could club you correctly for eighteen holes. An unforgettable character with his outrageous wardrobe and dreadlocks, Randy looked like he had been outfitted at Goodwill or some other mix-and-match thrift store. Not one item of his clothes coordinated. Randy created the impression of a scruffy anti-fashion statement.

His flashy smile exposed his gold-capped incisors. Ugly keloid scars on his face and arms upset some golfers, until they recognized his talent. The scars on his arms represented needle tracks, those on his face resulted from bar fights. Nevertheless, it was difficult not to like the skinny little guy, so full of life.

Two industrial giants, "Masters of the Universe" from San Francisco, hired Randy to caddy for them while on vacation in Bermuda. They were initially put-off by his appearance but, as the game progressed, became very impressed with his skills.

Acting on a mischievous whim, they conceived a prank: to bring Randy back to caddy for them at their prestigious golf club in San Francisco during the upcoming invitation four-ball tournament. They both thought it would be a hilarious interlude to the staid environment of their golf club and to see their friends' reactions to Randy. Today, the idea would be considered insensitive but, back then, a lot of weird behavior passed for an innocuous prank, tolerated as off-beat humor.

They paid for Randy's airfare, plus a generous 2,000-dollar bonus. They instructed him to come just as he was, not to change a thing. Randy hadn't left the island since his parents brought him over from Jamaica. He thought it sounded like fun, not appreciating his host's motives. So, off Randy went to San Francisco.

He was met by his hosts at the SFO International airport. They dropped his duffel bag off at the hotel arranged for him, and took him over to the golf club for lunch and practice. They were really amped up for the member/guest four-ball.

Randy took their instructions seriously. He had not changed his outfit from the Mid-Ocean Club, but he hadn't bathed either. He looked a little haggard from the overnight flight, but still wore his flashy smile with gold-capped teeth, and brimmed with his usual enthusiasm.

Randy seemed impressed upon his arrival at the posh golf club. Members and guests, however, looked astonished. Provincial, aristocratic San Francisco ... meet the Rastafarian islander. One couldn't tell whether they were more upset by his dreadlocks or his outfit, probably the latter. The prank obviously backfired among the austere and humorless club members. They felt their privacy had been invaded. They resented the inappropriateness and insensitivity of the "joke."

With their delicate sensibilities offended, a few members summoned the club manager. He came out to assess the situation first-hand. It did not go well.

He addressed the businessmen, "What in the world are you doing? What are you thinking?"

They confessed that they considered it a joke, and thought it would be fun to see everyone's reactions.

The club president suspended the two members on the spot, and apologized to Randy. He explained that the caddy could not come into the club dressed as he was. The fact the Randy was black with flowing wild dreadlocks had nothing to do with the decision, of course.

The two chastised members took Randy to lunch at Trader Vic's, raising a few more eyebrows. They felt sorry about embarrassing Randy, gave him another 2,000 dollars, and told him to have a good vacation in San

Francisco before returning to Bermuda. They hoped to see him on their return next year for their golf vacation in Bermuda.

Vacation he did. Randy had never possessed so much cash. It was party time, and San Francisco was a great place for it. Alcohol, drugs, and women were plentiful, with some even legal.

Randy hung out in small bars around Union Square and Market Street. He was mesmerized by the Hari Krishna's and read their literature. He learned they believed in the personification of God, while Buddhists did not. He even considered becoming a monk while on one of his LSD trips. One thing he knew for sure, he wasn't going to use the return plane ticket to Bermuda after finding San Francisco his kind of world. Except for those country club folks, no one cared who he was, what he was, or looked like. Randy was going to whoop it up as long as the money lasted.

His party raged on for several months, rarely with a sober day. When the money ran short, Randy considered finding a job, but he only knew how to caddy. Fat chance of landing that job here.

San Francisco had been a wonderful experience for him. He enjoyed his small room in the Mission District flop house, including a bath and three square meals a day. He still didn't dress conventionally, but finally bought some jeans, a couple of tie-dyed t-shirts, and a moth-holed sweater at a thrift shop. This comprised his "office" attire. Wearing a multi-colored cotton Reggae knit cap with his dreadlocks hanging out, he fit right in with the Union Square panhandlers and druggies ... just one of the gang. They were pretenders, but he was the real deal.

One day out of the blue, opportunity knocked. While having a beer and burger at Lefty O'Doul's Bar off of Union Square, a man approached. The thin, well-dressed Hispanic sported a pencil-thin mustache punctuated by a permanent sneer. He was accompanied by a short, fat, balding Hispanic wearing a Guyabara, formal Latino wedding shirt. They definitely looked out of place in San Francisco, where most things go unnoticed unless completely outrageous.

Randy braced for a confrontation. "Who are you guys?"

Ricardo Sandoval, the man with the fixed sneer, introduced himself and his partner Jorge Gomez. He politely inquired if they could join Randy at his table and buy him a beer.

Randy had reservations, but did not object quickly enough, and they sat down across from him.

Ricardo immediately asked Randy if he was interested in a job.

Randy raised his eyebrows in surprise. "What kind of job?"

"You'll be sort of like a street merchant."

"What's that?"

"We have a little business in San Francisco selling drugs."

"Really?" Randy replied, his interest perking up.

"I noticed your needle tracks, and thought you might be interested."

"I noticed your mouth is pretty fucked up. What's up with that, dude?" Randy countered, offended.

He ignored the insult. "Complication from a childhood palsy ... You interested in a job or not?"

"How much will you pay me?" Randy inquired, wondering if this was too good to be true.

"We work on a percentage basis. You can make several hundred a day or two to three thousand a week, if you're good at it."

Street-smart, he had to ask, "How do I know you're not cops setting me up?"

Ricardo smiled. " Couldn't be further from the truth, man. What d'ya say? Give it a whirl?"

"Who do you work for? Who pays me?"

"I work for the Rajah. He pays me, then I pay you every Saturday for the rest of your life."

Randy still wasn't convinced. He had a lot of questions.

"How big an opportunity is this? How do I know you'll come through on your word? Where do I get the stuff to sell? And actually, what is the stuff you want me to sell? Who's this dude, Rajah?"

"Here's the skinny. In time, you'll meet the guys in the cartel and get the big picture. That's only after we trust you and evaluate your performance. If you get busted, you're on your own. So, be careful who you deal with, okay? We'll supply you with pot and LSD to start. If you do well, we'll let you go big time and push Burma Gold."

"What the hell is that?"

"It's the finest grade of pure heroin in the world, man. We bring it in from Laos and Vietnam. It's potent dope with a big street value. Gotta warn you though, if you start using it instead of selling it, we'll take you out. Got it? Screw up once and we'll whack you. Got it? We'll dump your body in the bay."

"Right on, brother, you got a deal. When do I start?"

CHAPTER TWELVE
MIRAMAR NAVAL AIR STATION

1964

After Al Ruey graduated from the University of Virginia, he applied for flight school at Miramar Naval Air Station outside of San Diego. His ROTC training allowed him to enlist in the Marine Corp at the rank of lieutenant. The Naval Air Station had received its first delivery of the A-4 Skyhawks, a modern aircraft slated to replace the A-1 Sky Raider in squadrons and, eventually, be deployed to Vietnam.

When Al arrived in 1964, the training program was going full bore. The Marine pilots and ground crews loved the A-4, a sleek lightweight delta-winged design with a single turbo jet in the rear fuselage. The plane was fast, nimble, easy to operate and maintain, and adaptable for carrier or ground duty. The fighter's design facilitated carrier storage, as its wings did not require folding. It was affectionately nicknamed "Scooter," or "Heinemann's Hot Rod" after the famous Douglas aircraft designer. Armament included two colt MK 20 millimeter cannons under each wing, capable of 200 rounds. Hard points in the fuselage and wings allowed for a variety of rockets, missiles, and bombs.

The Air Force flew the supersonic F-105 Thunder chiefs, nicknamed "Thuds." The F-105 was faster and carried more fire-power, but was heavier and not suitable for carrier duty. The Skyhawk perfectly suited the Marine's mission of ground and sea attacks, close air support, and long-range bombing missions. The aircraft was fitted for air refueling in a unique buddy-system fashion. This system allowed the A-4s to take off with more armament and less fuel, with the intent to fill up their tanks while in the sky.

Al's training course was intense, with his instructors intolerant of even the most minor lapse on the ground or in the air. Discipline and military decorum were strictly indoctrinated, and those lacking them quickly washed out. Every pilot who graduated genuinely earned his wings. Every pilot personified "Duty, Honor and Country." The Marine Corps indoctrinated the spirit of Semper Fidelis, and it became ingrained in core beliefs for life.

Al Ruey had the "right stuff" in his superior's evaluation report, and was soon promoted to captain. Soon after, the squadron commander summoned Captain Ruey to his office to offer a proposition.

"Vietnam is heating up. CINCPAC plans to deploy two or three aircraft carriers to the China Sea off Vietnam's coast sometime in the near future, probably in early 1964. The Seventh Fleet has proposed sending out the carriers *USS Bon Homme Richard*, the *Constellation*, and most likely the *Forrestal*. Interested in a tour of duty?"

The commander explained that Marine Skyhawks would be carrier-based at first, but plans included moving to a ground squadron at Chu Lai sometime shortly thereafter, then Danang. The squadron commander inquired if Captain Ruey would accept the deployment.

"Yes, sir! Count me in, Commander."

The commander informed him he would receive a promotion to lieutenant colonel upon satisfactory completion of the squadron's formation, and training, including carrier-landing proficiency.

"As a gifted flyer and a natural leader, you've earned this jump promotion, and will concurrently assume the command of a squadron," the commander explained.

Al didn't need to consider the opportunity long ... it fit him perfectly. "That would be great, sir. I'm honored. Thank you, sir."

Prior to deployment to Vietnam, more intensive training would be necessary. Captain Ruey started forming his squadron by hand-picking his pilots from the outstanding trainees at the Naval Air Station with advice from the commander.

He emphasized to his new lieutenant colonel that squadron commanders would be allowed some autonomy, but most of the orders would come down through CINCPAC. He might also receive orders from generals on the ground in the central highlands—far from Chu Lai's northern coastal location on the South China Sea—or from Yankee Station aircraft carriers off the coast. He instructed Ruey to go with the flow, the Corps was not running the show.

Al understood perfectly what the proposal and his duties entailed. He saluted the commander and thanked him again for the opportunity. Elated at the prospect of commanding his own fighter squadron, he left the office with a big smile on his face.

The Naval Air Station assigned thirty prospective pilots to Ruey. From those, over the next year, he must select only twenty, based on skills, compatibility, and any intangibles he considered an asset. He knew he would find it difficult to eliminate a third of such gifted pilots to retain a score of elite fliers, but that was his task.

Captain Ruey addressed his prospective squadron candidates and opened with the old Air Force adage: "There are old pilots, and bold pilots, but no old, bold pilots."

This familiar joke broke the ice with the men, who laughed heartily despite the fact they had heard the same joke many times. They knew Ruey, and respected him and his exceptional flying skills. No one was jealous he earned the job. He was the real deal, a genuine squadron commander, a natural leader.

Ruey then proceeded to define their Vietnam mission precisely.

One: Tactical close ground support.
Two: Protection for Asian allies' aircraft.
Three: Light fighter-bomber missions.
Four: Proficiency in both carrier and ground landings—day, night, and under any weather conditions.
Five: Become expert in armament—specifically bombs, rockets, and Sidewinder and Zuni missiles.
Six: Develop a close relationship and knowledge of aircraft maintenance. Double-check everything, every time.
Seven: Although the current armament on the A-4A was for self-defense, develop skills for air-to-air combat. One could never know when it may come in handy.

Eight: Do not hesitate to ask questions. Do not assume anything. If you break down the word "assume," it makes an "ass" out of "u" and "me."

Al was fortunate to have assembled a group of gifted and dedicated flyers, all steeped in Marine traditions despite their young ages. The Marine Corps had a way of indoctrinating their men. This disciplined tradition would serve them well in Vietnam. Ruey's squadron was destined for greatness in battle, excelling in close-air support.

CHAPTER THIRTEEN
SAIGON REUNION

Brinks Bachelor Officer's Quarters

Nothing about the Brinks Hotel building in downtown Saigon looked inspiring. In fact, it appeared rather ordinary. In contrast, its ground floor patio bar and surrounding gardens truly impressed, and served as an excellent watering hole for officers visiting the base officers' quarters (BOQ).

CIA Deputy Station Manager Biff Roberts surveyed his surroundings, not familiar with this particular transit military hangout. After entering the ground floor gate, a stone path led through the manicured lawn to the patio bar, an open-air, palm-frond thatched roof bar housing monkey-pod furniture, mixed with rattan bar stools. Multiple tables scattered throughout the bar accommodated a large, thirsty crowd, and the varnished table tops withstood drunken revelry.

The most impressive feature about the bar was its floral arrangements. Jasmine scents filled the bar. Vines climbed up to the roof and the supports for the plantation shutters. The shutters were open tonight since the monsoon season was waning. The surrounding gardens showcased a tropical paradise displaying plumeria trees, jasmine vines, birds of paradise, and various colors of bougainvillea climbing the walls. Overhead, suspended teak ceiling fans circulated the heavy evening air. The fans moved slowly, methodically, in a mesmerizing fashion. Further out in the garden, palm trees lined the perimeter, protected by a ten-foot high wrought-iron fence.

"Seems like a beautiful setting to kick back, relax, and enjoy a drink and conversation on an overnight stay. I'll give it a try."

A lot of action took place here apparently. Although some fifty yards from the road, exhaust fumes competed with the native flowers' fragrances. The traffic noise was inescapable, despite the piped-in elevator music in the bar.

Hi-fi could use an update, Biff noted. *Hope the music is better upstairs on the roof garden.*

The BOQ's rooftop restaurant served first-class American and Vietnamese food and boasted a good wine list, a vestige of the French colonial period. The smaller roof garden bar also offered a tropical flair. He'd heard that a Filipino combo played GI favorites up there. Since respectable females didn't hang out at the BOQ, they didn't need a big dance floor. The ladies of the night didn't come here to dance.

He sat at the piano bar, sipping a gin and tonic, and reflected on his hectic Saigon experience since his arrival last year. Finally, he had a few moments to relax and ponder his present circumstances. He had a lot of balls in the air. Vietnam defined the spy business, mind blowing in a dimension he never anticipated. He realized he was still on the learning curve facing a final exam of his capability—executing the Phoenix program.

He recognized he must pick up his game in the clandestine war that the Special Activity Division (SAD) waged under his leadership, meet the demands, and succeed where his predecessor failed. Shadow wars are never easy. Many South Vietnamese intel officers could not be trusted to collaborate with CIA's covert missions, so he decided to go it alone with his reliable SAD staff. It became a heavy burden with success difficult to measure when facing an unpredictable enemy that lurked everywhere, but nowhere at the same time.

This apparent contradiction occurred on a daily basis somewhere in MR IV, the Saigon war sector. Difficult to identify without uniforms, the VC attacked sporadically day or night in street clothes or pajama outfits with captured U.S. armaments or Chinese/North Vietnam-supplied guns. Asymmetric warfare challenged his adaptability in this unpredictable environment. No game plan could be set in stone. Flexibility became the key with backup plans a necessity in Vietnam's confused milieu.

Early on, it became clear the military suffered under self-imposed restrictions requiring them to jump through hoops to engage the enemy. So, Biff planned for SAD to pick up much of the slack, not bound by such limitations on rules of engagement. Not hampered by chain-of-command restrictions, SAD would engage the enemy proactively, based on actionable HUMINT. His paramilitary SAD officers enjoyed this tactical advantage.

Most of his days in Vietnam lasted more than twenty-four hours. His job demanded more, one challenge following another, allowing for little downtime. Tonight, he'd have some leisure time when his guest arrived. Maybe he'd relax for a few hours. Hoping to drown out the traffic noise over the garden wall, he asked the bartender to amp up the piped-in music, which he gratefully noted had changed to oldies but goodies.

The ceiling fans dispersed most of the road fumes, but not the cigarette smoke in the patio bar. Preferring his cigar aroma, he lit a Cohiba, and ordered another G and T. He sat back and blew out a puff of smoke.

Vietnam was getting to him.

He'd correctly predicted that U.S. involvement in Vietnam would pick up after the Congress passed the Tonkin Resolution on Aug. 7th. The Resolution gave LBJ broad powers after North Vietnamese PT boats attacked two U.S. destroyers off the coast of Haiphong. Essentially, LBJ received a blank check from the Congress to conduct battle without an official declaration of war. That move fit well with the president's nebulous program. It was obvious to Biff that LBJ lacked commitment to the Vietnam War and feared congressional resolutions could get messy. The current POTUS had mastered political manipulation. He harbored other ambitions, favoring his "Great Society" programs. LBJ never referred to Vietnam as a war, but rather as a "conflict."

That pissed off Biff, along with most of his friends.

It's a war, and poorly conducted at that. What are they smoking? Even with all the American advisors JFK sent over since '61, the ARVN lacks discipline and the will to win, he thought. *What the fuck is going on over here? That gal Summerville, made a good point. If we knew the history of Vietnam, we probably would never have been in this friggin' war in the first place. To be fair, the restrictions placed on our advisors in'61 and '62 limited success big-time. Muddled planning…*

Biff's misgivings never left his consciousness… they gnawed at him even on his rare night off. DC decisions were hard to fathom. Mixed signals. Confusing. One dumbfounding decision followed another. But, muddle had become the order of the day, not boding well for successful operations.

The greatest military in history marched to DC's tune. American advisors could retaliate only if fired upon. The advisors could suggest operative plans and strategies to the ARVN, but lacked authority to command or co-op missions. Preemptive strikes against the VC were forbidden to U.S. advisors under these self-imposed restrictions.

There's an awe-inspiring strategy, he mused sarcastically. *Guess it's hard to see the big picture with your head up your ass.*

Needless to say, these restrictions frustrated the American advisors in their vigorous attempts to inspire the ARVN to action. It seemed the ARVN lacked the required aggressiveness to preempt the enemy or finish the battle by pursuing the fleeing Viet Cong.

So much for our technological advantage, Biff mused. *The ARVN's lack of will offsets that benefit.*

It appeared the VC had some kind of "psych" on the ARVN. As if the ARVN regarded the descendants of former Viet Minh guerrillas, who defeated the French, as a superior foe.

Biff recalled from past intel reports that Colonel John Vann had been critical of the South Viet military performance in the Ap Bac debacle. General Maxwell Taylor had ignored Vann's recommendations to rectify the situation. Now, the VC controlled almost all of the southern part of the Mekong Delta. The Viet Cong recently scored similar victories in the rubber plantation areas west of Saigon… MR IV, Biff's bailiwick. He planned for the SAD to pick up some of ARVN's slack. They had the assets.

He sipped his drink, but rarely tasted it, preoccupied with his thoughts. The South Vietnamese Government lacked significant leadership since Diem's assassination a year ago. Actually, it remained dysfunctional under the succeeding military junta, maybe worse.

He wondered if the CIA's complicity would be discovered in that Black Op. Any recriminations? Keeping secrets in Vietnam was near to impossible. He dreaded the blowback if that skeleton got out of the closet.

"Vietnam is a country in turmoil. Damn it! It's their war, not ours," Biff vented under his breath. "Why can't they get their act together?"

The reality of the circumstances struck him heavily. The South Vietnamese performance, politically and militarily, did not portend an optimal outcome. The CIA's recommendations and intelligence estimates to General Taylor were generally disregarded, as were Colonel Vann's. Taylor marched to Washington's orders.

In Biffs' estimation, the war was a case study of mismanagement at many levels of command. His stream of CIA intelligence opened multiple avenues for military success, but they were infrequently implemented, resulting in lost opportunities.

Who knew Indochina better than the CIA, after all those years preceding the current Vietnam War, dating back to the post-WWII OSS covert actions? The CIA's predecessor, the OSS, had passed on remarkable knowledge laying the groundwork early on for undercover actions in Laos and clandestine efforts in Vietnam.

The CIA had a long history in Indochina dating back to Lansdale in the late '40s, followed by his protégé, Conein, in the '50s. These two operatives personally knew Chang Kai Chek, Ho Chi Minh, Diem, and most of the major French colonial military and government leaders preceding the humbling French defeat at Dien Bien Phu in 1954. And, Biff knew the CIA was intimately aware of the facts and failures of Vietnam's partition in the Geneva Agreement of 1954.

He ran those historical facts through his mind while ordering another G and T from the Vietnamese BOQ bartender, his mind filled with recrimination. *What's DC's problem?* Before JFK introduced military advisors in 1961, the CIA maintained a paramilitary, covert support system for Diem's ten-year reign. It seemed ridiculous to Biff that Washington continually ignored the CIA's expert advice at this critical juncture. No one knew the Vietnam situation as well as the CIA at this time. They knew the backstory, saw the big picture, and suggested a bleak predictable future based on their intel estimates.

Biff's frustration level often caused him to spontaneously vent aloud. He muttered through clenched teeth, "Another SNAFU!"

A few officers overheard him and looked up from their bar stools, probably thinking him deranged at worst, or stressed out at best. They resumed drinking and smoking.

On his third round, Biff switched to a Tom Collins, oblivious to any reactions around him. His guest was late. Might as well tie one on, no telling when he'd have another night off in Saigon. He had just returned from a CINCPAC committee meeting at Hickam AFB, Hawaii. It was obvious from that conference that other intelligence branches shared his personal frustration with current Vietnam policy. Hopefully, their recent recommendations would be more carefully considered by the U.S. Command in Vietnam than in the past, and passed up the chain of command with more conviction. Their reasoned advice seemed to fall on deaf ears here in the wartime theater, also.

"Time to put all this aside and have an enjoyable evening with an old friend," he murmured. "Good ol' Roe MacDonald. He must be tied up in traffic."

He sipped his drink and his mind automatically slipped back into his ruminations. Nothing happening in Saigon or its environs escaped Biff's CIA links. His diplomatic cover at the U.S. Embassy was becoming a not-so-well-kept secret. Biff mixed in high circles with the local movers and shakers, both American and South Vietnamese. They knew his connections and respected his role in the clandestine war, and were learning not to mess with this young man.

Recently going over routine Tan Son Nhut AB, TSN, intelligence reports, Biff noticed Roe's name listed as a flight surgeon attached to 86th MAC out of Travis AFB California. He noted Roe currently was TDY to Clark AFB in the Philippines and Tan Son Nhut for fifteen months. The 86th MAC regularly brought ammo, 81mm mortars, and armament into Tan Son Nhut, Bien Hoa, and Danang. The aircraft then reconfigured for air evacuation of wounded to hospitals at Clark, P.I.; Naha or Kadena, Okinawa; or Tachikawa, Japan.

The aircraft commonly used by the squadron were C130s, C135s and, later on, C141s. Biff observed that Roe was logging more than 300 flying hours per month. Both of them needed a break. Many of the Air Force officers stayed overnight at the Brinks BOQ in downtown Saigon. Brinks seemed like a secure location to meet his old buddy for a drink on the patio, followed by dinner on the roof garden.

Biff had arranged the occasion with Roe through the flight commander at Tan Son Nhut, who saw Roe on his frequent missions. Biff had booked an overnight room for Roe on the top floor at Brinks, and looked forward to the reunion with great anticipation. The years since they had last met had passed quickly without communication. Biff considered Roe a close friend since high school, when he caught Biff's last-minute pass and scored the winning TD to assure the championship. But as their career paths diverged over the past ten years, they'd lost contact.

***

Right on schedule, over an hour late, Biff noted sarcastically five minutes later as his friend arrived. Roe had pulled up to the guard station in an NCO chauffeur-driven USAF Dodge Six Pack.

Punctuality was obviously not a big feature in Roe's life at this point, Biff figured. Or maybe traffic, or his duties at Tan Son Nhut delayed his arrival.

Whatever.

Roe jumped out of the vehicle and headed up the path approaching the patio. He looked fit in his khaki tropical dress. Captain's bars adorned his shoulders and cap. He wore his flight wings proudly over his breast pocket.

He really looks professional in uniform. In fact, Biff thought he looked "spiffy" using their high school terminology.

Roe spotted Biff in the bar and threw a mock salute in his direction. Biff rose from his table grinning ear to ear, as usual. Some things never change, despite Vietnam. His friend looked natty in his light-blue cord suit with his Yale regimental school tie over his Oxford button-down shirt.

The quintessential Ivy Leaguer, Roe observed. *He's one sharp dude.*

The two old buddies rushed to greet each other, shaking hands and warmly patting each other on the back to express their genuine friendship.

Roe drew back and looked at his friend for a few moments. "Long way from Wicomico, dude, you're lookin' good."

Biff held his gaze steady. "Ain't it though? You can't beat a paid vacation, Roe. How's your old wazzoo?"

Roe laughed. "Haven't heard that phrase for over ten years, man."

Biff laughed, too. "Got you the best room in the house, partner. Have you stayed at the BOQ before?"

"No, for security reasons our crews usually RON in Bangkok, but most often we return to Clark with wounded the same day. Turn-around flights are becoming more common. The Air Force thinks it is safer over in Thailand. This will be my first stay here at Brinks. Nice looking patio bar. I love the tropical plants and atmosphere. Sorta reminds me of Hawaii."

"Actually, downtown Saigon is more impressive with its tree-lined boulevards and its French Colonial architecture. The French lived high on the hog during their halcyon days."

"I wouldn't include this building in that category," Roe chuckled.

Biff scanned the room. "Got that right. Let's have a drink and catch up on old times. What's your preference?"

"Gin and tonic, Bombay Sapphire gin."

"You got it."

"You know, Biff, it's a little bit more humid here tonight, reminds me of the Chesapeake Bay in late August."

"At least it's not raining. The G and T will refresh you. Drink up."

"Out on the flight line it's like a sauna. I took a shower and changed clothes at TSN air base. It feels good to get out of that flight suit. I smelled like Goose Tatum's sneaker after a double header!"

Both laughed at this old high school joke.

Biff knew Roe had already earned several decorations for his Vietnam service. Nothing escaped the CIA's notice. But Biff didn't want to go there. He planned to just keep it light, talk about the good old days, sports, and women.

"So, my friend, here's a toast to the good ol' days down home, a long ways from this RF, huh?"

Roe donned a puzzled expression. "RF?"

Biff translated, "Rat fuck."

Roe, mused to himself, *Biff, always the master of acronyms, fits right in with the military lingo in Vietnam. He speaks their language.*

He smiled and punched Biff on the shoulder in a friendly fashion. "You're still a joker."

"Yeah, everything's a BFD over here in Saigon. Oh, by the way Roe, BFD means a 'big fucking deal.' We can't get the friendlies and the military command on the same page, and the ambassadors are on yet another page. Believe me it's a real circle jerk."

"Gotta be frustrating, Biff."

"You bet your sweet ass. So, what's happening in the States?"

"I hardly get back there unless we air evac some severely burned GIs to Brooks' Burn Center in San Antonio. We stop by Travis and Hickam on the way back. All I know about back home is what I read in the *Stars and Stripes.* That's about it for my information source."

"How's your love life, Roe?" He didn't let on that he had an ulterior motive for switching to that topic.

"You gotta be kidding, Biff. Gotta say it's limited to a couple of one-night stands with horny RNs at Clark. I don't mess with locals, too big a risk of getting the clap. On the bright side, I met a nice Qantas stewardess over in Bangkok. We try to meet whenever we can at the Mandarin Oriental Hotel. Love their terrace and pool. It's really an oasis. She's a hoot, full of life. Good lookin' gal. We have fun together. How about you?"

"Well, I still have my high school sweetheart, Mary Beth. She lives in San Francisco now. I plan to marry her, if I ever get out of here. Meanwhile, there's a nice secretary at the embassy…my mistress, or 'moose' as the GI's say." He chuckled.

"She's a sophisticated Eurasian beauty, French educated. She's fluent in four languages: English, French, Vietnamese, and Chinese. But, there is still nobody like the love of my life, Beth."

"I wish I had someone to go home to. That's assuming I don't buy the farm over here in 'Nam. The guerrillas are getting bolder and better equipped every month. We're getting more scattered ground fire on our landing approaches. Thank God they don't have SAM missiles yet and few anti-aircraft guns."

"Our intelligence tells us the Soviets plan to give Charlie some SAMs soon. That may spell disaster for us. SAMs are a game changer."

"Hope to be outta here before then, Biff."

"Let's get back to women, Roe. I thought of you last week. I was back in Hawaii at a CINCPAC intelligence meeting. They invited this PhD consultant, Ann Summerville, to challenge us with some Southeast Asian history and discuss the Domino Theory. She shared some very interesting information in respect to the threat of spreading of communism in Southeast Asia. She's one sharp cookie. Good lookin' California gal. I'd like to fix you up with her. She's intelligent and quite attractive, a real knock out when she takes off her granny glasses. I don't know how approachable she is, but I suspect she's not a one-night-stand type. She's the marrying kind. If you're interested, I'll set it up."

"Okay, sounds like a plan. I get to Hawaii fairly often on air evac's to the States. I'm game for a stopover."

"I'll let you know when our next meeting is taking place in Hawaii. Maybe you can take a couple of days of R and R and meet us there. I really think you two would be a good fit, if you're up to the intellectual challenge."

"That would be bitchin'. Count me in. Just give me some lead time, okay?"

Biff nodded and decided to shift topics again. "Miss the Eastern Shore?"

"Sure do. Ever wonder how we ended up here?"

"Not a day goes by, Roe. Beats the hell outta me, man."

"Hard to believe, sorta like a bad dream. I wake up sometimes wondering where I am."

"Don't feel like the Lone Ranger, pal. I've had the same experience, waking up in some really weird places. Let me tell ya, Vietnam's a bit of a culture shock."

"Got that right. This place is really far-out."

"Speaking of far out, did you know that Cody's up in the central highland boondocks? He started out as a ranger, but now he's a Green Beret, gets involved now in unconventional warfare. Cody's a snake eater now."

"Nope, I lost track of Cody. So he's Special Op's?"

"Yep, and, I hear Al Ruey may soon be deployed to carrier duty in the South China Sea, flying A-4s off the carrier deck for close air support from Yankee Station. Word is, Marines are planning a land-based squadron at Chu Lai, so he may end up there after the Seabees lay down one of those short aluminum runways. Either way he'll be in the thick of it."

"No kidding. Can you believe that? All four of us over here fighting VC 'gooks' in the jungles and rice paddies… don't you find that incredible? Did you ever imagine such a strange coincidence? Ten years or so ago we were in a huddle trying to win a football championship. Now we're trying to win a war."

Biff shook his head. "No way that I could have seen this coming. It's really weird, all of us ending up here in Vietnam. We're talking a seriously *foreign* country. I rode a bike around Europe after college, but those countries really didn't strike me as foreign, nothing like this place. Just a decade after high school and the good ol' days back home, here we are involved in a crazy war half way 'round the friggin' world."

"It would blow most down homers away, if they could see this. We were brought up in such a tranquil, conservative environment. It takes *some* adjustment to adapt and survive over here. Some of the Vietnamese working on your flight line during the day will change into their black pajamas after dark in hopes of killing you or causing some serious damage to our aircraft. We post a guard twenty-four seven. When no one wears uniforms, you can't tell the good guys from the bad."

"Unless they are shooting at you," Biff wisecracked with another signature grin. He immediately grew serious again. "What you just described happens a lot. No joke, Roe."

His buddy ran a finger through the condensation on his drink glass. "We really had it pretty good down home, looking back. Compared to this mindboggling experience, down home seems quite provincial. We were really lucky. Look how these poor folks are struggling to cope with all the chaotic mess going on over here."

A commotion out on the street drew both men's attention.

"Grenade!" One of the MP guards yelled.

Reflexively, Biff and Roe ducked under the table to avoid the explosion fifty yards away on the far corner of the bar patio. The concussion knocked glasses and liquor off the bar shelves and demolished several empty tables. Fortunately at 1900 hours the bar was almost empty, so no casualties resulted. An hour earlier, the grenade would have killed or injured at least a dozen or so. At 1700 hours, it would have amounted to a "Happy Hour" massacre. Most military in Saigon liked to eat dinner around 1830, so had already departed the patio bar.

Biff turned back to Roe, who had ducked to the ground, still fixated on the street scene. His grim expression said it all… "Near miss."

Biff held out a hand to help his buddy to his feet. "That SOB coulda killed us. But, timing is everything in war and peace. We lucked out."

Out in the street MPs quickly apprehended the culprit, a young teenaged VC, no more than fifteen years old. He had fallen off his motor scooter when he lobbed the grenade, foiling his getaway. The MPS were beating the crap out of him.

This was not an isolated incident in Saigon and Cholon of late. Terrorist acts were becoming a common threat, intended to send a message that no one was safe under the Nationalist Saigon regime. Consequently, the popularity of rooftop bars escalated at a rapid pace. Even Willie Mays couldn't lob a grenade four or five stories high.

Roe dusted off his uniform. "Wow. The VC shoot at our planes all the time, but that was up close and personal. Enough to piss off the Good Humor Man."

His attempt to lighten the mood worked, but the event had served as a scary close call.

"How 'bout we adjourn to dinner on the rooftop? Just in case he has a buddy tied up in traffic down the street. Someone who might have a better arm…"

"Sounds like a plan to me. Let's go."

***

Biff ordered a bottle of wine, a Chateau Mouton, 1958. Over dinner, the two pals caught up on more news and related several war stories.

As Biff finished his last bite, he remembered their previous line of conversation. "Hey, before that kid lobbed a grenade, I believe I was bringing you up to date about Al and Cody."

"That's right. Fill me in."

"Well, Al's over in Miramar organizing an A-4 Skyhawk squadron. I think they'll soon deploy to Vietnam, either off a carrier in Yankee Station or Chu Lai, maybe Danang."

Roe's eyebrows raised, "I didn't even know Al had his wings."

"Oh, yeah, Al's becoming a rock star in the Marine Air Force. He's got a lot of talent ... Word has that he's one hell of a flyer, plus he's always been such a likable guy to boot. Naturally, he's moving quickly up in the ranks."

"Great. Good for him. And, Cody, what's up with him? You said he's a snake eater."

"Johansson's on his second tour now. He spent last year down in the Mekong Delta under Colonel Vann's advisory group as a ranger. Cody turned in his black beret for a Special Forces green one thanks to Vann's recommendation. His reports raved about Cody's leadership and sharp-shooting skills, and how Cody excelled in fire fights down there in the rice paddies and jungles."

"Where's he now?

"Good news, bad news...Vann promoted him to captain. After he got his bars, command sent him to the boondocks."

"The boondocks?"

"You know, the jungles and rainforests in the central highlands up near Pleiku. Only worse assignment would have been Khe Sanh."

"What's Cody's mission up there?"

"He commands three platoons in his company in the forward command post at Pleiku, a TAC base. They have 5,000 feet of runway, a rudimentary dirt-based strip with perforated metallic PSP cover. Camp Holliday is two or three miles away. Their recon mission is to keep an eye on the Ho Chi Minh trail traffic coming down from North Vietnam, but they're forbidden to enter Laos to effectively shut down the VC traffic. Can you believe that? Another brilliant strategy out of Command. Those VC bastards maintain trails and tunnels all the way to Saigon, our intelligence indicates. And, our troops are forbidden to go over the fence after them. Is that crazy or what?"

"Yep, crazy. Sounds like a hairy assignment for Cody, managing another ill-conceived policy. Our self-imposed restrictions sure give the enemy a tactical advantage."

"Well put. You hit the nail on the head, man. You can't chase 'em over the border. How dumb is that?"

"Real dumb and frustrating. Another typical DC policy decision dictating to MACV." Roe shook his head in disgust.

"Got that right. It's a dangerous assignment, but Cody thrives on it. He's hunting VC now instead of birds and rabbits back home. You can bet he's going over the fence into Laos. Unconventional warfare, that's what Green Berets do, pal."

"Guess he's right at home in the jungles out on S&D missions, loving real front-line stuff." Roe inclined his head slightly to one side, picturing Cody out in the boondocks. "Bet he fits right in."

"Right down his alley. Ya'know, I bumped into Cody last month. We both nearly fainted at the surprise encounter."

"How's that? What'd' ya mean?"

"Chance meeting, I didn't expect to see him in Cholon. We have the opium dens and narcotraffic under surveillance in Cholon out near our PX. The Viet underworld descendants of Binh Xuyenn are running beaucoup illicit operations over there, which, by the way, we intend to bust. I bumped into Cody in a local body shop. He was drinking the lousy local beer, Ba Muoi Ba. It's known as 'Thirty-Three' in Vietnamese. They say the French brewmaster had that many mistresses, so they came up with that catchy name. On R&R in Cholon, the troops order a 'Thirty-Three' and exchange war stories."

"No kidding? That's great little piece of local history. So, how was Cody?"

"Cool, smoking a joint, drinking beers with several of his ranger and beret buddies who had their pot bowls out, puffing away. You wouldn't recognize him in his crew cut, Roe. He had a tan complexion to begin with, now he's really dark brown from the sun and weather over here. Looks and acts tough as nails. He was very cordial and friendly with me, but I certainly would not want to mess with him, has a gnarly look about him."

"Cody into drugs? He hardly ever even drank beer."

"Not the hard core stuff, just recreational marijuana, I'd say. Bar's a popular R&R escape for GIs down in Cholon. They get high, get laid, then they go back to killing 'gooks,' as they call 'em."

"Sounds disrespectful to the enemy. Not nice to put 'em down and call 'em bad names." Roe laughed at his own sarcasm.

Biff shared a hearty laugh. Roe was quite a character, still able to joke around despite flying more than 300 hours a month and dealing with the wounded day in, day out.

Biff scratched the stubble on one cheek. "Here's my concern. The opium dens are a big worry. If our GIs get into the hard stuff, we'll have a big problem on our hands."

"No argument there."

"Seriously, Roe, I'm concerned about the negative influence of Cholon on our GIs. Most of these kids have never been out of the country, a lot of 'em probably never even been out of their state. We've thrown them into a war they really don't understand in a foreign country thousands of miles away from home. Some of the soldiers are still boys, not men. They'll screw anything from a gnat's ass to a horse's collar, drink heavily, and do drugs. Anything to get away from this war for a few hours."

"Gnat's ass..." Roe chuckled. "That's an old down-home expression. Haven't heard that one in quite a while either."

Biff needed to vent his nagging frustration about this topic, and Roe realized it. He listened politely even though he'd heard it all before. Vietnam had a way of getting to you. He'd treated his flight crews for everything from hangovers to the clap following R&Rs. Trivial problems compared to his air evac missions, but he understood where Biff was coming from.

"Most guys are only dicking around with pot, Roe. But, if they get on the hard-core stuff, opium and heroin, we'll soon have a serious discipline problem in the armed forces. Everybody knows this is not a uniformly professional army... a third are draftees. They don't give a rat's ass about Southeast Asia, much less the Domino Theory. Some can't even spell 'communism.' That's not to denigrate the career armed forces and those draftees who take their tour of duty as an obligation to their country. They're patriotic. But, let me tell you, pal, we've got a lot more problems over here than just the war. The ARVN is poorly disciplined, and we're supposed to advise them and provide support with poorly disciplined troops? Gimme a friggin' break, man! How's that gonna work out?"

"Not going to end well. I didn't realize most this shit was going on, Biff. You sound really frustrated." Roe leaned slightly forward. "Doesn't look like a good long-term prognosis."

Biff raised his hands above his head briefly. "I'm up to my ass in alligators. It's hard to remember I came here to drain the swamp."

Biff lit a Cohiba cigar, eliciting Roe's rebuke about smoking contraband cigars. They shared another friendly laugh together when Biff reminded him Cuban cigars were legal in Vietnam.

Biff blew out a puff of smoke. "Seems to me like we are fighting this war with our hands tied behind our backs, with too many self-imposed restrictions."

"You got that right, pal."

"As I told you, judging from what our intelligence reports tell us, this is one fucked up deal."

"Couldn't agree more." Roe could see Vietnam was getting to him.

Biff took a long drag on the cigar, and snuffed it out in an ash tray. Roe checked his watch, regretting he had no more time to console his buddy.

"Well, Biff, sorry to break this off, but it's getting late. Good you got that off your chest. Vietnam grinds you, I understand. Gotta get some rest. Out at 0600, better turn in. Thanks for the dinner and good times. It was great to see you again, pal."

"Really good to see you, too, Roe. Next time we'll meet at Cercle Sportif. It's a lot classier place, and certainly much safer from guys on motor scooters tossing grenades. I'll keep in touch. Thanks for listening to my bitching."

"No problem. Let's meet at Cercle Sportif. I've heard good things about the club. I'm in and out of 'Nam all the time. Just give me enough notice, okay? Also, let me know next time you're going to be in Hawaii. I'd like to meet this gal, Ann. Set it up. OK? This was a fun get together tonight, except for the explosion. I thought we were in deep kimchi."

"A miss is as good as a mile, but this place is vulnerable to terror attacks. We'll hit Cercle next time."

Biff grinned widely as he shook hands with his kindred spirit, and they parted ways.

***

Biff must have possessed extraordinary prescience. Three months later, on Christmas Eve 1964, two VC saboteurs disguised as ARVN officers in uniforms, parked a car in the Brinks Hotel lot. The car was loaded with explosives timed to go off just before dinnertime at 1730 hours. The bomb's explosion blew off a huge section of the BOQ, killing two officers and wounding many others.

Biff and Roe read all about it in the *Stars and Stripes.*

CHAPTER FOURTEEN
INTEL MEETING II

Hickam AFB, Hawaii May 1964

After the last joint meeting of the intelligence agencies in November 1963, committee co-chairman Captain Noreika had sent a blunt consensus statement to CINCPAC commander Admiral Sparks.

Following his review, the admiral forwarded this document to the Joint Chiefs of Staff (JCS) at the Pentagon. Essentially, the document asserted that, based on current intelligence information and estimates, the Vietnam conflict was a saga of "misguidance, mismanagement, and misgovernment."

The report directly stated that ARVN possessed an 'unnatural propensity' to bungle field operations despite the input of 15,000 experienced U.S. military advisors. The report cited the Ap Bac debacle as the prime example where American expertise and advice were largely ignored, resulting in casualties and a lost opportunity for a resounding victory. The document warned that the U.S. faced "a confluence of pivotal events" if the military and political situation continued to deteriorate.

American leadership searched for a sound strategy in its quest to stem the tide of communist insurrection in Vietnam, led by North Vietnam's proxy, the Viet Cong. Their intelligence document warned emphatically that the VC continued to gain control of the countryside, and stressed that ideologies clashed, predictably deterring inroads to their hearts and minds.

The committee recommended that the USAF favored bombing of North Vietnam's strategic targets in Hanoi and Haiphong. General Curtis LeMay was the most hawkish, advocating "bombing the communists back into the stone age."

The Marines advanced the idea proposed by Colonel Krulak: instituting a counterinsurgency action in North Vietnam employing mercenary guerrillas.

The Navy urged the blockade of Haiphong Harbor.

The Army repeated its request for more troops and authorization to launch preemptive strikes to attack the enemy in their safe havens, particularly the Ho Chi Minh trail in Laos.

In the committee's opinion, all options seemed prudent and reasonable. With the admiral's endorsement, all these recommendations had merit and were forwarded. The JCS agreed and recommended the report to the NSC, and on to President Johnson's administration, for serious consideration.

After winding its way up the chain of command, the administration offered a wimpy response: a proposed visit to Saigon by Secretary of Defense McNamara, and a proposal for a Honolulu conference in June 1964. Again they procrastinated, taking no definitive or specific action on the CINPAC committee's sound intelligence estimates and recommendations.

***

Captain Noreika brought the conference to order by announcing that, once again, their recommendations were essentially tabled, citing the tepid response. The officers groaned, grumbled, pissed, and moaned in frustration.

Biff whispered to the captain, "No big surprise there. What's fucking new?"

When the group finally settled down, Capt. Noreika informed them that a second coup d'état, led by General Khanh, had ousted the junta of four generals who had taken over after Diem's assassination last year, initiating round three of successive Saigon governments. He questioned if they were in for another round of ineptitude.

That announcement set off the committee again, causing the officers to stir in their seats, unsettled and annoyed.

"This bullshit is getting old." Marine Colonel Andres Rodriguez muttered loudly enough for others to hear.

Biff immediately recognized the general who led the takeover as "Big Minh," who represented nothing more than a figurehead Chief of State in Saigon's second government since Diem's assassination. The CIA deputy station manager predicted the political turmoil in Saigon would continue to be matched only by the inconsistent performance of the ARVN. Nothing surprised Biff anymore in Vietnam. He was becoming cynical. He thought "FUBAR" best described the circumstances.

Captain Noreika asked Biff to give his current status report based on CIA field operations in Vietnam, hoping that would settle the gathering down, or at least distract them from their rage.

Biff took the stage, smiling as usual in his sanguine manner. He always presented himself before this committee congenially, never showing the pressure or frustrations of his challenging position in Saigon. Under the façade, he seethed... almost like a grenade with the pin out, ready to explode. But, he maintained self-control despite knowing his accurate CIA assessments and recommendations continued to fall on deaf ears in Washington DC. It seemed no one could make a decision back there. For them, waffling was the order of the day.

"Many of you may not know CIA's history in Southeast Asia. It's relevant. It goes all the way back to the OSS role in Burma and the company's involvement with the Chinese conflicts following World War II. The OSS was the precursor to the CIA, formed in 1947. You may recall the OSS agency's most notable accomplishment was the support of Chiang Kai-shek, a nationalist general in China, but that's a long story for another day.

"Later on, the OSS proposed the Patti mission in Indochina to support and forward Ho Chi Minh's proposal for a phased independence of Vietnam. It seemed a reasonable solution. Ho proposed the French and the United States as transitional partners. Unfortunately, the strict U.S. policy of containment of communism torpedoed any consideration of negotiation with communist-tainted governments—a missed opportunity, as we look back.

"In hindsight, if managed correctly, the present situation in Vietnam may have been averted. Think about it. Of course, hindsight is always twenty-twenty."

Biff briefly studied each face in the room, assuring himself that the "Patti mission" message registered.

"Moving to the decade of the '50s, consider the Saigon military mission, a classified CIA mission under Edward Landsdale set up to evaluate the political power structure after the '54 agreement. The two scenarios were evaluated: the merger of North and South Vietnam versus keeping them as independent states.

"You recall the outcome—a divided Vietnam, the second scenario. Ho leading in the North, Diem reigning in the South. The CIA attempted to broker an agreement for a united Vietnam, but as I mentioned, Washington DC vetoed any consideration of a 'united government containing communists.'

"This rigid ideology prevailed during the fifties when the U.S. focused on Laos, not Vietnam. Again, you may recall, in Laos, another north/south conflict raged between the communists Pathet Lao in the north, assisted by the NVA, versus the U.S.-supported Loyalist Vientiane government under General Phoumi in the south. Thailand joined the U.S. in this support. The CIA paramilitary and Special Forces engaged the enemy side by side with the Loyalist army. And, for full disclosure, you may recall the Loyalists were supplied by Air America, CIA flights."

Army Colonel David Turner snickered, while USAF Josh Havenmeyer uttered a subdued "ahem."

Biff leveled his gaze at them. "Contrary to the rumor, the CIA did not engage in opium traffic to support their covert activities. I'd like to dispel that ugly rumor. The CIA enlisted mercenary tribesmen in the battle against the communists in the north who may have trafficked using Air America. We deny involvement."

Rodriguez chuckled. "Of course you do, but was it *plausible deniability*?" His friendly heckling took a dig at the classic CIA byword, with no malice intended. The other officers laughed, or cleared their throats.

Biff grinned, but continued without pursuing that line of thought. He got their collective message, *Yeah, right.*

"Okay, moving on … During the '50s, our field officers or operatives supported the Diem nationalist government … propped it up basically. This was facilitated by Lansdale and Conein, living legends in this bit of CIA history. Note, the agency recruited U.S. government support under the Truman/Eisenhower/JFK administrations. We operated with universal blessing from them, so no blame to lay.

"The exploits of Landsdale and Conein achieved mythical status among company old-timers during this period. They were indispensable to the Indochina mission, conducted under the three successive administrations, as I mentioned. Why is this history relevant? I present all this historical background as a prelude to the current pessimistic assessment I intend to relate to you."

Turner mumbled, "Not again, Roberts."

"Yep, steady on. Based on our long history in Southeast Asia evaluating and collating extensive intelligence data provided by our extensive network of sources, our estimates remain cynical."

"What's new?" Turner commented.

Biff nodded, but ignored the remark. He was used to taking flak at these often-contentious meetings.

Captain Noreika hit a spoon against his glass, indicating he wanted order restored.

"At the risk of appearing like Nostradamus, I offer the following observations. I again emphasize to you that this is based on our twenty-year perspective of CIA intelligence experience in Indochina. It's a stark message. Most of this data has been formulated by Harold Ford, former Saigon CIA station chief, an esteemed and respected CIA colleague. It has been updated by the present CIA staff for today's presentation. The CIA offers A, B and C caveats to our increasing involvement in Southeast Asia.

"Starting with A: Do not underestimate the North Vietnamese strength and national appeal. The Viet Minh defeated the French. They are viewed as liberators. The VC are their successors. They are resolute, resilient, and can be ruthless in their pursuit of liberation. Their goal is to reunite Vietnam under communism. The north maintains an extensive network of spy assets in the south. They have infiltrated the government, the military, and even the Buddhists.

"B: Do not underestimate the enemy's staying power. They are in this for the long haul. They are confident that the U.S. efforts to prevail will fade as morale dissipates. Ho's game plan is to simply outlast us, irrespective of the cost in North Vietnamese lives. The NVA understands the concept of 'limited war, a war of attrition.' If we escalate, expect the enemy to escalate. The agency's position on this intelligence is fixed in stone, you can count on it. It will be a 'tit for tat.' Our reliable assets confirm this as North Vietnam's long-term blueprint for success.

"And, C: Another word of caution, don't overrate the South Vietnamese military and political potential despite our considerable influence."

He looked up and noticed Ann Summerville nodding in agreement.

"To illustrate the Vietnamese's capricious and often inept performance, let me describe three notable failures. First, consider the Ap Bac debacle. This abysmal ARVN military failure is well documented in Colonel Vann's report, an embarrassment that General Harkins buried."

"Second, the government's mismanagement of the Buddhist uprising using hostile repression is reminiscent of the communist's actions in the north. Buddhist self-immolation has generated bad press in the States. Madam Nhu has handled the current crisis with the delicacy of Marie Antoinette. She essentially has encouraged immolation by the Buddhists. That response doesn't go down well back home."

"The third failure involves the flop of the strategic hamlet experiment. The program seriously disrupts the normal pattern of life for the peasants, and engenders disrespect toward the government. Peasants do not identify with Saigon, or Hanoi for that matter. They are basically apolitical and want to be left alone. Dislocation of their way of life is unlikely to win their hearts and minds. They feel insecure. The VC intimidates them. Their choices are limited. They can cooperate with the VC, or be shot.

"So, in the final analysis, it should come as no great surprise that support for Saigon's government is dwindling at home and abroad. Our intelligence estimates lead us to reach the same conclusion presented by our civilian consultant, Professor Ann Summerville last November of '63. Without radical changes in the dynamics, this war will not be won."

He paused and inclined his head to the professor, who returned his nod of approval.

He went on to explain that the war in Vietnam was essentially a civil war. In the CIA's opinion, Ho was not motivated by a monolithic communist plot to take over the world, not even Southeast Asia. Though Ho may seek Soviet or Chinese monetary or military support, he has no interest in bringing foreigners into his country to fight the U.S.

"Ho Chi Minh knows Vietnamese history and had been down that road before confronting the French. He's a devoted nationalist, but committed to communism, which is the essence of our contentious relationship with him as our enemy."

Biff paused to let that sink in.

"That presents the U.S. with a quandary. How do we deal with Ho Chi Minh? How do we best conduct the war? How do we manage the Buddhists and peasant dilemma?"

The uncomfortable challenge caused the audience to shift and stir in their seats, murmuring muffled comments to each other. As fighters, not nation builders or reconstruction project facilitators, a ready solution eluded them, but all had opinions.

In the following question-and-answer session, the various intelligence services proved clearly divided over the CIA's pessimistic assessment. Everybody rehashed their viewpoints. Intense exchanges ensued. Fiery turf wars became apparent.

Colonel Rodriquez challenged Biff. "Think maybe the CIA screwed up by whacking Diem?"

Biff smiled, but declined to respond to the taunt.

At that point, Captain Noreika called a halt to the increasingly overheated discussion. He suggested perhaps Professor Summerville, with her state department's connections, could enlighten the committee on the question of why no definitive action had resulted from their prior recommendations, tabled seven months ago.

Biff conceded the podium to her.

The professor hastened to say she understood the committee's frustration at what appeared to be the appalling cognitive dissonance of LBJ's administration. The chain of command dictated that this committee report its best intelligence data and estimates to CINCPAC who channeled to the JCS, who then would refer their consensus to the DOD, and finally up the chain of command to the NSC and the administration.

Ann related that Washington D.C. insiders had informed her that LBJ chose to adopt the prior JFK administration's strategy of limited war. To effectively pursue this strategy, LBJ's team added McNamara as SECDEF to the picture. An analytic person with a unique defense perspective, he committed to systemic analysis of a war that simply did not lend itself to systemic analysis. His policies further complicated the limited war strategy.

Just like his predecessor, LBJ did not want to become the first president to lose a war, but he failed to commit to a strategy to win it.

"Let's face it, LBJ games traditional procedural processes. Bypassing the JCS recommendations to conduct a war ignores decades of experience shared by veteran flag officers," Ann pronounced. "Declaring he knows better inserts arrogance."

Nearly everyone in the room responded with an audible sigh.

"If the truth be known, LBJ's focus is on the domestic front to institute his 'Great Society' programs. He wants that to be his legacy, not Vietnam. FDR's New Deal programs represent Johnson's ideology and goal. The Vietnam conflict he inherited is viewed more as a nuisance. 'Wars are too important to be left to generals,' word is, he told his inner circle."

She waited for the eruption of derisive reactions against Johnson to subside.

"Is this hubris, or just plain ordinary arrogance? Draw your own conclusions. The pervading mindset of LBJ's administration is that America's superior firepower will prevail without a large commitment of combat troops. A war of attrition will suffice—maybe not to win the war, but at least not to lose it. In essence, LBJ's administration believes it can succeed where the French failed. Recall Santayana's admonition? 'Those who cannot remember the past are condemned to repeat it,' Ann paraphrased. "I guess LBJ's inner circle didn't get the memo."

A few guffaws followed the humorous remark.

"My state department contacts tell me LBJ shares JFK's original concern that American credibility among our allies is at stake in Vietnam.

The U.S. must fulfill its commitments some way, somehow. He's looking for shortcuts. There seems to be a concerted effort by his administration to avoid presenting Congress and the American public with a full knowledge of the facts. These disingenuous actions suggest deceit. The administration continues to underplay the potential costs and consequences of the war at best. At worst, they distort the facts by misrepresentation and ambiguity."

Colonel Turner clapped. "Right on!"

His spontaneity reflected the prevailing general frustration among this distinguished military group. In calling out Washington's leaders, Ann elicited the committee's undisguised delight at her assessment.

"It's my view that the LBJ administration, at this point in time, has no sound plan for victory, militarily or politically. The administration continues to ignore the JCS input, so the military experts are effectively sidetracked. This administration seems fixated on short-term expedience, with no comprehensive estimate of the long-term costs of the Vietnam war in lives, money, or credibility."

"Amen, sister," Colonel Havenmeyer blurted in a low tone.

Noreika glared at him, shocked at his uncharacteristic lack of decorum.

Havenmeyer shrugged and returned his focus on the consultant who was starting to make inroads with the officers by offering opinions that resonated with them.

Unfazed by the outburst, she went on to say the conventional chain of command to conduct the war had been abrogated, going back to the JFK administration, and continuing through the present administration.

"In his inaugural address JFK said, 'Let us begin anew—pay any price ... bear any burden.' Are these eloquent platitudes or conventional wisdom? After articulating these lofty goals, why would JFK dismantle a system that has served the nation well in previous wars, especially in matters of national security? Who has the credentials to manage war? The JCS in consultation with the NSC? Or, a newly elected president who surrounds himself with close advisors inexperienced in military affairs of state? Must we abide by untested 'yes men?'"

"JFK reached his decisions after closed meetings with his coterie of the best and brightest—the Ivy Leaguers, whiz kids, and the team.

Was this the opening scene of the 'New Frontier'... soon to be dubbed 'Camelot?'"

Camelot, my ass, Biff thought.

Ann pursed her lips. "If you think I am being sarcastic, I am. I'm a civilian consultant without the restrictions on free political speech or opinions that constrain the military. I'm not expressing a Democrat or Republican viewpoint. I'm an equal opportunity critic."

Biff had to contain himself from laughing out loud. *This woman is full of piss and vinegar today. She must have some good resources back in DC. Maybe I can tap into them.*

He glanced over at Captain Noreika, smiling at Ann's comments. The others didn't look so positive. In this audience, surely some suspected Ann might be a communist mole.

Better check it out. Some of her comments are off the wall. Perhaps she is more than just a "Berkeley whacko."

Ann continued her summation by establishing timelines in the context of the geopolitical considerations following World War II and the Korean conflict. Before the conference, she had distributed detailed references in handouts in case someone wanted to check her facts, careful to document her statements. She referred them to one section so they could follow along as she provided her next evaluation.

"President Kennedy's inner circle consisted of Secretary of Defense Robert McNamara, Secretary of State Dean Rusk, National Security Advisor McGeorge Bundy, and Army Chief of Staff Maxwell Taylor. This 'Old Boys Network' bypassed the JCS and NSC in planning the 'Bay of Pigs' invasion. The fiasco occurred after just two months after JFK assumed office. Proper air cover was not provided during the landing assault, resulting in the casualties and capture of CIA trained troops."

She said if the routine structure of the JCS and NSC channels had not been dismantled by JFK, the outcome might have been favorable... certainly not as dismal.

"Unfortunately, the LBJ administration didn't learn the lesson of this tragic outcome. The tension from the fractured relationship between the JCS and JFK's administration continued well into LBJ's term. Decision and policy-making did not allow for systematic review and input from those more experienced in the ways of war ... generals and admirals. JFK tried to lay the 'Bay of Pigs' failure onto the JCS and the CIA. In fact, the JCS was consulted only after JFK had made the decision to give the CIA the go ahead for the invasion. Unfortunately, the CIA did not coordinate the covert paramilitary activity with the JCS. Not an auspicious beginning to JFK's presidency. A mutual distrust between them followed for years into the LBJ term."

Biff scratched his chin. *Ann really has her facts in line. She's not holding anything back. Good to get that out there, remind the military of historical facts.*

"Kennedy was not satisfied with American progress in Laos attempting to stem the communist tide of the Pathet Lao. Therefore, JFK and his inner circle decided to take a stand in South Vietnam. Ever hear much about that? Instead of committing U.S. combat troops, he planned to insert Special Force advisors. This would be under the newly formed command, MACV. There had been a gradual escalation in the number of advisors since 1961. By 1963, it numbered 15,000. Gradually a change in their mission occurred, authorizing them to respond to an attack by defending themselves. Why did it take two years to develop that brilliant strategy?"

She paused and scanned their reaction, though the question was rhetorical. "This inner circle management concept, I fear, may get us into more trouble. Why would any rational person ignore the input of the NSC and the JCS? Why would the administration ignore the CIA intelligence estimates and recommendations of this committee? Perhaps, we can still hold out hope for a positive outcome for the June meeting in Honolulu with McNamara."

***

No one could have anticipated that one of the seminal events of the Vietnam era would occur August 2, 1964, in the Tonkin Gulf, rather than that June in Honolulu. It destined the entire complexion of the Vietnam conflict to change dramatically.

CHAPTER FIFTEEN
NUMAZU SEA SURVIVAL SCHOOL

July 1964

Roe MacDonald received orders to report to Numazu, Japan, for sea survival training. With Vietnam heating up, someone in the USAF command had the foresight to set up this survival school. Overwater bailouts were becoming a realistic prediction. With two or three carriers at all times in the South China Sea's Yankee Station off North Vietnam, and increasing air traffic at three major South Vietnam air bases, it was inevitable that some pilots or flight crews would use this training to survive the ordeal of an overwater bailout.

The Soviets were now supplying the enemy in the north with SAMs. So, the stakes were rising as the odds of being shot down increased. Four events had increased the likelihood: the deployment of more U.S. aircraft to forward air bases adjacent to the sea, North Vietnam PT boats attacks on the destroyer Maddox, Marines on patrol boats offshore, and spotter planes offshore. All were susceptible to ground fire and missiles. If an aircraft is forced to ditch in the sea, this training becomes invaluable, needless to say.

Roe flew to Tachikawa Air Base in Tokyo. From there, he caught a bullet train to Numazu, seventy miles to the south on the Japanese peninsula. The survival school and barracks were just outside of town of Numazu on the coast. Even though it was July, it was cold and rainy. Not ideal for jumping in the ocean.

Roe knew some of the USAF personnel attending the course from various bases in the Pacific theater and Southeast Asia. From what he'd heard, this was not going to be anything like a summer camp. The choppy Sea of Japan awaited their arrival on the Izu peninsula. Roe wasn't really sure whether that was the Sea of Japan or Suruga Bay. It didn't matter, it was damn cold water. They would practice over-water bailouts for one week under various scenarios.

Upon arrival Roe met an outgoing flight surgeon, Captain Johnson, who gave him a briefing of what to expect.

"The first activity simulates an over-water bailout, involving jumping into the sea from a thirty-foot-high, rear platform of a moving LSD. The landing ship dock rocks in the heavy seas and, at times, it becomes very exciting," his colleague warned him.

"Dressed in your flight suit and jump boots, hanging from a harness, you wait for the command. Then you jump, feet first, plummeting into the sea. Your survival pack is strapped on. You submerge deep into the sea for two or three seconds, which seems like an eternity. The cold water takes your breath away, Roe."

"Sounds hairy, man."

His new best friend, Captain Johnson smiled. "It gets worse, pal. Resurfacing, you bob up and down like a cork, while being dragged by the harness attached to the moving LSD. It's up to you to roll over on your back and release your harness. Otherwise you risk aspirating sea water or drowning."

"That would sorta motivate you." Roe commented.

Both men laughed.

"You betcha! Next, you inflate your life raft and Mae West life preserver, and start paddling to shore."

"That's the reason they call it, sea survival school, I suppose," Roe joked.

"No problem, you can handle it. Good luck."

The two doctors shook hands and departed.

***

On a clear day, the famous snow-covered Fujiyama volcano is clearly visible about eighty miles to the west. If the sea is not too choppy, the view is an enjoyable aspect of the training course. One of the few.

If lucky enough to have a day off when the hammerhead sharks cancel the classes, Fujiyama is a nice place to visit. Roe lucked out one day. The Japanese village had good restaurants serving sukiyaki, rice, and refreshing Kirin beer. Roe had time to enjoy the communal "hotsy bath," a real foreign experience, after he played a nice eighteen-hole golf course for ten U.S. dollars That included a set of rental clubs and a young Japanese girl caddy.

On his third day of actual training. Roe noted that the short chop of the sea with four- or five-foot waves created an unusual effect with trainees bobbing up and down, visible to each other one moment and gone the next. It resembled a carnival shooting arcade, but it was no carnival. It was indeed a challenge, man against the elements, making his way to shore in a small life raft with paddles about the size of small sticks used to stir paint. Somebody's bright idea, someone who'd obviously not had to perform the task. It was not only difficult to climb into the raft in pitching seas but, once in, difficult to maintain balance and not tip over. One had to be extremely motivated as a survivalist. To Roe, paddling to shore seemed to be the longest two miles ever recorded.

Once reaching the shore, a challenging landing awaited. The waves crashed near to a shoreline with a steep drop-off to a rocky, pebble beach. It was a classic shore break, full of risks. If you got too far ahead of the wave, you'd crash, break a bone, dislocate your shoulder, or even break your neck. Timing the landing was important. The prudent survivalist would jump out of his raft and surf ashore with the raft ahead of him as a buffer to avoid a disastrous crash landing.

If that exercise wasn't challenging enough, the next day this process repeated *blindfolded* to simulate a bail-out on a dark or stormy night, or eye injuries suffered during the bail-out.

Once Roe mastered this arduous task, the survival school instructors put him into a helicopter rescue simulation in high seas. A chopper hovering fifty yards or so above the sea lowers a basket or harness to simulate a rescue. The helicopter crew hoists him up from the turbulent ocean and pulls him inside. This rescue seemed a little scary, but it got more challenging in the next scenario.

On the final rescue simulation, Roe had to pretend one arm or shoulder was broken and, while disabled, climb into the raft he'd just inflated.

Then the real test came, getting into the helicopter's harness and securing it, using only one arm and hand. If you failed the test, you repeated it until you got it right. If you really bungled it, you could fall fifty feet or so into the sea. Some did. Not a pleasant experience.

Saturday was wrap-up day at Numazu, a summarizing experience. They dropped Roe and his fellow trainees off the back of a fast-moving LSD to simulate a windy situation. He had to roll onto his back to avoid aspiration of seawater while being dragged behind the LSD. The next step required him to release his harness and inflate the life raft retrieved from his sea survival kit. This time, he must paddle three miles through a four-foot chop to the rocky shoreline.

Saturday was an unusually clear day for this time of the year, so Fujiyama's snowy peak became visible with the crest of each wave. Roe could not wait to complete this course. As a lifeguard in high school, he swam in the ocean one mile each day. But, this definitely was not Ocean City, Maryland.

He watched his fellow trainees paddling slowly to shore. Those who had rocky landings the first time picked up on the technique of surfing to shore with their raft ahead of them, proving experience is the best teacher. One pilot never got the hang of it and dislocated his shoulder, which Roe relocated for him on the beach.

Captain Johnson did not exaggerate the "exciting experience."

As a reward for your endeavors, you received a certificate and a 5th Air Force patch signifying completion of the Numazu Sea Survival School, a proud achievement.

Once Roe survived the rigorous days, he appreciated the training, realizing it might save his life someday, certainly others.

***

The course instructor met Roe shortly after his final landing and handed him a TWX (telex) message from Clark Air Base.

<Capt. Roe McDonald, Flight Surgeon, 86th MAC:

Meet Colonel Mason at Tachikawa Air Base at 1300 hrs tomorrow. You have a humanitarian mission on Cheju Do Island. Colonel Mason will fill you in on the details. He has all the necessary medical material and personnel on the C-47.

/ Colonel J.T. Anderson, USAF – 86th MAC – Clark AFB, PI.>

Roe thought, *No let up! C-47? What's that all about?*

He arrived early at Tachikawa AB to meet his old pal, Colonel Howard Mason. Roe greeted him warmly, as the colonel was one of his favorite pilots, a personal friend, and an unforgettable character known for his quick wit, ready smile and unflappable nature.

"What's with the C-47? Didn't know you flew old gooney birds. Thought you were married to your C-130."

Colonel Mason grinned. "Can't land or take off in a C-130 on a beach, Roe, or I would."

"A beach? You putting me on?"

The colonel laughed. "The island where we're going has no airstrip. The Cheju Do tide ebbs at 1400 hours, about twenty-seven feet. The sand is hard and compacted. We've got a good four hours to complete the mission and then we've got to get out of there."

The cheerful officer took everything in stride, nothing fazed him, not even landing on a beach. This affable, chubby, forty-two-year old Midwesterner lived to fly, loved steak and potatoes, a couple of scotch on the rocks, followed by a bottle of California Merlot with no ice bucket. No one ever saw him with a hangover. Not a single incident report marred his career during eighteen years of duty.

Roe knew his friend would soon make "Bird" if he didn't buy the farm in 'Nam. But, best of all, if they needed to land on a beach on a small island in the middle of the Sea of Japan, he was in good hands with this pilot.

"Exactly what is the mission, Colonel?

"Diphtheria outbreak among Asian kids on the isolated island, none are immunized. You're to supervise the medics on board who will inoculate the kids with DPT vaccine. Three kids are in serious condition at the little six-bed hospital there. I requested you take a look at them. They have one doc', one nurse, no vaccine, and limited antibiotics. We got everything you need on the plane, according to my manifest."

They finished their coffee and jumped aboard the C-47 for the hour-long flight. On approach, Roe spied the tiny island off the south coast of

Japan and Korea. The tide was indeed out, leaving a pristine, wide, flat beach with compacted sand having the consistency of cement.

Colonel Mason flew "a 180" overhead, surveying the island for the best landing spot. Perfect weather for a visual landing.

"Good thing... no tower, so have to deal with it. Good old-fashioned flying. Plus, a good story for the O-Club." He spotted a good landing area and started his descent.

He eased the C-47 down gently, as if he landed on beaches every day.

"No sweaty-da, Roe," he remarked with his usual good humor. "Grease job.

This guy really loved to fly. No challenge too great, no weather too inclement. It was all second nature to the colonel.

"At least no one's shooting at us on approach." he joked.

"Got that right, not like 'Nam. Nice landing, Colonel. We should be able to walk away from this one." Roe quipped. The old Air Force joke always elicited a laugh, no matter how many times you heard it.

"Don't mean to sound like an old lady, Roe, but you've only got four hours. Gooney Birds don't take off too well at high tide."

"We won't cut it close. We'll get right on it. I spoke with the four medics, they seem experienced. Hope the locals have all 380 kids lined up for us. That could be a major glitch in the immunization process."

"That was part of the deal, you can count on it. They'll be organized and waiting at the small hospital."

"I'll check in there with the Korean doc' to see if he needs any help first," Roe stated. "The medics will get started on the immunizations."

An old World War II jeep ferried Roe and his four cramped medics to the small hospital, a rustic structure of cinderblock concrete walls, small windows, and a palm-frond and bamboo thatched roof. The floors were hard clay dirt, no tiles or hard wood. Very primitive for 1964.

He greeted Roe with the traditional Korean greeting. "Anya hashamica."

Roe nodded at the doc. "Chosume da."

He knew a little bit of several Asian languages, enough to obtain medical information and to exchange a few polite phrases.

The Korean doctor, who had trained at a missionary hospital in Seoul, Korea, switched to fluent English. As with most Asians, he was extremely polite and differential to Americans. He led Roe through the small hospital. One child was recovering nicely from a ruptured appendix. An IV dripped slowly, infusing antibiotics into his system to prevent sepsis. Another young girl in a leg cast was receiving treatment for a non-displaced fracture of her fibula. An elderly man was being treated for pneumonia and required nasal oxygen.

A drama unfolded with a case Roe had never witnessed before. Three young children in various stages of diphtheria showed the classic black membrane covering their posterior pharynx. They were receiving IV antibiotics, but what concerned Roe was one youngster was experiencing difficulty breathing. In fact, he had stridor, an ominous sign of impending airway obstruction.

Roe expressed his concern to the local physician, suggesting an emergency bedside tracheotomy. The Korean doc said he had never performed one, and wasn't sure he had a tube to fit the child's airway.

Roe responded, with the Korean doctor's permission, he would perform the ten- to fifteen-minute procedure under local anesthesia. The doc concurred and found an antiquated steel trach tube sterilized many months before. Roe was accustomed to the plastic, high-tech tracheostomy tubes used in Vietnam and San Francisco. Necessity was the mother of invention, though ... it would have to do.

Roe deftly made a small transverse slit in the child's lower neck and, using a small hook, inserted the tube and suctioned out the trachea, clearing the child's airway. An O2 cannula at two liters a minute was attached to the trach tube. The child's stridor ceased and his breathing became normal within minutes.

The Korean doctor bowed gratefully and thanked Roe profusely for performing the tracheostomy so skillfully. "The village will appreciate your good deed. Can you stay for dinner?"

Roe apologized, "We must take off before the tide comes back in.

"Ah so..." The Korean doctor had forgotten the tide's importance to their beach landing. "Yes, of course, you must."

Outside the clinic, the medics conducted their DPT inoculations with great dispatch. They didn't want to be stranded on this remote Pacific island by tempting the incoming tide on takeoff.

Roe double-checked all the DPT documents against the patient list. He gave a copy to the local doctor for his files. A horse-drawn carriage ferried them back to the beach where Colonel Mason and his crew were kicking back and smoking their Marlboros.

A bad habit," Roe thought, *but I'll never break him of it.*

***

Roe left the island with an appreciation of just how good Americans have it: all the modern amenities and first-class American medical care they enjoy. He felt they might have prevented an epidemic on this tiny island, which would have affected future generations. It was a typical humanitarian mission that newspapers and TVs rarely reported. Random good deeds often went unnoticed. The media were heavy into the negative or dark side of life, so it seemed to Roe. Photos of a Buddhist monk burning in self-immolation on a Saigon street sold more newspapers. Bottom line, sensational events sold more copies, attracted a larger audience.

Maybe he was too much of an idealist in that respect. He could still distinguish between perception and reality in most cases. What the medical team had accomplished today contrasted in stark reality to the routine care affluent America enjoyed. An impoverished sector of a remote Asian society lucked out, receiving immunizations to prevent a disaster. If Americans could experience this situation up-close-and-personal, maybe they wouldn't bitch so much about the good old U.S.A.

Our country has its faults but, in the final analysis, we've got it pretty good, Roe reflected as he climbed aboard the Gooney Bird.

***

They landed safely at Clark Air Base, PI at 1800 hours. Not a coincidence. Colonel Mason filed that flight plan. He announced it was happy hour at the Officer's Club. Dinner and drinks were on him.

Big deal, Roe thought. All drinks only cost twenty-five cents, and a steak dinner with wine cost five dollars.

Every night was TGIF at Clark AB O-Club. Usually, the club rocked with jovial activity until someone announced Lt. So and So had "bought the farm" in Vietnam. That halted the festivity and brought a moment of silence followed by sincere toast to for his service to his country.

"Here, here!"

MAC began suffering losses in the war, not so much from attacks on the transport aircraft crews and planes, but from USAF lieutenants transferred out of the squadrons, drafted to fly helicopters in Vietnam. Their high attrition rate plus the Warrant Officers flying multiple chopper missions a day dampened many nights at the O-Club. Nasty reminders of the war had a way of creeping into the lives of those trying to forget it for a night.

After a solemn reflection on the increasing mortality rate of chopper pilots, Roe concluded it was the colonel's generous thought that counted more than his generosity. He'd air evac'ed their wounded and too many in body bags.

Actually, Roe was looking forward to sacking out after a quick meal. He'd had another tough week. It sure was good to be "home," if you could consider Clark AB in the PI as such. He lived out of a B-4 bag. No telling what he would confront next. His tour of duty consisted of facing one unpredictable challenge after another.

CHAPTER SIXTEEN
INTEL MEETING III

Hickam AFB, Hawaii August 1964

Captain Noreika observed that, despite the differences in opinion, the group was forming a bond. Though interservice rivalries still persisted, and all continued to act with enlightened self-interest to protect their respective turfs, the officers were drawn together by their professional commitment to do what was best for their country. These officers took their oath to protect America seriously. Highly disciplined, they were trained to plan, conduct, and win a war. Every officer in attendance was decorated for some distinguished service or accomplishment. War was in their DNA. That's what they did.

Captain Noreika announced that the U.S. was approaching a "fork in the road."

Biff chuckled to himself. *Should they follow Yogi Berra's advice and take it?*

As Captain Noreika saw the Vietnam situation, America should either abandon a protracted and somewhat ambiguous war, or take over the responsibility from the South Vietnamese and commit to winning. In military parlance, Vietnam was an asymmetrical war, or, in simple terms, guerilla warfare, winnable only with the right strategy.

So far, that strategy remained elusive to those calling the shots in Washington, D C. Senior military recommendations based on comprehensive intelligence estimates were generally ignored, which served as a constant source of consternation to the committee.

American forces excelled in conventional warfare: frontal attacks involving battalions and divisions facing off in decisive confrontations. Guerilla warfare was another matter. Vietnam required new strategies and tactics. Helicopter assaults of otherwise inaccessible enemy locations were emerging as a viable option, but in relatively small operations at this phase of the war.

Pragmatic, Biff saw no choice but to introduce a massive infusion of U.S. combat troops, accompanied by sustained bombing, which would give the enemy no sanctuary in North Vietnam, Laos, or Cambodia. That would be the easy part of the solution. The difficult task eluding them would be to politically win the hearts and minds of the peasants. How can you convert or influence an essentially apolitical population to your way of thinking?

This presented a conundrum for the committee, but there must be a way out of the quandary. The outcome had implications for both national security policy, as well as civilian-military relations. It would determine if the war was winnable.

The sticking point: how to convince D.C. of a cogent policy? JFK and LBJ had essentially dismantled the traditional relationship with the NSC and JCS advisory personnel. This reality hampered the war effort, the hindrance increasingly obvious to all on the committee. It left them perplexed and frustrated. Executive decisions were hobbled by ignoring input from those with extensive professional experience in war and security. The administration's new buzzword was "flexible response," ironic in view of their inflexible, rigid attitude. Their reluctance to deal with the complexity of a "new kind of war" in Vietnam further hampered the endeavor to thwart the threat of communism spread in S.E. Asia.

Biff thought "vacillation" more aptly described their buzz. The dynamics between the administration and the military remained in constant flux, each jockeying for position. But, in the end, a classic Hobson's choice prevailed: a distinction without a difference, a take-it-or-leave-it proposition.

The administration played a zero-option game, pretending that military input was important to issues and strategies, despite the fact the administration had already committed to another policy. This effectively reduced the JCS and NSC to rubber stamp preconceived administration policy. If there ever was a misguided policy, this arrogant, deceitful practice—words not backed by action—superseded all others.

Clearly, the current situation in Vietnam called for a coherent, strategic flexibility if the U.S. wanted to win the war. But, how was that defined in specific terms? For some politicians, it was the "wrong war in the wrong place." In contrast, many of the military officers never saw a war they couldn't win. This disconnect in perspectives further hindered the war effort. Perhaps "hindered" in this context is euphemistic. LBJ's objectives remained nebulous to allow for wiggle room. LBJ turned it into an art form.

This was the situation in late August of 1964 when Captain Noreika convened the third joint intelligent committee, three months after its May conference. Before this sober gathering—earlier in the month on 7 August 1965—Congress had just passed the Tonkin Bay resolution. It gave LBJ carte blanch to conduct the Vietnam War with little or no Congressional oversight. The Tonkin Bay incident became a pivotal event. Who could predict what was next in the prosecution of the Vietnam War? The committee was tasked to forecast future events, to predict the unpredictable based on intelligence reports.

Captain Noreika's job obligated him to present Admiral Sparks with up-to-date intelligence estimates and recommendations from the committee following the Tonkin Bay incident. CINCPAC then would advise the JCS, then the recommendation would go on up the chain of command to formulate policy, supposedly…

He astutely noted uneasiness in the group. "Well, I suppose you all suspect why I called this conference so soon after we last met. In case you don't, let me put it into perspective. In June, Rusk and McNamara met here in Honolulu with CINCPAC commanders. The outcome of the meeting was the adoption of a 'graduated pressure' strategy, supposedly to allow multiple, flexible responses and retaliatory bombing of North Vietnam. I don't have to tell this group that this represents a major escalation of the war. The attack on the USS Mattox last week by North Viet PT boats led Congress to pass the Tonkin Gulf resolution five days later. This means retaliatory bombing will begin sooner, rather than later.

Admiral Sparks requests a concise compilation of our latest intelligence estimates."

He surveyed the committee. "Has anything changed from anyone's previous recommendations? We'll go around the room by service and agency. Don't be long-winded. I can predict what most of you will say. This is a procedural thing. I doubt that your estimates will have changed radically in three months. This meeting is for the record to offer our most current intelligence estimates."

Colonel Turner spoke first, representing the Army. "Our position has not changed. Our intelligence data indicates that limited bombing will not do the job. In the last meeting, Colonel Havermeyer related Air Force General Curtis LeMay's comment, 'Bomb them into the stone age.' We endorse that recommendation since we have no credible information supporting a limited bombing campaign. We should go all out. 'We're swatting flies when we should clean up the manure!' as LeMay said."

This elicited a loud round of laughter, some almost rolling over at a remark like this from a sober West Pointer not generally known for his mirth.

Colonel Turner waited for the jovial atmosphere to subside. "Army intelligence essentially agrees with the Air Force assessment of the situation. Our estimates suggest that nothing less than a massive infusion of U.S. forces in a combat role, rather than an advisory role, will win this war."

Colonel Havermeyer raised his hand to comment. "I concur with Colonel Turner. His quotes were certainly appropriate. Our estimates support his assessment, as you know, since I related General LeMay's opinions and recommendations in our last meeting. Nothing has changed from our perspective. We need to move on."

Colonel Rodriguez, U.S. Marines, agreed with both officers, but emphasized that his boss, Colonel Krulak still recommended mounting a counter-insurgency force in North Vietnam.

"As stated earlier, this is an asymmetric war. Conventional military tactics will fail, simply because the enemy will not stand and fight, and confront us like wars in our past. We are fighting guerillas who hit and run. We need to adapt to this style of warfare. I could not agree more with the CIA assessment in this regard. Earlier, Col. Krulak submitted to this committee his detailed plans to change strategies. Therefore, I see no need for further elaboration. I only urge serious reevaluation of how we are managing this conflict and consideration of his strategy."

Biff Roberts followed with his appraisal. "I personally agree with all of the officers' assessments. The agency, however, remains very pessimistic regarding the conflict's outcome without radical changes. That would include a massive influx of U.S. combat troops, a sustained bombing campaign allowing no sanctuaries, and a naval blockade of Haiphong Harbor. But, the harbor blockade comes with geopolitical risks and must proceed with caution. There is always the chance that a Soviet or Chinese ship might inadvertently become involved."

"The final CIA consideration concerns our political shortcomings. It involves the pacification of South Viet hamlets and villages. We liberate the peasants' homes, chase the VC out, but fail to secure the villages long-term. As soon as the protective troops move out, the VC will return. The poor populace is stranded in between, helpless. The AVRN refuses to secure the hamlets over any lengthy period. We are not authorized to perform this task. We are restricted to 'S and D' missions in a war of attrition. Much of the problem stems from our inability to solve the political infighting in Saigon, and coordinating our pacification efforts, not our participation on the battlefield."

"Agreed," Turner grunted.

Biff acknowledged him with a nod. "All things considered, we can win the war militarily, but lose it politically. Therefore, the CIA maintains a pessimistic outlook if the current strategies continue. We're fighting a war with self-imposed limitations. The peasants fall into the VC camp by default. The VC resupply in these sanctuaries. Let's face it. The war has not been taken to the enemy in North Vietnam, Laos, and Cambodia in full force. They enjoy an unlimited supply of off-limit sanctuaries."

The audience cheered this remark. They concurred that self-imposed restrictions were counter-productive to winning. Allowing enemy sanctuaries made absolutely no sense. Some expressed it in profane terms causing Noreika to tingle his glass to restore order.

"Biff continues to hit the nail smack on the head," Captain Noreika commented to his attaché. Nice summation.

The captain thanked Biff and asked Ann Summerville to give her political insight into this current situation before the committee adjourned.

"I'm not a military expert by any means," she started, "but the viewpoints expressed today make imminent sense. We should focus on maintaining security in the countryside. Why liberate a hamlet if there is no intention of securing the village? Why not hold your ground? Personally, I don't think much of the proposed 'gradual pressure policy.' I anticipate it will not be implemented until after the November elections because of stateside political considerations. If you recall, I remarked in prior meetings that LBJ's major focus is domestic. He focused primarily on his Great Society ambitions, not Vietnam. I predict LBJ will go into a holding pattern until next December, unless an unforeseen event forces him to act otherwise. In my opinion, his inaction indicates he's not willing to deal with it."

Her predictions proved to be absolutely correct as events unfolded. The committee's consultant read LBJ's motives better than the military. Her role as the Devil's Advocate started to open some eyes and minds.

CHAPTER SEVENTEEN
INTEL MEETING IV

Hickam AFB, Hawaii January 1965

Captain Noreika called the committee to order. The situation in Vietnam continued to not go well. He asked Ann Summerville to summarize the timeline since their hastily arranged meeting since five and a half months before, last August 1964. The chairman requested her perspective on the key events of the Vietnam War, and policy-making following the Tonkin Bay incident. He found her take more objective than the military opinions, and refreshing. She usually was right on target. Amazing for a civilian.

Ann spread her index cards out on the lectern. She inquired if everyone had received their summary outline updating recent significant events. Receiving nods of acknowledgement, the consultant smiled and began her summation.

"Almost six months have passed, and the same question remains: Are we winning the war?" This elicited the customary grumbles, as expected.

"As you recall, last June, Secretary of State Dean Rusk and Director of Defense Robert McNamara, visited Honolulu for a special CINCPAC conference. I sat in on the meeting and took detailed notes. Their discussion centered on two subjects: one, increasing aid to South Vietnam; and two, reviewing the Pentagon's strategic plans to bomb North Vietnam.

"At present, they state the plans require refinement. Our committee's recommendation and intel estimates were considered but, once again, no specific action taken ... basically shelved. I reviewed numerous memos and recommendations from the Rusk-McNamara meeting. Here's my candid assessment, gentlemen, cutting through the nuanced language."

"Rusk and McNamara discussed the CIA's contrarian stance, citing its 'pessimistic position' regarding the administration's decision to 'go big' in North Vietnam. As stated in the CIA's memorandum addressed to DCI John McCone, the memo questions the assumption that limited bombing in North Vietnam would materially affect the enemy's capacity to supply South Vietnamese insurgents, the VC. In the CIA's view, graduated bombing would be ineffective. Mr. Roberts can elaborate on that viewpoint later." She nodded in his direction.

"The high-level meeting concluded that the DRV efforts and bellicose attitude would not be deterred by limited bombing, according to current CIA intelligence estimates. Allow me to pause for a moment. DRV? Democratic Republic of Vietnam? Isn't that an oxymoron?"

Her audience chuckled at the inference.

"At any rate, the CIA memo was discussed at length in the Honolulu meeting. The memo suggests that limited bombing would achieve just the opposite effect by increasing DRV resolve and determination. CIA estimates suggest this action would harden their resolve and lead to escalation of the DRV war effort, as we increase ours. And, gentlemen, this CIA memo also strongly suggests the action would risk a wider war."

She paused to let this sink in, ignoring the audible moans in the room.

"In my opinion, CIA intelligence estimates have been right on target. Again, I'll let Mr. Roberts elaborate on that major assumption later. The outcome of the Rusk-McNamara conference has resulted in increased South Vietnamese aid, but at this point they are continuing to 'refine' the North Vietnam bombing plans. Does this sound familiar? Come as a surprise? Is it a ruse to procrastinate yet again? At the risk of being judged as a cynic, I still think 'refine' was a code word to allow LBJ to stall, not to act before last November's presidential election. LBJ is much attuned to public opinion and the general perception that the Democrats are 'soft' on communism and war, so he dithers, playing both ends against the middle."

"Amen," Colonel Turner cracked.

His response elicited a few snickers, followed by Noreika tapping his glass once again to restore order.

"LBJ's opponent, Barry Goldwater, is an unabashed 'Hawk,' who even suggested using our nuclear arsenal in Vietnam. As I've stated before, there is no doubt in my mind that LBJ's Great Society plans remain his major focus, not Vietnam. President Johnson is a very clever politician, and a master at ambivalence. He equivocated and wavered until the election was over. Why else would he refuse to retaliate in response to the VC attacks on American installations? There was no retaliation for attacks for the Brinks BOQ last Christmas, or the Bien Hoa Air Base attack outside Saigon. How else do you explain this lack of response? I believe it is unprecedented for an American president.

"You'll note new buzz words emerged as a byproduct of last June's Rusk-McNamara conference, representing General Maxwell Taylor's national security strategy: 'flexible response' and 'graduated pressure.' Those terms ought to stimulate a lot of discussion in our Q&A later today."

She noted approval in the officers' expressions and body language.

"Here are the questions this committee should ask: Is this another perplexing administration blueprint for an increased American commitment and involvement in Vietnam? What price should America pay to maintain South Vietnam's independence?"

"Once again, not to be repetitious, do you recall JFK's rhetoric? 'Pay any price and bear any burden.' Has the time arrived for a definitive decision on Vietnam? This is January 1965, decision time, gentlemen. Should we cut and run? Or, should we increase American commitment in a combat role? Should we reevaluate the Domino Theory, our pretext for involvement? Is that pretext still a valid assumption based on our experience? Should we go the ultimate step and re-examine our national strategy regarding containment of global communism? How big a price will we pay? How much burden should we bear?"

"I have pondered these questions since last August when North Vietnam PT boats attacked our destroyer, the *Maddox*, in the Gulf of Tonkin. When Congress passed the Tonkin Gulf Resolution half a year ago, it essentially granted LBJ carte blanche to conduct the Vietnam War without Congress' explicit oversight. Giving LBJ this extraordinary war power was a serious mistake, in my humble opinion. Shouldn't the president's war power be limited by some oversight?"

Murmurs of agreement followed her observation.

"LBJ's deceptive practices, along with his inner circle of advisors' have repeatedly pre-empted JCS and NSC input in the war's prosecution. Now, compounding the problem, Congress has essentially abrogated their collective oversight responsibility. Can you believe that?"

She knew no one in the room could even remotely justify that act of irresponsibility. It smacked a double whammy to the military.

"Whatever happened to the system of checks and balances in our government? By law, the JCS are the principal military advisors to the president, along with the NSC, and the DOD. This does not appear to be the case in this imperial presidency. In my opinion, we face an escalation of the war without the proper traditional channels of command ... normal checks and balances."

"McNamara has stated there are 'no experts on Vietnam.' I beg to differ. The JCS is comprised of decorated, experienced generals, veterans who have reached the pinnacles of their careers. Their input is critical to an optimal outcome in Vietnam, as well as the future of Southeast Asia. Why would any rational person ignore this valuable consultative resource? Answer that pithy question."

She consulted her index cards and scanned the room. Her answer came as officers nodded in agreement. A few smiled.

"As retaliation to the Tonkin Gulf incident, American aircraft have bombed North Vietnam for the first time. The strategy of graduated pressure with limited bombing has been set in motion. We have crossed the critical threshold, taking direct military action against the DVR. I'll leave it there for your consideration."

Ann's lecture was received with approbation by the committee. For the first time in her four briefings they politely applauded, acknowledging their agreement and respect.

Her take is prudent and, I bet, prophetic, Biff thought as he leaned toward Captain Noreika. "What do you think, Rich?"

"She's a sharp cookie. She has a clever way of putting things into perspective with observations apropos to our current situation. Professor

Summerville is very deliberative in her presentation and collation of facts. I'm very impressed. She's been a good investment by CINCPAC. She thinks with clarity, and outside our military mindsets."

"Refreshing, isn't it?"

"Yes, it certainly is. We're on the horns of a dilemma. Our committee seriously needs to influence DC policy based on our sound intelligence data…to make them listen reasoned recommendations based on factual data, not some ivory tower concept. My impression is our national strategy regarding Vietnam is rudderless. I personally find Professor Summerville's viewpoints challenging, and generally on the mark. Especially her comments regarding the contrived diminution of JCS's role by LBJ. Pointing out LBJ's conceit probably won everybody over to her point of view. Even some of these crusty old vets are starting to come around to her way of thinking."

"That's saying a lot. Summerville does her homework. I'd like to get to know some of her sources. She's getting inside the beltway information somehow," Biff replied.

Captain Noreika smiled. "It's interesting that one of my attachés thought she was a commie mole after her first presentation here. He's now in her camp. But, I must confide he had the FBI check her out. He associated her with Berkeley's SDA, a pinko outfit on that University of California campus."

Biff chuckled, "I guarantee you she's not a commie. She's a dyed-in-the-wool Libertarian. Her IQ is off the charts. She won a lot of debates at Berkeley with radicals, I understand. Coming from that liberal university, naturally bells and whistles went off. I confess I also had the CIA vet her. She's legitimate, the real deal."

Both men chuckled at their unfounded suspicions of the consultant who emerged out of nowhere to have a profound influence on their committee.

"Well, Biff, I'm calling you up next. What do you have for us today?"

"More iconoclastic babble, designed to give 'artistic verisimilitude to an otherwise bald and unconvincing error.'"

"I assume you are referring to Vietnam policy? I didn't know you were schooled in Gilbert and Sullivan. Was that quotation from *The Mikado* or *Pirates of Penzance*?"

"Honestly, I'm not sure, Rich. I'm a little shaky on operettas, just always liked that line."

"I think maybe it was *The Mikado*."

"Okay, you're up, Biff."

With his trademark grin, Biff took the podium. "Brace yourselves, fellows. I've handed out three classified memos for your consideration and consternation."

"What's new, Roberts?" Rodriquez had a feisty reputation and loved to tweak the CIA rep.

"Plenty, pal." He smiled in good nature at the Marine Colonel.

"First, consider the NSC action memorandum number 288, dated 17 March 1964. That memo states that major objective in the Vietnam War is to 'achieve an independent, non-Communist government in South Vietnam.' The NSC's stance is that, unless this objective is achieved, almost all of Southeast Asia will fall under Communist domination. Basically, this is an expression of their belief and a categorical endorsement of the Domino Theory in respect to Communist aggression in Indochina. The NSC is clearly on board with their uncompromising stance regarding the pessimistic future of Southeast Asia if Vietnam falls into communist control. They maintain an unwavering stance on this issue."

"Next, look at our second CIA memo expressing our contrarian opinion to the NSC assessment of the Domino Theory. It's labeled the *one* memorandum compiled for our DCI, John McCone, dated June 1964. With me, got it?"

He paused until they nodded affirmation.

Biff went on to cite in detail intelligence data collected over twenty years of experience in Indochina. In conclusion, he stated the CIA seriously doubted the loss of Laos and Vietnam would result in a rapid, successive Communist takeover of other sovereign states in Southeast Asia.

"In other words, our intelligence data does not support the Domino Theory. The CIA contends that any further spread of communism outside Laos and Vietnam would take considerable time. Time in which the balance of power might change in ways unfavorable to communism. I stand by this assessment in contraposition to that held by the NSC. We simply disagree."

"Care to elaborate on that, Biff?" Captain Noreika asked.

"The CIA takes this position...The extent to which individual countries would distance themselves from the United States to embrace communism would be significantly affected by the substance and manner of U.S. policy following the loss of Laos and South Vietnam. That is precisely why sound American policy is so important, and why this committee's input should count in influencing judicious decisions in Washington DC. We must impact the decision makers with our constructive input if we hope to attain an optimal outcome."

"How do we accomplish that?" Noreika challenged him.

"By overwhelming them with valid data, and irrefutable facts. We must impugn fuzzy thinking leading to false assumptions and unintended consequences of misguided actions or inactions. For example, the third memo I'm presenting today is a composite of CIA officers' comments on the JCS war games conducted in April 1964. There was widespread assumption at the war games that attacks against the DRV would interrupt their capability to supply the insurgent VC forces in South Vietnam. Another major assumption was that the DRV would call off the support of the VC if cities were bombed in North Vietnam."

He held the committee's full attention regarding these key assumptions as they located the third CIA memo. Their expressions told him they were interested where Biff was going with this contrarian case.

"The CIA finds these assumptions highly dubious and risky given the nature of the war with the Viet Cong. The enemy guerillas have captured enough American and ARVN weapons and munitions to last a considerable time. Time to independently conduct an asymmetric war, employing hit and run tactics for years. The peasant population residing in their hamlets is intimidated by the Viet Cong. They are forced to supply them food and shelter on an intermittent basis as the VC pass through their villages. The Viet Cong are continually on the move. Moving targets are hard to hit, especially if residing over the fence in safe havens in Laos and Cambodia."

"Got that right," Noreika chimed in.

Others murmured agreement.

Biff quoted JFK when he was a U.S. Senator, "No amount of military assistance in Indochina can conquer an enemy which is everywhere, and sometimes nowhere." His follow-up statement about the quote identified it as a perfect description encompassing the CIA's viewpoint regarding VC operations in Vietnam.

"Technically, we're dealing with a new form of warfare employing guerilla tactics . . . the VC engaging in asymmetric warfare strategies. The rules of engagement restrict appropriate retaliation, much less undertaking proactive military action. Different tactics require different solutions, new methods. So far, no one seems to be on the same page. It is becoming apparent we lack a comprehensive Vietnam strategy, gentlemen.

"Let me point out that an independent Pentagon intelligence working group recently reached essentially the same conclusion as the CIA. This group would not concede a very strong chance of breaking Hanoi's will by instituting a program of sustained bombing of North Vietnam. Their intelligence estimates concluded that the DRV is willing to sustain significant damage to pursue their cause of reuniting Vietnam under communism. It all comes down to a test of wills. Recall the Vietnamese have a long history of strong wills, tested over millennia, according to Professor Summerville. Americans don't deal in millennia."

He inclined his head to her in approval.

"Go back to the history of Dien Bien Phu in 1954. Recall how reluctant the JCS and the U.S. Army were to supply forces to bail out the French? Why? Mainly because the JCS realized at that time the hostile terrain in Indochina was not suited for effective, conventional military action and supply. The jungle geography shields enemy supply lines, but not allied airlifts. What changed? Let me tell you . . ."

Biff leaned forward on the lectern. "We face a similar situation today along the Ho Chi Minh Trail supply line from North Vietnam through Laos and Cambodia to South Vietnam. The trail winds through heavy jungle and mountains. Our agency's intelligence estimates and recommendations back in 1954 are just as pertinent today. Nothing has changed. Their major supply lines are shielded by the jungles and protected by our self-imposed restriction of engagement of the target over the arbitrary fence. Our DCI has made this case to the JCS and NSC as well as the president's Cabinet. He expressed this observation as a caveat to U.S. expansion of the war in Vietnam."

"The DCI also emphasized the imperative of winning the peasants' support. The CIA also raised these questions, 'Is there enough political and military potential in South Vietnam to make increased U.S. commitments worthwhile? What is the risk and /or benefit analysis of escalating U.S. involvement?"

He paused for them to consider that equation. Ponder the politics.

"I suspect you're wondering how all this will shake out? Consider the administration's reaction to our DCI's input? Their response will blow you away. Somewhat dismissively, Director McCone was urged to 'get on the team.' This appears to be the standard form of intimidation for LBJ's administration's coercive tactics. The DCI was effectively frozen out of the inner circle of advisers. Our mission will definitely be impaired with this sort of negative attitude, freezing out our nation's major foreign security agency, the CIA. The administration doesn't seek opposing viewpoints. They tell us to 'get on the team,' but ignore our input."

Those comments caused a universal cranky response.

"The CIA's job is to collect and collate intelligence data, analyze it, and produce concise intelligence estimates to enable sound policy formulation in Washington DC. Frankly, this Administration's attitude is counter-productive to the war cause. They made that clear to our DCI. In fact, they insulted his personal intelligence and the CIA's."

Biff gritted his teeth and took a long breath, his irritation uncharacteristically visible.

"I have to tell you off the record, sound policy formation ain't happening, guys. Is this a winnable war? Not with this friggin' insular approach. Someone has to get real in DC. They seriously need an epiphany."

The following discussion reached a new level of robust contention. Everyone had an ax to grind, typically along military service lines-of-interest with each inbred bias. Confronted with conflicting and competing intelligence data, it was difficult to reach consensus decisions, even in this select committee.

If a committee of this small size experiences so much difficulty in recommending plans of actions, just image the mess in Washington DC, Biff thought.

Captain Noreika abruptly adjourned the meeting before it became too acrimonious. As they left, he murmured to Biff, "Way too much pissing and moaning for this old sailor to tolerate."

Biff nodded in agreement.

***

After the meeting, Biff chatted with Ann. More impressed with her after each conference, he also grew more assured she and Roe would really hit it off considering their intellectual similarities. She was an attractive woman in many respects.

Typically, even while trying his hand at matchmaking, he came straight to the point.

"Ann, I'd like you to meet a close friend of mine, Dr. Roe MacDonald. He's an Air Force Flight Surgeon flying air evacuation missions between Tan Son Nhut, Danang, and Clark AFB in the Philippines. We go back to high school days together. I think you two would enjoy each other's company. Think you might have any interest?"

Her eyes widened and she smiled warily.

"I haven't met Prince Charming on this island yet, so I'm open to your offer to fix me up, although I'm not a strong advocate of blind dates."

He grinned. "Trust me, only your intellect will blind him."

She tilted her head and gave him an amused stare.

"All kidding aside, though, Ann, I think you two have a lot in common and would make a good match. He's a perfect gentleman, so there's no worry."

"Okay, let's give it a whirl. Set it up, Biff. I'm game. I'll see you at our next conference."

She smiled and bustled off to her office with a stack of papers under her arm.

***

Neither knew that while they were meeting in Hawaii, Roe MacDonald was about to become involved in a major air evacuation in Pleiku,

Vietnam. The course of the war would soon again impact their lives with a further escalation of the Southeast Asian conflict following the devastating surprise dawn attack at Pleiku by the VC and NVA in early February 1965.

CHAPTER EIGHTEEN
PLEIKU, VIETNAM

February 1965

"Incoming!" The startled sentry jumped over the berm and ducked for cover in the closest bunker. He quickly sounded the base's general alarm. Horns blared, followed a split second later by loud concussions of an artillery barrage shattering the silence of the night.

A battalion of VC troops reinforced by a company of NVA commandos and sappers were conducting a coordinated, predawn surprise assault from six klicks away. A massive barrage, launched under the cover of the adjacent rainforest, announced the onset.

The Pleiku military installation consisted of Camp Holloway—the billeting area, headquarters, and a TAC airbase—two-and-a-half miles south of the camp. The camp was surrounded by a heavily fortified, ten-foot-high barbed wire fence. The base represented a critical link in the defense of the central highlands sector and interdiction of enemy supply routes along the Ho Chi Minh trail to the west in Laos. Exactly the reason it became a major target on that early morning.

Naturally, the attack caught most of the camp asleep or off guard. Abruptly awakened, the men hastened to battle following a brief moment of confusion.

Incoming 81mm mortars took out a large portion of the northwest perimeter fence, exploding many mines and magnesium trip flares strategically placed along the protective barrier. This damage created a breach at the north end of the camp. Fortunately, none of the incoming artillery hit the ammo dump near the middle of the installation, but the breach made the base vulnerable.

The command post immediately sprung to action. Colonel Franklin Pettyjohn barked a barrage of orders over the camp's loudspeakers to counter the strike threatening to overrun the camp. He was astonished at the magnitude and accuracy of Charlie's siege, along with the fact that the enemy could amass such a large force so close to the base without discovery. Pleiku was designated as a recon base. How could that happen? He realized the enemy enjoyed the element of surprise, and he must act quickly to avoid them overrunning the base.

"Scramble our planes to avoid hits by enemy artillery. Get our O-1 Bird Dog spotters airborne immediately to locate source of the incoming and staging areas. We'll need FAC support. Place a call to Colonel Ruey over at Chu Lai. I'll request close combat air support with his A-4s. I'll relay the enemy's present positions to him. Scramble the helicopter gunships to interdict the frontal assault on the north perimeter."

UH-B Huey choppers armed with two banks of rockets and four quad MGOC machine guns were airborne within minutes to head off the frontal attack at the north perimeter. This was no ordinary hit-and-run attack by the Viet Cong. It was a major frontal assault in battalion strength attempting to score a major military victory, an unusual tactic for the VC.

"Instruct Captain Johansson to get his company up to the northwest perimeter *stat* with armored personnel carriers to fill the breach. Get another platoon to reinforce all peripheral sentry positions and machine gun nests. Have the tank company move into position to counterattack. Send half of the tanks over to the air base to secure the area. Instruct the TAC aircraft spotters to keep us apprised of VC troop movements. We'll need accurate information for the A-4s ETA [arrival]."

His staff scurried, carrying out his rapid-fire orders. Walkie-talkies hummed with action instructions.

The colonel's instincts were correct. The enemy attacked through the breach in waves of company numbers—120 plus men—a very aggressive tactic considering the formidable perimeter defense. However, the VC underestimated the huge number of claymore and Bouncing Betty mines. Their reckless onslaught resulted in a massive fireworks display of explosions as onrushing VC soldiers tripped the buried landmines blowing them five to ten feet in the air, some of them to bits. It was an awesome display of deterrent munitions firepower.

Despite that folly, VC continued to advance through this lethal array of mines, recklessly rushing through the breach in a suicidal frenzy to overrun the camp. Their exploding bodies silhouetted in the air against the bursts of tripped magnesium flares. However, some defied the odds and slipped through the minefield to reach the interior of the camp, posing a serious threat.

The ARVN sentries in their nests rapidly fired their .50 caliber machine guns raking the onrushing enemy, killing many. The machine gunners were well protected in concrete revetments, reinforced by large sand bags. Only a direct hit would disable the bunker with its trained gunners. This random event occurred just as Captain Cody Johansson arrived with his company of American special force advisors and ARVN commandos.

He quickly assessed the situation, noting the machine gun nest closest to the breach was no longer firing after a direct hit from a VC grenade launcher. It became imperative for him to rectify the situation, as masses of VC continued to pour through the destroyed section of fence in waves, without apparent concern for casualties. Cody realized they must plug the gap despite being outnumbered. They must get the critically positioned machine-gun nest firing again. Their survival depended on it.

The conflagration from the continual explosions of incoming artillery and mortars, plus successive detonations of tripped mines and magnesium flares produced an eerie atmosphere. The sound was deafening. It felt like his eardrums would pop. The concoction of fumes and smoke reeked of sulfur, cordite, magnesium, and human body parts. The smell triggered coughing jags among the base defenders, and some gagged at the repulsive odors. Cody knew they were in for a close-quarter battle and ordered his three platoons to rapidly fan out to stop the onrush. His radio man could hardly keep with the steady stream of orders over walkie-talkies.

The successive detonations produced sudden, blinding-bright flashes of light against the dark, predawn sky. It compromised targeting of the onrushing enemy determined to overrun the camp. The explosions sucked oxygen out of the humid highland night air and made it difficult to breathe. Nevertheless, Cody's troops kept firing at the onrushing enemy at relatively close range. No time for anxiety. The confrontation was brutal. It was simply kill or be killed. This horrific scene distilled the essence of battle into its basic raw physical nature: the sights, the sounds, the smells of war.

Cody recognized that peripheral defense impediments would soon be exhausted. He swiftly moved with his platoon to get the critically positioned machine-gun nest firing again. He knew close range .50 caliber firepower would deter the VC onslaught.

Incoming mortars and bullets continued to fill the air, producing confusion among some of the inexperienced ARVN troops. Cody rallied his platoon through the hail of bullets, directing them through the firefight to the gunners' nest.

Fortunately, base gunship helicopters arrived, quickly exhibiting their massive firepower with a hell-storm of rockets and machine gun fire, raking the attacking VC and NVR who continued to amass for another blitz through the perimeter breach. The choppers' firepower allowed Cody time to act.

The American Special Ops advisors were accustomed to war scenes like this, however, the new AVRN troops were not. The intensity of the battle awed them. A short break in the action allowed Cody to quickly appraise the situation and bark more orders.

"Get the wounded out of the bunker, Sergeant Nyo! Take two trained gunners to replace the .50 caliber team that went down. Get that gun firing again right away! I'll cover you with a platoon of AR-15 riflemen with RPGs. Move out now!"

They responded professionally and promptly, as Cody commanded tremendous respect. They trusted his judgment. For most it was the first live-fire test of their skills, but they did not panic, they were disciplined, moving swiftly in response to his orders. Cody moved about, rapidly deploying the three platoons comprising his company along the northern perimeter. He then chose to stay at the most vulnerable point of attack, the breach, leading a platoon he'd personally trained. This real-life encounter would soon determine their mettle. Cody was confident they were up to the task, promising himself this would not become another Ap Bac debacle.

Within a few minutes, the platoon's confidence in Cody was substantiated with his awesome display of frontline courage and expert marksmanship skills. As the platoon advanced to the disabled machine gun bunker, they encountered remnants of a VC platoon coming through the breach directly at them. Somehow, these troops had avoided the remaining mines and chopper gunships. They threw grenades at the bunker and fired their AK-47s wildly from fifty yards away. They were closing rapidly in on the wounded gunners in the bunker, making up with their poor shooting skills with blind courage. This quickly became an intense up-close-and-personal encounter.

Dawn was just about to break. Visibility remained limited for most, except Cody and a few other Americans who wore infrared night goggles. Cody lifted his M-16 rifle and proceeded to single-handedly annihilate well over two dozen or so oncoming VC, picking them off like clay pigeons. It reminded him of his youthful days of trap-shooting competitions, the larger targets actually made it easier. He sensed a strange sensation of superiority, shooting in a zone, firing rapidly as if he could not miss. And he did not. It was a weird sensation, without pleasure or remorse, just a well-trained mechanical act devoid of emotion. Macabre in a sense of precision to him, and awe inspiring to those observing his skill with an M-16.

Several charging VCs tripped over their fallen comrades. One of the VCs managed to launch an RPG grenade in Cody's direction, instantly killing the two ARVN's to his right side. These two commandos shielded Cody, saving his life, but losing theirs. Not an uncommon happenstance in war where inches often determine survival or death.

Cody glanced at the two dead AVRNs at his side, crossed himself, and slipped a new clip into his M-16. He was not a particularly religious man, but much more of this battle and he would become one... The old saying, "No atheists in a foxhole," came to mind.

Close friggin' call! Man, I really lucked out!

Blood steamed down his face and oozed through his camo's down to his canvas jungle boots. Shrapnel fragments had ripped into Cody's shoulder, face, right arm, and leg. Half of his right earlobe was blown off, but Cody ignored the injuries. He was alive and functioning … that was all that mattered. He plugged on, nailing one attacker after another.

He slipped in another clip, took aim, and dropped two more VC charging at him while his men got the machine gun nest up and running. For a Green Beret, this was what it was all about. Courage never crossed his mind, nor did fear, he simply demonstrated his concept of company commander's duty to lead by example. Cody thrived in the field, his actions spoke volumes, and were duly noted. His platoon tried to emulate his performance boldly resisting the enemy onslaught.

"Cody's bleeding like a stuck pig," his platoon lieutenant told a sergeant.

"Is he going to be okay?"

"Don't worry, he'll be the last man to die fighting."

In between shots, Cody shouted to his men, "Stay down and continue firing. Advance on my orders only. Take good aim and maintain a low-profile target."

Cody dropped to one knee to steady his M-16, leveling his rifle at another group of rapidly closing VCs attempting to encircle his platoon. His company had spread out along the perimeter to thwart the VC attack, so his squad was slightly under-manned. He continued to drop one after another, rarely using more than one bullet, swinging his M-16 like he was skeet shooting back on the Eastern Shore of Maryland. The side advantage quickly shifted to Cody's favor with his astounding marksmanship. Several of the men of his platoon paused shooting momentarily to watch his remarkable deadly display.

"Like watching a friggin' action movie!" one American sergeant exclaimed to three ARVN riflemen next to him. "Holy shit!"

The platoon lieutenant later noted in his action report, "Cody never missed! He must have killed twenty-five or thirty VC singlehandedly. You had to see it to believe it. Cody killed most of them. We killed the rest."

The brown bars' AAR report stated they may have underestimated Captain Johansson's "kills" by at least a dozen or so. "In two 'Nam tours, I never saw such an awesome display of marksmanship." He stated for the record.

In what seemed an eternity, but lasted only about thirty minutes, the perimeter battle went on with overwhelming intensity. The first two VC assaults were over for now, but another was expected soon. Company reinforcements and tanks arrived.

Cody took this lull in fighting to reposition his men, re-arm the machine gun nests, and evacuate the wounded. He directed them to park the tank and M-113 armed personnel carrier that had just arrived in the breached barbed wire perimeter to block the next expected assault.

A demolition team arrived to place new claymore mines and magnesium trip flares and concertina wire on the outside of the breached perimeter. Most of the mines had been exploded by the waves of VC attackers, but this was still a treacherous exercise for the explosive experts. One inadvertently stepped on a mine and was instantly killed, with two others seriously wounded by "friendly fire."

Receiving reinforcements, a full company now braced for the next VC attack. A field medic managed Cody's bleeding wounds. He refused to go back to the small base hospital for treatment. This man lived for encounters like this. War apparently was in his DNA. For Cody, this was why he became a Ranger, then a Green Beret. There was no high like an intense fire-fight. The adrenalin rush was indescribable. He thrived on the intense encounter.

Meanwhile, the remaining helicopter gunships not disabled earlier by the airfield attack had scrambled, and joined the initial choppers. They busily carried the battle to the enemy preparing for a second round with a wave of perimeter attacks. The chopper firepower overwhelmed them, forcing a retreat to the adjacent jungle.

As the VC tried to regroup under the rainforest foliage, the roar of jets was heard overhead. Colonel Ruey's squadron of A-4 Skyhawks were arriving on scene from Chu Lai. Now, some concentrated firepower would take place. The TAC spotter aircraft, Cessna 0–1s nicknamed "Sopwith Camels," accurately relayed the location of the enemy fire base. The Skyhawks would rely on their forward air control (FAC) for targeting. GPS coordinates were not operational during the Vietnam War. The standard operating procedure assigned FAC control of all close air support. No ordinance could be fired or dropped without FAC clearance.

As Colonel Ruey's A-4 squadron approached Pleiku the conflagration of the firefight came into his cockpit's view. Less than a minute later his VHF-Uniform channel blared. FAC's Cessna O-1s spotted them and promptly checked in using their squadron call signs. Strict policy dictated coordination of close air support with forward air control who remained in close contact with the ground troops on Fox Mike. Avoiding friendly fire required precise management and skill. No attacks were initiated without FAC clearance. These spotters, also known as "Bird Dogs", were the unsung heroes in Vietnam taking big risks flying at low altitude and slow airspeed to locate enemy targets. They often took heavy ground fire, but at other times the enemy was reluctant to give away its position by firing on the spotters.

The colonel's VHF-Uniform channel squawked again, relaying FAC's instructions for the attack plan.

"Checkertail, Bird Dog One. Condition hot. Willey Pete's will vector two primary targets in about five. Standby. Follow the puff and light 'em up."

"Read you, Bird Dog. Guarantee no friendlies in strike zone?"

"Affirmative. You are cleared in hot. Follow the smoke. Fire away and await our next FAC clearance."

"Roger that. Out," Ruey replied and switched to another channel.

He issued orders to his squadron on his UHF channel, using their individual call signs: 'Hotshot,' his wing man Neelson, and 'Sandy,' Alex, a third pilot.

"This is 'Shoreman' actual. FAC has cleared us. Willey Pete's will vector two primary targets in five. Hotshot, take your two wings and peel off to attack target two. Sandy, you and your three Checkertails, follow me to eliminate target one."

"Roger, Shoreman," Neelson replied, not hiding his enthusiasm to lead the attack on the second target.

Sandy followed, "Will be hot and heavy on your tail, Shoreman."

"Adjust airspeed to three hundred knots and set attack angle. Allow plenty of space to pull out after dropping your ordinance. Don't want anyone fragging themselves."

"We got it, Shoreman," Hotshot chirped.

"Okay, here we go, guys. Happy hunting." Ruey smiled as he peeled off and started to dive, leading VMA-211 Skyhawk squadron into close air support of the besieged base. They vectored in on the spotter planes' white phosphorous rockets' puff identifying their targets.

The intensity of firepower took a quantum leap at that point. The explosions were almost deafening following the Marine squadron's bombing. The earth shook. Large plumes of smoke and fire shot a mile up into the air. Two other A-4s strafed the adjacent jungle, disrupting the VC plans for another attack. The Skyhawks expended half of their 85,000 pounds of ordinance on the first two targets highlighted by the "Willey Pete's", the military phonetic nickname for the white phosphorous markers released on targets by the fixed wing spotter planes referred to as "Bird Dogs."

The A4s pulled up and out, and reassembled in squadron formation. They circled over the targets behind Ruey awaiting the next FAC target clearance.

Secondary explosions from the enemy's ammo dump in the rain forest lit up the dawn sky like the four of July.

"This is fucking awesome, Shoreman!" Hotshot exclaimed over the UHF intercom.

Colonel Ruey chuckled in his O2 mask. "This is what we do, Hotshot. Standby for the finale."

***

The battle will soon be over," Cody observed… "Go get 'em, fly boys!"

As the battle subsided, Cody designated authority to his lieutenant and went to the base hospital for further treatment. He was still bleeding through bandages the field medic had applied. Absorbed in the firefight, he neglected his bleeding wounds, typical for a seasoned Special Ops officer. He now felt a little woozy and figured he better go in for treatment. The worse was over.

The dawning sky was illuminated for miles around by intermittent explosions from direct hits on enemy munitions stockpiled in the rainforest. The attack choppers and Skyhawks continued to do a job on "Charlie"

The base took a significant hit. The Zulu tolled eight American advisors killed and more than a hundred ARVN killed or wounded. Twenty aircraft were destroyed and others were disabled. The enemy's well-coordinated attack on Camp Holloway and the nearby Tactical Air Base inflicted considerable damage. Fortunately, the TAC wing and gunship helicopters had rehearsed for a wartime scenario like this. Most were airborne within fifteen minutes during the surprise pre-dawn attack and took the attack to the enemy, avoiding a disastrous overrun of the base.

Word of this shocking attack was immediately relayed to MACV and CINCPAC command, setting off a cascade of responses.

***

On the jeep ride back to the base hospital, Cody reflected that his ARVN Company had performed well under the pressure of a surprise attack. Maybe the American advisory training was starting to pay dividends on his second tour of duty.

Upon arrival at the base hospital, he was astonished to see that the northern half of the large Quonset hut hospital building had been blown away. A medic told him that several direct hits had wiped out two surgical teams who were busily caring for the wounded. Cody reflected for a moment. For long-range rockets and mortars to score direct hits on vital structures required accurate coordinates. This implied that spies had infiltrated the base... something that needed to be investigated. He planned to discuss it with the commander in the debriefing.

Firemen were busily extinguishing the fires and making makeshift arrangements for the base hospital's two remaining surgical teams. Medics scurried around in all directions assisting the wounded. Courageous surgeons, including the hospital commander Lt. Colonel J. B. Baldwin, continued to operate on the wounded despite the tragic loss of their colleagues just yards away. Although grieving, he continued to do what he did best, organizing his triage and surgical staff. He assembled a backup team creating a makeshift third operative team, and scrubbed in. Nobody could save lives under pressure like this outstanding surgeon.

Cody took his place in the triage line. A medic administered a shot of morphine sulfate. The morphine produced a euphoria Cody had never experienced before.

Wow, he thought, *great stuff!*

Though still coming down off the high adrenalin rush of a full-blown firefight, this topped it all. He could wait all day for medical treatment in his present state of mind: comfortable, weakened, and stoned.

***

Meanwhile, over at Tan Son Nhut airbase near Saigon, the sun rose and the humidity picked up. Flight Surgeon Roe McDonald was eating breakfast at Papa San's Quonset hut by the flight line. The Vietnamese cook was preparing some seasoned beef and rice with eggs over easy. The flight crews devoured Papa San's spicy meals at wooden picnic tables under a plain tin roof, nothing fancy. A large sandbagged bunker stood a few yards away to provide shelter in the event of a firefight or surprise mortar attack. Ten-foot-high barbed wire fencing fifty yards from the Quonset hut provided a buffer zone of rice paddies northwest of the flight line. Sentries patrolled the perimeter with watch dogs.

Out on the flight line, the crew chief busily reconfigured the C-130 for air evacuation of the wounded. The plane had just hauled in a load of 81mm mortars, M-16 and .50-caliber ammo, from Clark Air Base PI. The day was starting off like any other, a routine exercise: ammo in, wounded out. They had this routine down pat.

The squawk of the walkie-talkie intercom interrupted their meal, announcing that Pleiku was under siege, one half of the base hospital blown up, and a hundred or so wounded.

New orders sounded from 86th MAC: "Proceed to Pleiku ASAP. Plan assault landing. Take all precautions with treetop approach and descent. Anticipate ground fire. Expect a full load of injured. Bring as many medics and medical supplies as possible. Camp Holloway base hospital partially disabled."

Roe and the crew left their last bites and scurried over to their MAC C-130. They were airborne to Pleiku in thirty minutes, escorted by two

F105s from nearby Bien Hoa to insure a safe arrival. Everyone understood the importance of this air evacuation mission. Roe noted it was the first time that America had suffered so many serious injuries and casualties in battle with the Viet Cong. The war was escalating.

***

Despite scattered ground fire, Lt. Colonel Howard Mason made a textbook assault landing at Pleiku. Full flaps, treetop, the "whole nine yards," as the colonel described it in his customary jolly fashion.

"No sweaty-da," he used a favorite expression from his Korean tour at Kimpo Air Base.

Under any circumstances, he was the eternal optimist. Since he wasn't killed in Korea, why would he expect to die in Vietnam?

As he taxied to the hangar, Roe noticed that a dozen or so planes still burning. Firemen were frantically trying to extinguish their charred skeletons. Several adjacent Quonset huts were still smoldering along the flight line. It was not a pretty sight, very upsetting, even to a veteran surgeon like Roe.

Roe had quickly assembled a surgical evacuation team from base support at Tan Son Nhut, supplied for any eventuality, including blood transfusion. They carried a large supply of type O, the universal donor, and plasma. ARVN ambulances met them at the flight-line hangar for the short drive to Camp Holloway. The ambulances were escorted by commandos and jeeps sporting mounted .50 caliber machine guns.

As they drove through the airfield, the devastation all around sickened Roe. Upon their arrival at Camp Holloway, more damage greeted them. Burning Quonset huts, once billets for the ARVN commandos and their American advisors, had taken direct hits from the incoming. The fire squads busily worked to dose the lingering fires and retrieve the dead.

The morning haze obscured by smoke burned his eyes and a pungent acrid odor enveloped Camp Holloway. The fumes of cordite, magnesium, burning rubber and JP-4 mixed with the smoke of smoldering vehicles and buildings made him cough. The chaotic scene was the worst Roe had ever witnessed. Anger and remorse competed for his emotional reaction to this level of enemy destruction, the loss of life. It was a grim reminder that this war was far from over. In fact, this surprise attack indicated it was growing worse.

As they drove on, Roe saw a makeshift mortuary for the dead set up in a field tent. The sight punctuated his dismay.

Fortunately, the VC had missed the base ammo dump next to it, otherwise more mortuaries would be required.

Upon arrival at the billeting area, the most shocking sight was the total demolition of half of the base hospital. As Roe walked up, he noticed a dispirited surgeon in scrubs sitting outside smoking a cigarette and sipping from a canteen. He appeared exhausted, taking a short break between cases. As Roe came closer, he recognized the surgeon from UCSF.

JB had been his favorite senior resident while in training, a great guy and terrific surgeon. JB obviously had his hands full here with the number of wounded.

Roe commiserated with JB's emotional task.

"JB, looks like all hell broke loose here."

JB looked up dejectedly, then his eyes widened in surprise. "Roe, Things are not going well … not well at all." JB was so emotionally drained he could hardly speak. His voice sounded weak, surely from unimaginable stress. "The gooks killed half our OR team. What a bitch … and, what the hell are you … doing here … in the middle of this?" A puzzled look on his face.

"Brought in a plane load of personnel and supplies to set up an air evacuation, and to help you out, pal."

Roe had never seen JB so filled with emotion, so devastated. A surge of anger overcame him. "Good God, JB, what a friggin' mess. It had to be a direct hit by those bastards."

"It was … unbelievable. All four teams were operating up a storm." His voice grew a bit stronger, but he still spoke with hesitation of being overwhelmed with grief.

"The attack surprised us, but we mobilized quickly. We were operating twenty minutes after onset. I still can't believe my colleagues are gone. Blown to bits by a direct hit! The forensic team is trying to put all the pieces together. Really …"

"What a disaster." Roe patted JB on his shoulder, attempting to console him.

"You've got that right. Those SOBs really caught us sleeping. This installation is set up as a forward tactical base to interdict the Ho Chi Minh trail supply line. Some friggin' tactical base, huh? Got our ass handed to us in a hand basket!"

"Someone should have recon'ed the VC grouping up for this attack," Roe responded. "After all, this is a forward TAC air base, isn't it?"

"You picked up on that?" JB said with undisguised sarcasm and bitterness. He raised his head and glanced around at the chaos.

"Look, old buddy, I've gotta get back to work. Appreciate you giving us a hand and air evac'ing the wounded. Heard you are pretty good at that. Thank you, Roe. Gotta run, man."

They shook hands firmly and hugged ... a poignant moment for the two surgeons. There was no way they could have ever imagined this grim scenario happening back in those halcyon San Francisco days at the University hospital up on Parnassus Heights.

"War is Hell," Roe repeated the old cliché, "but it doesn't come close to describing this mess. JB, I'm really sorry about your colleagues."

JB simply pivoted away from his friend to return to the OR, still shaking his head in disbelief. Halfway there he turned and said, "See ya, Roe." and continued on.

Roe swore he had tears in his eyes. That's why he left abruptly.

Surgeons are tough men, but everyone has their stress limits.

Roe and his medics entered the triage area and started prioritizing the wounded and sorting them out for air evacuation. During this process, he suddenly recognized his high school buddy, Cody Johansson, sitting on a bench, hunched over—spaced out or exhausted. He'd heard, on the jeep ride over, about Cody's remarkable feat defending the base perimeter breach. The driver could not stop talking about it.

Blood seeped through Cody's bandages and clothing, with clots thickly coated and smattered on his camo uniform. Half of his right ear had been blown off. Deep gashes caked with blood pocked his face and arms. Blood oozed through his torn pant legs and stained his canvas boots.

Shrapnel injuries... Roe immediately recognized. *Here's a man who just experienced a battlefront. These commandoes are tough dudes.*

Roe went over to check his friend's pulse. Seeing Cody in short hair without his ponytail surprised Roe more than finding him among the injured here.

"Hey, Cody, looks like you caught a little flak, old buddy."

Cody looked up, confused, but finally recognized the voice and the speaker.

"No shit. Almost bought the farm out there. It was friggin' brutal. What the hell are you doing out here in the boondocks, Roe?"

"I'm going to haul you out of here, dude, along with your wounded pals. We're going to get you fixed up at Clark then you're going to have a little R&R."

"Sounds like a plan."

"One of the medics told me you shot up a storm out there. Heard you took out several coveys of VC."

Cody picked up on Roe's bird-hunting analogy. "Was a helluva lot easier than shooting quail or rabbits, let me tell you, Roe. You should have seen it, man. Those crazy bastards just came charging through the mined perimeter breach, setting off magnesium trip flares and blowing themselves up on our claymore mines, two or three at a time. Fucking nuts! The M-113 APC arrived quickly to fill the breach. They killed the few remaining gooks we hadn't already shot. It was a wild-ass experience, pal, let me tell ya'. It was suicide for them to just keep charging through. It was like shooting ducks on a pond.... unsporting, but this is war and anything goes, you know. Good to see you, Roe. You've got a lot of wounded to haul out of here. Can you believe what those bastards did to the field hospital?"

Cody usually was pretty quiet. Now he was talking up a storm, animated, and blurting out words excitedly as he skipped from one subject to another, relating a disconnected word salad of topics. He was on an emotional roller coaster, or perhaps morphine, so not too unusual in wartime. He appeared to be taking everything in stride, though.

Roe reflected for a moment. *He's one tough guy. Seems such a short time ago we were playing for a football championship together down home... It's funny how we ended up here, thousands of miles away.*

"It's unbelievable, Cody. Friggin' unreal."

After a moment, Cody came back around to Roe's original statement. "Honestly, Roe, getting out of here now seems like a good plan, a real good plan."

"We're all over it. Are you okay? Need anything for pain?"

"Nurse gave me a morphine shot. I feel like I've been to some Cholon opium den. Higher than a kite. I could fly to Tan Son Nhut without a plane." He laughed.

Despite all his wounds, he still has a sense of humor. But, what does Cody know about Cholon opium dens?

"That morphine sulfate does the trick, Cody. I'll get this triage organized and get the show on the road. We'll be on our way within an hour."

"Right on, Roe, I sure could use some R&R. This war's becoming a bitch, man."

***

The flight to Tan Son Nhut was uneventful. After refueling, the C-130 pushed on to Clark, P.I. only a two-and-a-half-hour flight with good tailwinds.

At Clark, the USAF hospital staff rushed to meet the air evac team. Ambulances ferried the wounded to the base hospital for definitive care. It was a case study in efficient triage and emergency medical care.

C-130 flight engineers, after unloading the wounded, reconfigured the aircraft to haul more ammo back to Tan Son Nhut in a swift turnaround flight back to the war zone. Not much let up. Roe had just enough time to check on Cody, catch a bite, and go to the bathroom. A new group of pilots would normally take the next leg, but Roe had no replacement. He and other flight surgeons were stretched thin. It was back to Vietnam for him on another round of triage and air evacuations.

***

Weeks later in Saigon, Roe heard from Biff that Cody had been highly decorated for his courageous service at Pleiku. Cody earned the Silver

Star and a Purple Heart. After treatment for his wounds at Clark, Cody could have gone home, but he requested to return to the central highlands for some "unfinished business," as he put it. Naturally, his request was granted. Company field commanders of his quality were hard to come by. Cody was a special sort of Special Ops officer, devoted to his duty. He returned to the war zone one month to the day after his shrapnel injuries.

***

In response to the surprise attack on Pleiku, CINCPAC dispatched two battalions of Marines and a support helicopter squadron to Danang. They arrived a month or so later, in March. Their mission, perimeter defense of the air base, now included preemptive strikes against Charlie, a new dimension in the escalating conflict.

For the first time in Vietnam, U.S. troops were authorized to "search and destroy" the enemy, designated as "S&D" missions.

American troops were going on the offence. Vietnam would soon become America's war, which meant more air evac's for Roe MacDonald.

CHAPTER NINETEEN
CERCLE SPORTIF SAIGONNAIS

1965

The lush French Colonial country club occupied thirty beautifully landscaped acres in the middle of Saigon, not far from the Presidential Palace. Built in 1920 at the height of the French Colonial era, Cercle still functioned as an exclusive club and a private playground for the aristocracy forty-five years later, despite the ongoing war. This idyllic parkland stood as an enclave of privilege, a virtual paradise in stark contrast to the turmoil taking place in the busy city of Saigon and throughout South Vietnam. American officers considered the club a mirage in a desert of chaos outside its gates.

The Saigon police, Quan Canh, QC, guarded the club's entrance on Hong Trap Tu Street from terrorist attacks. Dubbed "White Mice" for their attire and pompous behavior, they paraded around in their tailored white uniforms wearing aviator sunglasses reserved for Vietnamese air force crews. Their pretention deserved the derisive description. But, nevertheless they maintained a semblance of order in the madness of downtown Saigon.

Blue and white Renault taxis beeped incessantly trying to negotiate the busy thoroughfare clogged with Honda scooters, pedicabs, bicycles, and crowds of pedestrians attempting to cross the intersection. Diesel and castor oil fumes hung heavily in the humidity, but traffic slowly progressed with a touch of Asian patience and a modicum of manners.

Outside of Cercle's high walls, occasional tanks and troops would move slowly through the streets already jammed with vehicles of every description, their destination unknown to the public. But, once inside the club's grounds, jets screaming overhead were the only reminder of the war. This sanctuary insulated the select few from stark reality of fighting the VC, if only for a few hours. It ranked first on Biff Roberts' shortlist of getaways. But, he often came here often for other reasons, mainly clandestine in nature.

French, Chinese, and Vietnamese rubber-plantation owners, wealthy businessmen, and of course, generals and politicians escaped both the heat and the conflict here. The elegant setting featured a white wooden-framed colonial clubhouse with its classic orange terra cotta tiled roof. This magnificent two-story edifice perched on the hillside overlooked the manicured grounds. Fenestrated balconies with shaded porches overlooked the pool, tennis courts and expansive terraces below. Brilliant red flamed trees interspersed among the palms and tropical flora highlighted the grounds' vista, a tropical delight that created a pacifying effect for its visitors. A place to sooth raw nerves, a place well suited to privately discuss business, politics, and the ongoing conflict. And, an ideal place to pursue Saigon's quintessential pastime, conspiracy.

Naturally, Cercle Sportif fit right into Biff's agenda, a perfect place to escape, a spot to relax and reenergize, a secluded hangout to gather one's thoughts, and foremost, a perfect place to spy on those conspiring.

While relaxing on the porch, Biff sipped a gin and tonic and listened to the distant ping pong sound of tennis balls, mixed with the chatter of children playing in the Olympic size pool. The laughter drifted by as if no one had a care in the world. Tennis players, sunbathers, and formally dressed waiters scurried across the plush lawn terraces to pursue their activities with not a care in the world. Meanwhile, conversations on the porch took place, many not carefully guarded, conducted in different languages within his earshot. He recorded them on a small, hidden eavesdropping device, a practice that yielded valuable information for the CIA when later translated at the Embassy.

This club's competitors across town—Cercle Hippique Saigonnais, or Club Nautique—while classy, could not compare to Cercle Sportif's impressive ambiance, impeccable service, and quality cuisine. Sportif embodied an especially enjoyable experience for an expat to relax. Today's visitor would love it.

Biff arrived an hour or so earlier than his get together with Roe. He wanted some time to take some mental notes on today's guests. And, and more importantly who was meeting with whom. Biff unobtrusively evaluated the chances of discovering the next big conspiracy or coup d'état. Saigon was a city of intrigues, most nefarious. Something sinister seemed always in the works. No one understood conspiracies like Biff. Whatever the mission required, Biff was up to the task, the consummate spy.

He wondered if anyone here knew that he was deputy CIA station manager in Saigon, an attaché to the U.S. Embassy under diplomatic cover. On second thought, he laughed to himself. The CIA was kidding itself if it really believed that "diplomatic cover" was possible in Saigon. He doubted the word "secret" was even in Saigon's lexicon, or that the Vietnamese even had a word for "secret." The Chinese had a word for it: *mi*. Biff was still a little shaky in his Asian languages, especially Vietnamese, not an easy language to pick up.

While he watched two sparrows fighting over a bread crumb under a table on the terrace, he called the waiter over and ordered another gin and tonic.

"Please add some smoked salmon hors d' oeuvres, most ricky-tick."

Biff tried a few GI phrases, not knowing if it was proper Vietnamese or not. Ricky-tick was probably slang, meaning "sooner if not immediately."

"Yes, sir."

He raised a hand to stall the waiter. "Is there a Vietnamese word for 'secret'?"

Without hesitation the waiter responded, "Kinh, K-I-N-H," as he spelled it out.

It wouldn't surprise Biff if the waiter was a spy. The guy radiated bad vibes Biff couldn't put a finger on, but his intuition flared. This waiter apparently was fluent in Chinese, Vietnamese, English, and French judging from overhearing his conversations at other tables. The ethnic language mix seemed not to challenge him, possibly a tip off. His answer to the question had arrived so promptly that Biff became suspicious. But then, Biff was always suspicious. That was the nature of his job, and his personality, and the key to his survival in Vietnam's hostile environment. The question remained... who was he spying for, the north or south?

After the waiter left, Biff reflexively checked under the table and chairs for a bug.

One can't be too careful in Saigon, he thought.

Finding no hidden listening devices, Biff relaxed a bit. His small hi tech eavesdropping devise fit snug in his inside vest pocket equipped with a directional app to capture targeted chatter. No need for conventional bugs.

Maybe he was overly cautious and suspicious, but always ascribed to the "better safe than sorry" philosophy. Sloppy CIA officers in Saigon didn't last long. Biff trusted few people in his life, and this waiter was not one of them. The waiters here were professional, always the most courteous. But, there was something about this one, a new guy, something that immediately aroused suspicion, a sixth sense that Biff possessed. He doubted this man was an ordinary waiter.

Moments later, two well-dressed Asian couples arrived with two teenage children, a skinny Asian boy and an attractive young girl. They sat at a table next to his, just a few discreet feet away. While usually reserved to the point of diffidence, the elder Chinese gentleman smiled and greeted Biff in perfect English in a friendly manner. They exchanged pleasantries and small talk. He introduced himself as Bill Hsu.

The wives sat quietly involved in muffled in conversation with the children. No one bothered to introduce them. The teenagers were well behaved, obviously thirsty after playing tennis in Saigon's heat and humidity. They looked sharp in their traditional all-white outfits. Biff did not usually engage in conversation with strangers, but this family piqued his interest. Even more unusual, they responded to his overture.

He asked, "Are the children good players?"

He thought this enquiry an innocuous way to strike up a conversation. Everyone is proud of their children, especially Asians. Biff had a keen interest in Asian culture. He had learned a lot during his brief Southeast Asian posting. Chinese families are usually limited to one or two children. Among the elite, there is a tremendous cultural drive to excel in academics. The Chinese are a polite, homogenous society, very family oriented, and very private, if not xenophobic. This pleasant family dispelled this notion with their outgoing manners.

Biff was impressed with the cordiality and openness of these two families. Obviously, they had been around a lot of Americans, not reluctant to engage in conversation.

In fact, they too had a keen interest in foreigners, especially Americans. Mr. Hsu responded, in a British accent, that the boy's name was Guy Lau and the girl, Eva Hsu. Both were fifteen years old and excellent players.

"They've done well in tennis competitions here." He hastily added, "They are going to pine for Cercle Sportif and their friends here."

"Why is that?"

"We'll be moving to Paris next month. The children are enrolled in one of the top Lycees. Both are excellent students, fluent in four languages.

I bet I know which four. "Wonderful. What a great experience for them. Why are leaving Saigon, if I may enquire?" Biff tried not to appear probing or nosy, but could not restrain his curiosity.

"Saigon is dying. As the local saying goes, 'She's dying like a whore who is desperately trying to turn her last trick.' Mr. Hsu smiled at his colorful metaphor.

"Just look at To Do Street. Sleazy bars, prostitutes all over, infested with drug peddlers. Saigon is becoming like Cholon. It's disgraceful that mama-sans who run the family noodle shop take to the streets once they find prostitution more profitable than their business. Most soon find the competition from young peasant girls overwhelming and soon return to their mundane life and their noodle shops. It's a sad commentary."

Biff grasped the message of Mr. Hsu's compelling story and offered a comforting comment to illustrate that he commiserated with Mr. Hsu's situation.

"Wars always disrupt and dislocate normal life with its ravaging and pillaging. The Vietnamese have suffered for decades, if not centuries with the incursions of foreign invaders. Now the Vietnamese are involved in a civil war between the North and South, communists versus nationalists. Toss in American politicians and military into this fray, and you have a recipe for Vietnam to come apart at the seams."

"I don't understand the phrase, 'Come apart at the seams'," Mr. Hsu admitted.

"Disorder, confusion, chaos... It's an American colloquial expression. Americans have a tendency to speak in metaphors, clichés, aphorisms, and slang. It's a vernacular way of speaking, called "colloquial language." It's certainly not the King's English. We have a lot of colorful expressions, some of which would offend you."

Mr. Hsu, still looked somewhat puzzled, simply replied. "I see."

Did he?

Decades of war bred a resilient population. Those who adapt, survive. Darwin had it right, "Survival of the fittest." Many Chinese ethnic Vietnamese passed this severe test of natural selection. They were a hearty lot, self-determined. If only they had benefitted from sound leadership, and corruption was not endemic, life might have turned out better for them.

Another squadron of fighter jets roared over the club, briefly damping out all conversation, a reminder that war continued to rage on outside this tranquil sanctuary. Cercle remained one of the last bastions for the privileged set, a vestige of the halcyon days the French enjoyed in Saigon for over a century. Those halcyon days that now seemed like centuries ago, but they passed only a little over one decade ago with France's defeat at Dien Bien Phu, prompting their departure from Indochina in 1954. Life went on for a select part of society acclimatized and sheltered from war...

Biff gazed down from the balcony at the veranda below, absorbing the splendor. He noted that the jet noise only briefly interrupted the clubhouse conversations of those inured to war. The tennis matches still progressed. Laughing children continued to frolic and splash around in the pool. The rich and famous, movers and shakers of Saigon society, sunbathed, and sipped their citron and soda, gin and tonics far removed from war's reality.

The life of the elite and gentry.

Just outside the club's gates, pill boxes with machine gunners protected the chosen few. The flyover had distracted him. He daydreamed, his thoughts drifting off.

Saigon and Cholon, Sodom and Gomorrah. He reflected on the dichotomy of Vietnamese society, the vast gulf between the chosen few and the masses. Was God punishing wicked behavior?

Not far from this posh club women living in small hamlets, who never owned a bikini, or even dreamed of lounging by a poolside, are probably fleeing mortars and firefights with their children in tow. In the midst of all the wartime chaos, Biff knew peasants would continue to tend their rice paddies where the bodies of dead soldiers decayed in the hot sun, not retrieved by their comrades. This was in stark contrast to the American practice of never leaving a fallen solider behind.

Biff found the disconnect mindboggling. Juxtaposing Cercle Sportif's close knit world of elites with Saigon's wartime environs and the peasants' struggle for existence, he found the disparities of the two realities striking and depressing.

His thoughts had drifted off in the midst of a conversation, which did not unnoticed by the Chinese gentleman who patiently waited for a response.

Biff's apologetic gaze focused on the Asian man. "Sorry, I was daydreaming."

"The planes are quite loud, aren't they? Quite impossible to talk, you were saying?" Mr. Hsu asked.

"Let me recover my train of thought. Oh, yes. You said you were leaving because Saigon is dying, and you arranged for your children to attend school in Paris. Not a bad decision to get away from the war."

"That is part of our motivation. The main reason is that our business was taken over by the Viet Cong. Mr. Lau and my family, for several generations, have owned a lumber mill above Kien Phong where the Mekong River branches into the Delta. Our company's timber men cut trees in the central highlands and float the logs down the Mekong River to the large island where we have our lumber mill. We mill the logs and provide Saigon with building materials. We've decided it no longer suits the family's purposes. We have relatives in Paris and look forward to our new life abroad."

"What an interesting story, but tragic how it ended for you. I wish you all the best. It sounds like a judicious move."

"Thank you. We must run along now. The children have enjoyed their lemonade. May I give you my card?"

"Yes, please. Thank you."

"Of course. I enjoyed meeting you and our conversation."

Biff glanced at the embossed card. It read, "Hsu and Lau. Mekong Lumber LTD" with phone numbers listed in Saigon and Kien Phong. And, of course, the neatly printed information was available in four languages on the back of the fancy business card.

***

Biff later checked the company's credentials at the Embassy. Their lumber business was one of the oldest and most profitable in South Vietnam. War had disrupted yet another productive enterprise. Biff admired the Chinese businessmen for picking up and moving on, doing what was best for their families.

The pleasant Chinese families departed the terrace just as Roe strode up to the verandah in civilian clothes, looking spiffy.

He must be on R &R, Biff thought. Roe looked handsomely casual in his madras sport shirt, khakis, and old white buck shoes.

He rushed to the porch railing, grinned and waved. "Come on up, Roe."

The two old buddies shook hands, patted each other on the back, repeating the same ritual greeting since high school.

"How you doing, Roe?"

"Fine, old buddy. Some place you have here, Biff. Posh! The Air Force doesn't provide us digs like this to hang out. Pretty impressive, nothing like this in Baltimore or Philly either," he joked.

"A haven from war's hell. Having your usual?"

"Sure, gin and tonic, Sapphire Gin."

"Looking pretty casual, Roe. Got some time off?"

"As a matter of fact, I'm flying to Bangkok tonight after our dinner. Got some jump orders with a C-135 crew outta Tan Son Nhut. I plan a little R& R with my Aussie sweetheart, Lynne. After that I have some consultations and flight physicals up at our airbase up in Takhli, Thailand. The flight surgeon up there is swamped with the buildup of the fighter bomber squadrons at 355th TAC Fighter Wing."

"Sounds like fun. What have we got up at Takhli?" Biff knew the answer, it was a rhetorical question.

"Supersonic F-105 THUDs, and the newer version two seat F-105G fighter bomber. They are conducting some intensive North Vietnam bombing missions out of Thailand. Unfortunately, they're taking some big-time losses from NVN antiaircraft, SAMs, and MiGs."

"Operation Wild Weasel, Roe? Or Rolling Thunder?"

"That's classified information, Biff, but you're cleared top secret, so I guess we can discuss it. It has some important implications for the conduct of the war, a topic you can discuss in your CINCPAC intel meetings in Hawaii."

Roe suspected the CIA was aware of every detail of the escalating bombing plans on the drawing board for North Vietnam airstrikes, including the six zone NVN attack plan dictated by CINCPAC and MACV. He knew Biff was just messing with him.

"I've got my sources," Biff grinned and chuckled. "I didn't know until recently how powerful a fighter bomber the F-105 really is. Has a bomb bay big enough to carry an atomic bomb. F-105s can pack more wallop than a WWII B-17 or B-24 with conventional bombs."

"You're very knowledgeable, Biff. You never cease to amaze me with the scope of your technical detail. Add this vital information to your data bank. It will blow you away. The NVN targets are selected, not by the JCS military experts based on actionable intel like the CIA's, but by LBJ's inner circle, who don't know jack shit."

"I suspected as much."

"Here's the skinny. NVN prime targets are heavily fortified with SAMs, Zu-33 anti-aircraft, and MiGs. Consequently, the F-4 target suppression aircraft and our F-105 bombers are taking heavy losses. Pilots complain it's almost like NVN knows their targets ahead of time, even know their call signs and ETA. They suspect something is fishy since NVN intel is definitely not that good. Over the last two years, the Navy has lost 160 planes, and the USAF 280. Planes can be replaced, but not the 300 pilots who ejected and ended up POWs or MIA. This has the potential to inflict psychological damage on our fighter command and defeat the mission. The pilots complain they take high risks to bomb marginally significant targets, while critical targets nearby and easily accessible are restricted, designated as off limits for political reasons."

He shook his head in disgust and took a sip of his G and T. Biff could see Roe was very upset about this situation.

"Naturally this BS pisses off TAC wing commanders and their pilots. Flyers at Danang, carrier squadrons in Yankee Station, and those at eleven other airbases have registered similar complaints to Takhli's 355th TAC Wing, which has suffered the major brunt of our losses. This DC nonsense seriously affects morale. No one can understand why politicians are picking the targets, not the JCS. They wonder why there are so many self-imposed restrictions on those critical targets so obvious to them and easily accessible to their ordinance. They question why we don't inflict a real impact on the enemy and get this war over. They want to go all out, since they realize they have the capability to cripple the enemy."

Roe leaned back and looked Biff in the eye. "Their frustration keeps flight surgeons busy accessing if the air crews are still fit psychologically to fly, or won't go rogue in a fit of anger when their wingman is shot down. That's the situation I have to deal with at Takhli Royal Thai Airbase. The 3555th TAC wing has been hit the hardest. It's starting to get to them. Their flight surgeons are swamped with depressed, frustrated, and angry pilots' complaints."

"Didn't know those stats, Roe. A big morale problem could compromise their mission, I agree. Can't keep sustaining those losses very much longer. Sounds like the frustration is building to the boiling point."

"That's the big picture DC doesn't get, Biff. If the pilots are taking that much risk, why not make it worthwhile by targeting vital installations? Hit 'em where it hurts. More of a risk/reward equation. This strategy is counter-productive to winning a war."

"I like the way you think, Roe. LBJ and his boys think they know more than the generals and admirals. That's the basic problem, as I see it. We'll discuss the problem at our next CINCPAC intel meeting. Register our complaint through channels. Maybe they'll get it. Thanks for your input, pal."

"I'm impressed with Cercle Sportif." Roe abruptly changed the subject.

He found this "Rolling Thunder" topic too painful to continue discussing. LBJ and his inner circle could fuck up a church picnic. The military was paying a steep price for their feckless decisions and hopeless indecision. They lacked a comprehensive strategy and will to win the war. They pecked away at it incrementally. Seemingly always in the reactive mode, never proactive with full force and resources of the U.S. military. They squandered the military's technologic advantage. It made him sick every time he air evac'ed the wounded and body bags on their MAC aircraft.

"You don't think anyone can lob a grenade this far from the street, do you, Biff? That was a little hairy at the Brinks BOQ last September!"

"Sure was. But, it's pretty safe here. Guess you heard about the sabotage last Christmas Eve at Brinks? Two sappers blew the side off the building."

"Read about it in the *Stars and Stripes*, quite a blast. We were lucky it didn't kill more officers."

"We were lucky, it's safer here. I wanted you to see this place and enjoy one of the best meals in Saigon. The cuisine is excellent and the French wine outstanding. The service is very sophisticated."

When it came to the "noble rot," Biff demonstrated another side of his renaissance man personality."

"You live a tough life, dude."

Biff, still grinning, "Someone's got to support the local economy."

"On the serious side, I've got to tell you about my experience last week in Pleiku. I air-evac'ed our old buddy, Cody, to Clark AFB."

"What? I heard about the surprise attack by the VC, but I didn't know Cody was hurt bad enough to be air evac'ed."

"Our down-homer distinguished himself in battle, but paid a price, got fragged by the VC. Cody did us proud. Word has it that he personally wasted well over two- or three-dozen VCs coming through the north perimeter breach. I've read the after action report. Maybe not an exaggeration, knowing is skill with a rifle. Cody's receiving a Purple Heart and a Silver Star."

"Wow! Deserves the decorations. How bad was he injured?"

"Multiple mortar fragments, MFW's we call 'em. Incoming killed two ARVN standing next to Cody. They must have shielded Cody, taking the brunt of the blast. Blew off half of Cody's right ear and left a big gash in his face, arms and legs. Not life threatening, but a scary close call. He lost a lot of blood. They are fixing him up at Clark now. They've recommended plastic surgery at our Presidio Hospital in San Francisco, but Cody has elected to return to active duty next month in the central highlands. He's one hard-core guy... Green Beret. Didn't want to wear the 'million-dollar wounded' label."

"What's that?"

"A non-crippling wound considered serious enough to return to the States."

"Cody's not a woozy for sure. No way a Green Beret would fake it to get orders to go back home."

Biff lifted his glass to toast Roe. "Here's to you and Cody, fellow. I admire your good work. It seems like we were playing football together just short while ago. Now we are over here in Southeast Asia trying to sort out a big mess, fighting gooks, killing communists."

"Got that right, pal." Roe raised his glass of gin and clinked it with Biff's before continuing to relate the inside story on Pleiku.

"Evidently Charlie had two well trained and armed battalions, plus a company of seasoned NVA Commandoes. They conducted the well-coordinated surprise attack just before dawn, inflicting a lot of damage. Serious mass-cal... attack killed eight Americans, wounded more than a hundred. They destroyed twenty aircraft the crews couldn't scramble quick enough to avoid the mortars."

"I read that report, a sore spot with me. But, I didn't know the full extent of Cody's injuries. I'm glad the command praised his battlefield actions. I'm sure he earned his decorations."

"Cody did earn them. Not a bullshit recommendation in his case. Some game the system to get the hell outta here with three Purples. Ironically, our high school football circle is now closed, Biff. Think about that?"

"How's that, Roe?"

"A Marine squadron of A-4 Skyhawks led by our high school wide receiver, Al Ruey, flew in from Chu Lai to provide close air support. They laid the hammer on the VC with cannon fire, rockets, and bombs. His squadron continued strafing the retreating VC back into the jungles, blew up their ammo dumps in the jungle, and nap'ed them."

"Actually, I'd received a summary of that report, but without all the details. Small world, isn't it? You, me, Cody, and Al over here fighting communism," Biff commented sarcastically, and paused. "Ever wonder why we got involved over here, Roe?"

"I figure it's a carryover from the cold war psyche, Biff. That's probably as good an explanation as any. Seems we're always trying to thwart communism no matter where it pops up."

"That's one way to look at it. The party line justifying this action is the 'Domino Theory."

"I understand that, but this war is an expensive way to prove or disprove a theory'

"You've got a point, Roe." He'd never looked at it that way. Roe pressed the point with a down-home analogy.

"Fighting an abstract like communism is sort of like being 'up shit creek without a paddle'. You can spend a lot of time trying to get somewhere in unpleasant circumstances and surroundings. Progress is difficult, if not impossible. You may be lucky just to get back to where you started." Roe shook his head. "*Nothing* about our involvement in Vietnam seems defined to me."

"I agree, things are screwed up over here, but I believe our military superiority will eventually prevail, don't you?"

"I'm not concerned about our military performance. Politics, ours and theirs, will determine the outcome in my opinion, Biff … not the military."

"That is an interesting perspective. I have conflicting opinions, wavering between positive and pessimistic. My CIA reports color my perception. Maybe I should get some rose-colored lens."

"Might help, pal."

"Sorry to hear about the extent of Cody's injuries. I heard he had just been promoted to captain."

"Cody's tough as nails. He'll be okay. I'm not worried about him, he's a tiger. He sure earned that promotion serving out in those jungles and rice paddies."

"What do you say we have some dinner, Roe? Enough of the war stories."

"I'm up for that. I'm sort of hungry."

"You'll love the shrimp, crab, and rice dish. It's one of my favorites. The seafood is fresh from the Delta. Not as good as our blue fin crabs back home on the Chesapeake Bay, but pretty damned good."

"I'll follow you. Lead the way."

They went down the porch stairway escorted by Biff's waiter, the one he'd already nicknamed "the Spy" on a hunch.

Entering a formal dining room Biff selected a table over in a private corner with a view of the verandah and doorways.

Roe noted that Biff never sat with his back to the door, sort of a Wild West habit of his. He knew Biff carried a .9 mm Beretta automatic under his jacket. That's why he always wore an oversize lightweight jacket despite the Saigon heat and humidity. Roe was qualified to carry a pistol, but he didn't. He kept an M-16 on his Air force missions close at hand on the plane. Roe was a good shot with a rifle, but couldn't hit a barn door with a .45 pistol. Too much recoil.

Table service was efficient, as expected. This time Biff ordered a 1958 Cheval Blanc. Roe found it educational to dine with a fine-wine connoisseur and epicurean, and Roe allowed him to order all his favorite French and Vietnamese dishes.

Roe was still a 'down homer.' He enjoyed a good meal and wine, but he never indulged in extravagancies. Biff had a certain zest for life with all its good things. Biff lived as if there were no tomorrow.

Probably a good idea in his profession, Roe mused. Maybe that isn't a bad philosophy over here in Vietnam, come to think of it.

Roe's deference to Biff's recommendations paid off as he enjoyed one of the most delightful meals he'd ever experienced. The seafood courses arrived in orderly fashion with a perfect sense of timing. It was a dining experience. Biff introduced him to a Vietnamese condiment, nuoc-mam, a fermented fish sauce.

Roe tried it. "Not bad… but, got to admit just the thought of it tends to turn me off."

Biff laughed at his reaction.

Halfway through the leisurely meal, a Vietnamese Combo took the stage. They opened with their version of Brubeck's "Take Five." The pianist was proficient, but the saxophonist was a far cry from Paul Desmond.

The drummer ... well, he really lacked the talent for the drum solo. He was no Joe Morello, not even close.

That number received only polite applause from the diners, but it was still early ... maybe the combo would warm up.

A lovely young Asian woman joined them on the stage in the traditional Ao-dai attire. The next number was their version of the Beatles' "Yellow Submarine." She had a nice voice, but her Asian accent distracted from the British tune.

Beatle mania was sweeping the U.S., but just drifting into Southeast Asia. The combo struggled to keep in synch with her lyrics, but everyone got the general idea and politely applauded. Except for a couple of American civilians across the room. They were rudely laughing and putting her down, which was considered insulting behavior in polite Asian society.

Biff stood up abruptly and approached their table to reprimand them.

Uh-oh, Roe thought, *Fireworks?*

Always the gentleman, Biff reached over the table to whisper in their ears. Roe could only imagine what message he delivered.

Roe noticed Biff had unbuttoned his blue blazer jacket so the two unruly men could glimpse his Beretta in its vest holster. Biff embodied all things intimidating: a big, imposing fellow who happened to "carry." He noted his buddy didn't act the least bit confrontational. He just politely instructed them to get their act together. Something to the effect they shouldn't perpetuate the image of the "Ugly American," a short lecture in manners for foreign visitors.

Biff returned to the table completely poised and unflustered. He remarked, "I don't know who let those two characters off the reservation. Xin loi, sorry about that, Roe."

Then Biff casually resumed his meal.

"That was pretty smooth, Biff." So, Biff was picking up Vietnamese catch phrases like the guys used on the flight line at Tan son Nhut.

"Not my first rodeo." he chuckled. "When in Rome..."

The singer continued to belt out the lyrics, "We all live in a yellow submarine, a yellow submarine..."

This was a reference to the British MI6 subterranean file of communists, activists, subversives, anyone they might suspect of anarchy. Great

Britain had its share of problems with the Warsaw Pact, Suez crisis, and the Malaysia insurgency, plus dealing with its own activists at the present time.

Like most Filipino bands in Cholon, the local combo couldn't quite get the beat either. A poor imitation of the Beatles … but, boy, did they try. Most of the Filipino singers lip-synched along with the band—probably a good idea. Someone should have recommended it to this young vocalist.

Roe glanced at his watch. Time had flown by. He thanked Biff for a lovely meal, but asked for a raincheck on dessert. He needed to get out to Tan son Nhut to catch his flight. Anxious to get to Bangkok and see Lynne, he begged off. He pictured her in his mind.

She was quite a joker. Lately, she had been kidding him, paraphrasing the old country western lyrics, "You're not as good as you once were, but you're good once as you always were."

When he related the joke to Biff, the old pals shared a hearty laugh.

"Must be some gal, Roe."

"One hell of a woman, Biff."

Biff suggested the next dinner in May at Hickam's Officers Club. He still wanted to introduce Ann Summerville to Roe, who had agreed to the invitation. Biff promised to send the dates when he would be in Hawaii. Told Roe he was usually there two or three times a month. Both friends were looking forward to the trip, just set the date.

Biff stayed for dessert. He met some friends from the Embassy and shared a bottle of Napoleon Cognac. And, of course, he enjoyed one of his prized Cuban Cohiba cigars.

It reminded him how Roe always ribbed him about smoking contraband cigars.

"Khong Xau", don't worry about it, he chuckled to himself.

His CIA colleague in Havana kept him well supplied if not available on Saigon's black market.

After an hour or so of imbibing, the Embassy group called it a night.

***

Biff returned to his Saigon apartment across the park from the U.S. Embassy. In keeping with the neighborhood, it was a white stucco colonial building with a terra cotta -tiled roof, dark green shutters, with a small wrought-iron balcony in the front and back. A ten-foot wall surrounded the property providing security and privacy. The property had nice front and back yard patios. Lovely gardens lined with palm trees and flowering plants provided shade from the hot Saigon days.

He approached his second-floor flat—above the apartment of two elderly Vietnamese—about midnight. Biff was exhausted and a bit tipsy from the last glass of Cognac and all the wine with dinner. As usual, he was suspicious. He sensed trouble, but couldn't identify the threat. Regardless, he never ignored his intuition.

Biff entered his apartment, reflexively scanning the room for any evidence of intrusion, small traps he routinely set to tip him off. He checked his reliable, ultramodern security monitors provided by the CIA. In Saigon, a deputy station manager couldn't be too cautious. He quickly ascertained his apartment was secure.

After a hot shower, he crashed, confident his quarters were safe and sound. In minutes he fell into a deep slumber.

He awoke with a start when the bedside monitor emitted small intermittent beeps, indicating a potential intrusion. Biff checked the fluorescent bedside clock: *"3:10 a.m."*

Biff always kept his .9 mm Beretta under the pillow next to him. He slipped off the safety of the pistol, chambered a bullet, and checked the hallway monitor. In the second-floor hallway, two dark figures in black pajamas stood by his door, ready to pick his door lock with a standard "jimmying" device.

Biff took up a position beside the living room couch, where he would have a clear view of both men once they entered, and rested his right forearm to steady his semi-automatic's aim. The monitor revealed both men carried pistols, indicating a plan to assassinate, rather than rob him.

Biff was now fully awake and alert. He grinned. These two yahoos were in for the surprise of their about-to-be short lives.

They skillfully opened the door lock with little sound. As the door started to slowly swing open. Biff steadied his Beretta.

The two Vietnamese intruders rushed into the room, their pistols raised to fire. That action tripped a blinding flash at the doorway, stopping them in their tracks, a vital element of surprise. Biff took good aim at their silhouettes and fired two accurate shots into their chests. Both dropped to the floor face first, mortally wounded.

Biff fired .9 mm hollow-point bullets. Hollow points enter with a small hole, but splatter, reeking massive damage, and the fragments exit with a large hole. These bullets intend to kill, not wound. Both victims lay motionless on the floor, blood seeping from their black pajama tops. Two Chinese pistols lay beside them.

Biff, remained calm and collected, as if he had just caught a pick-pocket on the streets of Saigon. He turned over the two dead bodies. The first was a nondescript twenty-year-old male with multiple body scars indicating previous scrapes or VC activity.

When Biff turned over the second body, he gasped uncharacteristically.

"Holy shit! The Cercle waiter."

His premonition earlier in the evening had been well founded. The waiter was, indeed, a spy and a would-be assassin.

Thank you, Langley, for the surveillance system. It works.

Biff needed to get rid of the bodies and clean up the bloody mess without concerning his neighbors. The gunshots and commotion had awakened the Vietnamese couple on the ground floor. They were yelling frantically upstairs to assure themselves that Biff was okay, and didn't need any help.

The sincere, concerned couple looked after the mysterious American visitor to their country. Their regard of Biff included not only curiosity, but parental sensitivity. They liked this polite American who brought them small gifts from the American PX on holidays—theirs and his. Mr. Roberts was a considerate tenant.

Biff assured them he was fine, just a small accident had occurred. He'd take care of everything, apologizing for the disturbance. Biff placed a call to a colleague at the Embassy. The Embassy provided twenty-four-hour coverage for circumstances like this.

"James, I've got a situation over here at my apartment. Need a direct exchange. Yeah, a DX. I've got bodies of two would-be assassins to dispose of as soon as possible. Now is as good a time as any. Send a couple of boys over to take care of this, okay?"

"Right, boss. Consider it done."

Biff pondered the events of last evening at Cercle, considering motives for this assassination attempt. *What's the connection with this waiter?* Though a matter of speculation, he bet it was someone at the Palace, not the VC, who plotted to take him out. The Chinese pistols indicated the Viet Cong, but presidential palace assassins could have used them as a ruse.

The Vietnamese specialize in intrigue. In Saigon, conspiracy thrives. It could have been a retaliatory action following Diem's assassination last year, as CIA had been implicated. Or, it could have been part of the elaborate VC spy network.

God! Who knows in this country?

CHAPTER TWENTY
BANGKOK RENDEZVOUS

March 1965

Captain Roe MacDonald deplaned the C-135 sweating profusely in his flight suit. He touted his B-4 bag containing his civilian clothes to the hangar's flight-planning section to hitch a ride downtown.

The Bangkok heat was oppressive, even in the late evening. Not the slightest breeze stirred the dense humidity and the temperature registered ninety degrees. Southeast Asia's weather resembled a sauna. It seemed much more uncomfortable than the muggy Chesapeake Bay area in August.

Roe had spent two previous R&Rs in Bangkok with his Qantas airline companion, Lynne Andrews, at the Mandarin Oriental Hotel. On R&R, he usually sought non-stop action, hitting the ground running, but tonight he was beat. Lynne shared his enthusiasm for Bangkok, but would understand his fatigue. A good time awaited him tomorrow after a good night's rest. It was a relief to get away from the constant tension in Vietnam. He really needed a break.

He crossed the tarmac, anticipating that Jimmy, the jeweler, would greet him as he did most Air Force flights. The hustler, was a 24/7 businessman. Actually, his jewelry was top-notch quality at one half the U.S. price. Roe had a gold bracelet appraised in San Francisco just to be sure it wasn't a fake. It was certified as high quality and authentic.

On the flight over from Saigon, he thought he might buy Lynne an emerald-studded gold bracelet. She had been a really nice companion to him on his R&R trips. Roe wasn't deeply in love with her, but he was definitely attracted and wanted to do something nice for her.

As predicted, Jimmy showed up with a wide smile on his face. "Buy anything, Captain? I give you good price."

"How about a nice emerald bracelet?"

"Come out to my car," Jimmy replied, smiling ear to ear. He remembered Roe.

They proceeded to Jimmy's old jalopy with more dents than could be counted, cracking paint, and rusting battle scars. Jimmy unlocked his trunk to reveal a dazzling display of jewelry. Roe figured it contained conservatively about a quarter of a million dollars' worth of bracelets, necklaces, rings—all featuring the world-class rubies and emeralds for which Thailand was famous. Nothing about Jimmy surprised Roe. This was one true, enterprising capitalist operating out of his car trunk.

"That one over there looks good, the emerald and gold bracelet. How much do you want for that one, Jimmy?"

"One thousand dollars U.S.," he quickly replied.

"How about seven hundred?" Roe replied.

Bartering was an art form in Southeast Asia.

"Nine hundred," Jimmy countered.

"Eight hundred, final offer."

"Okay. Done. Sold. Eight hundred U.S. Want a gift box, Captain?"

"Sure. Thanks."

The bartering routine was an Asian ritual. Everyone expected a deal. Roe knew this bracelet would cost at least $2,000 in San Francisco, if you could find one of this quality and design. He thought Lynne would love it.

He smiled and slapped Jimmy gently on his shoulder, signifying how much he enjoyed this exercise. The salesman grinned, confident he had come out on top in this transaction.

"Wrap it up, Jimmy." He counted out eight crisp one hundred dollar bills.

"Want a ride to your hotel, Captain? I'm going into town for a late dinner date."

"Sure, thank you. That works for me. Mandarin Orient Hotel."

Roe had received a telex from Lynne before departure that she had arrived earlier that day, hit the pool, and planned to take a nap in the room she'd reserved for them. Lynne was a very organized woman.

Roe figured he'd arrive at the hotel too late to go out on the town. They'd do that tomorrow night. He wasn't hungry. He'd already had an early dinner with Biff at Cercle Sportif, and the food and drink contributed to his exhaustion. The action in Vietnam was picking up and he'd put in some long, grueling hours without much sleep. Sacking out early worked for him. He wasn't ready for a command performance and hoped she'd be asleep when he arrived.

Roe chuckled, recalling how she had kidded him on his last trip about the old country western tune lyrics he shared with Biff earlier at dinner.

Lynne was a hoot, and happened to be an Australian free spirit who really enjoyed sex. That suited Roe just fine, if he was rested. She had no hang-ups, made no demands, expected no promises, and offered no corny "Was it good for you?" stuff. Lynne was a great gal to be with.

The night desk clerk at the classy hotel recognized him from prior trips, smiled, and handed him a note from Lynne. He efficiently checked Roe in for two nights.

Roe opened the hotel envelope. Her message read, *"Come up and see me, big boy. Love, Lynne."*

Roe guessed this was her humorous Mae West invitation. Lynne was a character and he loved her great sense of humor and vibrant personality. Plus, she was a real looker—a medium-height brunette with hazel eyes, who came across as an athletic, outdoor type. Certainly not an artsy-crafty type woman with a library card. Lynne possessed a certain sophistication associated with her extensive travel and prolific reading habits on her long trips, and maintained a cosmopolitan outlook on life. She was the perfect companion for Roe, very compatible. No drama, no pretenses, just plain old-fashioned fun.

Roe took the elevator to the fifth floor, followed the hallway to the end room overlooking the river and city lights.

Perfect, he thought. *She's got good taste.*

He unlocked the door and quietly entered. She had remembered not to set the door chain, so his entry did not awaken her. The air-conditioned room was a perfect sixty-eight degrees, refreshing after the day's oppressive heat and humidity.

As Roe entered the corner suite, he immediately noticed the fragrance of jasmine and fresh-cut tropical flowers. The ceiling fan rotated slowly. A small balcony overlooked the river and city lights below—an adornment, since it was much too hot to sit out on the balcony. The room was tastefully decorated with rattan furniture, attractive batik prints on the wall, and small oriental rugs scattered across the white-tiled floors. The décor impressed him, hinting at a professional touch.

Across the sitting room he observed Lynne sleeping quietly in the adjoining bedroom in her thin negligee, the covers turned back. A bottle of her favorite Dom Perignon champagne rested in the ice bucket next to the bed, an inviting scene.

Should he awaken her? No, he'd take a shower before quietly slipping in beside her.

Lynne must have taken in too much sun or had one too many cocktails this afternoon, Roe thought. *She's usually roaring and ready to go party when I arrive. Now, she's out like a light.*

It surprised him, but did not disappoint him.

The warm shower was refreshing. He put on some clean boxer shorts and slipped into bed beside her. She had a lovely fragrance. She slept soundly, never stirred. Roe joined her in a deep slumber minutes later.

***

"Maid service..."

The knock on the door announced it was ten in the morning. Rise and shine. Roe and Lynne had slept eleven hours without waking once. She turned to him, smiled, and gave him a kiss.

"About time you got here, fella."

Roe laughed at the enticing tone in her Aussie accent. "I'll tell the maid to come back at eleven, okay?"

"Sounds like a grand idea. I've missed you, Roe."

"Oh. I brought you a little gift, Lynne."

He got out of bed, dismissed the maid, and retrieved the gift from his B-4 bag. Jimmy had attractively gift wrapped the present to impress her.

"Roe, you didn't have to bring me a gift," she protested, purring softly like a kitten.

"I wanted to get you something nice. You have been so good to me. Just my way of telling you how much you mean to me."

"Oh my gosh, Roe, it's beautiful!"

She gave him a big hug and kiss, put on the bracelet, and displayed it to Roe like a grand prize.

"But really, Roe, this is too much. Just being with you is enough of a gift. Thank you so much."

"You're welcome, Lynne. Let's celebrate. Do you think the champagne is still cold? How 'bout a toast?"

"Sure, why not?"

They toasted in bed and finished off the bottle.

Roe watched her beautiful body through her flimsy negligee. It complimented her vivacious personality, and she knew it.

Lynne picked up on his building arousal. "Anything I can do for you?"

"As a matter of fact…"

Lynne gave him a naughty smile and laughed. "I bet I know what you want. I'll give you a little gift."

At eleven o'clock sharp, the maid returned. Roe got out of bed and called through the door, instructing her not to return until evening turndown.

"We're fine, just fine. Come back this evening."

Roe jumped back into bed, smiling at Lynne.

What a woman!

He turned over and whispered in her ear. "How about a nooner?"

"Bring it on. Keep this up and I'll stop singing your favorite country western song." Lynne laughed mischievously.

"I don't want to spoil you, but I've had a good night's rest. I'm ready for a toss in the hay with my little Aussie lass."

She raised an eyebrow, maybe at his fake Australian accent, or maybe at his rare inclination to clown around. "You're a good man, Roe. I love being with you, even if you are a Yank. You're so good to me. I promise not to tease you anymore on this trip, but don't get used to my affectionate treatment."

Roe thought he'd really enjoy hearing a conversation between Lynne and Biff. Both were masters of *bon mot* and *repartee*. He could imagine the scene now: Lynne would send off a zinger and Biff would come back with a clever parry or retort. Both full-of-life characters embodied a genuine zest for life and two of his favorite people.

Lynne and Roe showered together and dressed for the pool and a late lunch. Since it was mid-week, they had the pool mostly to themselves. Roe, relaxing in the shade, glanced over to her contently reclining on a chaise lounge by the pool with an Australian magazine. She wore the emerald bracelet Roe had given her. Obviously, she really appreciated his token of affection.

Lynne sensed his gaze, looked up, and smiled. She had the most engaging smile ... lovely, in fact.

"What's up, mate? Want to swim? Bet I can beat you, two lengths of the pool, free style ... You up for that?"

"Okay. You're on. You better put on your bikini top. That's a lot of drag," he joked.

Lynne perched at the edge of the pool ready to dive in and challenge Roe with her impressive, powerful stroke.

"Let's go, fella. On three. One, two, three!"

They dove into the pool with a huge splash.

She smoked him by three strokes.

"What is it about Australian swimmers? Maybe they have webs between their toes."

Lynne laughed heartily, followed by an engaging, teasing smile. "You're out of shape, Roe. You've got to keep up with me."

"You're just in much better condition that I am. Frankly, I didn't know you were that good a swimmer. In high school I was a lifeguard at Ocean City, Maryland, and swam one mile a day in the ocean. I probably would have beaten you in those days."

"Try outracing a great white shark on a surfboard. It's a huge incentive to develop your freestyle, believe me."

Roe didn't doubt she and her friends in Bondi had actually experienced shark encounters. Lynne never embellished her stories.

"I'll *pass* on that experience, Lynne."

Lynne adopted her "ball of fire" look, ready to pursue one activity after another.

"Some of our Qantas flight crews are meeting up at the Barracuda Disco tonight. It's party time. I think you'll enjoy meeting them. We could have an early dinner and link up around nine-thirty, okay?

"Sure, sounds like a good idea. I'm ready for a little party time. The past month has been rough."

She pulled herself up out of the water in one fluid motion to sit on the pool's edge with her feet dangling in the water, and squeezed water from her hair. "Okay, we're on. I don't know why our flight crews hang out at the Barracuda. It's a bit bawdy and raucous."

He hung on the pool's ladder railing, looking up at her. Even soaking wet she looked pretty damn great. "How's that?"

"It strikes me as weird that so many men enjoy looking up through the glass floors at the women dancers above them. That's kinky. But, the Filipino band is good and really cranks out some good music, great for dancing."

"Okay, let's do it. Why don't we have a light meal at the Bamboo Club after a drink at Lolita's. I've never been there, but my pilots say it's a colorful place. Both are a short taxi ride over on Sukhumvit Road."

"I'll dress for the occasion. I want you to see the new outfit I bought in Singapore on my last trip."

"I can't wait, love. You always look great. You'll turn a lot of heads, I'm sure. I'm proud to escort you."

That's the first time Roe used the word "love" when referring to Lynne. It sort of slipped out.

"Well, thank you, Prince Charming. "Hah! Just kidding," she added. "I forgot I promised to be nice."

"We better go up to the room and get ready," Biff suggested.

After cleaning up from the pool, Lynne came out into the sitting room in a stylish batik sarong showing a lot of leg, visible through the side slits with every stride. She used very little make-up, as it would be difficult to improve on her healthy complexion. She coifed her hair in a perfect pixie style.

She did a small pirouette, like a model, seeking Roe's approval, and held up her wrist to show off her new bracelet.

She looked like a happy, fulfilled woman, and Roe felt he'd really done a good thing. *She's on cloud nine.*

She'd told him before about how Australian men she'd known often came across as rough and tumble, viewing a show of sentiment as unmanly somehow.

Well, he wasn't going to allow her to question this American's manliness and sentiment.

He felt he was a man she respected, if not loved. He only wanted to show her his appreciation and affection for her. She was not a particularly emotional or sentimental woman but, deep down inside, Roe suspected he'd touched her heart. Her worshipping looks indicated he'd done a good thing, and had made her happy. He wondered if she was falling in love with him. Time would tell.

"You look absolutely marvelous, darling. Maybe I should call for MP escorts to keep would-be rivals away from you."

Lynne ignored his joke. "This is the outfit I told you about. I was in Singapore and Malaysia last week and thought you'd enjoy seeing me in this sarong."

"If I may ask, what do you wear under a sarong?"

"Nothing. Absolutely nothing, my dear."

He'd think about that comment all night.

"If you get me turned on again, we'll never make it out of here, Lynne."

"Flattery will get you everything, Roe. Absolutely, everything you desire ..." Her eyes sparkled. "Later."

She's as sexy as it gets, he thought. *Does this woman ever get angry? Cranky? Maybe not.*

He smiled at her. "You're such a flirt."

"And, you love every minute of it. Let's go party."

After a twenty-minute taxi ride without air conditioning in Bangkok's hot climate, and congested traffic, both felt in need of another shower.

The fragrance of Lynne's perfume permeated the cab, dampening the odor of stale smoke. Nearly everyone smoked in Bangkok.

He took Lynne's hand and pulled her closer to him. "You smell great. What are you wearing?"

"L'air du temp. It's French."

"Then it's expensive, isn't it?"

"Not in the airports' duty-free stores. Remember, I'm flying a lot. I'm glad you like it. It's one of my favorites."

"I'm glad I came over to Bangkok to see you. You are quite a gal, Lynne. The more I know you, the more I realize how lucky I am to be with you."

Lynne fluttered her eye lashes flirtatiously. "You really know how to say all the right things. That makes you either one smooth operator, or a rare find ... a sincere man. Is that an oxymoron?"

She winked emphatically. "Why don't you just come live in Bondi with me so we can share a little bit of heaven together?"

He gave her a dubious look, taking her invitation as a joke. *Or was it?*

She ran a finger gently down his cheek. "Seriously, though, thank you, Roe. What a nice thing to say. I assure you that I adore being with you. You make me so happy. I consider it my good fortune that we met by chance here last year."

Roe pondered her brilliant smile. *How can you make someone who's perennially happy, happier? I guess I succeeded.*

He returned her beaning smile. "You deserve it, Lynne. I really mean it."

Though not given to public displays of affection, Lynne leaned over and gave Roe a peck on the cheek. He met her intense gaze and squeezed her hand affectionately.

They arrived at Lolita's about eight o'clock. The bar was air-conditioned, thank goodness. They entered through the hanging bead doorway, popular in Southeast Asia, into a dimly lit saloon. The sign on the reception desk read, *"Lolita's—one of the best executive BJ and full-service bars in Asia."*

Roe turned wide eyes toward Lynne. "Does that mean what I think it means?"

"Yes, of course. Are you some kind of Puritan?" She laughed heartily.

Now Roe understood why a lot of 86th MAC crews hung out here on Bangkok layovers.

They selected a table over in the corner and Roe handed her the exotic drink list. "Want a cocktail with a small umbrella in it?"

"Not into that. I'll stick to good old gin and tonic."

"Let's make it two of them. Sapphire gin?"

"Sure, Bombay is better than Beefeaters."

The server came over. Roe, puzzled, tried to determine the individual's sex. His clinical instincts settled on a "transvestite lesbian."

What the hell kind of bar was this anyway?

Things started out with that impression and proceeded steadily downhill. The drinks arrived promptly, and the lesbian made her initial foray, politely hitting on Lynne, who ignored it. Roe wondered if Lynne knew that this transvestite was actually a woman…

A disc jockey played American records in the background for the sparse early crowd.

Five minutes later, the transvestite made a second, bolder incursion, brushing up closely to Lynne to inquire if she needed anything. Lynne recoiled. Visibly annoyed, she obviously didn't like her space invaded. Though she didn't express any displeasure to Roe, he picked up on it.

The third intrusion was quite a bit more overt. She rubbed Lynne's buttock and leaned over to whisper a proposition in her ear. Lynne abruptly sprang up out of her chair, grabbled the lesbian tightly by her left arm, and spun her. She delivered a brisk, powerful right upper cut to the lesbian's jaw, and absolutely cold cocked the annoying interloper who had intruded on her life and their wonderful evening.

The waitress slumped to the floor, knocked out cold.

"Holy shit! What did she say to you?"

"You don't want to know, Roe. You really don't want to know."

"Let's get out of here."

On the way out, the bouncer approached to inquire what had happened.

Lynne piped up immediately. "I think our waiter is on drugs. She slipped on an icy wet spot, crashed into our table, and spilled a drink on my dress. We're leaving. This place sucks!"

Roe chuckled at the unintended pun. "Let's head over to the Bamboo Club. It's just up the street. Walk or take a cab?"

"Let's walk. I need to cool off. I'm still pissed."

"Did you realize she was a transvestite lesbian?"

"Yes, of course. Roe, I wasn't born yesterday. I live in Sydney. It's the San Francisco of the South Pacific. But, usually, they are subtle, not overtly intrusive and rude."

"What did she say to you?"

"She said something very rude, to which I took great exception."

"Where did you develop that professional right upper-cut?"

"I teach a self-defense course for women in Bondi, when I'm not flying."

"Pretty impressive. You really nailed her."

He'd not seen this side of Lynne. You never know, sometimes, who you are sleeping with ... or how very special they might be.

***

The Bamboo Club was a welcome relief, and more suited to their style. Roe had been there before and enjoyed the club's ambience. It was more of an Asian style bar for young people. The food wasn't fancy, but tasteful and very substantial. They'd eaten a late snack at the pool, so they weren't very hungry. He hoped the calm atmosphere would allow Lynne to unwind. The relaxing, pleasant music playing in the background should help.

They were served by Thai women in lovely silk dresses, called cheongsams, whose mandarin collars created a sense of formality. The waitresses were polite, efficient, and spoke good English.

Roe and Lynne shared a large bowl of shrimp and noodles, delicious beyond description.

The lighting was indirect with well-placed Chinese lanterns interspersed over the bamboo-motif tables and booths. Roe thought maybe they ought to call them "Thai lanterns" here. Anyway, it provided a nice Asian touch. What a contrast to Lolita's.

Lynne recovered her composure nicely from her unpleasant encounter. Out of the blue, she turned to Roe. "Wasn't Lolita some girl in a novel who had sex with older men?"

"Yes. In fact, 'Lolita Syndrome' refers to older men who have a predilection for young women, girls and teenagers. It's an abnormality just this side of a pedophile or statutory rape."

"Thank you, doctor. You're so smart."

He got her sarcasm ... and that she wasn't trying to be mean. Roe gave Lynne plenty of time to calm down. He engaged her in small talk, and avoided a recap of the ugly encounter. He even tried a diversionary tactic.

"Want to play pool in the back room?"

"I've already beaten you in a swimming *pool* once. Wouldn't it be hard on your ego if I waxed you in billiards, too?"

Roe, chuckled at the clever comparison. "You're too much. How about another cocktail?"

"We'll be drinking a lot with my friends at the Barracuda. You're not trying to get me drunk and take advantage of me, are you?" She always kept a step ahead of him.

"All we've had today was a bottle of Dom Perignon. That worked pretty well, didn't it?"

"Sure did the job." She licked her lips. "I'll pass ... but feel free."

"I think I'll do something uncharacteristic." He ordered a three-layer rum Mai Tai with a small Japanese umbrella in it.

Lynne laughed. "I can't wait to see this. What's come over you?"

***

When ten o'clock rolled around, Roe paid the bill and they snagged a taxi for a short hop over to the Barracuda Bar at its Soi Cowboy location. The bar featured a transparent glass floor between two dance stages. It was the biggest "go go" bar in the district, advertising four classes of girls—all available for a price. Schoolgirls upstairs on the glass floor, beach bikini girls on the dance floor, hostesses in black dresses, and waitresses. All quite attractive.

The Barracuda Bar served as a perfect retreat for a sex maniac. This establishment was anything but Asian in architecture. The décor was modern. Red vinyl booths and seat covers, plastic chairs. It was an ultra-modern bar/disco on par with those in Los Angeles or New York City. The only Asian aspect of the establishment was the race of the employees and most of the clientele, mostly Japanese.

The whole atmosphere was illusory, a dark, smoke-filled room with scintillating disco lighting. The flashy, multi-colored disco lights created a weird, psychedelic illusion through the swirling clouds of smoke. Party goers appeared as apparitions among the flashing lights of the disco, creating a surreal atmosphere.

The glass floors made it a voyeur's paradise, as the women and girls wore no undergarments while they pole danced or gyrated to the deafening disco music, decibels above safety levels. The disco's flashing lights added to the raunchy party atmosphere.

Roe thought to himself that this place must have been the proving ground for Wharfdale speakers and woofers. And, a haven for the depraved.

Actually, the bar was nothing more than a front for organized prostitution. Pick and choose. Buy two drinks with a girl at 200 baht a drink, pay a "bar fine," and she's yours for the night—after negotiating her professional fee, of course.

The crowd was going wild at ten at night, drinking, negotiating, and enjoying the sexually explicit floor shows. Clients apparently didn't mind practically cutting their way through the thick clouds of cigarette fumes.

Roe turned to Lynne and yelled over the din. "Do you think we'll need an oxygen mask?"

"Maybe… Oh, I see my crowd over there in the far corner. Let's join them."

As they walked across the floor to join Lynne's friends, Roe noted Asian women dancing bare breasted. Asian woman aren't noted for large breasts. This bar, however, was a contradiction, attributable to silicone implants.

Better living through chemistry.

The Asian pole dancers performed Las Vegas style, non-stop, as the visitors wove their way through the bar.

Lynne and Roe joined her friends: two pilots and three stewardesses. They sat away from the major commotion and the huge speakers at the far end of the room.

They already had a load on when Roe and Lynne arrived. Lynne was right. This place was wild, bawdy, and raucous. A sociologist could spend a month analyzing this bar and its occupants' hedonistic activities, bordering on debauchery.

After the customary introductions, Roe and Lynne sat between the pilots and stewardesses. They were an affable Australian lot, the party sort. Roe was glad he got a lot of sleep last night. He and Lynne were sober compared to her friends. He ordered two gin and tonics.

One senior pilot, George, slapped Roe on the back. "Wait until you see the next show, pal. She's the best stripper I've ever seen!"

"Swell," Roe replied. He hoped they weren't going to be here all night as he had already experienced the unpleasant incident at Lolita's, and the smoke was getting to him.

The stage darkened and the spotlight appeared. A Scandinavian stripper with large, enhanced breasts appeared. Tassels dangled from each nipple.

Lynne nudged Roe. "Are they real?"

"No. See the sub-mammary scars? She's had implants. But I must say, for a stripper, she doesn't look too worse for the wear."

George, well into his cups, exclaimed, "Wait until you see this, mate. It'll knock your socks off!"

The sexy bump and grind music started. The stripper gyrated, simulating sex. *She had to do something,* Roe thought, *she was already half naked. How much more could she strip off?*

After a minute or so, she was down to her G string, so he could see her pubic hair was shaved. Roe, the surgeon and a student of anatomy, analyzed more than her performance. He noted her pubic structure and firm buttocks, probably resulting from years of dancing. This was one sturdy stripper.

Even so, he thought Lynne was sexier covered in her sarong.

George leaned forward. "Now comes the best part." As if on cue, he yelled, "Feather the right one!"

The pilot's reference described a twin-engine plane with one propeller firing and the other one shut down.

The stripper laughed and smiled, accommodating George's request. While she twirled the right tassel, her left breast tassel dangled straight down ... "feathered" in flyers' jargon.

"Remarkable," Roe muttered.

George applauded loudly, hooting and hollering while his buddy giggled uncontrollably. The three stewardesses were talking about the shopping tomorrow, completely disinterested in the performance, not even watching.

Lynne poked Roe in the ribs with her elbow. "I can do that."

"Yeah, right, sure you can."

"Roe, can we go back to the hotel? I'll tell them my dinner upset my stomach. I'm not really enjoying myself. The smoke is too thick, it's nauseating. Can we leave?"

"I agree. It's so loud in here I'm going deaf."

Roe took the initiative and announced that Lynne wasn't feeling well ... it must have been a bad shrimp at the Bamboo Club. Everyone understood. They'd been there, done that.

"We'll take a rain check," Roe announced. "Nice meeting you."

Outside the Barracuda, cabs waited. They hopped in one and off they went back to the Mandarin Oriental hotel.

Lynne rested her head on his shoulder and her hand on his thigh. "Thanks, Roe. You're so sweet."

She fell asleep on the twenty-minute ride home. When they pulled up in front of the hotel, he rubbed her arm, "We're home, sweetheart. Wake up."

"I'm sorry. I must have dozed off."

With no wait for the elevator, a rare occurrence, up to the fifth floor they went. The maid had finally gotten her chance to turn down the bed. She had left fragrant fresh-cut flowers and, of course, the obligatory mint candies by the bedside table lamp.

Lynne raised an eyebrow at Roe. "You didn't believe me in the bar, did you?"

"I'm not sure which bar, or what you mean, Lynne."

"About feathering one tassel while the other one twirls and jiggles. It's all about coordination and muscle control."

Witty, sassy, and a tease.

"Really?"

"Watch me."

Lynne pulled off her sarong and let it drift to the floor. She wasn't kidding him earlier. She was completely naked beneath the sarong. Even without the tassels, she did a good imitation of the stripper. She really could do what she claimed—with her bump and grind gyrations, she feathered one breast.

Roe applauded. "You might put the stripper out of a job, Lynne. Unbelievable. You never cease to amaze me."

"See, I told you I could do it. I'm pretty tired, interested in going to bed with me?"

"It's that time of night."

They slept the next morning until the maid arrived at eleven o'clock, the newly arranged time. On this occasion, they donned their bathrobes and let her in the room to clean.

Roe suggested breakfast, followed by a sampan trip in the afternoon up the rivers and canals. Shops, bars, and restaurants along the way offered a variety of activities and diversions.

Lynne said she heard the trip was a lot of fun and she'd love to go. Both had early evening flights, Roe to Takhli and Udorn airbases in northern Thailand, and Lynne a return leg to Sydney.

The weather was cloudy, hot and humid as usual, but a light breeze cooled them on their motorized sampan trip. Fortunately, they didn't have to share the space on the boat. The chatty boatman was knowledgeable in local history giving them a capsule summary while motoring upstream.

Lynne inquired about the best shops in Bangkok. It turned out they were twenty minutes upriver and one block west. The boatman said he'd wait at the dock. He also made some suggestions for lunch at "The Deck."

They weren't particularly hungry, but they were hooked on noodles and barbecued shrimp. The boatman said the best place was forty minutes up river. They agreed to shop for an hour or so, and then go upriver for lunch at The Deck.

Lynne was not a picky shopper or one given to impulse purchases. Roe observed her manner as she assessed quality, not confusing price with the value of the merchandise. She was really looking for something for her two-year-old niece. She finally found a children's shop with typical Thai clothing and selected a nice outfit. She said it was half the going price in Sydney. Now satisfied, she suggested they head upriver.

The boatman waited by the shore where he had docked the sampan, smoking and chatting with another boatman. Roe wondered if they got a kickback from the stores and restaurants. Probably.

As they went up the river, areas of jungle encroached between the different districts of Bangkok. Roe thought he certainly would never do a trip like this in Vietnam, he'd be ambushed for sure.

The Deck came into view, a bamboo structure with a thatched palm roof, essentially an open-air restaurant with a huge deck overlooking the river. It was a travelogue, picture-perfect establishment for visitors and locals.

The boatman told them it had been in business for more than forty years and had world-class noodles and shrimp, fresh every day. The water buffalo steak wasn't bad either, just very expensive.

They docked and went up the rustic path covered with fragments of oyster and clam shells. It reminded Roe of the Eastern shore of Maryland, almost making him homesick for a moment.

Lynne tugged at his arm. "Roe, look over there. If you love kids, you'll love that scene." She pointed to another deck about fifty feet away.

Roe glanced over. Six young boys were trying to conduct a turtle race with the small terrapins they'd caught on the riverbank.

"Hah! That's great. Reminds me of Sausalito across the Golden Gate Bridge. They race turtles every Wednesday night at Zack's Happy Hour. I didn't realize it was an international sport. I don't see anyone taking wagers like they do at Zack's. You've got to come for a visit to San Francisco and see it firsthand. Spend enough time to ski in Tahoe with me, if you come in the winter."

Lynne perked up. "I'd really like to do that with you. I've never been to the States. The senior gals outbid us on the San Francisco and Los Angeles trips. If you're really serious, Roe, I'll save up my vacation time."

"I'll get out of the Air Force in eight months or so. I'll set it up and we'll have a ball, okay?"

"You're on."

The Deck turned out to be a great recommendation. The meal was even better than last night's dinner at the Bamboo Club, and certainly a lot quieter and cheaper. It gave them a chance to talk, and the conversation wandered into his involvement in Vietnam.

Roe explained to her that the war situation in Vietnam was getting worse. The Viet Cong were getting bolder and better equipped. Their attacks were increasing and inflicting more casualties, including American advisors. He gave Lynne a little background history.

"In mid-1963, the U.S. had 12,000 military advisors in Vietnam. That number increased gradually, but after last months' attack at Pleiku I anticipate a greater U.S. commitment, probably in the range of 200,000 combat trips by the end of 1965."

Roe predicted that the South Vietnam conflict would soon become America's war. In that case, Australia and other Southeast Asia and Pacific allies could potentially become involved. He painted less than a pretty picture, as he saw a very ominous future ahead. He was going to be busy, very busy.

"My R&R time will be unpredictable, Lynne."

Lynne had never seen this serious side of Roe. She sensed where the conversation was leading. Their precious time together was strictly for rest and recreation. They had a close relationship, but because of their different life pathways, and the distance, it may never be more than a few days together. With an unpredictable calendar, a lasting relationship was improbable. If that was the case, so be it. She would enjoy every moment with him and strive to make him the happiest man in the world. Lynne listened intently as he continued in a serious note.

"Last month, I air-evac'd one of my high school buddies out of Pleiku to Clark AFB. He was wounded in a surprise VC attack. Let me tell you, Charlie did some serious damage to our TAC ops base in the central highlands. My CIA buddy told me he expected the U.S. to retaliate by increasing our combat commitment. There's no way this won't be our war within the next six months. I expect you to keep this confidential, Lynne," he added, knowing he could trust her.

"Scary proposition, Roe, I won't make a peep to anyone."

"It sure is scary. My point in telling you all of this is that I'll get over to see you when I can, but certainly not very often. The USAF owns me. I'm flying over three hundred hours a month. I see things getting worse, not better, in Vietnam. The situation is spiraling out of control. The South Vietnam government and military are dysfunctional, riddled by graft and corruption at high levels. Jealousies, plots, and intrigues, coups, you name it, they've got it all. Don't get me started."

Lynne sensed his growing irritation. She squeezed his hand reassuringly.

"I didn't set you off. It was sort of a spontaneous combustion on your part." She giggled lightly to try to lessen the tension.

Roe joined in with a short laugh. "I guess I got on my high horse. Sorry. With so much BS going on over there, it really burns my ass."

"I can see it really bothers you. I'll be here for you, whenever. Just give me some advance notice to arrange my schedule. I promise I'll be here for you, Roe."

"I'll do my best. You're a great gal and I enjoy being with you. You make me almost forget the friggin' war. You're a breath of fresh air, believe me."

"I can't imagine what you and the Americans are going through in Vietnam. We'll get together from time to time…" She placed her napkin on the table. "We better go now. I've got to shower and dress for my flight. I don't trust the traffic, so I leave a lot of time to get to the airport."

"Okay, we're out of here. It was a fun day, wasn't it?"

"It was, and the boatman deserves a very big tip."

Back at the hotel, they showered and dressed: Roe in his flight suit, Lynne in her stylist Qantas outfit. He never had seen her in uniform.

"You look sharp, lady. They'll be ordering extra booze just to watch you walk down the aisle."

"Oh, come on. Cut it out, flattery will get you…" She sighed. "Well, that's out of the question now."

"I've arranged an air-conditioned Lincoln Continental to drop you off at the airport and to take me to the flight line for my Takhli trip."

At the airport, she gave him a particularly long kiss and hug goodbye. Roe thought she had a tear in her eye. It might not be love, but it sure felt like it.

Neither knew it would be their last rendezvous in Bangkok.

CHAPTER TWENTY-ONE
INTEL MEETING V

Hickam AFB, Hawaii May 1965

Departing from his customary routine, Captain Noreika summarized the pertinent international events since their last meeting. He emphasized the noteworthy events of late 1964 and early 1965. They represented turbulent times worldwide, punctuated by more seminal events than he could recall in any other period of his long military experience.

His recap noted that China exploded its first atomic bomb in October of 1964. In the USSR, Khrushchev was ousted, and Kosygin and Brezhnev took control.

He described how, meanwhile, in Saigon, riots convulsed the streets protesting the political role of General Khanh. Buddhist unrest reached another level of intensity. Immolations escalated. Photos of the horrid scenes appeared on the front pages of U.S. newspapers, causing much dismay and anti-war sentiment in the United States.

On the Vietnam military front, VC combat engineers known as "sappers," mortared Bien Hoa outside Saigon, inflicting considerable damage to the TAC airbase. Maxwell Taylor replaced Cabot Lodge as Ambassador in the early Fall. Lodge returned to the U.S. to run against LBJ, but lost the primary to Goldwater who, in turn, lost to LBJ in a landslide sixty-one percent margin in '64, attributable to Goldwater's threats of nuclear war in Vietnam.

Later in November '64, Noreika explained, Ambassador Taylor offered General Khanh safe exit out of Vietnam. By refusing, Khanh created an awkward diplomatic situation. South Vietnam's leader would not step down and leave. Now what?

To top off the end of a tumultuous year in 1964, two VC insurgents blew up a good portion of the Brinks Bachelor Officers Quarters on Christmas Eve, killing two American officers and injuring others.

The audience listened in solemn silence, uncomfortable by the stream of bad news from the Navy captain who recounted these events in a grim, serious tone.

"Finally, a dramatic event occurred in February 1965 that jarred LBJ into action. One incident he could not ignore. A VC battalion, reinforced by a NVA company, staged a devastating, surprise attack on Pleiku air base in the central highlands, Corps II area. The damage to Camp Holloway and the nearby airfield was significant. Eight Americans were killed and more than a hundred wounded, ten aircraft destroyed, and half of the base hospital blown away."

Noreika described how LBJ's national security advisor, McGeorge Bundy, happened to be in Saigon at the time assessing the over-all war situation with Ambassador Taylor and MACV commander, General Westmorland. It was reported that Bundy was visibly upset when receiving the news of the Pleiku attack during his departure meeting.

Bundy immediately cabled LBJ urging retaliation, informing him that the Ambassador and the MACV commanders concurred. Bundy was one of the few who could influence the president's decisions.

For once, LBJ moved into swift action, trusting Bundy. He met with his inner circle of national security advisors and ordered air strikes in North Vietnam.

"He couldn't worm out of this predicament," Captain Noreika commented.

Bundy was a trusted presidential ally who thought the prospects of winning in Vietnam were grim. The prevailing viewpoint in Saigon was that the U.S. lacked the will and perseverance to stay the course. Bundy counseled the president not to negotiate a withdrawal. That would constitute "surrender on an installment plan." Bundy further urged continuous bombing, not episodic responses as postulated under the "graduated pressure" strategy.

"Clearly, the Pleiku attack in February 1965 was a pivotal event triggering America's escalation of the war," Captain Noreika noted. "Jets took off from the decks of the aircraft carrier *Ranger* within hours in 'Operation Flaming Dart.' The target, an NVA camp near Dong Hoi, a coastal town sixty miles above the 17th Parallel, which constituted the DMZ between North and South Vietnam. By the end of February '65, 'Operation Rolling Thunder' began with sustained bombing of North Vietnam."

Captain Noreika explained he had taken the liberty of relating all these events, because he was privy to some highly classified information that may not have filtered down through the general intelligence system yet. He wanted the events evaluated in the context of the entire geopolitical situation, urging them to focus on "the big picture."

Of course, he did not divulge his CIA source, Biff Roberts. He had called this meeting to assess the status of American intelligence readiness, as the war reached a new level of U.S. commitment.

"Well, Biff, does the CIA have anything new we can relate to the command? You didn't have much notice of the conference. It was a rather hasty arrangement."

Biff took his place on the podium. "Captain, you've summarized major events up to March '65 for the committee's consideration. Let me pick up from there. The 9th Marine Expeditionary Brigade landed two battalions at Danang in late March for perimeter defense of the airbase, which is just eighty-five miles south of the 17th Parallel DMZ. A squadron of helicopters will provide support for their 'Search and Destroy' operations. It's noteworthy that this is the first deployment of U.S. combat forces with authorization to search out and kill VCs."

"Hoorah!" Marine Colonel Rodriguez cheered.

Biff laughed. "I am heading up to Danang soon to coordinate delivery of four AC-47 gunships. We're talking major firepower for close air support with this aircraft armed with Gatling guns. These deployments will enhance U.S. combat presence in Corps I North Central Highlands. They will facilitate S&D missions against the VC. Rapid deployment by assault helicopters will keep the VC off-guard and interrupt their hit-and-run tactics. The Marines' mission is to create a nightmare, denying the VC sanctuary. They will interrupt safe havens that the VC rely on to regroup."

"These deployments represent a major change in the complexion of the war. It also admits that the U.S. advisory program with the ARVN has been ineffectual. That may be an understatement. In recent months, the VC with NVA companies put five South Vietnamese combat regiments and nine battalions out of action. This represents an astounding number of military losses by South Vietnam."

This statement elicited collective sighs.

"General Westmoreland has requested forty-four more combat battalions to supplement the eighteen battalions now in South Vietnam, that's about 50,000 new troops. Clearly, this escalation "Americanizes" the war, something many did not anticipate with the LBJ administration's history of vacillating policies since he took office."

"Amen!" Turner, the Army officer commented.

The committee laughed and Biff grinned in response. Even Captain Noreika smiled at their reaction. He understood their frustrations, welcoming LBJ's surprising about-face.

"The question remains, will this change the course of the war? The short answer is, militarily yes, politically no. CIA intelligent estimates have not changed our long-term view, for the pessimistic reasons I presented at these conferences in earlier sessions. CIA doubts concur with General Bruce Palmer's independent assessment that escalating the air offensive against North Vietnam's major economic targets will not substantially affect the DRV's capacity to supply its forces in South Vietnam. Nor will escalated bombing bring Hanoi to the negotiating table. The DRV is determined and resolute in this battle of wills. They are dedicated to a program of perseverance, to outlast the U.S. regardless of all costs and time required. While the VC benefit from North Viet supplies, they basically can survive and fight for protracted periods autonomously. That's our CIA estimate."

"Nothing new there," the USAF's Havenmeyer murmured just loud enough for the room to hear.

Biff raised a pam in acknowledgment. "You'll recall, the VC performed remarkably well without DRV support for years, and they certainly can again with the huge amount of captured armaments. As the U.S. increases the ante, the enemy is prepared to meet the call 'chip for chip.' Take that to the bank," Biff declared.

He referred the officers to the CIA Office of National Estimates memo from the previous month: April 1965.

"This memo was submitted shortly after the Marine deployment at Danang, and at the onset of the sustained bombing campaign of North Vietnam. To quote the report, 'Based on present realities, we are proceeding with far more courage than wisdom to unknown ends.' So, once again, it seems the U.S. is underestimating the resolve of our enemies."

The military men groaned at this revelation, but Biff ignored their negative reaction. He'd expected it.

"It appears unrealistic to expect that this particular bombing campaign will bring them to the negotiating table on our terms. We predict the DRV plans to weather the storm, according to our reliable sources. Based on CIA estimates, the odds are considerably better-than-even that the U.S. eventually will have to disengage from Vietnam on terms quite short of our present objective. Not an encouraging estimate or prognosis, by any means, gentlemen."

The officers shifted in their seats, muttering among themselves, as this pronouncement represented a foreign concept to them. Biff understood their dedication to winning all too well.

"Withdraw? Are you out of your mind?" Rodriguez asked sarcastically.

Collectively, Biff knew they respected him and his record with the CIA, but, to a man, thought the CIA was absolutely wrong about this. No way would their superior military lose to this ragtag guerilla army. No way!

Biff shrugged at the consternation he had created, waited for it to subside, and continued dispassionately, concentrating on just presenting the facts and letting the "chips fall where they may."

"Furthermore, it appears to the CIA that the current Johnson administration's mindset and attitude of 'get on the team' forestalls objective assessments. They continue their elitist attitude, wanting to hear only good news, stifling the bad. So, naturally, I suspect our recommendations will continue to fall on deaf ears, except perhaps on Bundy's. He seems open and receptive to new ideas and approaches to the Vietnam problem. Unfortunately, he's a lone voice of reason back there in DC.

"The CIA maintains that these are accurate and intelligent judgments. We stand by our data, gentlemen."

Biff took a dramatic pause, letting the audience settle down. He had something else very important to relate to this intelligence committee, news that would rock them back on their heels. He desired their full attention for the announcement.

Quiet eventually fell.

"Obviously the Johnson administration has strong differences with our CIA recommendations, despite our DCI's urging. That is why our DCI, John McCone, will be resigning his post as Director of the CIA."

A shudder of astonishment reverberated through the committee.

"The DCI will be the first major political casualty of not being on the team. America's role in South Vietnam has been transformed by the recent events I have mentioned. The ball is now in our court. It's now America's war without CIA input providing essential intelligence to conduct the war."

You could have heard a pin drop in the conference room. For the CIA's DCI to resign over policy matters was astounding.

After the disruption, the committee became receptive to Biff's perspective, but with qualifications. They knew they could win the war militarily, absolutely without question. But, the CIA had a good point. Could they win it politically? No one was willing to commit to nation-building in Vietnam.

South Vietnam was a country with an army, but no effectual government. Each succeeding governments' performance seemed as dysfunctional as the one it replaced, riddled with factions, schemes, and corruption. It always seemed like a coup d'état waited in the wings.

Biff concluded his presentation. "Maxwell Taylor again offered General Khanh asylum outside Vietnam, an offer he finally accepted. Air Vice-Marshall Nguyen Cao Ky is rumored ready to take over the military regime in June, the fourth change in government since Diem's assassination in November of 1963. At least this coup is relatively peaceful. It is also rumored that Henry Cabot Lodge is returning to replace Maxwell

Taylor as Ambassador. Political upheaval is the one Saigon constant you can count on. It is the way of life over here, gentlemen."

The audience sat stunned, while Captain Noreika stared at Biff.

"That was some bombshell you just dropped on us, Biff. That must have been hard for you to deal with. McCone is a good man, an effective leader." He turned to the committee members. "You fellas taking any notes?"

He laughed at the sarcastic remark, and shook his head. Nothing in this war fazed him.

He turned to Ann Summerville. "What political insights do you have for us today? Any gems? Can you top Mr. Roberts' revelation?"

Ann moved up to the podium.

"As a matter of fact, I do have some gems, but Biff's announcement would be difficult to top. There are serious political determinants that will influence the performance of the war outside of the military considerations noted by Mr. Roberts today. With little or no fanfare, General Khánh finally left at Ambassador Taylor's urging. Dr. Quat assumed interim control of the government in Saigon last February. It appears he will step down peacefully in June when Air Marshal Ky will become Prime Minister. Ky will rule with a military junta following the bloodless coup.

"On the war front, it might be argued that the U.S. commitment of combat troops is not tantamount to an American war, but is certainly a major transformation headed in that direction."

She pointed out that South Vietnam was on its fourth government in three years, their military was failing, and the strategic hamlet program was in shambles. Buddhist riots and student protests continued, and the lack of determination to defeat the VC was quite evident to anyone willing to take an objective assessment. All this negativity had occurred despite considerable aid to prop up their army and government.

"In fact, it seems the Vietnam government actually resents our intrusion into their internal affairs. This leads me to question, is this war effort really worth it? Geopolitically, U.S. policy dictates we must take our stand against communism in Southeast Asia. The Johnson administration cites the risk of losing America's image and power in the world if we lose in Vietnam. It is quite obvious that LBJ is sold on the flawed Domino Theory."

Ann paused to let this statement sink in. She then shared that in April, at the Johns Hopkins University, LBJ offered a proposition for Ho Chi Minh's participation in a Southeast Asia development plan in exchange for a negotiated peace. Pham Van Don, the Prime Minister of North Vietnam rejected the proposal the following day. He stated any settlement in Vietnam must include the Viet Cong.

"Despite the sustained bombing, the DRV is not willing to negotiate a peaceful settlement. This is precisely the point Mr. Roberts and the CIA have been making to this committee and Washington for months. And, at the present rate of troop commitments, I extrapolate that the U.S. will have close to 200,000 troops in Vietnam by the end of 1965. All in full combat status, another major escalation."

She asked the group, for a moment, to put themselves in North Vietnam's position and in Ho's shoes. She posed the question: Why would the U.S. offer to negotiate a settlement after only two months of bombing if they thought the U.S. was winning the war?

"Ho realizes this is a war of attrition, fought essentially on his terms. Like the French, Ho views the Americans as ill-suited for guerilla warfare, especially in this hostile terrain. Furthermore, for years the U.S. has operated with self-imposed restrictions regarding its enemy's sanctuaries. I predict Ho will wait for the right moment before committing to a large-scale, conventional assault in South Vietnam. Pleiku was just a prelude, gentlemen."

This remark created a stir. The officers glanced at one another in concern, before returning their attention to hear what the consultant thought would come next.

"Ho is in no hurry. He has waited his entire lifetime for this opportunity. The Viet Minh outlasted the French. Ho figures the Americans will suffer a similar fate. This is the prediction he's betting on. His whole war plan is predicated on this conviction. At this point, it doesn't appear the bombing has inflicted serious damage to the DRV infrastructure. There are ample explanations for this failure that we've discussed before. There has been no blockage of the harbors, as our committee offered for consideration. Our proposals to bomb the dams in the northern part of the country, flooding most of the country and destroying their hydroelectric power sources have also been rejected. Other strategic targets are off-limits. And, despite repeated bombings, the Ho Chi Minh trail is essentially intact. The NVA and VC still enjoy sanctuary in Cambodia and Laos. I've been informed the VC have tunnels and trails all the way to Saigon. Our lack of a comprehensive strategy has led us to this point, to the brink of failure.

"In summary, Ho has no reason to negotiate with the U.S. Time and history are on his side. He firmly believes North Vietnamese determination will prevail in the end. He understands his armies are no match for U.S. firepower and conventional warfare. He will go back to the textbook history of Vietnam: to continue guerilla warfare to demoralize the enemy until the appropriate time arrives for the invasion of South Vietnam."

She gathered her notes and returned to her seat without further discussion. She'd made her statement. Let them absorb it.

The captain thanked Ann for her thoughtful insights and opened the floor for discussion.

Their discussion revealed overwhelming approval of the war's escalation... the feeling that it was about time. They thought the CIA was unduly pessimistic in its prognosis, though approved of Ann's political insights. The meeting was adjourned with less rancor than usual.

***

After the meeting Biff chatted with Ann. He was becoming more and more impressed with her and reminded her his friend Roe McDonald was arriving tomorrow.

Biff had arranged for dinner at the Hickam Officers' Club tomorrow evening at seven o'clock. He would make all the appropriate introductions, and repeated his conviction the two of them would absolutely hit it off.

Ann replied that she was looking forward to the evening and the introduction. "Nothing ventured, nothing gained, right? Besides, you wouldn't dare fix me up with a loser, would you?"

Biff laughed, noting her face quickly returned to a pensive expression. No doubt she shared his and the committee's frustrations with the conduct of the war.

She obviously was ready for a break. He hoped his Vietnam flight surgeon friend would provide a new spark in her life and she'd return the favor to Roe. He could use a good woman in his life.

CHAPTER TWENTY-TWO
THE INTRODUCTION

Hickam AFB, Hawaii May 1965

Roe felt like he'd been on a treadmill for the last few months or so, with one air evacuation after another. From Vietnam to Clark, P.I., or on to Tachikawa, Japan, or Kadena, Okinawa—depending on which hospital had space and operating teams available. The primary base hospital at Clark was becoming swamped with wounded from Vietnam as the war picked up. A new addition was underway to manage the load. Under the standard operating (SOP) procedures, Vietnam field hospitals—MASH units in many cases—would stabilize the wounded. As soon as possible, USAF MAC planes transported the wounded to Clark, P.I. or other major hospitals, usually within a day or so.

Clark's overload could be attributed to successful helicopter med-evac's from a frontline landing zone (LZ) to a field hospital, usually within an hour on average, with resuscitation being performed en route. The innovative practice of using well-trained medics on the Huey choppers with the call sign, "dust off," yielded more battlefield survivors than any prior war. It reduced mortality to around two percent. If a wounded man survived the first twenty-four hours, he could expect only a one percent chance of dying.

Once stabilized in field hospitals, MAC C-130s, C-135s, or C-141s transported the wounded for definitive treatment. Many, still fresh out of the field, landed in one of the hospitals noted above within one or two flying hours. That became almost a daily duty for flight surgeons like Roe. He routinely logged more than 300 flying hours a month.

At the moment, he sat in the jump seat of a USAF C-135 winging to Hickam AB on a deadhead flight to Hawaii for some well-deserved R&R. He would meet this gal Biff was fixing him up with ... Ann somebody-or-other. His tired brain couldn't even remember her last name. He hoped Biff had gotten this one right, sometimes he tended to hype women.

Roe needed someone in his life, a lasting, more meaningful relationship. Between chatter and jokes with the pilots and navigator, he let his mind roam, thinking about all that had transpired recently in his hectic life, if you could call it a life. Recollections and random thoughts whirled like a cyclone through his mind. Near exhaustion and constant tension had a way of doing that.

Outside of his flight surgeon duties, not much exciting happened. He lived out of a B-4 bag, and ate at the various airbase O clubs wherever the day's mission ended up, in or out of Vietnam. Usually he'd share a few beers and war stories with the boys, many of the same recycled tales, but usually involving different officers at different clubs each night. Too often recently, he'd discover to his dismay that a great guy he'd met on a prior visit had "bought the farm" in 'Nam.

Following a short evening, he'd crash at the BOQ in a standard small, cheerless USAF room ... uniformly painted in a faded shade of avocado green and furnished with an uncomfortable cot draped with mosquito netting. A broken or malfunctioning A/C also appeared standard issue. Sometimes the BOQ included a burned-out bedside light bulb, or a toilet that hardly flushed. That glum scenario became his routine.

However, the shower usually worked fine and the price was right. He took every opportunity to shower, as he lived in a sweat-soaked flight suit or fatigues. Vietnam was a virtual sauna. Hot and humid as a bitch.

It reminded him that he hadn't had athlete's foot or jock itch like this since hot summers in high school. If the itch was not annoying enough, the daily preventive anti-malarial pills upset his stomach when not taken with meals, and he missed a lot of meals in this job. He'd lost ten pounds on his Vietnam tour with occasional bouts of diarrhea. Once he swore he had cholera and treated himself with tetracycline, Lomotil, and had a medic give him IV hydration. In Vietnam, a lot more was going on behind the war scene. He never missed a mission despite this malady.

These were minor concerns compared to what was really bugging him: dealing with Vietnam's turmoil—the mortality and morbidity suffered by young fighters in an ill-defined war. Many were only nineteen years old. He was amazed no one ever bitched on his evac's. The wounded were glad to have survived Vietnam and looked forward to going home.

The Pleiku attack had emotionally drained Roe. Seeing his San Francisco surgery pal, JB, sitting dejectedly by the field hospital had bothered him deeply. Minutes later, tending to his injured high school buddy's wounds had overwhelmed his emotions even more. Then, the week at Numazu sea survival school had been an unexpected physical challenge.

His R&R in Bangkok with Lynne briefly restored his state of mind and perspective, but it had been too short a respite from the realities of war. Vietnam's grind had started to wear on him. Roe was just plain beat.

The short stint at Takhli Royal Thai Air Base following his Bangkok breather had been an eye opener. He spent three days with 355th TAC combat flight crews, and their squadron and wing commanders. He agreed with the resident Thailand flight surgeons that operation "Rolling Thunder" was taking an emotional toll on the combat pilots, as well as physical.

Roe learned these bomb runs into NVN's dangerous Route Pack Alpha 6 sector had already approached a thousand sorties. He also saw that the staging of huge numbers of planes and armaments at three airbases in northern Thailand foretold the war's escalation in future operations. It also indicated to him that the war would soon move to another level of intensity with increased U.S. involvement.

The buildup of supersonic F-105 fighter-bomber squadrons, "Thuds," posed an ominous threat to North Vietnam, Unfortunately, it also cost a huge unforeseen expense not factored in on the drawing boards. The strike forces were incurring terrific losses of aircraft and flight crews from NVN anti-aircraft, SAMs, and MiG intercepts on their NVN missions. The planes carried RHAW homing and warning systems to detect enemy radar, and employed electronic warfare radar jamming, known as "music" in flyer jargon. Despite these additional electronic counter measures (ECM), and target suppression by Udorn, Thailand and Navy F-4s flying off carriers in Yankee Station in the North China Sea, the Thuds took a significant amount of enemy fire.

The F-105s were often crippled, forcing pilot ejections. Under the best circumstances, the combat pilots could fly the damaged plane out of the Alpha 6 sector, punch out, and parachute northwest of the Red River in northern Laos or South Vietnam. This gave them a chance of survival when picked up by "Jolly Greens" rescue choppers. Otherwise, pilots risked capture and brutal treatment as a POWs, or being listed as MIA or KIA.

Their efforts were complicated by distance-to-target logistics dictating aerial refueling from KC-135s on the way back to base. Loaded with heavy bombs en route to NVN, the F-105s could not carry enough JP-4 to make the round-trip return to base (RTB). The daily, long, perilous sorties were stressful. Flying NVN combat missions east of the Red River to attack targets in the Hanoi/Haiphong harbor sector required considerable skill and nerve, aka "cojones."

Fighter pilots are a tough, special breed willing to take great risks if the reward justifies the action, but increasing losses of comrades took an emotional impact. Mounting aircrew and aircraft losses, plus the fact CINCPAC placed vital targets off limits, affected Wing morale. They soon recognized the risk/reward equation in Alpha 6 was not tilted in their favor. In fact, it was out of whack.

Squadrons questioned wing commanders why they bombed non-critical NVN targets at such great risk when vital targets were ripe for the picking? Every day, they saw essential infrastructure on their multiple air strikes, assessed their vulnerability, and knew they could take them out.

Why place the MiG airbases at Hoa Luc, Gia Lam, Kep, and Phuc off limits? Why not bomb NVN steel mills, power plants, rail-head and lines, SAM sites, and harbor facilities? Strike vital targets to cripple the enemy? Bomb the hydroelectric plants and dams on the Chinese borders flooding much of NVN? They tried to figure out why they were prevented from doing so. What was so apparent to them clearly eluded the decision makers. Something definitely was not right. The self-imposed restrictions made no sense, a Whiskey Tango Foxtrot disconnect.

The TAC pilots soon figured out CINCPAC took orders from Washington DC regarding the targets. Word was out that LBJ's inner circle often ignored the JCS and the CIA's input. This deplorable situation and the lack of a comprehensive strategy to win the war appalled them. Frustration would only continue to build and their stress mount under these restrictive rules of engagement.

Flight surgeons had to address these stress factors when determining if the pilot was fit to fly, capable of making the right decision under fire without going rogue or freaking out. Roe held long conversations with them. Their resilience impressed him—despite the obstacles, the fighter jocks persevered and carried out their missions professionally.

Some pilots planned to address the threat factor in Alpha 6 sector. He'd heard a story from a reliable source that Colonel Robin Olds, stationed at Udorn AB, Thailand, devised a clever plan to intercept MiG-21s harassing the "Thuds" on their North Vietnam bomb runs. Hanoi SIGINT had learned the predictable identifying factors, or ID, of incoming F-105 flight patterns, including their call signs and radio frequencies. Olds set a trap, "Operation Bolo." He assembled a squadron of nimble F-4s, superior in air-to-air combat to the F-105. His squadron posed as F-105s using their ID en route to North Vietnam.

He pulled off the masquerade using Thud ID to take down MiGs expecting a sortie of F-105s, rather than these nimble F-4 aerial aces.

Olds went on to become a three-time ace—sixteen kills in two wars—and USAF awarded him a Flying Cross. And, they promoted him to general, every Wing commanders' dream.

***

Without hesitation, Roe had decided to take Biff up on his offer to meet Ann Summerville in Hawaii. Even if the blind date flopped, he'd escape the daily pressures of Vietnam and have some leisure time to recharge his battery. He saw no downside to the trip.

Biff and Ann were winding up an intelligence meeting at Hickam AB in Hawaii. Roe had accumulated a lot of leave time, so he planned to take a three-day vacation in Hawaii: one day to rest, one day to meet Biff and Ann, and one day to be with Ann if they hit it off. He exchanged telexes with Biff and arranged the dates. Roe's jump orders secured him a hop in the C-135 jump seat to Hickam.

It was a perfect day upon their arrival in Honolulu. Hickam air base was adjacent to the oceanfront international airport. The approach to the airstrip provided a spectacular view of Waikiki and Diamondhead. Pearl Harbor was visible, along with the monument to the wreck of the *USS Arizona* memorializing a Japanese sneak attack in 1941. There were only a few clouds against the pale blue sky, which contrasted to the verdant island's tropical foliage and dark-blue sea.

The pilot skillfully set the C-135 down in a westerly 20-knot crosswind. After a fairly long taxi to the hangar, Roe thanked the crew for the hop, grabbed his B-4 bag, and hitched a ride to Fort Derussy. He'd be there in time for lunch and a relaxing day at the beach.

Fort Derussy, with its officer's BOQ on the beach in downtown Honolulu, welcomed him. It was a lovely piece of real estate, comprised of a nice inland park and a white oceanfront sandy beach. The building was dated, anything but charming, but the quarters provided a comfortable bed, a fridge full of beer, TV, and a fabulous ocean view just a hundred yards from the sea. And, an A/C that worked perfectly.

The BOQ had an ocean veranda and bar patio for light meals. He made a beeline, and ordered a Coors beer and a burger. "Make that a cheeseburger," he told the Filipino waiter, "with an order of fries."

It was good to be back in the states. The TV reception wasn't very good, so the black-and-white set flickered. The aerial was weather-beaten and battered from twenty-knot sea breezes, but he could catch up to the news and sports on the mainland.

His cheeseburger promptly arrived, done to perfection, the fries great. Roe decided he was getting tired of Asian noodles and rice. The second and third ice-cold beers were even better than the meal.

After lunch, he took a long nap on the beach under the shade of an umbrella. When he woke up, he dove in for a refreshing swim in the ocean, followed by another nap. Roe wished for more moments like this.

Slightly sunburned, Roe returned to his quarters around seven in the evening, drank two more beers, showered, and hopped in bed to watch the news and sports channel. He had a slight buzz on from jet lag, beer, and a little too much sun. A night out on the town never crossed his mind, out of the question. He looked forward to sacking out without a phone ringing to summon him to duty in some far corner of Vietnam.

He slept till ten in the morning the next day, almost fifteen straight hours of uninterrupted rest. From Vietnam, he'd crossed the international-date line, flying several thousand miles through Pacific Time zones. Roe was a bit spaced out upon his arrival in Hawaii. The rest did him wonders. He felt invigorated and ready to take on the world again.

After a refreshing morning shower, Roe applied an extra layer of sun lotion, slipped into a bathing suit and t-shirt and went to the ocean veranda for breakfast. It was a beautiful morning with a light sea breeze. He ordered the real American version of bacon and eggs with hash browns, orange juice, and coffee. The meal hit the spot. This short-order cook had his act together.

The restaurant was almost empty, as everyone had eaten earlier while he slept in. After breakfast, he took a short swim and found the ocean refreshing, not hot like Vietnam's sea. It was great to be out of the oppressive humidity of Southeast Asia and into a relatively comfortable tropical climate of Oahu. The steady breeze cut the humidity.

No one will shoot at me here, Roe mused.

After the swim and another short nap on the beach, Roe called Biff to check on the dinner arrangements.

His buddy cheerfully answered after two rings, obviously expecting his call.

"Good to hear from you, Roe. How was the trip from the land of the coup?"

"Slept most of the way. Got to Derussy in time to catch up on some serious Zs. What's the game plan for tonight, Biff?"

"I reserved a table at the Hickam Officers Club with a view of the channel leading to Pearl Harbor. We can watch subs and ships arrive and depart during drinks and dinner, in case you and Ann don't hit it off."

Biff laughed and Roe joined in.

"And, the time would be?"

"How 'bout 1900 hours? That will allow us plenty of time for viewing our spectacular Hawaiian sunset. Ann will meet us there. She lives outside Honolulu, up on the north shore."

"She a surfer?"

"No. Just values her privacy and solitude."

"Looking forward to our evening together. It's great to get away for a few days, believe me."

"I bet. See ya tonight, pal."

Around 1800 hours, Roe put on his tan summer uniform that had been freshly pressed that afternoon by the same Filipino houseman who shined his shoes. Well rested for the first time in weeks, he was ready and raring to go. He couldn't recall the last time he felt this good, probably in Bangkok last March.

The Officers Club was packed at seven, 1900 hours. "Happy Hour" was just winding up, and no one was feeling any pain.

Roe spotted Biff sitting at a choice deck-area table by an attractive young blonde with a pageboy cut. She was beautifully attired, classy in a white sundress with a fine floral pattern. Her bare shoulders revealed a tan only locals could acquire over weeks of exposure to the tropical sun. Roe's anticipation of the introduction took a quantum leap immediately. He experienced a boyhood thrill. If her personality matched her great looks, credit Biff with a home run.

Biff recognized Roe's arrival in the expansive dining room's foyer. He stood, grinned widely, and waved Roe over for the long-awaited introduction.

Roe approached in a brisk stride. Biff noticed a bit more zip in his step, a good sign that Roe approved of his choice for a blind date, at least at first impression from a distance.

"Roe, I'd like you to meet Ann Summerville."

Quietly, Roe and Ann stared at each other, sizing each other up. Both parties obviously had harbored some apprehension about Biff's qualifications as a matchmaker. Coincidentally, both were searching for a meaningful relationship. And now, both were pleasantly surprised with Biff's good judgment, which rendered them momentarily speechless.

Biff gazed on in wonderment as they both took too way long to acknowledge his introduction. Was this an awkward moment?

What's up? Biff wondered. *Come on, man, speak up.*

After a seeming eternity, Roe managed to speak, "I've heard so many good things about you, Ann. Biff sings your praises."

Ann briefly glanced at Biff with an approving smile. "I'm very pleased to finally meet you, Roe. Biff speaks so highly of you that I expected some shining knight in armor to arrive on a white horse."

She laughed lightly. She nudged Biff in amicable fashion, acknowledging her appreciation of his choice for fixing her up, and Roe didn't miss the subtle communication.

Biff watched their interaction with amusement. Roe studied her lovely teeth, her engaging smile with a hint of a dimple. His pal couldn't take his eyes off her. She returned his approving gaze, her pale blue eyes staring into his, indicating a mutual attraction. No missing the fact of the instant magnetism. Ann was not only as a charming woman with great self-confidence, but a knockout... an elegant, beautiful woman with an engaging personality.

Biff realized he'd done well at his first attempt at matchmaking. He'd never seen Roe so at a loss for words. To keep the introduction from becoming more awkward, he decided to move it along by nudging Roe with his elbow.

"Come on, Roe. Sit down and share some champagne with us. You've been out in the boondocks too long, old buddy. Enjoy some Veuve Clicquot, relax, and have a good time."

He glanced out the window and pointed. "Look at that sub going up to Pearl Harbor, some happy sailors coming home."

They all looked out to the channel as a nuclear-class submarine glided up the narrow maritime byway for some shore duty after six months at sea.

Biff set a cheerful, positive tone for the evening. It was time to be lighthearted. He planned to ensure that levity prevailed tonight, and intended to go all out to make this work.

The champagne was delightful. Biff ordered a second bottle to break the ice, as if it was really required for that purpose. By this time, Roe and

Ann were cautiously engaging in conversation, each evaluating the quality of the other's intellect, Roe clinically, Ann emotionally.

It's just a matter of time, Biff thought. *Looks like a go.*

A quartet started to play some jazz across the room on a small stage above a large parquet dance floor. They were putting out some good sounds, in contrast to the Filipino group at Cercle Sportif in Saigon, the last time Biff and Roe got together. It was smooth, groovy music with a good rhythm.

Biff wondered if Roe would ask Ann to dance. Maybe after dinner? *Roe's a big boy who can take care of himself. Just not as aggressive as I thought he'd be with women.*

Things soon lightened up, erasing any early social tension. Gaiety and small talk took its place as the champagne flowed.

The Filipino waiter arrived for their dinner orders. Biff suggested a rib-eye, bone-in, or macadamia nut encrusted mahi-mahi. He knew Ann would order a salad and grilled fish, judging from previous dinners with her at the O Club after their contentious CINCPAC meetings.

Roe chose the mahi-mahi and raved about it. Biff ordered the same dish, accompanied by a delightful Chateau Montelena Napa Valley Chardonnay to go with their meals.

As the evening progressed, laughter and sharing of stories seemed to go on endlessly. One story prompted yet another between Biff and Roe.

Ann found their interaction entertaining. She enjoyed seeing them joke with each other. She laughed at their stories... some were downright hilarious. She studiously observed the joyful reunion of the two old friends exhibiting a genuine friendship. Indeed, they were kindred spirits, going way back.

Ann did not really know Roe yet, but found it reassuring that he was fast friends with Biff. She and Biff shared a pleasant, platonic relationship. Their ideology in the intel meetings meshed, promoting a respectful, collegial relationship. She knew about Biff's intentions to marry Mary Beth in San Francisco after the war. Actually, she found Biff handsome and interesting, but she was not physically attracted to him.

On the other hand, with Roe, *Certainly possibilities, and maybe a lot of potential.*

Ann had a mental checklist of desirable traits, and Roe was starting to meet a lot of her criteria and expectations. She decided to proceed with caution ... being much too analytical to become infatuated.

Nevertheless, she appreciated Biff's arranging this date for her. She was growing a bit weary of the local officers hitting on her. So, she spent most of her time alone, reading at her beach home in Haleiwa. That routine was beginning to grow old.

As a top-notch government consultant for Southeast Asian affairs, she took her high-pressure profession seriously. She spent hours reading and studying documents. Even though she had earned her PhD, Ann considered education a continual process. She went all-out to stay current with dynamic geopolitical situations, formulating options and developing algorithms for each conceivable scenario, much as they do in war colleges. She didn't know all the answers, of course, no one did. But she always kept a list of options as well as what questions must be asked, what decisions evaluated, and lastly, what would be the most pragmatic outcome of any course of action taken. Her intellect suited her well for the task.

Her reflections were interrupted by the upbeat music. Officers, wives, and escorts were dancing to the music of Sonny and Cher's new release, "I Got You, Babe." The dance floor grew crowded.

Biff thought it a good time to gracefully exit. Satisfied that he'd accomplished his mission, he faked a call and announced he had some business to attend to, politely excusing himself. He figured his buddy would recognize his polite way of bailing to give them some space.

He gave Ann a peck on the cheek and Roe a big bear hug with a, "See ya, pal."

"Good to see you, keep in touch, Biff."

Roe felt himself staring at Ann again. Once more she looked him squarely in the eyes. "Aren't you going to ask me to dance?"

Roe laughed heartily. "Of course, but I'm no Fred Astaire, I warn you."

"I'm no Ginger Rogers, either." She took the initiative by taking Roe's hand, tugging and motioning him to the dance floor.

Roe hadn't danced a step in more than a year, since his posting to Southeast Asia. Maybe it would all come back, just like riding a bike.

He responded in mock gallantry, "May I have this dance, madam, and the next one after that?"

Ann laughed engagingly. "I'll have to check my card."

Wouldn't you know, as soon as they reached the dance floor, the band switched to a lively Fats Domino tune ... time to jitterbug. Roe knew only two dance steps: slow and—fortunately—jitterbug.

He was a coordinated athlete and, at one time, quite good on the dance floor. In fact, at high school formals, only Biff received more offers to dance from the girls. However, that was an eternity ago. Now, it was his job to impress this lovely woman he had just met. Or, did he really need to impress her? That might be an outdated, high school thought.

Ann made it easy for him, following any dance step with ease. She'd considered ballet school until she got involved with poly-sci at Berkeley.

She made Roe look like a ballroom maestro. They laughed and twirled, sincerely enjoying the others' company, like kids again without any hang-ups. Fortunately, survival school at Numazu had gotten Roe back into good physical condition. He could dance all night with Ann. He was actually starting to relax and enjoy himself. The first time since Bangkok.

Next, the band played a slow dance to a romantic tune by George Shearing. Ann moved close, pressing lightly against him. Not seductively, but in a very friendly, cozy fashion. Her breasts pressed against his chest when she cradled her head on his shoulder. The couple slowly moved to the rhythm across the dance floor and back. Anyone looking at their comfortable ballroom style would assume they had been together for years. After dancing to a rendition of a Sinatra tune, they returned to their table, cheerfully chatting like old friends.

It would be an understatement to say Roe and Ann "hit it off" on their first date. It was a smashing, successful start. They enthusiastically made plans for the next day. Lunch at the "Pink Palace," the famous Sheridan Hotel on Waikiki, a return to Fort Derussy for an afternoon on the beach and a swim, followed by dinner at Ann's in Haleiwa so he could enjoy a rare home-cooked meal.

As they parted, Ann gave him a friendly peck on the cheek and squeezed his hand, signaling her enjoyment of the evening.

"Until tomorrow, see you then, Roe."

"I really enjoyed meeting you, Ann. It was a lovely evening. Shall I see you to your car?"

"No need. It's just outside the door. I have a reserved officer's parking space." She smiled and walked away, looking back once over her shoulder with a playful wink. She knew he'd be watching.

Wow. Biff came through. She's just what the doctor ordered, Roe reflected.

Another day in paradise, Ann thought as she climbed into her new cream-colored Corvette convertible. It was a balmy night, full moon, stars absolutely beautiful, especially after meeting Roe.

Thoughts raced through Ann's elated mind on her drive home. *He's an exceptional man, educated, athletic, and quite handsome. Has a warm, amicable personality, a bright future in surgery ahead of him in San Francisco.*

She couldn't help but to go through her mental checklist, noting he'd earned quite a few positive checkmarks. Ann knew what she wanted in a lifetime companion. She sensed he did also, well aware of their mutual attraction. She'd been picky and choosey about men since high school. She knew that she was not "easy," in fact, her intellect intimidated most men.

He must have some flaws, all people do. She just couldn't pick up on his. *I'm not going to let this one get away. I'll fix him a nice meal, enjoy a fine bottle of wine with him, and take it from there.*

Hopefully, she had just met "Mr. Perfect."

Departing Honolulu, she revved up the Corvette and headed up the North Shore along the spectacular ocean highway, her blonde hair blowing in the wind, classical music thrumming from her surround-sound stereo speakers.

Her two-bedroom home in Haleiwa was one of the two older homes on Papailoa Road. An elderly Chinese couple lived up the beach road three hundred yards away. They owned the local grocery store that had been there forever. In fact, it was the only store, unless you counted the gas station.

Haleiwa in the mid '60s was not "discovered." It was remote and secluded, compared to the environs of Honolulu where all the action took place. Ann sought seclusion. It was conducive to her work. She always thought it would be enjoyable to share this bungalow with a man, if only she could find the right one. With her high standards, they were hard to come by.

Maybe Roe will work out. I'll prepare him one of my favorite dishes, grilled Ono with papaya sauce. I bet he'll love that.

She could as easily prepare a gourmet meal as draft a thesis, possessing remarkable talents in the kitchen. *Am I plotting? Of course. I don't want to overwhelm this unsuspecting man, but I don't want to let him get away either.*

The next day, Ann arrived at the Sheridan "Pink Palace" for the afternoon lunch. Diet conscious, she declined having a burger and beer with Roe, and chose a fruit salad instead. She wore a classy Hawaiian mumu and flip flops. Roe had on Madras shorts, a white polo golf shirt, and canvas boat shoes. The Filipino waiter remarked to the bartender that they made a handsome couple, not the usual tourist or surfer types who frequented this popular beach bar. These two oozed class.

Roe glanced at Ann. "I haven't had a Mai Tai yet, how about you?"

Ann laughed, "I don't drink anything with an umbrella in it. Maybe I'll have a vodka tonic."

Roe thought, *Just like Lynne, no drinks with an umbrella. Must be a gender related thing.*"

After a pleasant lunch, Roe suggested they go over to Fort Derussy for some private beach time and a swim. Waikiki was much too crowded for him.

They drove in the Corvette convertible, top down, while Roe reflected how many Americans seemed to be enjoying this privileged lifestyle in Honolulu, a far cry from Saigon. Maybe someday he'd join them in this tropical paradise.

Luckily, they found a parking spot close by. They quickly changed clothes in Roe's quarters, and proceeded directly to the beach, hand in hand.

Roe grabbed two large terrycloth towels and selected a nice spot with two beach chairs, an umbrella, and a lovely ocean view. They talked for an hour about everything, until Roe suggested a swim.

She hopped up and lifted her mumu over her head. She wore a fashionable bikini with a floral motif, very Hawaiian. It exposed a lovely figure that her sundress only suggested last evening.

"Looking good, lady." Roe grinned in approval.

"Glad you like my bikini." Ann was not oblivious to him checking out her trim body, nor his horny expression.

Playfully, she dashed away from him. "Come on in, Roe," she yelled, "the water's fine." She dove into the gentle surf.

Her sudden vivacious attitude surprised Roe. She had been so reserved last night. For a moment, this vibrant aspect of her personality reminded him of Lynne's unpredictable fun-loving spontaneity.

Maybe I've been away from women too long. They certainly are not docile and demure anymore. They seem free-spirited, self-reliant, independent—all of the above, he thought, his analytical mind working as if in response a multiple-choice quiz.

Ann bobbed up and down in the ocean, treading water, waiting for Roe to slip off his Madras shorts. He had his boxer-style, nylon bathing suit underneath.

"I'll be right there, Ann."

Roe noticed Ann had taken some impressive, strong strokes after diving in the surf. She was fifty yards offshore. Biff said she was a "California girl," known to be outdoorsy and athletic. That suited him fine.

"You're not a bad swimmer for a PhD!" Roe shouted to her, smiling ear to ear.

He dove into the surf and swam out to meet her. The water was seventy-four degrees, the air eighty-two degrees ... perfect. Life was good.

They frolicked in the surf like kids, laughing and splashing. They soon tired and returned to the beach to sunbathe and take a nap. The Mai Tai's delayed punch hit Roe and he was out like a light within minutes.

Ann appraised his physique while he slept. He was a strong, well-built man who'd obviously taken good care of himself. He drank, but he didn't smoke, hardly swore, at least in her presence, and took naps to recharge his battery. Vietnam must be exhausting. I can't imagine what he's been through over there.

She thought this might be the start of something grand. It had been a long time since she had been with a man like Roe, someone with depth to their personality and physically attractive.

She turned her attention to a light novel while Roe napped.

After a couple of hours on the beach, Roe started to get sunburned, despite the all the lotion he'd applied. She woke him up to warn him, and they decided to get out of the sun.

Roe invited Ann to his room to shower. She showered first, Roe second, each providing proper privacy to the other.

She came out of the bathroom wrapped seductively in a large bath towel, her hair tussled. "Do you have a blow dryer, Roe?"

"Sorry, Ann, I'm just a visitor here. I apologize."

"No problem. My hair will dry on the drive up to the North Shore in the convertible. I'll spruce up at home."

Roe appreciated her go-with-the-flow attitude. Evidently she did not sweat the small things ... not a prima donna.

God, I love that, he mused.

It was a balmy early evening, a welcome relief from the swelter of Saigon. Roe envied the fact that some people actually enjoyed this laid-back lifestyle every day. What a pleasant contrast to Vietnam. This trip was just what he needed.

They jumped into Ann's Corvette and headed north, top down, hair blowing in the wind. Ann turned on the radio and selected a station playing light jazz by the Modern Jazz Quartet, the MJQ. Roe sat back and enjoyed the scenic drive with his new best friend. He really enjoyed being with her. It all felt so natural.

The next tune on the radio, as they sped up north, was a new Beatle tune, "All You Need is Love."

Roe chuckled. *Not a bad idea. Propitious tune at the most appropriate time. Things are looking very promising for this relationship.*

He smiled at Ann, who laughed mischievously like she'd read his mind. She gave him a warm inviting smile.

Forty-five minutes later they arrived in Haleiwa, a rustic beach-front town from another time, another place.

"Ann, you were not kidding. Haleiwa is indeed remote."

He noted the unspoiled look of the town, much as it must have been years ago. The harbor was in disarray with few active fishing boats. In fact, the town appeared a bit ramshackle, though modern compared to Vietnam.

Ann scooted through town and up Papailoa Road for a mile or so, carefully maneuvering the sports car around narrow curves of the unpaved, sandy road.

"Your place must be close to the ocean. I can hear the waves crashing on the shore."

"Wait till you see my home, Roe. I'm right on the oceanfront. You will love it."

Roe couldn't see the ocean yet because of the dense tropical overgrowth—palm trees, vines, bamboo, and thick underbrush.

Finally, they arrived at a clearing on a small peninsula. Roe glimpsed the ocean through the palms. An attractive, small bungalow stood on a rocky outreach about twenty feet above and sixty feet from the sea. Roe noticed a small cove and a sandy beach a short walk from the home. Thick grass provided a verdant, weather-resistant front lawn. The modest front porch, screened in to prevent insect invasions, offered a postcard view of the ocean. The bungalow was a small, attractive, white, wooden home with green shutters. It had a nice side yard adjoining the front with an assortment of tropical plants.

"What a nice place you have, Ann. Too bad about the view," he said sardonically with a beaming smile.

"Well, thank you, Roe. It's home sweet home to me. In about an hour or so, the sun will set right over there. Would you like dinner now, or a drink on the front porch overlooking the sea?"

"Why not have a drink, watch the sunset, and then we'll have dinner. How's that sound?"

"Sounds like a plan."

They entered the small home, decorated with good taste

"Very cozy, Ann. I like how you've furnished your home."

"A bit Spartan, but I'm not going to live here forever."

The kitchen was another matter. It offered every modern amenity, as if it was created in another generation. The kitchen opened up to the front porch through French doors. An old wooden table and four chairs rendered a spectacular view while dining. She had placed a colorful tablecloth with all the settings, including fresh-cut flowers for dinner *al fresco.*

"This is really cool!"

Clearly pleased at his response, she moved to the bar next to the pantry. "What's your preference, Roe?"

"Gin and tonic, thank you."

"Sounds good, I'll make it two. Would you go outside and select a ripe lime off my tree, please?"

"Sure, I'll be right back." *How neat is this, picking your own lime?*

She had already mixed the gin and tonic over crushed ice when he arrived with the fresh lime. She carefully washed it, sliced it into quarters, and squeezed one into each glass.

Gazing into his eyes, she held up her glass. "A toast... good to have you here. Welcome to my home."

"To our new friendship."

They clinked their glasses together, took a sip, and exchanged warm smiles. They enjoyed each other's company. Roe found it difficult to imagine they had just met the previous night.

"Biff was right, we do think a lot alike. I enjoyed our conversation on the beach."

"C'mon, you slept most of the afternoon." She chuckled.

"Well, you know what I mean. We share a common worldview about a lot of things."

"I attribute a lot of that to our educational backgrounds. I'm an academic PhD and you're a surgeon. That somewhat narrows it down to a small percentage of people on the bell-shaped curve, right? We're both at least a standard deviation to the right of the mean. I mean, think about it, few share our intellect and credentials."

Was Ann going professorial on him? Or just trying to flatter him? Roe didn't interpret her statement as self-aggrandizing. She was a competent woman, certainly not conceited...no reason to be.

He chose to change the topic. "I feel like I should apologize for staring at you last evening. I was leery at first. Most blind dates don't work out like ours. I must admit I was more than pleasantly surprised at Biff's ability at matchmaking."

"No need to apologize. To be honest, I was relieved Biff was just not fixing up some pal for a one-night stand. He said you were special. I would have to agree. Career-wise, both of us have accomplished a lot in a short period of time. I'm sorry you're immersed in such a fractious situation in Vietnam. We try to dissect the war policies and strategies at our conferences. I'm sure Biff has related to you that some on our committee thinks we're getting into a quagmire over there."

Roe became cautious. He needed to protect Biff in case Ann was probing for some reason.

"Biff's reluctant to discuss classified information with me, although I'm cleared for Top Secret. But, in private, he's intimated the fragmented nature of our overall policy in Vietnam. In essence, it's a case of lacking a comprehensive strategy. The administration, CIA, JCS, and NSC can't seem to get on the same page."

"Well stated, Roe. A succinct viewpoint, one that I happen to share whole heartedly." She smiled warmly. "I think you've grasped one of the fundamental problems with the Vietnam policy. Mix politicians in Washington DC with the Vietnamese government's intrigue and corruption, and you've got a recipe for disaster. I've had enough of that. Please don't get me started on Vietnam."

Roe sensed her rising irritation. "I won't, you can count on that. Mind if I fix us another G&T while we watch the sun sink into the sea?"

"Poetic alliteration. Go right ahead, I'll save you a place."

They watched the sunset and afterglow, while shifting from one topic to another, probing the others' knowledge on a vast array of subjects and disciplines: art, music, politics, academics, science, views on children and family.

As promised, the Vietnam War discussion never arose again, much to Roe's delight. It was too nice an evening and good company to waste on that topic. He knew, back in Vietnam, one of his fellow flight surgeons was out on a mission right now, while he kicked back here on R&R.

Ann leaned in towards him, as if to confide a secret. "I've prepared a meal fit for a king. I'd be disappointed if you didn't rave about it."

"It's been a long time since I've had a home-cooked meal and I am so looking forward to it."

"I've chilled two bottles of wine in the fridge. Would you open one bottle while I get this dinner set? Thank you for helping me, the maid's off for the night."

She has a good sense of humor. "My pleasure, professor."

"Okay, now. No sarcasm."

"Just kidding."

He fetched the bottle of wine and held it up, appraising it. "This is a nice Marlborough wine from New Zealand, a great Sauvignon Blanc. Good choice."

"It's one of my very favorites. That's why I chilled two bottles. It's Saturday night. No work tomorrow."

She grilled fresh Ono, a delightful local white fish. She topped it with a papaya-pineapple sauce and served it over a bed of wild rice. A fresh salad accompanied the meal. The dinner she placed before Roe would make any chef envious.

"Where'd you get all this culinary talent?"

"Junior year abroad in London I attended the Cordon Bleu culinary school."

"Haute cuisine, my fair lady, gourmet quality," he said, faking a British accent. "I'm impressed with your many talents."

The small talk and chatter went on throughout the dinner. They consumed both bottles of white wine, enjoying its citrus taste with the fish. Along the way their relationship budded. And, the conversation became less formal as the joked like old friends. Obviously they were becoming a bit tipsy.

Ann served a lovely desert, vanilla bean ice cream with blueberries and a dash of Grand Marnier topping.

"This is a delightful meal. Thank you. It was very considerate of you to go to all the trouble. I really mean that, Ann."

"My pleasure to serve an armed forces officer," she said facetiously. "Seriously, Roe, I'm glad you enjoyed it. I'm surrounded by men all day, but I don't cook for any of them."

Is that a thinly veiled admission of loneliness from this sweet gal?

"You weren't kidding. You really did prepare a meal for a king. I'll have to fly back here more often."

Ann smiled, "I sincerely wish you would. It's nice to share a meal with someone so enjoyable... who appreciates a good meal, wine, and conversation."

He sighed and looked out over the ocean. "Well, it's getting late. Maybe I should call a taxi."

Ann feigned sorrow. "Are you going to leave me here all alone? I do have a guest room, you know."

How can I turn down that *invitation?*

Roe studied her face to determine the intent behind her offer. Could this be too good to be true?" I honestly don't want to intrude, but, if you don't mind..."

Go slow, man...

She didn't hesitate. "Okay, it's a done deal. You'll stay overnight. That means we can sit outside on the beach, talk, and enjoy a fine Cognac I bought at the BX. How's that sound?"

"Sounds like I lucked out meeting you. I could get use to this royal treatment. You're spoiling me."

Ann laughed, gave him an affectionate kiss on the cheek, and scurried off to get the Cognac and beach towels.

It was a perfect evening to sit out on the beach. After an hour or so of non-stop discussions, some of consequence, others with no redeeming value, both were on their third Cognac and getting more than a bit tipsy.

She turned to Roe, their eyes locked, and she boldly propositioned him.

"Up for a skinny dip in the ocean, Roe? It doesn't get any better weather-wise. It's balmy, a nice sea breeze, and a full moon. Here we are in our private little cove. It's such a grand night for a swim."

Her bold offer seemed out of character and the role reversal caught him by surprise. He'd been thinking along that same line, but hadn't pumped up the courage yet. He knew her inhibitions were down following the night's alcohol consumption, just like his.

He shot her a wide grin that would have made Biff proud. "I didn't think you'd ever ask, Ann."

Their strong mutual attraction was gradually blossoming into an affair. They clearly shared an irresistible, natural attraction to each other and sensed they needed each other at that moment.

Roe knew from Biff that Ann was not promiscuous. She had no steady boyfriend and rarely went out. She was a high-powered woman who unintentionally intimidated most men. Roe was her match. Biff was right. She was a good fit for him.

Hand-in-hand they sauntered down the small sandy cove, towels in hand, and undressed. She smiled, kissed him, and dove into the still sea. He followed. They swam out about fifty yards, then treaded water. She gave him a seductive smile, requiring no words.

They swam ashore, toweled off, and passionately embraced without a word. They'd connected throughout the evening, probing each other's intellect and worldview. He picked up on her receptive signals for companionship, and she perceived his need for someone strong to share the rest of his life. It was as if they'd know each other for years. Both knew what they were searching for and hoped they'd found it. This romantic moment was the natural progression, the emerging bond. Deep emotions took control.

Without a word, Roe spread the towels on the soft sand and beckoned her to join him.

Ann turned out to be an amorous and cuddly lover, passionate, but controlled.

Roe chuckled with the thought, *This isn't exactly like the beach scene in* From Here to Eternity, *but it's a reasonable facsimile. What a difference a day can make in one's life.*

They slept together that night in her bedroom, cuddling up like lovers of many years.

The next morning neither rehashed the past evening, and they avoided the corny, "Was it good for you?" stuff. In that respect she resembled Lynne.

They showered and dressed, allowing time for a leisurely morning before heading back to town. Roe's flight out of Hickam was scheduled for 1400 hours, no rush. Ann prepared a nice breakfast for him. They chatted, but he noted she was unusually quiet. Was she upset, or guilty about something?

Roe took a bold step and inquired. "Did I do or say something wrong, Ann? You're so quiet."

"No, not at all. I'm just so sad that you're leaving. It's just so lovely to be here with you in this beautiful spot. I finally find someone I enjoy being with, and now you're back off to war. What if I never see you again, Roe?"

"I'll come back to see you every chance I get. I've got six more months to go on my tour. I'll come back every chance I get, and try my best not to buy the farm."

He wasn't being macho, just realistic. He'd lost a lot of his buddies over in 'Nam ... it was a totally unpredictable circumstance.

Ann turned abruptly. "Don't even go there. Please promise me you'll come back."

"I promise. How could I go on without your good cooking?" He tried to lighten the tension.

He thought of a popular tune, "Hey, good looking, what ya got cookin?" but it wasn't a good time for a joke. She was serious.

She drove him to Fort Derussy, waited for him to check out, and drove him to the Hickam flight line.

Roe could tell from the sweep of her sparkling eyes that she admired the way he looked in his flight suit. Her expression clearly conveyed she had finally found her man and could barely stand to send him off to war again. The thought of losing him was insufferable.

As Roe jumped out of her convertible and gave her a warm goodbye kiss, a Fleetwood Mac lyric blared from her radio, "Don't stop thinking about tomorrow."

Roe and Ann took it to heart. They would not.

CHAPTER TWENTY-THREE
SILVER BAYONET, IA DRANG, CTZ II

November 1965

As the dry season began in the mountain section of the central highlands, military action started picking up. MACV assigned the First Air Cavalry a search and destroy mission to locate the NVA regiments that had attacked a Special Forces camp outside of the Mantagarde village of Pleime. The commanding officers of the First Cav—Colonel Tim Brown, and Lt. Colonels Meyer and Moore—planned to retaliate in force in one of the first major offensive battles involving American troops. The battle would go down in the annals of Army history as an example of innovative helicopter tactics, FAC coordinated close air support (CAS), and American adaptation to guerrilla jungle warfare.

This chapter is based on documented accounts of America's first major offensive in Vietnam and presented to give the reader an idea of the complexity of conducting a major battle in Vietnam, and details the vital role played by technology, tactics, and innovative med-evacuation. Flight surgeons managing those injured during the encounter developed modern triage techniques resulting in decreased mortality and morbidity, many used to this day.

It all started when the First Cav captured a Viet Cong whose interrogation led to intelligence later confirmed by tactical air reconnaissance missions. This information indicated that three NVA battalions, numbering about 1,700 soldiers, with several companies of VC were occupying

Prong Mountain above the Ia Drang valley and threatening more attacks on SF encampments.

"Ia" translates to "river" in Vietnamese. Above the river, the terrain was as hostile as imaginable: dense rain forests, jungles, elephant grass five feet high, huge sand hills, vines, and heavy underbrush. The harsh terrain was inaccessible by road. The well-armed and camouflaged enemy, dug into hillside trenches, would offer stiff resistance. They'd constructed a network of spider holes and disguised gun emplacements to repel the suspected attack. In fact, it appeared the enemy had lured the Americans into this harsh environment to set a trap favoring guerilla warfare. At the onset, it quickly became apparent that was indeed the case. The location conferred the VC/ NVA a "home field advantage," a milieu in which the VC and NVA were comfortable. This maneuver had worked successfully against the French, why not the Americans?

That deception would deter First Cav. Despite having a well-conceived attack plan they fell into a trap.

The slopes of Prong Mountain would be the first real test of American combat effectiveness in its first major offensive role in Vietnam. The advance intelligence reports greatly underestimated the number of enemy troops, however. Almost twice as many NVA and VC awaited the American attack. It would not be a cakewalk, as they would soon discover. The operation did not get off to a good start despite modern military tactics and equipment.

U.S. innovation in jungle warfare conferred several tactical advantages: the rapid delivery of combat forces and armament by UH-1D helicopters into formerly inaccessible environments. The First Cav attacked Ia Drang in division strength, more than 15,000 men, utilizing support squadrons of 435 helicopters all trained in rapid deployment search-and-destroy missions.

Huey gunships armed with M-60 machine guns and belt-fed M-75 grenade launchers escorted companies into combat. The large UH-1D choppers could transport a small platoon of twelve men and two crew. The Bell turboshaft engine powered two main and tail rotors with an air speed of 110 knots. Known as "Iroquois" these choppers replaced the older H-21 "flying bananas." In addition, the huge workhorse CH-47

Chinook choppers had a troop capacity of thirty-six, or the capacity to transport a battery of six 105-millimeter howitzers over dense jungles into landing zones (LZs) cleared by advance troops. The Chinook could clock 120 knots. Rapid deployment conferred a tactical advantage even in hostile terrain, leaving virtually no place in Vietnam inaccessible, plus added other vital advantages.

Advanced navigation systems on these choppers facilitated both night and foul-weather operations. Chopper delivery of an artillery battery provided the capability to commence firing within an hour at the battle site. Logistic chopper support provided regular delivery of ammunition from base camps. "Dust offs" Huey's rapidly evacuated wounded for medical care. This practice resulted in timely medical care and consequently less mortality and morbidity among the injured troops. A UH-1H helicopter could manage six stretchers and medics for air evacuation from a secure LZ. Medics initiated trauma treatment in the field and medical stabilization while en route on the choppers.

These modern military factors combined to produce an efficient fighting force like the First Cav, but upon arrival they encountered an entrenched, clever adversary accustomed to asymmetric warfare. In many respects, the Vietnamese wrote the book on guerilla warfare over centuries. With the American's arrival anticipated, the enemy sprung the trap.

The battle was intense from the onset. The enemy encircled our troops in the LZs shortly after "Silver Bayonet" got underway. Not an auspicious beginning to the first major U.S. offensive, they were pinned down.

Desperate, the First Cav called in CAS to bail them out. FAC Cessna 0–1 spotters saved the day, as they would many times during the war, by coordinating the CAS targeting of the enemy encircling the First Cav, avoiding collateral damage. These Bird Dog pilots were the unsung heroes in Vietnam, flying low and slow over enemy positions, often taking heavy fire to locate targets for CAS. The role FAC and CAS played in this battle turned out to be the determining factor.

A-4 and F-105 aircraft bombed and strafed the entrenched enemy positions on Prong Mountain marked by FAC mk5 smoke rockets. Aerial or ground FAC in UHF communication with the pilots would clear all close-air-support attacks to avoid friendly fire from their ordinance. In Vietnam parlance, the command, "bring smoke," set targeting into motion. Similarly, VHF or FM communication from FAC would direct Army artillery fire on enemy positions.

Prior to all this activity, B-52s had cluster-bombed the ridge—the action intended to soften the enemy defense. But, the bombing only resulted in a limited degree of deterrence. The intense fighting occurred in close quarters, sometimes involving hand-to-hand combat. Americans found themselves engaged in a new kind of war. The NVA and VC developed a tactic of close-in fighting to decrease the advantage the attackers' had with close air support. The closer the battlefronts, the less effective the air support. Because of the increased risk of friendly fire, FAC would not authorize CAS to attack.

Colonel Moore's three companies adapted to the challenge and distinguished themselves in battle. Reinforcements arrived and repulsed repeated enemy assaults in the valley below Prong Mountain that lasted three days. The after-action report detailed critical aspects leading to the victory. The highlights of the battle's analysis in the AAR are summarized in the remainder of the chapter to show the complexity of "Silver Bayonet," citing details few outside of the military know or understand. Actual war is a complicated dynamic, not like the movies. Behind the scenes a great deal goes on.

American technology proved key to the battle... essentially one of the deciding factors. Tactical field radios coordinated troop deployments, maneuvers, artillery targeting, and rapid responses to enemy action. Ground troops communicated and coordinated operations using Fox Mike—the phonetic military term for FM frequency radio—and newer AN/PRC-25 portable, battery charged VHF/FM combat net radios. The backpack transceiver provided a reliable, short-range, two-way communication system between ground troops and FAC during battles. Ground troops rarely, if ever, communicated directly with the pilots flying CAS. All CAS communications were managed by FAC.

For example, if troops needed close-air support while pinned down or encircled by the enemy, they called FAC on FM/VHF frequencies to arrange for CAS. FAC managed and monitored all close air support with

USAF and Marine strike aircraft on an entirely different frequency, UHF. The practice accurately targeted the enemy and prevented friendly fire on troops in close proximity. FAC followed a strict protocol, flying risky missions to make certain all this happened with as much safety possible. In this respect, they were unglorified heroes.

The FAC's low-flying planes moved slowly at 110 knots, always maintaining close contact with the ground on FM/VHF channels supplying updated intel. Ground could talk with strike fighter pilots directly only if they had UHF frequency channels on equipment like a PRC-71, VHF/UHF radio transmitter. But, that was not standard operating procedure (SOP) in Vietnam, as ground troops, not the strike-force pilots, were instructed to talk with FAC on FM/VHF radio. FAC control avoided confusion and mixed signals, and got the job done in a very complex communication environment. Few civilians realize that the multifaceted nature of war involves a lot more than gunfire. This background is intended only as a primer.

Bird Dogs, the nickname for spotter planes, represent another important facet of battle tactics. The spotter's aerial perspective allows him to integrate incoming ground intel with his observations from above, and enables him to make rapid adjustments if the situation suddenly changes on the ground. Locating the targets for the strike force is the job of the Bird Dogs.

FAC not only bridged the communication gap between ground troops and the strike pilots, but also knew the tactical area of responsibility (TAOR). During the entirety of the Vietnam War, all CAS ordinance drops went through FAC on UHF frequency, or "Uniform" in brevity code. Each and every ordinance drop required authorization. FAC basically ran the show. No one questioned its pilots' authority or exceptional skill and bravery, flying so low, very vulnerable to the enemy. They accepted the risk to sanction accurate targeting to avoid friendly fire.

Often the enemy would not fire on them for fear of disclosing their location. "Bringing the smoke" posed a danger, but bomb damage assessment (BDA) following the strike also presented hazards.

For the record: In the sixties, FAC lost 122 Bird Dog aircraft and crews in Vietnam, becoming less effective as enemy SAMs and anti-aircraft took the stage in later phases of the war. By the end of the war, six times as many tons of bombs had been dropped as during all of WWII! FAC played a major role. Overall, U.S. and allied aircraft losses in 'Nam numbered around 10,000—a ratio of 0.4/1000 sorties over the decade of engagement. Most losses occurred later in the sixties over North Vietnam and Laos, particularly the A Shau Valley when the enemy acquired SAMs from the Soviet Union and modern anti-aircraft artillery from China. Soviet Migs also played a major role in protecting Hanoi and Haiphong with an unknown number of kills.

As an example of how FAC works: a Cessna 0-/ L-19 Bird Dog would fly low and slow over targets at 1500 feet, and hopefully avoid ground fire while receiving ground reconnaissance to correlate and aid them in spotting targets from above. A Bird Dog typically would carry twelve white phosphorous smoke rockets, aka Willie Pete's, to mark enemy targets' positions identified by ground troops. Once everyone was on the same page, denoted by the ground request "bring the smoke," the spotter would fire the Willie Pete. That would set the CAS sortie into action to start their bomb runs after FAC's final clearance and command.

Strike force action commenced when forward air control said, "Hit my smoke." That term authorized strike pilots to drop ordinance on the white phosphorous smoke arising from a Willie Pete explosion marking the enemy target. The Bird Dog pilot followed this instruction to the fighter pilot with, "Cleared in hot." After the fighter runs, the spotter performed a BDA and correlated the results with the ground troops to determine if another CAS run would be necessary. BDA was not without further hazard to the FAC spotter. These spotter pilots were acknowledged by CAS as the toughest dogs in the fight.

This CAS tactic conferred a huge advantage, as the enemy had no air force, and only rudimentary anti-aircraft capability. SAMs and Soviet Dash-K 12.7 anti-aircraft guns were in limited use in the mid-1960s, fortunately. CAS became less effective in later phases of the war as a consequence of NVA acquiring modern defense armaments.

Another advantage for our troops on the ground involved M-16 rifles equipped with a new M-79 quick-loading grenade launcher that worked efficiently, like a single-barrel shotgun. This weapon was especially effective in close range combat. Constant FM-channel radio contact enabled mortar teams to effectively reposition themselves during the battles to accurately zero in on VC positions relayed by spotters. This tactic worked well to advance troops up the slopes of Prong Mountain.

In one memorable incident, the enemy hid .50 caliber machine gun nests along the ridge to prevent frontal assaults by the Americans. Nevertheless, Lt. Walter Marn Jr., won a Congressional Medal of Honor for destroying a strategic nest, killing eight NVA before being shot in the face. American heroism was on display during Operation Silver Bayonet by men like Lt. Marn who inspired others to carry on the fight.

Recounting the events in summary: On the first day of combat, Colonel Moore's three Air Cavalry Companies trapped in the LZ were bailed out by close air support, averting a disaster. They fought their way up the ridge from the chopper landing areas, code-named "X-Ray."

The fierce battle supported by 4,000 rounds of artillery and 300 fighter-bomber sorties continued nonstop into the second day with heavy casualties on both sides.

On the third day, the Second Battalion, Seventh Cavalry came to their relief north of the ridge in a flanking maneuver. Unfortunately, the battalion was ambushed and put out of fighting commission by the Third NVA Battalion. Ironically, the 7th Cavalry had been Custer's regiment at Little Big Horn. One of the survivors noted the historical parallel with the comment, "History repeated itself on November 17, 1965."

But, by the battle's end, America scored a decisive victory using SECDEF's McNamara's kill ratio criteria, aka body count: 300 Americans perished while more than 2,000 NVA and Viet Cong were killed in combat.

Huey and Iroquois helicopters evacuated the wounded, overwhelming the medical facilities at Pleiku and Danang. The emergency call went out for all available flight surgeons and medic assistance. Air evacuation crews were needed urgently for triage and air evacuation at Danang.

Tan Son Nhut AB November 1965

Captain Roe MacDonald received the TWX for help at Danang through Colonel Mason at the Tan Son Nhut Air Base outside Saigon. The usually jolly colonel sounded very serious.

"Got a big problem up north in the central highlands, Roe."

"What's up, Colonel?"

"Ferocious battle in the Ia Drang valley resulted in a lot of GI casualties and injured. The command put out an all-points call for medical assistance. We can cancel the mortar and ammo transport to our Thailand airbases and reconfigure the aircraft to give them a hand. What do you think, doc?"

"Wounded always have a lot higher priority in my book. If you can get MAC to round up some extra crews, C-130s, and C-135s, we can do some quick air evacs. Meanwhile, I'll get as many medics rounded up as I can and we'll head on up to Danang, okay?"

"I've already refueled the aircraft. The loadmasters can get the ammo off the plane in the next half hour, reconfigure the aircraft, and we're off. I'll go change the flight plan, get clearance, and brief the crew."

"You got it, Colonel. I understand that's the first major offensive battle for our U.S. troops. I hope they did well."

The colonel replied, "I heard the First Cav kicked some serious ass, but paid a price. We took a hit. A lot of wounded, Roe."

CHAPTER TWENTY-FOUR "DUST OFF" TRIAGE

Danang AB November 1965

Roe landed at Danang two hours later and surveyed a wartime scene destined to become all too familiar in the next eight years, and one inscribed in his mind. It would haunt him forever. The ramps next to the two runways were lined with "dust offs."

Dust offs arrived delivering Silver Bayonet wounded from Charlie Med, Camp Holloway, Pleiku... All diverted because the field hospital there was swamped. Medics unloaded stretchers of wounded from these choppers arriving from the battlefield LZs and fire bases.

In Vietnam, medical treatment was instituted en route to a field hospital, often proving lifesaving. The average transportation time was one hour compared to three hours in Korea, where helicopters were first introduced for air med evacuation of wounded to MASH units for treatment. In Vietnam, medics accompanied the Huey's, their medical skills and timely resuscitative treatment often determined the difference in survival rates along with the faster transport times from battle field to a field hospital. There were 4,000 choppers in Vietnam of many different makes at this time to perform different missions. The Bell UH-1H Iroquois were the workhorses for dust off missions.

As mentioned, the wounded arrived at field hospitals in one hour on average. If the wounded survived the first twenty-four hours with emergency treatment, he had less than a one percent chance of dying.

In WWII, the casualty/death rate was 4.5/100. In Korea it improved to 2.5/100. In Vietnam, it was reduced to 1/100.

A medic familiar to Roe welcomed him, and informed him that several dozen tents had been set up in a triage area adjacent to the taxiways. He added the field hospital already had all twelve operating rooms going around the clock. The Danang facility was overwhelmed. Roe recognized the urgent need for MAC air evacuation of those able to fly elsewhere for treatment. That required triage—categorizing the level of injury and prioritizing the urgency of treatment.

Roe immediately went to the triage area to join his colleagues tending to the wounded. Crews of medical NCOs and RNs were hustling all over the area with IV bottles and type O blood, the universal donor source. The entire area was bloodstained, including the medic's clothes.

A gory sight, masses of body bags with ID tags, greeted them at the makeshift mortuary, located next to tents full of wounded. Medics and RNs scurrying about created an atmosphere of organization despite the apparent chaos and carnage. Wounded crying out in pain swiftly received more IV morphine.

Roe thought, "*What a waste of a vital natural resource. There ought to be a practical, safe way to salvage this blood and give it back to the wounded.*"

Some primitive attempts had been made to recover blood lost in battle, but the techniques were fraught with too many complications.

He thought about developing safe auto transfusion techniques. Roe's scientific mind was always churning, looking for methods or techniques to improve surgical care. *If I ever get out of this Godforsaken place, that'll be my research project.*

With that consideration, he returned to focus on the job at hand, triage and care of the wounded.

The base hospital's senior medical officer, Lt. Colonel Casey Johnson, was busy operating with other surgeons of Roe's rank and above. That left Captain Roe MacDonald as the ranking officer in the triage area. The medical personnel recognized him from previous air evacuations, knew his reputation, and deferred to his decisions. When it came to triage, Roe was without peer.

In a calm and controlled manner, Roe took charge in a walk-through evaluation. At least a hundred wounded were scattered on stretchers along the taxiway. They awaited transfer into makeshift triage tents out of the intense sun baking the tarmac between rain showers. More tents were quickly being set up to avoid exposure of the wounded.

Gathering dark clouds indicated it was about to rain again at this coastal airbase on the South China Sea. Vietnam weather was fluky, with three different regional monsoon seasons. In this case, it was dry in the Ia Drang Mountains where these men were wounded in action, but wet on the coast at Danang where they were air evacuated.

Roe evaluated the wounded, constructing a checklist and giving orders to his staff. What he saw pleased him. Multiple IVs and blood were dripping through plastic lines inserted in the patients' veins. Bleeding was properly compressed and controlled. Morphine was being administered liberally to relieve the wounded soldiers' pain. The professional staff conducted their jobs efficiently in this compelling wartime scene.

Roe's job required priority categorizing—triage of the wounded according to not only severity, but whether or not they could be safely transported out to alleviate the overload crisis at Danang.

He assembled a small staff of NCOs and nurses to accompany him to take notes and orders. Roe ordered the wounded sorted into priorities for care. He instructed that those hypotensive from wounds, or threatening to go into shock, be placed in separate high-priority tents with two large bore lines placed. The lines infused Ringers lactate, keeping the IV running wide open until the patient's blood pressure was maintained to just over 100 systolic. Roe ordered the medics to put in Foley catheters to monitor and establish a urine output of 30 to 50 cc per hour. Establishing adequate perfusion was a key to survival, he reminded them. Urine output was a reliable indicator. Blood transfusions and colloid followed the Ringers to stabilize the injured.

From experience, Roe knew if they quickly established those parameters the patient had a better chance of living. That they would avoid going into multi-organ failure from shock, usually a fatal complication.

The dust offs had transported the wounded here from the battlefield in record time, giving IV fluids and medical care en route, another critical factor in survival. Now, it was the medics' job to see the soldiers survived.

"Be sure adequate O-negative blood and plasma are ready for transfusion. Most importantly, keep the wounded comfortable with small intermittent doses of IV morphine. There is no reason for any of the wounded to suffer in pain. Keep them comfortable. You think you're having a bad day..."

The medics understood his dark humor and acknowledged his orders, swiftly moving into action. He continued issuing orders in the walk-around as more choppers arrived with wounded, swamping the medical staff already operating on overload.

They came upon a soldier lying on a stretcher with obvious fracture dislocations of both legs and frag wounds. "Put those with fractures like this in a separate tent area, and splint them. Immediately reduce any fractures impeding circulation. Check for peripheral pulses to rule out vascular compromise like this soldier might have."

He stopped to examine him and determined he had palpable posterior pedal pulses. "He has no vascular compromise. Give him some MS and transfer him over to the ortho tent."

"Flag all open fractures and be sure they get a dose of tetanus and antibiotics, stat."

He turned to the next wounded and pointed out his neck wound.

"High priority, be sure all patients with neck wounds like this are checked periodically for potential airway problems. Have endotrachial tubes and trach sets ready by the bedsides for an emergency. Slow bleeding can compress his trachea."

He fired one order after another to various medics as he moved swiftly through his assessment.

"Clamp all actively bleeding pumpers in open wounds with hemostats and cover the wounds with a compress and sterile gauze wrap after irrigating the wound with dilute betadine solution. This is expedient, we'll ligate them later. Check everyone for suspected rib fractures or pneumothorax. Any doubt, put in a chest tube and put it on water seal and suction."

"Any wounded arriving with sucking chest wounds, shock, airway obstruction, or on the verge of bleeding out, call me Stat, OK? Remember your priorities: airway precautions, stabilizing blood pressure, and relief of pain."

"Yes, sir." They collectively replied.

"Regarding the walking wounded, give them first aid, analgesia, and send them with a medic over to another tent out of this immediate area for later evaluation, low priority."

"Regarding those with head trauma, those with waxing and waning consciousness, check their neuro signs for subdural hematoma. If the injured soldier blows a pupil and an operating room is not immediately available for craniotomy, we'll burr hole him right out here on the tarmac to relieve the intracranial pressure. Not a big deal, I'll handle it. Be certain I have the proper equipment to perform the procedure out here, got it?"

"Yes, sir," a NCO replied.

"I can't emphasize enough the importance of checking all unconscious patients for airway obstruction. CPRs take valuable time and personnel, triage requires expediency. Any doubt at all, tube 'em, okay? We don't have the time or enough personnel to get tied up in multiple CPRs, many preventable with proper triage and anticipation of what could go wrong given the patient's injury."

"Yes, sir." The chief medic replied.

"We always need to think ahead." He checked his staff's attention, making sure they got it. They nodded affirmatively to the NCO.

"Got that right. Start sorting now into those groups while I continue my triage I'll soon give you a list of patient priorities regarding air evac status. Those to remain here, those we'll fly out, and those too injured to survive, the expectants. Just keep the severely injured comfortable until an operating room becomes available, and keep me posted on their status. Okay, people. Let's do what you do best."

"What about the crispies?" one medic asked.

"Separate the badly burned into expectant and survival groups. Keep 'em loaded up with IV morphine and fluids. The ones who can make it, we'll evacuate to Brooks burn unit in Texas. Keeping them out of pain, hydrated, and their BP stable are your primary concerns."

The medical team was a model of professional efficiency and expertise. Each patient's medical status was prioritized and tagged by color code. The most severely injured expected to survive during transport were evacuated on the first planes out, if emergency care was not available at the airbase hospital. Some were so severely injured they would not survive a two-hour flight anywhere. They received supportive care in hopes an operating room became available on base, otherwise their prognosis was dismal.

Roe observed a lot of carnage on the Danang tarmac, the price of victory. A future generation of trauma surgeons, RNs, and medics were being trained on the job here today. A horrific day first-timers would never forget.

One of the striking features Roe always noted in these situations was that none of the wounded ever whined, pissed, or moaned. It was remarkable. These were really tough soldiers who put it on the line for their country. If the medical team could save them, they were going home. Their overwhelming emotional response was, "I'm alive, I survived Vietnam, and I'm going home."

God bless 'em! Roe thought to himself as he continued the triage.

MAC C-130s and C-135s started arriving from Tan Son Nhut, Ben Hoa, and other airbases. Roe and his team supervised the loading of the transportable wounded. The Seventh Airforce Headquarters at TSN coordinated flights with aircraft commanders, designating destination hospitals for delivery of the wounded. Clark AB, PI was quickly filling up. Soon, backup hospitals at Kadena, Okinawa, and Tachikawa, Japan would also be fully occupied. Everyone suffered from overload, but plugged along. Adrenalin is a powerful stimulant.

Roe worked steadily for the next thirty-six hours as wounded kept arriving in choppers from the battlefield. The twelve operating teams at Danang would continue to operate day and night without let-up. No one slept. MAC evacuations took off every hour loaded with wounded to a predetermined destination facility for further care.

The macabre scene distilled war into a snapshot in time. A tableau of sacrifice that would remain with Roe for life. Images that would recur unannounced at the mention of Vietnam.

Finally, things calmed down on the third day as the battle at Ia Drang became decided in the U.S.'s favor. The First Cav distinguished itself in America's first major offensive battle in Vietnam.

But, a steep price was paid.

CHAPTER TWENTY-FIVE
HEADING BACK TO TAN SON NHUT

Three Days Later

After flying ten air-evac missions, Colonel Mason returned to pick up Roe and his medical team at Danang. They air-lifted a few remaining late arrivals from the Ia Drang battlefield to Saigon facilities, loading them on stretchers through the tail ramp of the C-130 for the short flight south to Tan Son Nhut base outside Saigon.

Ambulances met them on the tarmac to undergo a second triage before undertaking the next leg to Clark AB, in the Philippine Islands. Roe needed to determine if any patients had deteriorated in flight before giving his okay for them to proceed to Clark. Another Mac crew had arrived to fly the next leg with a fresh, rested flight surgeon.

Any unstable wounded troops would be offloaded and transported to Ben Hoa, thirty-five miles northwest of Saigon, and Long Binh 3rd Surgical Unit, just across the road, for further care. Both field hospitals were fifteen miles northwest of Tan Son Nhut. Those stable and transportable would go on to Clark PI after refueling the aircraft, and Roe's final inspection of their current status with his replacement flight surgeon.

After Roe supervised the offload, a weary Colonel Mason asked him, "Beer?"

"Sure. I could surely use one. No sleep for over forty-eight hours. I could use a break and a cold one, maybe two." He managed a smile even on the verge of exhaustion.

A sergeant took them in an Air Force jeep to the flight line café near their aircraft. The colonel liked to keep an eye on his C-130 and designated his crew chief to supervise the Vietnamese ground crew while the next MAC crew cranked up for the next leg to Clark. He didn't trust some of the foreign ground crew. Workers by day, VC by night. Who knows? Transition of crews allowed time for sabotage. Vietnam was that kind of country.

They deferred going to the O Club until they showered and changed out of their grubby flight suits.

Papa San's café was nothing fancy, a standard Quonset hut with four picnic tables under an open-sided, heavy tin roof supported by four-by-fours. Papa San cooked good burgers on an open-air grill, and the beer was always ice cold. It was a refreshing respite following a long flight or mission, despite being outside in the oppressive heat.

Colonel Mason joked you could fry an egg on the C-130's wing. Actually, the temp could reach 160 degrees on the aircraft's metal skin unless the plane was shaded by a tarp or in a hanger.

They would have twenty-four hours off until their next mission, they hoped. Tonight, they planned to live it up big time, and tie one on at the O Club.

Adjacent to the Quonset hut café, a large concrete revetment reinforced by sandbags piled ten feet high provided emergency shelter. Built decades ago during the French Colonial period, the bunker had no amenities other than a safe refuge in an emergency. No lights, no A/C, no BR, only a few survival supplies. The hot, dark interior provided only one thing—security from most VC attacks short of a direct hit. Basically, the large room-sized bunker was a concrete structure with a recessed floor four feet below ground level, damp with stale air from condensate humidity. Walls of sandbags stacked deep on moldy, pierced- steel planking shelves supported a rickety wooden roof piled with more sandbags, somehow resisting caving in from the weight and spotty timber rot. The primitive confines of this cave would freak out a claustrophobe.

The café backed up to the northwest perimeter of the flight line and aircraft parking tarmac. An old deserted rice paddy on the outer side separated the café from a high electronic fence and rows of concertino barbed wire. The jungle had been cut back a hundred yards for security. The perimeter of the base was patrolled 24/7 by armed sentries and guard dogs.

A thirty-foot wooden guard tower, manned by two sentries armed with M-16s and RPGs, stood fifty yards away inside the fence. Nungs, ethnic Vietnamese-Chinese mercenaries, kept a close eye on the jungle outside the perimeter from the tower. Trained by the SF, they often accompanied them on patrols. Nungs were trusted, reliable soldiers throughout the long war, and excellent sentries.

Suddenly, a blaring siren pierced the air, interrupting their pleasant interlude just five minutes after placing their order for a second round of beers. The disruption came from the north end of the air base indicating an emergency condition.

Within minutes the *whomp-whomp* of scrambling attack helicopters' rotors filled the air, a firefight imminent. The VC were at it again.

Colonel Mason looked at Roe and exclaimed, "Jesus, it never ends! Guess we better take shelter, Roe."

The words were hardly out of the colonel's mouth when the unmistakable whine of an incoming 81-millimeter mortar pierced the air, exploding in the deserted rice paddy thirty or forty yards away. The VC had a huge supply of captured American mortars from overrunning ARVN camps and were becoming pretty good at targeting them.

A moment later, the next incoming mortar demolished the guard tower, instantly killing the two Nungs. They never knew what hit them.

The base sirens blared in alarm indicating a DEFCON situation. The warning signal was soon joined by military fire-engine blasts warning personnel to get out of the way as they responded to fires. The major VC attack on TSN accelerated as whooshes and whines of incoming 122mm Katyusha rockets and mortars whizzed overhead. Explosions rocked the airbase in a random pattern. Security forces rapidly mobilized. More choppers left their hot pads to respond to the attack followed by the roar of jet afterburners clearing the base runways and tarmacs to avoid damage from the incoming barrage.

"Holy shit!" a pilot exclaimed. He knocked over his coffee as he ran for shelter.

The pilots and crews dispersed rapidly towards the large protective bunker. Within seconds, the next mortar caught a tardy pilot with shrapnel, piercing his leg and chest. He screamed in pain and fell four picnic tables away from Roe. He started to crawl to the bunker, groaning, breathing heavily, unable to scramble to safety.

Roe instinctively rushed to his aid, and lifted him over his shoulder in a rescue carry position. They headed for the safety of the bunker.

Colonel Mason waited and yelled, "Hurry up, doc! This could get real ugly!"

It did. The fourth mortar scored a direct hit on the café Quonset hut, exploding debris in Roe's direction, collapsing the tin roof and mountains of debris on him and the wounded pilot carried on his shoulder. The explosion's concussion and flying debris knocked Roe off balance. He fell forward onto the concrete floor. The weight of the pilot forced Roe's head into the floor, rendering him unconscious.

***

"My God! The doc's hit!" exclaimed Colonel Mason.

He and others ran out to rescue the two injured men, ignoring the danger of incoming mortars. They pulled Roe and the wounded pilot into the bunker just in time, as a fifth mortar exploded nearby on the tarmac.

Colonel Mason couldn't get Roe to respond. The flight surgeon lay unconscious, flat out on the revetment floor, bleeding from a big gash on his forehead and scalp. Fresh blood oozed through his hair already caked with matted, coagulated blood. The colonel compressed the wound firmly with a towel, took off his shirt and put it under Roe's head for support. Sweat streamed down his brow, stinging his eyes. He could feel his heart about to leap out of his chest. He was a flyer, not a medic. He couldn't bear the thought of his good pal dying. Though not a religious man, he muttered a prayer for Roe's survival, proving the adage there are no atheists in a foxhole.

"Someone call an ambulance, a medic!" He ducked as a rocket explosion shook the bunker with its concussion. His stress mounted. "Don't want to lose these two guys. We need help."

Several of the air crews carried small pocket flashlights that barely illuminated the interior while several others searched their flight bags for a field phone to call for help.

Similar poignant wartime scenes like this played out in bunkers, rice paddies, and jungle patrols daily all over Vietnam. No matter how often you witness trauma, the drama still stuns you. Nothing can prepare you to face life or death in real-time circumstances. It hardens you to the stark reality of war. You don't take time to consider dying, you exist as if in abstract, detached, in the moment, as if looking in on the scene disjoined from your participation. Like an out of body experience, you wonder if this really could be happening, and find it strange your concern is focused on the wounded in your presence, not your own mortality. Time slows down, nothing else matters but the present. Empathy for another man's suffering defines the experience.

That was the nature of a true warrior. The measure of a man facing adversity. That human characteristic distinguished most of the fighting men and women in Vietnam enmeshed in an incomprehensible war. Strong bonds form in wartime, making it difficult to compartmentalize episodes like this. A life-threatening experience is not something easily boxed away in the attic never to be revisited. The memory will come back to haunt you. Men will risk their lives to rescue another in peril. Wounded have priority, no one is ever left behind. Even those who perished in battle are retrieved at personal hazard, without regard to the risk.

The fighting men lived by that eternal American mantra: There are no noble wars, only noble warriors who care about their fellow man, their comrades.

The wounded pilot Roe had rescued minutes earlier sat five feet away, conscious, but coughing up bright red blood. He wheezed, propped up against the bunker's wall. He struggled to breathe and moaned in pain. A pilot tried to assist him by compressing the bleeding frag wound on his leg. He lacked medical skill, but made up for it by offering compassion, reassuring the wounded pilot he'd pull through, repeating, "Just hang on, buddy. The medics will soon be here."

"Holy shit!" the wounded pilot muttered, "I can't breathe!"

Another pilot found a walkie-talkie in the bunker and sent a distress call.

"Good Lord! Is a medic available? Need a medic, stat, to the flight line café bunker. We've got two seriously wounded and we're taking heavy fire."

The call went through, "We're sending help. Be there in five."

At the same time, another pilot in the bunker found a tactical radio and also called for emergency help on the Guard channel. "We have a pilot and a flight surgeon down. Send help immediately to the TSN flight line café bunker!"

Reserved usually for aircraft emergencies, he knew someone in the control tower would monitor the Guard channel frequency in the midst of an attack on the airbase.

"Read you. Help on the way." Came the rapid response from the tower.

Despite the firefight, an emergency ambulance arrived across the flight line within minutes. An NCO medic evaluated the two wounded. He diagnosed that Roe had suffered a severe concussion, and determined his airway was clear. His vital were signs stable and pupils equal and responsive to light and accommodation. No more to do in this case, at this point, as his wound had been compressed to stop the bleeding. He turned his attention to the pilot gasping for air across the bunker.

He suspected the pilot had sustained a hemopneumothorax and needed a chest tube inserted to relieve the pressure threatening cardiac arrest. The NCO quickly performed the procedure with standard ambulance equipment available in war zones. Under local anesthesia, he performed a deft stab wound between the ribs. He inserted a large plastic chest tube laterally through the fifth intercostal space while others held large field lights from the ambulance to aid exposure for his procedure. Blood gushed out of the pilot's chest with a loud hiss from the tension associated with the injury. The medic placed the tube under water seal to rush him to the base hospital for suction to re-expand the lung.

The two wounded were placed on stretchers, loaded, and the ambulance crew sped off to the base dispensary on the east side of the flight line. All the while mortar and rocket shells continued to crash all around them. Attack choppers continually roared overhead, responding to the enemy attack. Their arsenal of weapons would soon hammer the VC.

Colonel Mason marveled at the courage and expertise of the medics as they hunkered down in the bunker. The medics were absolutely fearless, keeping their composure under the most challenging circumstances. His plane had taken ground fire many times, but he'd never been shot down or felt threatened in his big C-130. Flying was no "sweaty-da" as far as he was concerned. But, what he had just observed was up close and personal, serious deep kimchi. These mortar attacks scared the crap out of him. The VC sappers just took down his squadron's best flight surgeon and a pilot in a surprise attack. He gained a new respect for the enemy ground troops.

At the north end of the runway all hell continued to break loose. Huey gunship helicopters strafed and rocketed the VC sappers who were launching their mortars and rockets from rice paddies adjacent to the base's north perimeter.

"Our Special Forces couldn't have done a better job reacting to this surprise attack. Thank God for the bunker," the colonel commented. "The VC are getting good at these assaults."

They would remain in the bunker until the sirens' intermittent beeps indicated all-clear. The attack Hueys and commandos would mop up this operation in about an hour, he anticipated. Until then, they would hunker down.

Colonel Mason was getting a real taste of what the "grunts" were going through in Vietnam.

Thank God I'm in the Air Force, the colonel thought.

***

An hour later, Colonel Mason sat in the field hospital waiting room until the surgeon came out with a status report. The door opened and a fatigued doctor in a scrub suit informed him, "Captain MacDonald has a severe concussion, but no evidence at this time of a subdural hematoma. His vital signs are stable. He's still unconscious. I'll keep him for observation tonight. He should be able to be flown to Clark early tomorrow morning. Can you arrange for that?"

"That will be no problem, Doc. Thank you. I'll take the remaining wounded you triaged from Danang over to Clark now, and return to pick up Roe and any other wounded tomorrow morning. Thank you for your good care of my old buddy, Dr. MacDonald. He's the best damned flight surgeon I've ever seen."

The doctor nodded agreement. "I heard about his courageous effort in saving the pilot. By the way, that pilot is going to be fine. He'll have a chest tube in for two days, but should be able to return to flight status in a month or so."

Colonel Mason replied, "Thanks a lot, Doc. You guys are doing a helluva good job over here."

He sighed in relief to hear Roe was stable. Though worried that Roe remained unconscious, he felt reassured that they had good neurosurgeons at Clark who would take good care of him.

If not, what would he do?

CHAPTER TWENTY-SIX
DANANG, VIETNAM

December 1965

Danang translates as "opening of the big river" in Vietnamese. The city is a major seaport on the South China Sea about 400 miles north of Saigon. By the Vietnam's standard of 4,000 years of history, it is a relatively young city dating back 400 years. Danang played a pivotal role in the country's modern history during both the French and American interventions in the twentieth century.

In 1858, French ships bombarded the city to protest Roman Catholic missionary persecution, a prelude and pretext to colonization under Napoleon III, leading to more than six decades of French occupation of Vietnam, Laos, and Cambodia—collectively, Indochina. The French called the city *Tourane*, one of five major cities in Indochina during the French Colonial period.

During the Vietnam War, Danang developed into a key air force hub because of its critical location on the North China Sea and strategic location eighty-five miles south of the 17th Parallel, the DMZ (Demilitarized Zone). It became the home of the second largest and busiest air base in the Republic of Vietnam with two airstrips shared by the VNAF, USAF, Navy, and Marines. The air base swelled to near capacity with arrival of two Marine battalions in response to the Pleiku attack in 1965. That brought the total contingency to 5,000 American troops stationed there as the war escalated.

U.S. commitment in Danang dated back to early 1961 when JFK authorized a long-range radar facility there to observe Soviet flights across the Laotian border. The Russians were supplying the Pathet Lao guerillas and North Vietnamese armies in the North Laos "Plain of Jars." The Americans were supporting the nationalist regime of General Phoumi in Laos. The CIA had a dog in that fight ten years before Vietnam heated up, a little-known fact.

In the decade before JFK's commitment to Danang, the CIA conducted a secret war in Laos. The CIA's paramilitary unit, the Special Activity Division, infiltrated "telephone repairmen" to organize local Hmong tribes to monitor Ho Chi Minh trail activity. The trail wove through dense jungles all the way to Saigon. Biff inherited and now managed SAD affairs in Vietnam and Laos. The relationship remained important to the intelligence agency because the Ho Chi Minh trail was "officially off limits" to the military, but not to the CIA, and they had critical tribal assets in Laos.

That situation had to change. Designating that part of the trail off limits was inane. Biff had new tactics in mind to interdict the VC supply route from North Vietnam. After his return from covert operations in Lima sites – clandestine landing sites near the dangerous Steel Tiger sector in northern Laos -he was encouraged. Still dressed in camouflage tiger suits and canvas jungle boots, his SAD unit looked like Special Forces. In fact, they were the CIA's paramilitary version of those elite warriors.

Biff planned a short stop over at Danang AB to brief the I Corps intel officers on his updated plans to curb the traffic of VC/NVA along the Ho Chi Minh trail. By upgrading "Search and Destroy" missions in CTZ II and Laos, Biff felt assured they could change the tide of the war by employing new tactics.

Bad weather delayed his arrival as his flight encountered severe turbulence The company's T-39 Sabreliner turbojet bounced through the turbulence and dark cumulus clouds en route to Danang until the plane climbed to 36,000 feet to fly above it.

The northern monsoon season on the coast raged in full force, making military reconnaissance and operations difficult in the I Corps northern zone. In contrast, up in the Central Highlands and Laos to the west where they just left, the dry season was beginning.

Biff thought, *What a weird weather system. But, Mother Nature always bats last.*

The courier jet provided subsonic transportation for two pilots and six passengers in plush airliner seats. The customized executive jet was armed with rockets in case of hostile encounters. The CIA pilots were ex-fighter jocks. All eight aboard were heavily armed, part of a select special activities staff responsible for covert paramilitary operations.

These men were capable of conducting high-threat operations where the U.S. government did not want to be in any way identified with their activities. In other words, the U.S. government and the CIA wanted to retain plausible deniability if they were caught and, if they were, they were on their own. No one would come to rescue them. A fact Biff always reminded them on these secret missions into Laos. So far, so good. They'd chalked up more than a dozen without incident.

It 1965, it was clear Vietnam was heating up with increased American commitment. Construction surged. Seabees were building eleven new airbases for USAF and Marine Squadrons. Three Navy carriers in Yankee Station deployed extra aircraft capability for NVN airstrikes. Three TAC bases were operating out of Thailand commencing NVN bomb runs in Operation Rolling Thunder. A total of fifty squadrons were envisioned to beef up the war effort.

It was also becoming clear to MACV that better reconnaissance intelligence information was required to interdict hostile movements and military shipments along the Ho Chi Minh trail if America was to succeed where the French had failed.

This is where Biff and SAD staff came into play. He had a specific plan to coordinate with military intelligence and command at Danang. He predicted his tactical plan's implementation would thwart enemy transit in both Laos and Vietnam.

***

"Danang tower, this is Scatback two three zero squawking one two-zero zero. Come in."

"Scatback, got you tracking 120 miles southeast of base. IFF activated."

"Request ILS landing instructions."

The T-39 pilot transmitted to the tower using the code sign "Scatback" identifying T-39 courier jets, and code "1200" indicated pilot flying visually above cloud cover. "IFF" identifies aircraft as friendly, and radar tracking activated and established. IFR is instrument landing protocol for bad weather, contra-indicating a visual approach (VFR)

"Scatback two three zero cleared for IFR straight-in approach to runway 17 L/35R. Conditions at minimum. Ceiling 900 feet, visibility less than one thousand feet with sporadic rain and winds out of the north gusting to 30 knots. Over."

"Roger that. Out."

"Just another routine day in Vietnam," the pilot joked to his co-pilot as he set the heading and started his decent.

"A little hairy, but at least no one will be shooting at us on approach."

Both laughed at the reference to their combat flying days. They could deal with weather any day.

"Prepare for landing," the pilot announced several minutes later over the intercom. Turbulence buffeted the jet descending at 400 knots through the stormy cloud cover.

Biff and the SAD staff buckled up.

Less than ten minutes later, after a few more bumps and jolts, the small two-engine jet touched down and glided to the end of the runway. The pilot taxied the plane into a restricted area, as the tower instructed, to a ramp. There, a jeep with a Marine manning a rear-mounted .50 caliber machine gun waited to ferry them. Their hosts, multi-service intelligence officers, stood in the rain to greet them before escorting them to a nearby Quonset hut that served as intelligence headquarters.

After the usual handshakes and arrival banter common among veteran officers, they sat down to business. Biff, while not the ranking officer, was obviously the 'commanding' officer. His reputation on the subject matter preceded him.

His role in the clandestine war was slowly attaining stature, reminding some of famous CIA spies Lansdale and Conein. Their legendary role in the prior decade of CIA involvement in Indochina still lingered among intelligence circle cognoscente. This group looked to Biff, as the new insider, for leadership. The restraints of military chains of command did not compromise CIA missions of his "staff." SAD enjoyed a high degree of autonomy, which served as a source of envy for military intelligence officers. They knew the CIA hierarchy arrangement and how things came down in Vietnam. SAD didn't deal with off-limits BS, nothing was off limits to them.

His hosts recognized Biff as an emerging heavy hitter. He had that dynamic force that defines a leader. Quite a contrast to his station manager in Saigon. Alex Chamberlain functioned as the "diplomat" who coordinated government policy, military command interaction, and managed Vietnamese politics within CIA operations. His boss was the overseer, the man who smoothed things over and greased the skids, avoiding getting his hands dirty. Biff was the heart and soul field officer who conducted the covert operations, some deep dark. In other words, the dirty work. These military intel officers envied Biff operating without their constraints.

With this background, Biff presented his latest plans for a new tactic to cope with problems "over the fence" in Laos.

"Let me brief you on a new aircraft concept for close air-support, gentlemen. Basically, our engineers have converted a low maintenance C-47 'gooney bird' into a gunship with tremendous firepower. The port side of the plane will be equipped with three new General Electric SUU-11A 7.62 millimeter, mini-pod Gatling guns. These are mounted on the left side of the aircraft aft of the door. The guns are situated in a position to fire through the open door and the fifth and sixth portside windows. Listen to this, it will blow you away… These guns can fire 6,000 rounds a minute times three, for a total of 18,000 rounds a minute! Normally, the gunner restricts the firing to short bursts of devastating fire for several seconds, which is quite effective. The guns are armed and fired by the pilot using a remote gun sight mounted on the left cockpit window. A team of gunners in the cargo compartment reload the guns."

This elicited more than a few oohs, ahs, and wows.

"For night operations, the plane drops MK-24 MOD-3 flares on the targets. Each flare lasts three minutes, producing two million candle-power of light, enough to read a newspaper. The pilot executes a python maneuver circling the target in an elliptical pattern, hovering at 120 knots over the target. This allows a concentration of devastating firepower. For example, one test-run hit nineteen of twenty-five mannequins scattered across three quarters of an acre with just a three-second burst of Gatling gun fire. Pretty impressive."

"I'll say," one officer commented.

"Big time wow factor," another added.

Biff grinned.

"Danang Air Base will be among the first to employ this awesome firepower. The downside is that the AC-47D is a slow prop plane subject to ground fire and hostile aircraft. Therefore, it may require some additional close air-support coverage from A-4 Skyhawks or your attack choppers. But, when it comes to night missions, this aircraft is in a class of its own."

Everyone listened intently, fascinated by the technology and its awesome firepower.

"The Fourth Air Commando Squadron's call sign is 'Spooky,' since they operate almost exclusively at night in camouflaged aircraft. The First Air Command calls their gunship 'Puff,' after the popular folk song, 'Puff the Magic Dragon.'

"FYI, a *Stars and Stripes* reporter came up with that nickname after he witnessed a night operation in the Mekong Delta. He reported that the visual effect of the tracers, one in every five rounds, or about twenty per second, gave the appearance of a dragon's fiery breath. When the AC-47D banks to the left and starts firing at night, it's an incredible sight. The flares, the aircraft's rotating beacon, and the tracer bullets produce an eerie cone of fire. Some captured VC thought it was a supernatural dragon attacking them. If it didn't kill them, it really spooked the hell out of them!"

Biff announced he'd arranged transfer of a few aircraft and experienced pilots to Danang within a month. They would now be better equipped to interdict the flow of supplies along the Ho Chi Minh trail through northern Laos into Vietnam with nightly attacks. Their activity would be coordinated with the CIA and U.S. Special Force troops in Laos. The new AC-47 squadron would fly combat support missions along the Laos border and provide close air-cover for classified missions day and night in all weather. It would facilitate air control and special clandestine missions against suitable targets in Laos, as well as provide cover for search and rescue support along the border and inside Laos during CIA classified operations.

"The AC-47D definitely is an exciting new tactical element," he noted.

Biff went on to explain that a second key contribution to the war effort would be the introduction of Falcon heat-seeking missiles. This innovative new missile had the capacity to lock on to heat sources over the Ho Chi Minh Trail at night, including small VC campfires. That would introduce a method to psychologically harass, as well as assault, the VC.

"This will impress upon the enemy that they have no safe haven at night."

Biff described his plans to coordinate Laos's CIA ground intelligence with Danang's Fourth Special Air Operations Squadron to maximize physical and psychological damage to the enemy. He emphasized they should anticipate many more night missions to utilize this weapon, and suggested they ramp up their training and planning for night operations to incorporate these two great innovations.

Biff looked around the room, "That's it, any questions?"

After a short Q&A, they compiled a consensus memo and adjourned for lunch at the mess hall. Biff anticipated chipped beef on toast. He was right. The lunch menu was quite predictable anywhere in Vietnam. But, it beat the hell out of K-rations, known as "K-rats," to the guys in the field and the snake eaters in Laos.

***

Before leaving Danang, Biff placed a phone call on a secure line to the U.S. Embassy in Saigon. The phone was answered by an Asian operator.

"U.S. Embassy, how may I direct your call?"

"Extension 22."

The phone rang three times and went directly to an answering machine. He left a message.

"Tonight, 2000 hours, Rex Hotel, Rooftop Garden Restaurant."

CHAPTER TWENTY-SEVEN
SAIGON RENDEZVOUS

That Evening

Biff strolled out of Danang's op center to the restricted parking area and jumped into the jeep for the brief ride to the CIA jet. As he climbed aboard, the ground crew saluted him. They didn't know this guy dressed in jungle gear, but if he parked his plane here, he certainly had to be a big shot.

Wheels in the well at 1600 hours, Biff and staff returned to Saigon for a debriefing with the boss at the Embassy. After that, Biff went to the Rex Hotel, accompanied by his two CIA bodyguards, Anton and James.

He planned to meet Cát Nguyen LePierre, an educated, beautiful Eurasian woman who worked in the U.S. Embassy as a private secretary/translator for Biff and his boss, Alex Chamberlain. She'd received Biff's message from Danang regarding dinner and a rendezvous at the Rex Hotel at eight o'clock, or 2000 hours.

She had not seen him in almost a month. Biff was constantly coming and going, in and out of the country. She knew he was a power broker in Saigon among U.S. and Vietnamese government and military bigwigs. Privy to his background, she knew he was the youngest operative ever to become a CIA deputy station manager—at twenty-one, less than a year out of Yale. He'd impressed his case managers at the Farm and they jump-promoted him to take the hot spot. His new Saigon assignment had suffered under his predecessor's detached performance, a xenophobic man Cát detested and was glad to see go.

Cát had a top-secret clearance with access to Buford Cavendish Roberts V's dossier. She was one of very few people at the Embassy who not only knew Biff's CIA identity, but his real name. As his devoted mistress for the past two years, she knew a lot about Biff, but not his status on the special activities staff. So far, that secret remained safe. To her, Biff was simply a kind, pleasant American gentleman. She had never witnessed his dark side, his killer instinct. In fact, Biff was quite a remarkable contrast to Alex, the staid CIA station manager at the Embassy.

Mr. Chamberlain, as he preferred to be addressed, came across as a studious, humorless man, always maintaining a very stiff, professorial manner. As an NSA officer, he worked with his techs deciphering codes day and night, and tended to the politics of the office. The man produced top-notch intelligence, first-rate at his vocation, but Alex was all work and no play. Indeed, he was a dull boy. He rarely attended Embassy social functions. In fact, Mr. Chamberlain was practically reclusive in his spare time, spending most of his time in his tenth-floor suite of the nearby Pittman Apartments, Number 22 Ly Troung Street.

The CIA station chief and many of his officers lived there, but not Biff. Station chiefs were generally recognized as spies while his deputy theoretically remained under the radar with diplomatic cover and immunity, as did an unspecified number of "attachés," or acknowledged CIA operatives also undercover at the Embassy.

That worked for Biff, although he worried how well secrets were kept in Saigon, and how long before his identity became public knowledge. That would set him up as a target, and the enemy played for keeps in Vietnam. Biff's special position in the CIA hierarchy rewarded him his own apartment across the park. His comings and goings were not to be observed by his peers or spies at the Embassy.

Mr. Chamberlain, regarded Biff highly, not as a loose cannon. On the basis of his outstanding performance reports, plus his personal observations, Biff's record was unassailable. The boss gave him a free rein, and encouraged him to enjoy his autonomy.

Even so, the boss maintained a detached relationship with Biff. He was NSA, Biff was CIA field ops. He recognized there wasn't a leash long enough to curtail Biff, so he didn't even try. Fortunately, Biff had never embarrassed the boss or let him down. They enjoyed a mutual trust and understanding. Each realized the sum of their talents was greater than their individual parts in their clandestine Saigon roles.

In contrast to her boss, Cát appreciated Biff who always escorted her proudly to Embassy functions and introduced her to his friends—American, Chinese, Vietnamese, and a few remaining influential Frenchmen. She never sensed a hint of a condescending attitude towards her, although they generally recognized she was his mistress. She was a loyal, non-promiscuous woman who enjoyed his company, and loved being a fine escort at these social gatherings. Their relationship was accepted as quite natural in a country with a long-established Colonial history of French philandering.

For more than sixty years, the French had established the tradition of maintaining a high-class mistress in Vietnam. Cát was as classy as they came. Her father was a French Diplomat who had owned a rubber plantation west of Saigon during his twenty-two-year posting to Indochina. Her mother was of Vietnamese ancestry with an educated, aristocratic background and carriage. This genetic combination produced a beautiful, slim Eurasian woman much taller than most Vietnamese women. The French referred to this mix as a *metisse.*

Her attractiveness demanded attention whenever she entered a room. Many of the officers in Saigon envied Biff's relationship with this lovely woman, someone who always dressed so elegantly and moved in social circles with refinement.

At the Embassy, Cát's education and language skills established her *bona fides*—in good faith. She was educated in Paris at the Sorbonne after her family left Saigon in 1955, one year after the French defeat at Dien Bien Phu. She had returned to Saigon as a young, single woman after becoming bored with Paris, preferring the Asian culture and lifestyle. She spoke fluent Vietnamese, English, French, and the Chinese dialects of Mandarin and Cantonese. She had a reasonable knowledge of Japanese as well. That opened doors. She had no difficulty obtaining a position as a translator of documents and memos at the U.S. Embassy. Her good looks didn't hurt her application, either. She conducted herself in a pleasant, cordial manner, aware of the multi-cultural nature of her job at the Embassy. Everyone liked her. Biff loved her, whenever he could find the time.

Cát allotted time after work to have her hair styled in an updo for a change. After that, she planned to go shopping at the boutique-lined Duong Nguyen Trail. At Zenplaza, she would purchase a designer Ao Dai dress by Trong Nguyen or Thanh Long. She could well afford to look good for Biff. She loved high fashion and, with her trim figure and attractiveness, she could easily pass for a model. She was approaching her twenty-fourth birthday, although she looked much younger.

Biff provided a generous monthly allowance for her to maintain a small villa and staff in the exclusive Binh Thanh District north of downtown Saigon. This was part of a CIA cover story. The villa was a stately four-bedroom French Colonial home of modest proportions surrounded by a high white stucco wall on three sides of two-and-a-half landscaped acres. The front of the home on the south side faced the Night Channel that fed into the Saigon River less than a mile downstream. A Riva inboard motor launch tied up to a small dock next to an adjacent boathouse could house two people. The home was about fifty years old, but in excellent restored condition.

Biff had bought the small estate with CIA funds with the intention of establishing a CIA safe house. Inflation was plaguing South Vietnam at the time. The highest denomination monetary bill was the 500-dong bank note. Biff paid in cash with three shoeboxes full of 500-dong bank notes, equivalent to less than 100,000 U.S. dollars. This was considered a steal at the time. It became a terrific deal for a safe house, used frequently. She and her staff provided the cover story. No one in the neighborhood caught on. She looked the part. That was the arrangement.

The company recently installed a high-tech security system and posted around-the-clock sentries after the recent assassination attempt on Biff's life. He visited the estate only when he had important dignitaries to entertain or house, or to conduct CIA business. He also used it to rendezvous with this attractive woman.

***

Promptly at 2000 hours, Biff entered the Rex Hotel lobby in downtown Saigon. His two bodyguards trailed a safe distance behind. He reflexively scanned the lobby, evaluating its occupants. By chance, he met a Vietnamese intelligence officer he knew and chatted briefly, but shared none of the day's activity at Danang with him. Frankly, Biff did not trust the Vietnamese intelligence agency.

He took the elevator to the sixth-floor roof garden. On the ride up, he reflected on his fast-paced day, jetting from Laos to Danang to Saigon. He was surprised no one at Danang appeared curious enough to inquire how he was pulling off the transfer of a Special Ops Squadron of AC-47s from Nha Trang. Or, how he obtained the commitment for the Falcon missiles? Did he run it past MACV? Or, did he bypass the bureaucracy?

Biff had valuable sources—lots of them, in fact—on a need-to-know basis. He could not, or would not have revealed his sources, even if they had enquired. Biff was the consummate field officer, and its code demanded strict allegiance to clandestine rules, a discipline ingrained in the staff. Not to mention the CIA had valuable resources like "black vaults" for him to tap. All non-traceable monetary sources, and, of course, backed by plausible deniability to conduct a shadow war.

Upon stepping out of the elevator, Biff was elated to find the weather surprisingly perfect. A ten-knot breeze cut the humidity. In the south of Vietnam, the monsoon rains arrived in May, and lasted usually until October. The southwest winds would soon carry storms from the Mekong Delta to the Central Highlands and coast. The local monsoon season was winding up with only occasional drizzle, or *crachin* as the French referred to it. It was a crazy weather pattern by anyone's standards. He had experienced all three Vietnam monsoon seasons in the last forty-eight hours.

Not one raindrop dared mar his evening with Cát. After a two-year relationship, he was anxious to see her. Though they shared a true affection for each other, she knew he had plans to marry Mary Beth in San Francisco after the war, but she never pressed the issue. She was terrific company for him in this God-forsaken country, a brief escape from reality of his job.

Adjacent to the pagoda dining area unfolded an open-air terrace with tables separated by attractive tropical potted plants, ferns, and flowers. The dim lighting lent a romantic tone to the restaurant. The Rex was a favorite with American war correspondents who hung out on warm

Saigon nights. The breeze rustled the fronds of the plants and palms on the deck. Biff loved that distinctive sound's pacifying effect.

The maître d' recognized him and came over to warmly greet him with a sincere handshake. One of the few remaining Frenchmen in Saigon, he probably could not afford to leave this high-paying job and tips to return to the high cost of living in Paris.

"Mademoiselle LePierre is awaiting your arrival, Monsieur. She is seated at your favorite table," he said with his distinct French accent.

Biff noted his two bodyguards had taken up residence in the Pagoda Bar with a clear view of their table or anyone with ill intentions. He spotted her at their table sipping a fruit cocktail.

Cát appeared stunning with her jet-black hair pulled up in a bun, wearing her dark blue, Chinese-patterned Ao dai—a tight-fitting silk dress worn over pantaloons. It emphasized her feminine beauty. She looked absolutely elegant. Her Eurasian features were even more striking in this fashionable Vietnamese traditional dress accented with a high mandarin collar.

Actually, she'd be a knockout in a burlap bag. He wondered once again why he didn't just live with this woman, but reason kicked in right afterward. *Too dangerous for both of us, And, she maintains the safe house front, living with her would blow the cover.*

He thought for a moment to kiss her on the cheek, but remembered that public displays of affection are taboo in Asian cultures. It was difficult, but he refrained.

They warmly exchanged pleasantries as he sat down. Over at a corner table, he caught two Chinese men gaping at her. He caught their eye for a fleeting moment and nodded his head slightly in disapproval. They looked away, embarrassed to be caught interloping.

As usual, the service and food were excellent. The expansive French wine list had some outstanding selections at bargain prices. They enjoyed a vintage Chateau Petrus together with their appetizing meal. The small string combo played old romantic tunes. Time seemed to fly by. The war was forgotten for a few brief moments as small talk occupied their attention.

Cát asked Biff if he wanted to go out on the town after dinner or come over to the Villa for a Cognac? She reminded him that she kept a humidor of his favorite Cohiba cigars there. Perhaps he'd enjoy a smoke and Cognac on the dock tonight?

"It is such pleasant weather, how often can one sit out on the dock at this time of year?"

He picked up immediately on the open invitation.

"You're very considerate, Cát. How could I turn down such a wonderful idea?"

Cát, smiled enticingly. "I thought you'd like that. You haven't seen the villa since Mama-san and I did a little decorating."

"No, it's been well over a month since our last agency visitors. How's Mama-san working out? The last group we entertained liked her cooking."

"Fine, she's a great housekeeper and chef."

Biff had provided Cát with the housekeeper and a chauffeur to drive her new black Peugeot sedan to the Embassy and back, and on shopping trips. Biff, of course, picked up this tab out of his personal account, not the CIA's. The villa's cash purchase, however, was a special deal, classified black vault funds, of course.

"I hope the home security system and the sentries are no bother to you."

"No bother at all. Things are changing here in Saigon. No one is safe from the Viet Cong. This was once such a lovely city. I'm sorry to see it deteriorate. I certainly feel more secure with the security system in place. And, the guards are unobtrusive."

"Maybe it will be a lovely city to live in again someday, Cát. I hope so. If only we can bring this war to a logical conclusion."

"I've known war in some phase or another my entire lifetime," Cát confessed, somewhat despondently. "I've never become used to it."

"That's an experience to ponder." Taken aback by her candor.

Biff could not imagine what a lifetime of war could be like. That's all she'd known. He admired this woman's resolve. He thought the Asians were extremely resilient, always finding some way to persevere. Cát was no exception, she was the rule. Her statement made him see her more compassionately and in an entirely different light. She rarely uttered personal, private inner feelings.

"I know life hasn't always been kind to you and your family. But, for now, I'll look after you, Cát," he said kindly and sincerely.

"You've been wonderful to me. I only wish we would spend more time together." She accepted and recognized her role as a mistress. It was not unusual or shameful in Saigon among the elite. Biff never demeaned her, or demanded anything. Their close relationship was based on a mutual understanding and unspoken loyalty to companionship. Cát had never cheated on him. She reflected on her good fortune in the midst of a war to associate with a true gentleman with a cultured personality.

She made good money at the Embassy, liked her job, and with Biff's provisions for her, she enjoyed a high-class lifestyle. But, most of all, Biff always lifted her spirits. Cát was truly glad to see him again. With élan she reached across the dinner table and touched his hand, smiling. She was very happy to be with him again, if only for an evening. She never knew when he would return to San Francisco to marry another woman. They both understood it would happen as soon as his mission in Vietnam wound down.

Cát smiled at him. "Will you be driving, or should I tell my chauffeur he is free for the evening?"

"My drivers, Anton and James, are over there at the bar." He inclined his head in that direction. "Your driver is free to go."

She glanced over and back. "You require two drivers? They look like hit men to me."

Biff laughed. *She's perceptive.*

"They are, my dear."

Cát inclined her head to one side. "Are you kidding me, Biff? I don't know sometimes!"

"Would I kid you, Cát?" Biff chuckled and grinned.

He paid the bill in dongs, and left a generous tip. The couple headed out together.

One of the bodyguards, James, left the bar to follow at a short distance behind them, while Anton lingered. He had noticed a Vietnamese rising from his table in the corner to follow Biff and Cát. The man was definitely packing, judging from the bulge under his jacket.

Friend? Or foe? Anton wondered. The company dictum came to his mind, *Suspect the worse ... foe.*

The man was surely up to no good, and Anton was assigned security. He got up from his barstool and intercepted the suspect from behind, near the end of the roof garden where one exits to the short passageway to the elevator bank. Anton nudged his .45 caliber into the man's ribs from behind and uttered in perfect Vietnamese-

"Going somewhere?"

In an instant, the Vietnamese whirled, trying to disarm the CIA field officer. The assailant was obviously a martial arts expert. Unfortunately for his opponent, Anton had been an instructor in martial arts and anticipated the move.

Anton did not want to shoot the assailant and cause a messy public scene. So, when the man coiled to disarm him, he instantaneously countered with a powerful karate chop to the assailant's forearm, breaking it with a forceful blow. The man whimpered and tried to continue the fight, but the CIA officer swiftly kneed him in the groin, tripping him to the floor while delivering another karate chop to the back of his neck.

The assailant crashed to the tile floor, gashing his head, which rendered him unconscious. This all happened in a few seconds.

The CIA officer, unharmed, searched the man. Indeed, the assailant was carrying a Chinese revolver, but no credentials. Anton identified him as a North Vietnamese spy. Fortunately, no one witnessed their fracas. They were too busy enjoying dinner and drinks over near the Pagoda fifty yards away.

The CIA officer quickly hoisted the assailant up and over the wall, throwing him six floors down into the busy streets of Saigon. He briefly looked down in time to see the assailant run over by three cars and a lorry.

"Let the police figure that one out," Anton sneered.

Just before this encounter, Biff, Cát, and their bodyguard, James, had reached the lobby. Cát wanted to window shop for a minute or two. Biff, in no particular hurry, accompanied her as she perused the hotel's extravagantly priced merchandise in the shop windows. Fortunately for him, the stores were closed at this hour. She soon became bored.

As they exited the hotel onto the busy street, Biff immediately noticed a commotion forty yards up the street. Two Saigon police cars quickly arrived, blue beacons blinking, creating a halo. The White Mice, as they were called derisively, started to cordon off the street. It appeared someone had either jumped from the building to his death, or been run over. Or, possibly, both events had occurred.

The second bodyguard, Anton, now joined them without comment, but with a smirk on his face. That answered that question.

His compatriot James inquired, "Where have you been?"

"I had some business to attend to upstairs."

James glanced down the street, and then nodded knowingly. "Well done."

Biff and his two guards understood the situation perfectly.

Cát groaned with obvious dismay. "People should drive more carefully and not run over pedestrians. That poor man just got killed."

"Yes, he did," Biff replied with a sardonic tone.

***

The parking attendant delivered their car, a bullet-proof black Mercedes sedan. The guards hopped in front, Cát and Biff in the back. Biff mixed a gin and tonic.

"Have one, Cát?"

"Sure," she replied, still visibly upset about the accident outside the Rex.

The Mercedes drove up the tree-lined avenue to the Duong Nguyen District. They headed north on the Thi Minh Khai Boulevard, which cuts diagonally across the entire city of Saigon, toward the bridge that crosses the Night Channel.

The driver was careful to check that no one was tailing them. The traffic ebbed and flowed with its semaphores and congestion but, at night, the commercial and pedestrian traffic subsided considerably. Once they crossed the canal into the ritzy Bienh Thanh district, they took a right turn and drove half a mile along the scenic north bank of the channel. Pulling up at the sentry station of Cát's villa, the driver flashed his credentials. A salute followed, with a wave through.

Biff instructed his guards to spend the night in the guest quarters by the boathouse on the river. There was a bath and a well-stocked kitchen and bar out there should they need anything. Also, he asked them to call

Tan Son Nhut flight control and postpone his 1000 flight to around 1400 and request another aircraft. He was heading to Hawaii the next day, he told them.

"Yes sir," they replied politely.

Cát noticed the deference in the voice of Biff's guards. They obviously held Biff in great regard.

Ten minutes later, in the lounge chairs on the dock, Cát and Biff enjoyed a brandy snifter of fine Cognac. She noticed how much Biff truly enjoyed his Cuban cigar.

Sentries patrolled unobtrusively fifty yards away with M-16 rifles slung casually over their shoulders. Small waves from passing yachts splashed against the dock. She couldn't be happier.

The Riva bounced lightly on and off the protective bumpers by the dockside. Biff chuckled to himself. He had acquired the expensive, pretentious Riviera motorboat from a French landowner who was forced to leave Vietnam abruptly. He got it at a bargain price, just like the villa. It was a beautiful luxury craft, with highly varnished sideboards and luxurious leather seats. Rivas were the rage on the French and Italian Rivera's among the wealthy. Biff used the boat on occasions when high-ranking visiting diplomats or Langley colleagues visited. It was a great way to safely see the city without traffic congestion, crowds, and to avoid threats.

Cát asked what he was chuckling about. Biff gave her his best grin, "Just thinking of an old friend who used to own this boat."

"Anyone important?"

"At one time, very affluent, but not anymore."

Biff had no intention of elaborating. That ended the conversation. Biff switched to small talk.

It was all very peaceful for the remainder of the evening. They engaged in light chatter. Finally, after forty minutes or so, Cát whispered in Biff's ear.

"I suggest we get some rest. You have a long journey to Hawaii tomorrow. You look a little tired, my dear."

"I've missed you. You're a good woman. A man needs a good woman." Biff lightly kissed her lips.

Cát knew exactly what he meant. Taking his hand, she led him up the stone path to the villa. Entering their bedroom, she closed the shutters to the master suite, dimmed the lights and put on some soft music.

Prior to leaving that evening for the Rex, she had laid out Biff's pajamas and kit with his shaving sundries.

Biff said he would enjoy a shower before he retired. Cát said she would join him.

They frolicked in the shower, soaping and bathing each other. They toweled off and went to bed together, snuggled, and enjoyed a tender moment. They fell asleep in each other's embrace. Biff was on the verge of exhaustion, not up for a bout of lovemaking. Not a problem. They shared a compatible relationship, no demands or pretenses.

A soft knock on the door at nine in the morning announced Mama-san's arrival. She inquired through the door if she could fix them breakfast.

Cát leaned up on one elbow. "Yes, of course. Prepare an American breakfast, if you would be so kind."

"Sounds good to me," Biff chimed.

His bedmate kissed him lightly. "You need a big breakfast before your long trip to Hawaii."

Cát was correct. Mama-san was indeed a good cook. The villa was immaculate, so Biff supposed she was good housekeeper also.

After breakfast, he kissed Cát goodbye, and told her he would keep in touch.

She looked on sadly as he walked down the lane to the waiting limo.

***

Off Biff went to Tan Son Nhut to catch a flight, but not the long one to Hawaii he'd told her about. The long flight to Hickam AFB on a USAF C-135 jet would have to wait. Some important SAD business had come up. Biff was heading out on a covert mission on a CIA T-39 jet to Vietnam's northern highlands and Laos with his "staff."

CHAPTER TWENTY-EIGHT REHABILITATION

Baguio, Philippine Islands January 1966

Biff Roberts' busy schedule with his SAD units in Laos kept him out of the Saigon loop for two months as they conducted covert field operations in hostile northern Laos territory. They trained more Hmong tribesmen as recon spotters with updated equipment, and he flew missions on C-47 gunships piloted by the Fourth Special Ops Squadron (SOS) to access, firsthand, the new weapon system designed to interdict the Ho Chi Minh trail.

The AC-47D's Gatling guns lethal spray looked promising to impede VC and NVR traffic along supply routes winding through the dense Laos jungle. Coupled with the deployment of Falcon heat-seeking missiles fired from Skyhawks flying night missions, Biff predicted—based on early results—they would further impact enemy sanctuaries. He felt they were on to something big. Conducting critical missions in territory "forbidden" by the military's restrictive rules of engagement, SAD and its native mercenaries effectively disrupted VC safe havens.

So, busy in this operation, Biff had no idea his flight surgeon pal, Roe MacDonald, had sustained serious injuries in a surprise VC mortar attack outside Tan Son Nhut in late November. Out of touch, undercover in the boondocks, SAD moved in areas so remote that, if they were captured, their existence would be denied. That condition was understood by the CIA paramilitary unit. They were on their own. Time flies when fighting covert wars in strange places where you are not supposed to be, like "across the fence" in Laos.

It was not until he arrived, two months later, for the late January intel meeting in Hawaii that a CIA colleague informed him about Roe's mishap. Biff had heard about the mortar attack at Tan Son Nhut in November, but not Roe's involvement, injury, and subsequent course of treatment.

As soon as Biff learned of Roe's injury, he immediately got on the phone. His Air Force contacts in Saigon informed him of Roe's whereabouts and present medical status, not good news. Follow up calls to Clark confirmed the situation.

The news shocked him, and he felt embarrassed he'd not kept track of his USAF buddy. The following morning before the meeting, he was mortified to break the news to Ann Summerville when she innocently asked him if he'd heard from Roe, whom she'd not heard a word from in over two months. Had he jilted her?

Biff had the unpleasant task of filling her in on the graphic details of Roe's injury in the Tan Son Nhut mortar attack. He told her all he knew, but added he planned to fly to Clark AB, PI right after the meeting to check on Roe personally, and promised to bring her up-to-date on his condition.

He told Ann that Roe had been air evacuated on one of his own 86th MAC C-135s to Clark AFB in the Philippines with other wounded soldiers in late November.

"Ironic," Biff commented to her. "Transported to Clark in one of his squadron's aircraft. Good Lord! That was over two months ago and neither of us knew about it. Here's a copy of the telex the Medical Information Officer at Clark AFB Hospital sent me after my phone call yesterday. It summarizes Roe's injuries and progress."

Ann's hands trembled as she read the report.

"CLARK AB HOSPITAL MEDICAL STATUS REPORT:

Captain Roe Mac Donald suffered a serious traumatic cerebral concussion complicated by a delayed subdural hematoma, 15 November, 1965. The injury required emergency neurosurgery two days later to relieve potentially fatal intracranial pressure. Doctor MacDonald remains stable post-operatively, but has significant memory loss. Several broken ribs and a clavicle are healing well as are several superficial fragmentation wounds.

His post op course has been rocky from a cognitive standpoint. The flight surgeon is suffering "battle fatigue" with a preoccupation and anxiety about returning to his profession as a surgeon.

In recent terminology, post-traumatic stress disorder, PTSD, affects Captain Macdonald. The syndrome will require extensive rehabilitation and psychiatric treatment. Arrangements are being made for his transfer to San Francisco for special care, but he is in no condition to travel that long distance yet. The doctors are following a very conservative course with him. His prognosis remains guarded.

—Lt. Col. JAMES DUDLEY, USAF/ MC."

Ann lost her composure and wept on Biff's shoulder. Her distress overwhelmed him, and it was tough for him not to shed a tear himself. The intelligence committee was scheduled to convene in an hour. Both had key roles, and needed to pull it together.

"Let's go get some coffee and settle down, Ann. I'm sorry for you both, but I'm confident Roe will pull through this setback. I'll cash in some chips and see to it personally he gets the best help available."

"I'll be praying for him, Biff. I love him. We'd built a lovely relationship during his visits, two or three times a month since you introduced us, so I had no idea why we lost communication. At least I know why now." Tears streaming down her face.

***

Right after the first day's meeting, Biff called Colonel Dudley at Clark's medical information office in the Philippines to make a special request. He had a plan, the wheels were churning.

The switchboard connected him to the colonel. Biff briefly, but convincingly, outlined his plan. He inquired if he could take Dr. MacDonald on less than an hour's flight up to Baguio for a change of scene and climate. He would arrange for continuing medical care up there at his company's facility near the Mansion House. Biff would arrange for private doctors and nurses to speed along his best friend's recovery in a private setting. He'd arranged for special consultation by a memory expert imported from the States to evaluate Roe in Baguio.

Colonel Dudley said he would check with the hospital administration, senior medical officer, and the base commander, and promised to respond to Biff's request promptly. He admitted he had never faced a proposition like this before. He would have to get proper authorization through channels.

Who the hell is this guy, Biff Roberts?

The colonel called back two hours later with an approval. The base commander briefed the hospital administration that Biff Roberts' offer was legitimate. Roberts was a top echelon CIA field officer with many resources. He'd checked with Langley. Staff doctors agreed the plan was feasible to facilitate Captain MacDonald's rehabilitation, especially if the CIA bigwig flew in a memory restoration expert from the States. With no need for further questions, they considered it done. Plus, as a secondary consideration, they always could use another bed at Clark.

Biff arrived at Clark AFB PI the next day. The base commander, General George Ambrose, met him on the flight line. Curious, he wanted to meet this heavy hitter with such impressive connections. He'd received several phone calls from Langley and even one from the JCS regarding this unusual proposal. Off-the-wall requests, like this CIA officer's, generally were never considered, but he'd listened to the rationale and went with the program.

The two alpha males hit it off after brief introductions on the flight docking area. In the interaction, neither deferential to the other, both kept eyes squarely locked and handshakes firm.

Pretty confident young man, the general assessed. *Likeable, not some cocky CIA cowboy. Man's got a great friendly grin.*

Biff sized up the general, too. *Old boy has a chest full of ribbons, been around the block. Keeps fit.*

"Where are you stationed, young man?"

Biff grinned at the rhetorical question. "Saigon, diplomatic corps, General."

"Yeah, right, our Embassy. How could that have slipped my mind?" The general chuckled. "Guess you'd have to kill me, if you told me what you did there."

Biff had no response, just grinned. He knew the general was just messing with him.

The base commander's jeep sped off the tarmac to the hospital. On the way, he remarked to Biff that Captain MacDonald had received a Silver Star and a Purple Heart for his heroic performance rescuing a wounded pilot under fire at great personal risk. He thanked Biff for his concern for this young flight surgeon, well known at Clark from his frequent med evac flights. The general related that he had met Roe on several occasions at the O- Club. Everyone at Clark spoke highly of the flight surgeon and regretted that the injury threatened to end his career.

The jeep stopped on the circle in front of the hospital, ending the conversation.

"Here's the entrance, Biff. I've arranged for a doctor to meet you at the information desk. I've got a staff meeting waiting, gotta go. Good luck on your endeavor. Hope things turn out well for MacDonald."

His jeep sped off towards headquarters.

The Clark Airbase hospital was undergoing massive renovation and expansion to accommodate the steady increase of war trauma coming in from Vietnam. It was extremely well staffed. A polite young surgeon escorted Biff to Roe's private room on the third floor. The entire building was air conditioned from the tropical heat and humidity in the Philippines. The facility's modernity impressed Biff. It was spic and span, smelling aseptically new.

"Stocked with the latest equipment," his escort proudly announced, noting Biff's interest.

"Nothing makeshift, like Vietnam. You could eat off the floor, clean as a whistle," Biff observed.

The distinctive smell of disinfectant common to hospitals pervaded the air, he noted as the doctor led him to Roe's room.

The hospital bustled with professional activity. The hallway traffic halted their progress several times as orderlies whizzed by with gurneys loaded with wounded on the way to the operating room.

As "load and go" evacuations from Vietnam increased, so did Clark's around-the-clock OR schedule. Doctors and nurses scurried in both directions, preoccupied with their next duty. The hubbub appeared nonstop, yet orderly in its own professional way.

Ten hallways, two elevators, and four turns later, they finally arrived at a private room with the name "Capt. Roe Macdonald" taped on the door, an expedient. The hospital had a big turnover rate on rooms and found using names safer than numbers to avoid mistaken identities and medical errors in the bustling facility.

Biff wondered if he would need a compass or escort to return to the foyer as he entered Roe's room.

Surprised, he found Roe sitting up in bed reading today's issue of the *Stars and Stripes. That's a good sign,* he mused.

He quickly noted an attractive young American RN in attendance, busying herself around the room.

Roe looked haggard and pale, like he'd been "dragged through a keyhole backward," to use an old down-home expression.

No doubt Roe had been through "hell and high water." Biff noted Roe's shaved scalp and healing scar, and felt remorse he'd taken so long to come to his best pal's bedside.

He greeted Roe with a wide grin. "How you doing, soldier?"

"I'm an airman, Biff. You never seem to get it straight, United States Air Force."

Biff had been informed that head injuries could cause personality changes. Roe appeared testy, out of character. He ignored Roe's edgy mood.

"You've still got your spirit, fella. I hear you had a close call."

"Got that right. That's an understatement. They mortared the crap out of us!"

Biff didn't expect this reception. He thought Roe would be more out of it, not irritable.

The pretty nurse continued straightening up his room, and Roe picked up on Biff's glance in her direction.

"Biff, meet Natasha, my nurse, I've known her since my early residency at San Francisco General Hospital. She's doing her patriotic duty over here."

"Small world. The Mission Hospital? Quite a good reputation."

He moved over to shake Natasha's hand.

She's absolutely beautiful, Biff thought.

Natasha, smiled, "Nice to meet you."

Biff picked up on her slight European accent. He inquired, "Were you raised in San Francisco?" He knew she wasn't.

"No, as a child my family moved from Prague to Palo Alto. My father is an engineer with Hewlett Packard."

Biff contemplated what a Prague CIA posting would be like, if all the women over there looked like Natasha.

He smiled. "You've covered a lot of territory in your young life."

"My family encouraged me to enlist to get the war-time experience on my résumé. Someday I may teach nursing at UCSF."

"Commendable ambition, Natasha. Are you taking good care of my old buddy, Roe?"

"Of course I am. He's a bit frustrated at his pace of recovery, but he hardly realizes how far he's progressed since arriving from Vietnam. He's able to read the newspaper, but forgets much of what he's read. We're working on that. I keep quizzing him. He's coming around." She gave her patient a pleasant look.

"Okay, Natasha. You're telling stories out of school," Roe said in a mock scolding tone. "You're taking great care of me. I'd just like to get out of here."

"That's where I come into play, Roe. I have arranged a month's intensive rehab up in Baguio," Biff announced.

"Who's footing that bill?" Roe snapped.

"The company has made all the arrangements. Maybe you could bring Natasha along."

"Sorry, sir, I'm assigned here and soon will be returning to San Francisco, but I appreciate the offer."

"You're spunky, Natasha."

"Spunky?"

"Spirited, know your own mind."

"I'll take that as a compliment."

"You should."

Roe observed this exchange between the two and realized Biff may have an ulterior motive. He broke it up with the curt statement, "Okay, you guys, enough of that."

Natasha excused herself, wondering, *Who's this big shot? Baguio is an exclusive summer resort in the mountains of the Philippine Islands. Why is he taking Roe there?*

She didn't understand Biff's extensive networks of connections. A "rainmaker," he could pull strings to make things happen. Roe was about to get the VIP rehab treatment courtesy of Biff's network. People in high places owed him favors. He was cashing in some chips to speed the recovery of his best friend. He had a game plan and some business to conduct in Baguio. He'd hired Filipino nurses and physiotherapists.

To top it off, he was flying in a professor from Langley Porter, Dr. Murray Robeson, one of the world's leading cognition experts on memory restoration. An unsolicited government research grant to study memory loss associated with wartime brain trauma arrived at Langley Porter in Doctor Murray Robeson's name, with the provision that the doctor visit Baguio for a month's consultation on a special case study associated with the grant.

Doctor Robeson secured a month's sabbatical leave from the San Francisco institute to fly to the Philippine Islands to personally attend to Roe's battle fatigue and stunning memory loss. The doctor hoped the flight surgeon's memory lapses were limited to short term and were reversible. Otherwise, Roe's promising surgical career was effectively over. The consultant looked forward to the challenge to clinically test his cognitive restoration theories in the treatment of PTSD. It was a great academic opportunity, one with national implications in wartime.

Good thing Biff had a big pile of chits to cash in. He'd paid his CIA and government dues, it was time for a withdrawal. He'd convinced superiors in the military medical corps that Roe's trial case could become a landmark case in treatment of PTSD. As Vietnam produced a steady stream of those injuries, they agreed. It was a go, and even thanked him for his foresight.

Roe's caretakers gave him a hearty send off the next day. No one patted Roe on the back, as he was still healing fractured ribs and still quite sore, but Natasha gave him a big gentle hug and a kiss, much to Biff's envy.

Roe's act of heroism at Tan Son Nhut and his past history in Vietnam as a flight surgeon had endeared him to the air base. Everyone was rooting for his recovery. They were proud of his achievements and his military decorations for bravery. They gave him a nice send off.

Biff flew Roe to Baguio in a small CIA plane that day. The pilot and copilot also served as Biff's bodyguards.

***

The twin-engine Cessna taxied to the runway, obtained clearance, and glided down the concrete runway. The flight was about one hour to Baguio, located at 5000 feet in the Cordillera mountain range in northern Luzon of the Philippine Islands.

On the way, Biff gave Roe a short history lesson, anxious to observe how much he could absorb. He wanted to see, firsthand, how his friend reacted.

"Baguio was established in 1900 after the Spanish-American War as a summer capital for the American governor general to escape the sultry Manila summer. The Spanish had maintained a garrison or commandant nearby forty-five years earlier."

"Baguio is where the Japanese surrendered at the High Commissioner's residence in Camp John Hay on September 3, 1945. This historic event marked the end of World War II. You will get to see the mansion that was the governor general's home. It's an impressive structure by Filipino standards."

Roe nodded, but said nothing.

Biff persisted, hoping to get a rise out of him.

"The CIA maintains a small plantation home, a safe house, not far from there. That's where you will recuperate under the guidance of a professional staff in very pleasant surroundings."

Still no response.

"The native language here is Tagalog, while English is the lingua franca. Many residents still speak Spanish as a third language. No worry, your staff speaks perfect English. You will have no communication problems, Roe."

"My staff?"

Finally, a response.

Roe's attention span had drifted off, demonstrating that a long road to recovery lay ahead. He had difficulty with retention, and simple cognition of even basic things. He lagged in the conversation's progress, missing the language comments, and didn't engage. But, surprisingly, at other times he seemed coherent and tuned in.

Roe inquired, out of the blue, "Can you drive from Manila?" Clark Airbase was located near Manila.

"It's over a six-hour trip, Roe, on one narrow road. Kennon Road is scenic, but a risky trip by vehicle. The road winds through the rice paddies, and traffic must dodge wandering water buffalo. Then the road climbs into the mountain foothills and winds through torturous hilly terrain to 5,000 feet. It's a spectacular ride, but dangerous. At that altitude, the dense jungle is replaced by moist tropical pine forests. Vines and ferns flourish in that climate. In fact, Roe, the name Baguio is derived from the local Ibaloi tribal word, "bagius," which means moss. The temperate, moist climate encourages mossy growth. Interesting, huh?"

"How do you know all of this, Biff? You sound like an ecologist."

His remark floored Biff. He regrouped.

"I've visited there a lot, part of my job, Roe. This area fascinates me. I've read up on it, pal. I'm a curious guy."

"Seems you are, Biff. I'm not into ferns, sorry."

"You'll come to love them. Let me tell you, pal, you'll be in a tropical paradise where wild orchids, tropical flora, and fruit flourish. The Baguio rice terraces are unique on the tilted hillsides, picture postcard stuff. The terraces give a quaint aspect to the town ... its signature aspect."

Biff tried to pump up his expectations and somehow lift his spirits. Roe's detachment was killing him deep down inside. He vowed not to give up on his best buddy.

The surgeon listened half-heartedly to Biff's dissertation, said little, but occasionally responded on target. Biff watched him gaze silently out of the plane's window at the changing terrain below. Strange behavior for someone he'd known since high school. The man had been robbed of his vitality, and had become a shell of his former self.

Biff noted this conduct and wondered how much actually registered in Roe's memory banks.

Holy shit! This PTSD is serious stuff!

***

After the Tan Son Nhut mortar attack, Roe had remained unconscious for five days. The medical team at Clark told Biff they'd lowered his body temperature on a thermal blanket to minimize brain damage following his emergency brain surgery to drain the subdural clot and relieve the intracranial pressure.

An alert doctor noted a change in Roe's neurologic status shortly after his admission at Clark. In medical parlance, Roe "blew a pupil," an ominous sign of increasing intracranial pressure, and an imperative for emergency craniotomy.

Biff appreciated their medical expertise, but worried about Roe's long-term prognosis. His pal was really out of it, sitting next to him looking like he'd been hit with a stun gun, a sign of "shell shock," as the doc's had explained.

Biff persisted with his monologue in hopes Roe would respond or comment in some appropriate manner. Roe remained mostly detached except for those occasional breakthroughs of rational responses. Though appropriate in manner, they also lacked affect. His emotional reactions were blunted, his normal vibrant personality flat, and appeared as a vestige of his former self.

Roe had evacuated hundreds of wounded. Ironically, now he'd joined them as a wartime casualty. A strange set of circumstances during his act of bravery had muted his best friend's emotional and cognitive resonance.

Biff had spared no cost or effort in his personal contribution to Roe's rehabilitation. Roe had served his country admirably and deserved every expedient to restore both his mental and physical health. Biff was grateful to be in such a privileged position to assure the attainment of this goal through a government PTSD research grant. He was giving this project his best shot to ameliorate the effects of Roe's tragedy.

Biff realized Roe was not interested in Baguio's history, so he tried another tack. "You'll love it, Roe. Baguio is a university town, full of college students, and nice restaurants. Be sure to go to the restaurants, especially the Rose Bowl and Patao's. The City Market is colorful. I suggest you also spend some time there while you recuperate. A lot of shops, an art colony, wood carvings, flower market, and unbelievable vegetable and fruit stands. The doctors want you to eat a healthy diet and build yourself up again. I've arranged a great staff to look after you. I'll be in and out of town, but you'll be well taken care of when I'm not there."

Roe stared at Biff for a moment with a puzzled expression. "Why are you doing all this for me, Biff?"

"You're my best buddy, like a brother to me, Roe."

"That's very kind of you, Biff, but I just need a long rest. I'm beat. Honestly, I'm having a tough time keeping it all together. I start to think or say something and just lose it. It's very frustrating. I can't remember shit. My thoughts are muddled. I have scary flashbacks and nightmares. My mind is jumbled. It's embarrassing. I'm really screwed up, Biff."

Biff noted Roe becoming emotional, something the doctors had forewarned him about.

"The Clark doctors told me, Roe. I've arranged for some professional help for you. When you are strong enough, we'll get you back to San Francisco for full recuperation."

"You're a real pal, Biff. I really appreciate your concern. I mean that."

Biff thought Roe's moist eyes looked a bit teary. The doctors said brain injury sometimes makes the victim emotionally labile. He'd never seen Roe cry.

Sure hope he doesn't. I couldn't handle that. He's always been such a tough guy.

"Buckle up, old buddy. We're on landing approach."

The pilot made a smooth landing on the short runway. This was a far cry from an international airport. They taxied to a small private hanger where a chauffeur-driven, black Mercedes met them on the tarmac. The chauffeur had a .9 millimeter strapped to his right hip. Both pilots were armed, and Biff carried, too. He never left home without his Beretta, just like his American Express card.

Roe picked up on this, "Is this a dangerous place?"

"Why do you ask?"

"Everyone is armed and the limo is bullet proof."

This cogent observation really pleased Biff. Roe was finally connecting.

"It's company policy. While you were out fighting wars, someone put out a hit contract on me in Saigon. Fortunately, so far, it has backfired."

He didn't tell Roe that he had personally whacked two would-be assassins breaking into his Saigon apartment. They climbed into the limo, equipped with a full bar and communication system. Biff had the chauffeur phone ahead to arrange for their arrival.

"It's definitely much cooler in the mountains," Roe commented.

Roe was finally talking. Biff started to pat Roe on the back, then remembered the healing fractured clavicle and ribs, and restrained himself.

"Drink, Roe?"

"I'll wait until we get to your place, thanks."

Biff and the two pilots enjoyed gin and tonics. The iced drinks with fresh lime hit the spot. After a twenty-minute drive, they arrived at an elaborate estate outside the north edge of town.

"There it is, Roe. Some beauty, huh?"

A large white stucco Colonial mansion perched on the hillside, framed by an impressive perimeter pattern of mature Norfolk pines. Three acres of manicured lawns surrounded the manor. At the far end of the property, an assortment of fruit trees and bougainvillea provided a scenic backdrop to the impressive estate. Adjacent to the home stood a large pool house with an Olympic-sized pool. Colorful beach umbrellas and white-cushioned lounge chairs completed this stately setting, fit for nobility.

"Pretty impressive, Biff, who lives here?"

"You do now, old pal."

"You're putting me on, Biff."

"Nope, not kidding! It's your home for the next month or so. Hope it speeds your recuperation."

The limo approached the mansion up a paved drive lined by hibiscus plants. The gate was staffed by two Filipino sentries with M-16s slung over their shoulders and .45s on their hips. They saluted cheerfully and waved the limo's occupants through the large wrought-iron gate. Passing the sentry post, the heavy iron fence protected the entire periphery of the property, yet the aesthetic Norfolk Pine landscaping made the fencing unobtrusive. Two additional armed guards with South African Ridgebacks patrolled the property.

The CIA maintained a virtual garrison here in Baguio, far removed from the hubbub and hustle of Manila. From Biff's perspective, it was all about security, a safe house for the CIA's P.I. operations.

The forty-year-old mansion's magnificent interior, furnished with all the modern amenities, matched the grounds in splendor. The home displayed a professional decorator's touch with provincial furniture and artwork by such Filipino notables as Cabebe and Cabrera. Area rugs covered the expansive tile floors in the sitting, dining, and entertainment rooms.

The home maintained a high-tech communication center in the basement which also served as a bomb shelter. CIA contacts worldwide could be reached almost instantaneously by satellite links. Large IBM computer banks lined the basement walls. The communication center was staffed around the clock by three M.I.T engineers, or "tech geeks" as Biff referred to them.

They also carried .45 caliber pistols, but were not required to wear uniforms. They worked shifts in Bermuda shorts, polo golf shirts and flip-flops. A uniformed sentry with a Thompson submachine gun guarded the stairwell entry to the communication center.

"Very impressive set-up," Roe remarked as they continued around the premises. He had finally initiated a conversation, emerging from his mute state, if only for a moment.

"Expecting another Japanese attack, Biff?" the comment was the first sign of his innate good humor since Biff picked him up at the Clark AFB hospital. "This place is an armed camp!"

"You can't be too cautious these days. This became an agency safe house after we moved out of Manila for security reasons, but there's no real secrecy or safety anymore out in the Pacific and Southeast Asia. They know we're here."

Biff was the type of guy who envisioned an insurgent, or communist behind every tree or under every rock. This instinctive CIA characteristic, or obsession, might have been the reason he had survived several assassination attempts.

Biff continued to explain the Baguio set-up. "This place is a major CIA communication command post for our operations in CINCPAC. Our satellite links give us current information and operational status of all our projects and assets, signals intelligence. SIGINT we call it."

"I'm familiar with our Pacific and Southeast Asian satellite links in Singapore; Perth and Sydney, Australia; American Samoa; Hawaii; and Guam. I traveled that circuit as a flight surgeon once a month for flight physicals and health maintenance programs."

Roe obviously hasn't forgotten everything, if he can still recall all that.

Roe had said more in the last five minutes than in the last twenty-four hours. He seems to be coming in and out of contact, relating to certain subjects."

"I didn't know you did that, too, in addition to all your Vietnam air evacuation duties. You've really been a busy man."

"Yes."

He regressed into his mute mode again, gazing off in space and lapsing into another episode of withdrawal.

I guess thoughts just come and go after serious head trauma. I sure hope Dr. Robeson can pull him together again.

"Now, Roe, let's go upstairs to your quarters and meet your staff."

"My staff?"

He still did not get it.

"Of course, you have your own personal staff for the next month. If you don't feel better by then, we may have to shoot you," Biff joked.

Roe actually reacted with a smile. "Biff, you're too much, dude."

"Nothing is too good for you, big fella."

They climbed the winding, marble staircase and entered the master suite.

"What do you think, Roe?"

"Top drawer, pretty impressive." The reply was again relevant.

"Okay. In each room is a panel of buttons for every eventuality or occasion. I'll start hitting them now. Your staff will arrive and I'll make the introductions. They will wear name tags, signifying their duties."

Roe mutely gazed at all the labeled punch buttons. Chef, Maid, Housekeeper, MD, RN, Physiotherapist, Psychiatrist, Dietician, and Security. Nine buttons in all.

Shortly, they arrived as a group, dressed in crisp white uniforms. All nine were Filipinos with excellent credentials. Roe was a bit overwhelmed with all of this attention.

"Biff, isn't this a bit extravagant?"

This reaction surprised Biff once more. With Roe mute one moment, engaged the next, Biff anticipated this would be a long process.

"We're going all out to get you back on your feet and your mind functioning. Next week, a Professor Murray Robeson from Langley Porter in San Francisco will arrive for a month to work on your memory restoration. He's a world expert."

"Biff, I can't afford all this care!"

"Tell you what, we'll just put it on the tab. Once you are a rich and famous surgeon you can buy me dinner, okay?

"Yeah, okay, right." He mustered a weak smile.

"If you're up to it, try to swim some laps each day. We also have a workout room next to the pool house. Also, the doctors at Clark emphasized how important your diet is to recuperation. You will have all the fresh fruit and vegetables grown locally, with several choices of meals daily, just like a restaurant. In case your choices aren't balanced, the dietician will balance the menu. Don't be bashful. The staff is here for one purpose only, to restore your health physically and mentally."

"We'll have dinner together tonight, but I must leave early in the morning to fly to Saigon."

"What's happening in 'Nam?"

"There's a lot going on over there now. Let me bring you up to date. Politically, Air Vice-Marshall Nguyen Cao Ky is now prime minister of the military regime in Saigon. Militarily, the Viet Cong and the VNA have put five South Vietnamese combat regiments and nine battalions out of action in the past two months while you were in the hospital."

"That indicates to me that we are losing the war, Biff."

"Maybe so, Roe." *He's getting it,* Biff thought. "It really means only one thing. It's going to come down to increased American intervention. We have eighteen American combat battalions in Vietnam now. LBJ has approved Westmoreland's request for forty-four more battalions. It's our war now, whether we want to admit it or not."

He wondered if Roe understood the implications.

"While you were in the hospital at Clark, LBJ reappointed Henry Cabot Lodge as Ambassador to South Vietnam to replace Maxwell Taylor. That's a major shake-up."

No response from Roe.

"My boss telexed me that the company needs to put out some fires. So, I'm returning to Saigon in the morning. I promise I'll periodically get back to personally check on you. I've laid out the game plan here for the staff. I've instructed them to care for you as if you were family. The Clark AB hospital staff typed out explicit instructions with a time-table. I don't expect any problems."

Biff wondered how much of this information Roe actually absorbed.

"You're one hell of a guy, Biff. How can I ever thank you?"

Roe's response indicated that maybe Biff's Vietnam update didn't register with Roe at all. He made no comment on the dramatic changes in Southeast Asia.

"Just get better. I'll be back next week with the professor."

"The professor?"

Roe had already forgotten that Biff told him about Professor Robeson.

"Dr. Murray Robeson from Langley Porter, UCSF, San Francisco."

"Oh, okay. I remember now."

Biff thought, *Did he? Really?*

***

The mansion staff launched into Roe's rehab like they were training him for the Olympics. His dietician carefully prepared his meals. He swam twice daily with a kickboard, and was starting to feel better, but he wasn't up to freestyle yet. The physiotherapist had him on a stationary bike and lifting light weights, and doing various other exercises. The Filipino psychiatrist gently took him through some routine memory tests and provided emotional encouragement and support.

Roe's recuperation entailed a concerted team effort. Each day marked some progress, marginal increments, but definitely progress. Physical improvement outpaced the emotional and mental, as the latter required more time and expertise.

***

As promised, Biff returned the following week with Dr. Robeson in tow. Roe thought the good doctor looked more like a symphony conductor. Once they chatted, Roe recognized the physician was a man of great compassion, the ultimate caregiver.

Dr. Robeson wasted no time explaining the psychodynamics and physical aspects of memory loss associated with PTSD, known as "battle fatigue" at that time. The doctor outlined his plans, expectations, and realistic outcomes of intensive therapy. The Baguio course of treatment would serve as an introduction to the intensive therapy Roe would start next month in San Francisco at Langley Porter.

Roe listened without comment.

That afternoon, Biff took Roe and Murray, now on a first-name basis, to lunch at the Rose Bowl Restaurant downtown. The two pilot/bodyguards, accompanied them. Roe and Murray didn't drink a cocktail, just a glass of Pinot Blanc. Biff ordered his customary gin and tonic with a slice of fresh lime.

He ordered a family-style meal of fish, rice, and local string beans to be followed by a strawberry dessert. This was a typical midday meal in Baguio. The preparation and service were excellent. No one ever left hungry from the Rose Bowl.

Midway through the lunch, Roe noticed a well-dressed Filipino gentleman in distress, gagging. His face was becoming slightly cyanotic.

Roe instinctively recognized his situation as airway obstruction, rose briskly from his chair and rushed to the man's aid. He stood the choking victim upright, wrapped his arms tightly around his lower chest from the back with hands clasped together over his lower sternum. With one strong squeezing motion, Roe performed the Heimlich maneuver.

The victim coughed up a large piece of meat, projecting it three feet across the table, to the surprise and relief of his guests. His color returned, and his apprehension subsided. He could breathe normally now.

He warmly shook Roe's hands and profusely thanked him in perfect English. He offered his business card, and Roe read the embossed engraving: *"Reinaldo Balisong, Mayor of Baguio.*

The mayor invited Roe and his friends to a dinner party at his home on the upcoming weekend. His wife would make the necessary arrangements. Roe didn't say much, other than to express he was glad the mayor felt fine now. He returned to his table.

Biff and Murray observed the entire incident that Roe managed with aplomb. His composure never changed and was in complete control of the situation. He knew what to do and accomplished the task smoothly, but like a robot.

Murray described it as a reflexive reaction to a potential catastrophe by someone well trained and experienced in medical emergencies. The doctor was delighted Roe had retained some of his basic skill sets and instinctive behavior. He said it was a favorable omen, portending successful memory restoration in Murray's program at Langley Porter.

Roe returned to the table without comment and started to finish his meal.

"Bravo, pal." Biff beamed at his buddy.

Murray chimed in, "Well done, Roe. That should boost your confidence in regaining your cognitive functions. That's a good start."

Roe looked up and smiled, "What?"

He retreated once more into his withdrawn state.

After an enjoyable meal, they browsed through the shops and marketplace. Murray skillfully kept Roe engaged in conversation with subtle comments and questions appropriate to the social situation.

It became apparent some of Roe's memory was surprisingly intact, while some was temporarily lost or scrambled. Murray recognized that a total relearning and recall process was necessary, in which key words and situations would trigger recall of an event or scene he predicted. Roe would require intensive "reprogramming." Murray was ready to accept the challenge and was quite optimistic of a positive outcome.

Biff observed Murray's very clever, subtle technique for getting Roe to connect. The doctor was a professional with a smooth balance between didactic and casual styles. Biff felt he'd made the right decision in choosing Murray to consult.

Langley Porter had some inpatient suites, one of which Biff had reserved for Roe. If Roe progressed satisfactorily, Biff planned to move him into an apartment in Parnassus Heights next to the University Hospital. Biff had coordinated these plans with the Chief of Surgery, Doctor Engels, along with Dr. Robeson. It would be an intensive endeavor to help Roe recall his past professional knowledge and skills.

Before Biff departed the next day, he arranged for Roe and Murray to attend the dinner function at the mayor's home the coming weekend. It would do Roe a world of good to get out and socialize, though Biff still hesitated to bring up Ann. He didn't know what effect that emotional topic might have on his friend. He was confident that Murray go into that topic would look after his buddy. He was in good hands.

Biff dreaded returning to Saigon, but someone had to put out the fires back there.

CHAPTER TWENTY-NINE
INTEL MEETING VI

Hickam AFB, Hawaii March 1966

Captain Noreika sensed the intelligence officers present were not only frustrated, but dispirited. He knew the committee's sound intelligence estimates consistently found little receptivity with LBJ, McNamara, and their inner circle of advisors in Washington, D.C. With normal communication channels disrupted, the NSC and the JCS were essentially out of LBJ's loop of close advisors. DCI McCone of the CIA retired in frustration, fed up with Johnson's policies and vacillation. Indecision had become the LBJ administration's management hallmark. This CINCPAC committee had difficulty dealing with such a breach of the traditional chain of command.

Captain Noreika addressed this select group of intelligence experts solemnly.

"Let me relate some excerpts from the letter that the CIA's new DCI Raborn wrote to the president, plus some other excerpts from another letter by presidential advisor Clark Clifford. Both are real eye openers, gentlemen.

"Six months ago, Raborn predicted, based on the French experience in Vietnam, we could soon find ourselves pinned down, our options limited. Of course, this comes as old news to this committee."

The captain shared how Raborn went on to state that the U.S. was approaching the position where few choices of action are left. The U.S. either had to disengage, at a very high cost, or broaden the conflict in quantum leaps. CIA's new DCI warned the administration not to become preoccupied with military action and lose sight of the political aspects of the war, which would be won or lost at the hamlet level.

"Basically, the DCI agreed with General Eisenhower's tenant that the critical factor was the loyalty and morale of the South Vietnamese. He based his assessment on Saigon station intelligence reports, Biff's bailiwick. No surprise there, gentlemen, it appears someone in the admin finally got the message."

The captain cleared his throat and took a sip of water before continuing. He could see the intel officers were starting to accept that reality.

"Maxwell Taylor, as usual, edited the intelligence report, deleting the worst news. Taylor likes to dress things up for the administration, it appears to me. He wants to be 'on the team,' not rattle them with bad news, so he sugarcoats it. Fortunately, we have access to the omitted or redacted text through back-channel sources. In other words, between Saigon station and CIA headquarters in Langley. This information provides a more comprehensive picture of the current Vietnam situation. A glimpse of their inside thinking. The truth hurts. I guess Taylor didn't think DC could handle the reality of the inherent problems between the South Vietnam government and its populace.

"Word has it that LBJ was so concerned with the DCI's report that he sent it over to Clark Clifford to evaluate. Again, through back channels, we've obtained a copy of Clifford's assessment of DCI Raborn's letter to the president, as well as his advice to him. Thank God for CIA back channels, gentlemen."

The committee cheered this statement. They were men of action. Indecision constituted a fatal flaw in their code of conduct. Unfortunately, indecision was a hallmark of LBJ's administration, the polar opposite of them, and the practice became a huge, recurring source of frustration.

He took another sip of water. His mouth got dry when he was angry. This situation upset him. He had no tolerance for duplicity and vacillation.

"Clifford's major point and advice to the president was, to quote him verbatim – "Keep the number of ground troops to a minimum, consistent with the protection of our installations and property in that country."

"In a colorful description, which may become memorable, Clifford warned, 'This could become a quagmire!' That's an interesting way to put it, wouldn't you say?"

Noreika smiled and surveyed the room. The word "quagmire" got them thinking deeply about getting mired in a war that LBJ's administration failed to offer the necessary proper direction and dedication to win.

"Clifford counseled the president, 'It could turn into an open-end commitment on our part that would take more ground troops without a realistic hope of victory,' and recommended the president pursue and negotiate a settlement that the U.S. could 'learn to live with.'"

"Gentlemen, that was the status over six months ago. Clifford and Raborn definitely saw the handwriting on the wall. Their premonitions are coming true, and their observations proving valid. North Vietnam bombing campaigns have been ineffective. Our troop levels reached 200,000 by the end of 1965 and are predicted to double by the end of this year. What do we have to show for our commitment?"

He shook his head in disgust.

"On another sour note, DeGaulle recently visited Cambodia and called for the U.S. to withdraw from Vietnam. I won't comment further on the typical French arrogance he displayed."

That comment elicited a few groans and profanities.

"Let's address the concept that we are in a 'quagmire.' I'd like your opinion. Let's start with Miss Summerville for a political perspective. Following her comments, let's go around the table for updated assessments by the various services represented here today.

"But, before Ann presents her perspective, I'd like to thank her for her valuable service as a civilian consultant to this committee. Ann will soon return to the States to pursue her career at a conservative think tank, the Hoover Institution at Stanford. The impetus for the sudden move revolves around Ann's other plan, which includes spending most of her time attending to the recuperation of a close friend, a wounded Vietnam flight surgeon undergoing intensive treatment in San Francisco for PTSD. This flight surgeon was decorated with a Purple Heart and awarded a Silver Star for his valor and bravery at Tan Son Nhut Air Base during the November 1965 VC mortar attack. I commend her for her efforts and contributions to our committee. We all wish her well, and thank her for her valuable service."

The group stood and gave Ann a hearty round of applause. They all had come to appreciate her objective input and academic challenges to their ingrained group-think, even though they often disagreed with her. They truly appreciated her dedication to a Vietnam veteran, impressed at her decision to return to the States to help him recuperate.

Biff almost fell out of his chair at the news. He had been so busy, in and out of Saigon on covert missions in Laos, that he'd lost track of Ann and Roe's relationship since he last spoke with Ann two months ago when she told him she loved Roe. She told Biff their relationship had blossomed, but suddenly stalled without any communication from him. She had no knowledge of the TSN mortar event and Roe's serious injury and surgery. Biff had the unpleasant task of filling her in on his situation, but lost track thereafter.

Evidently, the bond was much closer than he'd realized, and they'd reconnected while he was in the Philippines.

Obviously, Roe "forgot" to tell Biff how far their relationship had progressed. Of course, Biff never brought up the topic at Baguio, either, since he was unsure about his buddy's reaction to it. It planned to let the PTSD consultant MD manage their love life under the complex circumstances.

Currently, Roe was undergoing intensive memory restoration with cognitive enhancement at the Langley Porter Institute in San Francisco after his Baguio rehabilitation went well.

Ann, in her characteristic confident manner, approached the lectern and laid out her index cards containing her talking points. Not one to mince words, she proceeded to present her overview of the current political situation for the last time.

"I'd like to express my appreciation to the committee for considering the opinions of an outsider, the Devil's Advocate. I sincerely hope my consultation has promoted objectivity to the recommendations we offer to the administration. It has been an honor to serve on this committee."

Another round of applause from the group followed, showing how much they respected her.

"Here is my present viewpoint regarding our status in Vietnam. It is my basic conviction that the LBJ administration is backed into a corner. It is becoming apparent that all major decisions regarding Vietnam are based on political expediency. The process is further encumbered by LBJ's typical indecisiveness looking for a nonexistent consensus. War is murky, requiring judicious consideration of various options. But, eventually a timely decision and a sound commitment to action are required.

"I maintain that the policy of contained war and graduated pressure and response has actually led to an inescapable escalation of the conflict, an outcome that the administration's policy hoped to avert.

"The tipping point came in March of 1965 when the U.S. committed combat troops at Danang, their mission not only to protect U.S. installations, but to actively pursue and destroy the enemy. McNamara's body counts then became the litmus test of success. Once this happened, it was too late to turn back. The enemy would determine the future level of American commitment to prevent the collapse of the South Vietnam's regime. Time is on their side and they plan to outlast us."

She expressed her feelings that- "LBJ does not know Vietnam's history and played right into their hands, backing himself into a reactionary position by engaging in policies with self-imposed restrictions, trying to have it both ways.

"There is an appalling lack of a comprehensive strategy to win this war. They just seem not get it. Intelligence estimates and recommendations from this committee, passed on to the JCS and NSC, have repeatedly gone unheeded by the administration. The historical chain of command ignored. Civil and political unrest continues to increase in the U.S. with the general public's dissatisfaction with the war. This is typified by peace marches, campus protests, and draft card burning. What's wrong with this picture? The American consciousness is waking up to the fact that LBJ has gone to great extents to delude congress, the media, and the general public."

Ann looked the committee members straight in the eyes. "Mark my words, American public opinion will be the first domino to fall. Not Vietnam!"

She's certainly not holding back.

Biff glanced over to Captain Noreika who winked at him and smiled. The crusty old submariner was enjoying Ann's tirade. "Right on," he whispered.

Ann was declaring loud and clear what military officers could not do publicly: express political opinion or openly criticize administration policy. Ann's dissertation became a wonderful catharsis for the committee.

"As I said in my first lecture, ideas have consequences, some unintended. In my opinion, the Vietnam conflict is a case study in unintended consequences.

"The president and defense Secretary McNamara seem preoccupied with operational problems instead of focusing on the comprehensive picture. Policy objectives are not clarified. They are ambiguous, irresolute, and generally indecisive. The administration seems determined to quell internal dissent, especially from the JCS. Their mantra is, 'Get on the team!' This demoralizes the military leadership.

"*Gloria Patri!* Will I be shot for insurrection for lacking proper reverence for their policies?" she asked in a mocking tone. "Not on the team. Why would I support such misguided management of the war? Basically, I'm expressing intellectual outrage at the generational theft of our young people to fight in a war without a sound, comprehensive strategy to win. The entire situation strikes me as absurd!"

Ann took a moment to inhale deeply. "The initial Vietnam policy objective under General Eisenhower and JFK aimed to maintain a free and independent South Vietnam. The objective was to thwart communism's progress, as espoused by the Domino Theory."

Audible sighs followed. She hit the nail on the head.

"Now it becomes evident that the objective has shifted to maintaining America's global credibility. It is no longer necessary to win the war. A stalemate forcing negotiations will suffice. In essence, they promote a war of attrition with the goal, not so much to win, but not to lose the war. It's as if a show of force is tantamount to a form of diplomatic communication. If this is not cognitive dissonance, then what is it?

"I'll tell you what it is... It's the antithesis to Kantian supreme principle of pure reason. It lacks the unitary principle of thought. I guarantee eventually the American public will not buy into it. It's a failed policy!

Americans will always fight to win, if the cause is just. They will not condone fighting just *not to lose*. That's a foreign concept to American psyche."

The officers clapped and cheered, "Right on!"

The chairman tapped his glass, restoring order.

"American policy goals must be defined with clarity. How does McNamara's quantitative analysis of military success or failure contribute to ending this conflict? Body counts ignore other principle factors. How do political considerations in Saigon and in the countryside factor into the equation? The resoluteness of the enemy? The dwindling support of the war in the States? This war will not be lost militarily, absolutely not. It will be lost at the hamlet level. It will be lost on college campuses, in the streets of America, on TV, and on the front pages of newspapers!"

This dramatic presentation brought the committee to its feet with applause. Captain Noreika even clapped, smiling at Biff who wore a fixed expression, a wide grin.

Ann laughed at this reception and paused for a moment. She assured them she was not a subversive, just a Libertarian with a strong moral compass and a passionate concern for America's welfare, democratic conventions and traditions. She politely thanked the committee for their indulgence and expressed her gratitude for allowing her to freely present her opinions, even if they appeared somewhat outrageous.

Captain Noreika again thanked Ann for her service and wished her well. He opened the floor for discussion.

Colonel David Turner presented an update, emphasizing the importance of the major victory in the Ia Drang valley. He assured the committee that American troops would prevail in future engagements because of superior firepower, discipline, and the developing tactic of helicopter assaults and deployment. The Army conceded that the political factors in Saigon and the countryside remained unpredictable, and represented a cause for concern because of a lack of defined strategy to win the hearts and minds of the peasants.

The Air Force again pushed for unlimited bombing to include Red River Valley dikes and dams in North Vietnam, flooding vast areas and destroying critical hydroelectric power sources. They also urged that major MiG airfields and industrial targets be included. The Air Force maintained that if petroleum, oil and lubricant targets in Hanoi and Haiphong were destroyed, DRV war efforts would be effectively hampered. They admitted that collateral damage could be extensive. They also acknowledged that troublesome problems could arise if our bombs hit Russian or Chinese ships in the North Vietnam harbors. It was rumored the Chinese always left a ship in the harbor.

The State Department representative and the Marines dissented, stating the VC would still fight on as an autonomous unit, despite an all-out assault into North Vietnam. That was the nature of the enemy.

Biff restated the CIA's assessment that the DRV strategy, in a nutshell, was to achieve victory through a combination of three factors: a collapse of the Saigon government, the continued deterioration of the ARVN morale and battle effectiveness; but most importantly because of the exhaustion of the U.S. political will to persist in Vietnam, to fight the good fight to the end.

Biff restated that the communists were convinced that their staying power was inherently superior. This Vietnamese strategy worked against the French and the Japanese. Naturally, the enemy anticipated achieving an identical outcome with the Americans. "Why should it be any different?"

"CIA intelligence estimates predict more logistic and equipment support from the USSR in the form of MiGs and SAMs in response to the U.S. expansion of North Vietnam bombardment. Not a positive development, gentlemen. Our CIA sources also tell us that the DRV doubts that the U.S. will invade North Vietnam with combat troops, and that is also factored into their strategy."

On the political front, Biff related that Buddhist riots spread recently from Saigon to Danang and Hue. The Saigon government responded by sending in troops to quell dissent, troops that should have been out fighting the VC, in his opinion.

"South Vietnam will not survive without massive American intervention, I am absolutely convinced."

Colonel Rodriguez objected. In his usual abrupt, hawkish manner, he commented that the CIA was too pessimistic. America's military would prevail if the politicians just got the hell out of the way.

Biff let it go and concluded his remarks with, "We can win it militarily, but lose it politically, as Ms. Summerville has stated on several occasions. We are going to miss her."

***

After the meeting, Biff and Ann huddled for a heart-to-heart discussion of Roe's misfortune and future plans.

"Roe is everything you said he was, and more, Biff. Before his injury, he'd been flying back to Hickam two or three times a month for short visits with me. Our relationship blossomed, and I fell in love with him. We were very close to marriage when he was injured, and I didn't hear from him for two months. Not until you informed me of his circumstances in January did I understand the reason for the lapse in our communication. I feel compelled to return to San Francisco to stand by him through his ordeal. You stood by him and organized his rehab in Baguio for two months. Now, it's my turn."

Biff admired her devotion. He gave Ann his card, and wrote a private contact number on the back. He requested that Ann keep him posted on Roe's progress, and assured her he'd keep in contact with Dr. Robeson at Langley Porter. He gave her a big hug and wished her well.

It was a sad long flight back to Saigon.

Biff reflected on the day's events. Ann had turned out to be a real trooper. The Vietnam War was a mess as the spring of 1966 approached, with no end in sight. It would surely get worse before it got better.

It would. Tet was on the horizon.

CHAPTER THIRTY
U.S. EMBASSY SAIGON, VIETNAM

April 1966

Biff found a note from the boss on his desk when he returned to the Saigon Embassy from the recent Hawaii Joint Intelligence conference. It read: *"Something important has come up. Need to run it by you, a bit of a sticky wicket.—Alex Chamberlain, Saigon Station Manager"*

Biff thought the boss's note was informal until he signed it with his full name and title.

"Wonder what's up?" It struck Biff as a bit unusual for the boss to call him in for a chat. Biff enjoyed free rein in Saigon to conduct the business Chamberlain found "messy."

Biff entered the boss' outer office. His Asian secretary stood up immediately.

"Oh, Mr. Roberts, Mr. Chamberlain was hoping you'd arrive soon. Come right in, he's expecting you," she said in her sing-song Vietnamese-American accent.

Biff entered the Spartan inner office. Alex was a minimalist, his environment furnished with the bare basics. An obligatory, signed photograph of LBJ hung behind his desk. A small American flag graced a desk with only a bulky manila folder, marked "Classified," lying on its surface. A small plaque in one corner read: *"Non illegitimus carborundum."* Latin translation: "Don't let the bastards wear you down."

That pretty much sums up his worldview in these circumstances, Biff mused. *Man's got a tough job.*

"What's up, boss? You look concerned."

Actually he looked tired and stressed. The old man reminded him of Ichabod Crane, a lean and lanky schoolmaster, but he was not superstitious. He was a policy wonk with fastidious attention to details and an obsession with security matters.

"So glad you're back, Biff. I've got a problem to run by you. It must be handled delicately. I fear a log of ramifications, all of which are negative, if we botch it."

"How can I help?"

"Look, I know we've never openly discussed it, but I know you are SADs staff leader. I'm the only one in the Embassy who knows. That's why you have two bodyguards following you around after two assassination attempts on your life. The Democratic Republic of Vietnam has a network of agents in Saigon and you're a target. Also, we have some political enemies in the South Vietnamese government. For all I know, they may also have a contract out on you."

"I understand, sir." He was unsure where this conversation was going.

"But, that's not why I called you in today. I've always conferred a high degree of autonomy to you, and you've never let me or the company down."

Biff was starting to wonder if the boss was ever going to come to the point. He replied, "Thank you sir, I appreciate your expression of confidence."

"Okay, here's the story. We've got a serious opium-heroin problem brewing."

"I've noted that our military troops are frequenting opium dens in Cholon on R&R, and marijuana usage is becoming commonplace in the bars," Biff responded.

"It goes beyond that, Biff. Well beyond that. Drug cultivation and traffic thrives on poor governance, instability, and corruption. Laos and Vietnam have all three factors in common, in spades. It's becoming a breeding ground with ominous overtones."

"It could get out of hand with serious consequences, I understand, sir." His interest rose.

"Let me give you a brief historical overview, Biff, some relevant background. Then I'll come to the clandestine mission I'd like you to accept.

It'll take a few minutes of your time, so please make yourself comfortable. Coffee?"

He poured a cup for himself.

"Sure, thanks."

Biff wondered how it would be possible to get comfortable. The office only had straight back wooden chairs with no cushions. His boss wasn't into sofas, soft leather chairs, or any hint of comfort. He'd seen more comfort in an interrogation room.

Alex launched into a detailed historical synopsis of drug trafficking in Southeast Asia, as only a career NSA academic could, or would. The man knew his facts and rattled off a précis in an animated fashion. As an introvert, the boss rarely presented this spirited side, so it surprised Biff. He listened, while still attempting to get comfortable, squeezing his large frame into the chair's small fixed space.

His boss proceeded to explain that before the French arrived in Indochina in the late 1850s, only the Chinese locals smoked opium in small amounts and no problems existed. In other words, there was not a large demand. Most of the opium came from Laos and the Hmong tribal area of the central highlands along the Vietnamese border. Alex explained how the French changed that happy circumstance.

"The French Colonial period in Indochina was associated with enormous costs, as you might imagine. Huge budget deficits saddled the French in Tonkin, Annam, and Cochin China, the three provinces at that time. The financial problems were solved by a bit of irony."

He paused to see if he had Biff's attention. He did. Biff sat perched on the chair's edge, leaning forward since he couldn't fit in the chair.

"Paul Doumer, the French Minister of Finance, was exiled from Paris to Indochina as punishment after he attempted to impose income taxes on the French populace. He arrived around 1897 and set about promptly to exploit Indochina. An enterprising fellow, Doumer single-handedly turned Indochina's financial loss into a profitable French enterprise."

"How'd he accomplish that?" Biff tried to show interest, but wished Alex would explain why he called him in for a chat, and what his task would be?

"First, he centralized authority in Saigon and increased revenues for France's benefit. He accomplished this financial windfall by funneling taxes and custom duties into the central treasury." He took a sip of coffee, cold by now, and wiped his bifocals although he was not referring to notes.

"But, most of the financial assets were derived by monopolies Doumer created involving alcohol, salt, and opium. But, that didn't satisfy the man. An entrepreneur at heart, Doumer built an opium refinery in Saigon. The blend was produced for smoking, and burned quickly. Local consumption boomed, increased to the point that it soon accounted for *one-third* of the French Colonial income in Vietnam. Can you believe that, Biff?"

Biff nodded, but wondered what he would ever do with that interesting tidbit of information.

"Doumer didn't stop there. Under his guidance Vietnam became the world's third largest rice exporter after Burma and Thailand. An innovative Frenchman."

"Sure sounds like he turned things around financially, Alex. Quite an enterprising businessman. Odd that I've never heard of him."

"The Vietnamese will never forget him. Doumer definitely was a rainmaker. This background is essential and relevant to understand in the context of our current problem, your task. I'll get to that in a moment, as soon as I lay out everything for you."

"Okay, Alex."

"Drugs, namely opium, became more than just a lucrative enterprise to the French. The French used opium traffic to finance their military operations in Vietnam and Laos. They entered into multiple pro quid quo arrangements. They bought off Hmong and Meo tribes to assist their military endeavors. In turn, the French allowed these tribes to traffic and personally profit from their poppy fields' production. This mutually beneficial arrangement allowed the French to use opium profits to underwrite their military operations against the Communists.

"Finally, the French transgressed by backing the drug smuggling group, Binh Xuyen in an unsuccessful coup against Ngo Dinh Diem soon after the 1954 Geneva accord put him into office. That became his undoing. Bet you didn't know that?"

The boss glanced over at Biff who looked a little disinterested. "Don't get bored, Biff. There's more to come."

Biff replied coyly, "I find this history very interesting, boss. Please continue."

He never realized his boss was such a history buff.

"Okay. Now, let's go into the CIA's historical association with narcotic drug traffic in Southeast Asia, where we come into this picture. During the twenty years or so of the Cold War, the CIA paramilitary used Asian drug lords, dealers, and even gangsters as assets to fight Communism with a moderate amount of success. It is old classified information, but you must know that the CIA forged covert action alliances with key Asian opium traffickers, like the French did. The reason was that the CIA found ethnic war lords to be one of our most reliable and effective covert action assets."

"I've heard that, but not the details," Biff replied politely.

"The downside of this convenient *pro quid quo* arrangement has been a steady expansion of opium production in the Golden Triangle of Burma, Cambodia, Northern Thailand, and Laos to meet the increased demands for narcotics."

"Nothing like a capitalistic motive to drive production and sales, a basic supply-and-demand concept," Biff commented.

"Correct, here's how it all came down. The CIA tolerated this illicit drug traffic, even kept the lid on Congressional investigations, because we find that ruthless drug lords and ambitious tribal leaders of the Meo and Hmong are the most effective anti-Communists we could ever hope for to fight for our cause. Cost effective, in other words, Biff. We sort of look the other way, as long as they get our job done over there. It's simply a pragmatic solution to our sensitive problem in Southeast Asia. Success in covert, delicate operations is the bottom line in our line of work. The end justifies the means, however unsavory that may be. We get the job done, they profit."

"I'm following your line of reasoning, Alex."

"Listen, Biff, the numbers are mindboggling. It is estimated that the Golden Triangle has produced over 30,000 tons of opium a year since 1950. This large production is the result of two factors: prohibition and protection. Let me explain."

Biff readjusted his seat again. "Never realized you were so well informed on narcotrafficking."

Alex ignored the comment and pressed on with his comprehensive dissertation.

"Early in the fifties, the United Nation's pressure on Southeast Asia governments led to abolishing legal opium sales. These sales were a significant source of tax revenues. Legal opium dens were closed in the decade from 1950 to 1960. Due to prohibition, low cost, plentiful opium became unavailable despite the huge supply. Consequently, illicit trade arose to meet the demands of Southeast Asia. With prohibition, opium production increased in the Golden Triangle, much of it by the mountain tribes I've mentioned who operated in remote places difficult to control or monitor."

"I see."

"The second factor affecting opium production was governmental protection of narcotraffic by three intelligence agencies: Thai, U.S., and Nationalist Chinese. Again, Biff, a bit more of our history. Are you still with me?"

Biff still wondered where all this was going. "Yes sir. I'm following you closely with interest."

This was the most detailed conversation he'd ever had with his boss, especially involving uncharacteristic vigor. Obviously, he was turned on by the intrigue of why three different national intel agencies would protect narcotrafficking?

"During the early fifties, the CIA conducted covert operations in northern Burma near the Chinese border, the Shan Plateau, to be specific, in support of Nationalist Chinese. This action linked the poppy fields there with urban markets, another clever financial arrangement. I won't go into the details, but you can surmise the rest of the story. Following the Nationalist Chinese defeat in 1949, Nationalist Chinese forces fled into northern Burma where the CIA equipped them for several unsuccessful invasions of China in the early fifties. This was Truman's Burma equivalent of the Bay of Pigs, but less publicized."

"After being repulsed by the Communist Chinese Army, the Chinese Nationalists took up camp for another decade in Burma, hoping to launch another invasion of China. It never happened. Instead, they financed their operations and basic existence by trading opium on the Shan Plateau."

"Really?" Biff interjected to appear interested, but suffering from information overload at this point.

"During that decade, opium production doubled until the Burmese Army evicted the Nationalist Chinese in 1961. They migrated and took up camp across the border in northern Thailand. It was there that they started refining opium into a potent heroin. This began the era of the Golden Triangle's Burma Gold."

"Burma Gold?"

"The most potent narcotic ever manufactured," Alex declared.

"Now more to the point, the CIA picked up where the French left off, but was complicit in the drug trade only for political and military purposes. The company was not interested in profits, only in expediency. The CIA integrated the services of the Hmong and Meo tribes, funding covert paramilitary operations from opium sales. Just like the French did historically, they actually took a page out of Doumer's playbook."

Alex wiped his glasses again. Biff wondered if it was a penchant.

"In the early sixties, our CIA paramilitary in Laos had a secret army of 30,000 tribal highlanders, fierce fighters acquainted with the mountains, rain forests, and dense jungles. Biff, I emphasize... although the agency did not profit directly from the drug trade, we profited immensely from their military service fighting the Communist Pathet Lao and the NVA forces in northern Laos. Their covert actions in combat effectively held off Communist forces for a decade. Otherwise, Laos would have fallen into Communist hands. Our paramilitary and special forces could not have possibly accomplished this mission without their help. This is a critical piece of CIA history you never hear about."

"That's why Langley calls it The Secret War," Biff commented.

"Correct. Another positive aspect of our involvement with these tribes is that they assist us in rescuing downed pilots, interdict the Ho Chi Minh trail with ambushes, and protect radar installations that guide our fighter bombers out of Danang and our three airfields in northern Thailand. All invaluable services.

"Presently, we maintain one or two CIA paramilitary field officers to every one thousand or so tribal mercenaries. We also have experienced Special Forces in the field with them. Very frankly, Biff, we could not conduct this clandestine war without them. They are an extremely valuable resource for us. I might even say indispensable."

Biff sensed the boss might soon wind this up and explain his task.

"Now, let's get down to the nitty gritty. As a tradeoff in our priorities, we sort of look the other way while the tribes transport opium and heroin smuggled on our Air America and CAT flights. Our pilots are only indirectly complicit by flying the aircraft, you understand, the usual plausible deniability. We look the other way because their contribution to our basic mission far outweighs any considerations of illicit drug trafficking. Got it?"

"Got it, boss."

"Now, here are my three major concerns: First, we may get investigated over drug rumors, so I'd like you to go over to Laos and make certain our CIA operations are secure, secret, and not involved in any direct financial profiting from the drug traffic. Confirm nobody is personally siphoning off funds used to support the tribes.

"Second, I'm concerned regarding the increased use of illicit drugs by our troops on Saigon R&R. They are starting to frequent opium dens, instead of bars. It has the potential to affect negatively on military discipline and effectiveness. Conduct a comprehensive surveillance to monitor the situation."

"I understand the threat, the downside. I'll take care of it."

"Here are some facts you may or may not know. Marijuana use among the troops is increasing because of its general availability and low cost, but so far it has not presented a big problem. But, if our troops go for bigger highs with opium or heroin, they'll get hooked and we'll have major problems on our hands. There is every indication that drug abuse is trending in that direction. Some troops are experimenting with crude 'Number 3 granular heroin' in cigarettes. Not an auspicious prospect."

"Nor a good idea."

"Now, here's my third concern, Biff. It's my major worry. I suspect we may have a rogue operative in Laos who is deeply involved in drug traffic for personal gain. Recently, several well-documented incidents have been brought to my attention. They all implicate Sammy Wong, a CIA field officer trained in paramilitary tactics. He's been in Laos almost ten years. He is said to have established close relations with both the Meo and Hmong tribal leaders. Sammy lives with a Hmong woman who has supposedly borne him two children. She is a guerilla and, supposedly, a crack shot with an M-16 rifle. She and several other women travel camp to camp with the men in company strength to cook for them. They're always on the move. This particular company of mercenaries has built an excellent record of enemy kills. Unrivaled, you might say. This has granted them a great deal of autonomy. These two tribes are also implicated as kingpins in the narcotic trade to Saigon. All our leads trace back to Sammy Wong, identifying him as the majordomo providing a big-time supply line to Cholon opium dens from Laos."

"A rogue agent in the CIA ranks. Wow!"

"Yep, appears that is the case. As a counterinsurgency force, Sammy's company is on par with the very best VC companies. They are masters at hit-and-run ambushes, just like the Viet Cong. They live off the land and sleep in the jungles and rain forests. We hear from them only when they require munitions and more assault rifles, which we drop by helicopters in designated LZs. Otherwise, they are a self-sufficient unit willing to endure hardships and take out the enemy on a regular basis."

Biff started to say something, but his boss interrupted with a serious expression and tone.

"The bottom line, Biff, they are selling ten times the amounts of narcotics required to support their company, and buy off tribal leaders. We need to follow the money trail. Sammy Wong is elusive and probably indistinguishable from the Hmongs after living with them for so long. It won't be an easy task."

"Okay, what do you what me to do?"

"Take one of our planes over to Vientiane and check out the situation in Laos. I assume you have staff contacts there. Also, go with your pilot bodyguards. The Communists have agents and assets everywhere in Southeast Asia. You'll travel under diplomatic cover, of course, to visit

Ambassador Brown. I have all your documents prepared and channels cleared for your arrival tomorrow. Any questions, young man?"

"I know Ambassador Brown. He was just ahead of me at Yale. Also, Toby Collins is a U.S. Embassy attaché in Vientiane, and a good friend of mine from Yale. We both trained at the Farm, Camp Perry, Virginia. Are you aware he is a special activities staff member?"

"Yes. I've read his dossier. In that respect, you are two peas in a pod, Biff."

"If Toby can't find Sammy Wong, then Sammy's gone deep dark. Sammy was just leaving the Farm as an instructor in jungle survival when Toby and I arrived. He's a Chinese American, UCLA graduate in linguistics. He's fluent in Japanese, Thai, French, Vietnamese, and two dialects of Chinese. I'm sure he's now proficient in Laotian and tribal dialects after all those years in the boondocks with the tribes. He's got a great aptitude for languages. But, he's the last guy that I would suspect to be involved in drug trafficking for personal profit, Alex. That's a bit off the wall for him, but we'll check it out, okay? A CIA rogue is unheard of as far as I know."

"It's rare. All I ask, Biff, is just check it out with Toby."

"I have a sneaking suspicion I'll have a lot of luck. Toby knows the territory. I'll get him all over it. I better go pack my B-4 bag."

"It's all taken care of, new clothes and dopp kit on the jet in case you didn't get back from Hawaii to have time to pack. Wheels in the well 1000 tomorrow at Tan Son Nhut. Our Embassy driver will pick you up at 0845 at your place. Your pilots will be waiting."

Biff, glancing at his watch, it was 1500 hours. He thought about Cát, dinner, and spending the night with her. "Would you mind having the driver pick me up at Cát LePierre's place, boss?"

Alex flashed a rare smile. "You're one hell of a spy for a young fellow, Biff, a virtual James Bond. Absolutely, I'll relay the instructions to pick you up at Cát's tomorrow morning. In fact, she bought the new clothes and dopp kit, knowing your size and tastes. I trust she packed your new B-4 bag also ... I only paid for it."

"Thank you, sir." He managed to stand up straight, his back stiff from the uncomfortable chair. *The old man doesn't miss much.*

The case officer loved case management. The Saigon station manager had actionable intelligence for this exceptional field officer and tasked his deputy to track down a suspected rogue agent in the jungles of Laos. He chuckled to himself. *Might be like finding a needle in a hay stack.* "Good luck, Biff."

CHAPTER THIRTY-ONE

Vientiane, Laos April 1966

The CIA T-39 jet touched down softly on the Vientiane runway after an uneventful one-hour flight from Saigon. A Peugeot limo with a U.S. Embassy flag flying from the front bumper drove out to the flight line to greet them. Two Marine guards jumped out, armed with M-16s. They assisted Ambassador Brown and attaché Toby Collins out of the back seat.

Biff thought Toby had not changed a bit in appearance, but Ambassador Brown looked tired and worn out from his stressful job in Laos. Biff and his two bodyguards descended the plane's ramp, shook hands, and exchanged pleasantries. Biff scanned his surroundings, trying to match the dramatic descriptions of Laos in his briefing documents with his first impressions upon arrival.

It was a cloudy, muggy day in the "City of Sandalwood," Vientiane. Biff saw no sandalwood trees, just palms. Perhaps sandalwoods were plentiful in the countryside. Laos was once referred to as "The Kingdom of a Million Elephants," another interesting item Biff had read during the short flight, but he really didn't expect to see any elephants either.

So much hype in government docs these days, he reflected. *Who writes those verbose briefings anyways?*

The historical tidbits in his briefing papers failed to build up his expectations. He thought it might be helpful information if he was leading a tour, but he didn't know why someone included the information in his CIA briefing dealing essentially with clandestine matters in Laos.

Ah, you gotta love bureaucracy, Biff sighed. *People must justify their jobs somehow.*

They entered the limo, chatting and catching up on events and mutual friends. All talk avoided politics. The Lao driver turned up the A/C, exited the airport, and headed north up the main boulevard of the capital. As they approached city center, Biff noticed a Laotian version of the Arc de Triumphe.

"What's that?"

"It's called the Patuxay. It was built six years ago in 1960 to celebrate the struggle for independence in Laos."

"That's certainly an impressive structure with its pagoda tops and surrounding palm trees."

"I'll give you a brief history lesson at the Embassy," Toby offered.

Oh no, not another history lesson, Biff thought.

Biff noticed the streets were relatively empty of traffic and people, compared to the congestion of Saigon ... and a lot cleaner. In fact, there was no evidence here of the ongoing war up north in the Plain of Jars, a stark contrast to Saigon where military vehicles served as a constant reminder of the conflict.

Biff's initial impression included noting a certain calmness pervading Vientiane despite all the political maneuvering in Laos between the Loyalists, Neutralists, and Communist factions.

A short time later, the limo pulled up to the U.S. Embassy gate. Salutes were exchanged as the limo entered the well-fortressed Embassy compound. Ambassador Brown requested they join him for dinner. He asked them to excuse him for the daytime consultation, explaining,

"I have a lot of diplomatic affairs to attend to and telephone calls to make, gentlemen. I look forward to dining with you this evening."

Once inside the embassy, Biff and Toby adjourned to a secure area of the Embassy used by the CIA as a SCIF. Toby had all the modern electronic communication equipment uplinked to satellites. He had a modest staff, and an NSA cipher colleague, Angela Montero. Angela could have been a model. Biff wondered if Toby was having an affair with her. He wouldn't ask, too much of a dirty-old-man thought, even though Toby was known as quite a lady's man in New Haven.

"Drink, Biff?"

"Tom Collins, add a lime please. I usually drink gin and tonic, but when I'm with the Collins, I usually drink Collins." He laughed at his own lame joke.

Toby laughed too, "*I sure have missed Biff's grin. Not too many people smile and laugh around this Embassy. Not much joviality.*

"You haven't changed a bit since Yale, Biff. How's life treating you?"

"Busy. Tail's wagging the dog, Toby. I've got a lot of balls in the air. Now the boss has given me another job. I'm hoping you can help me out. I'm a little shaky on the Laos situation. We've got a serious problem brewing over here."

Biff uses a lot of similes and idioms, Toby thought. *Not the King's English.*

"Let me give you a brief background before you lay a task on me, okay, Biff?"

"Sure. Carry on. Bring me up to date." He settled into a soft, comfortable sofa, put his feet up on the coffee table, and scanned the room. Toby knew how to furnish an office. In contrast to his boss' Spartan quarters, Toby's plush furnishings, attractive Asian artwork, and a small library would make a Yale professor envious. Family photos were scattered on shelves and adorned his desk and coffee tables, creating a warm, pleasant atmosphere.

He realized his associate politely awaited his attention. "The Tom Collins hits the spot, Toby. Please go on with your briefing. I was just admiring your office, very tastefully decorated."

"Thank you. It's my home away from home. Keeps me grounded. Stay with my briefing, this country's history is a bit complicated because of multiple factors, but here is the Laos situation in a nutshell, some background to current events." Toby launched into a 101 primer course.

"The Laos Kingdom dates back to the 14th Century. But, from our standpoint, not much of consequence happened until the 19th Century when it became a French Protectorate or colony like much of Indochina. So, let's start there, okay?"

"Shoot, Toby."

"The French maintained de facto control of Laos from that early period until 1954, except for a short period of Japanese occupation during World War II.

"In 1954, Laos became a constitutional monarchy with full independence under the Geneva Accord. The French military training mission, however, continued to support the Royal Laos Army under a special exemption to the Geneva Convention. This French influence lasted until 1955, when the U.S. Department of Defense replaced the French. Recall the French were forced out of Vietnam about the same time. Guess it was an off decade for them."

Biff laughed at Toby's description. He'd somehow maintained his sense of humor in this remote posting.

"Under the U.S. policy to contain Communism, we picked up the slack when the French left Indochina. We trained and equipped the Royal Laotian Army to continue the fight with the Communist Pathet Lao. Basically, a civil war, most of the battles took place up north, not here. The North Vietnam Army, the NVA, backed the Pathet Lao insurgency with tanks and heavy artillery, as you recall from our early CIA involvement back then. And, of course, there were a series of coup d`etats during this period. Coups seem to be a big thing in Indochina."

"Big thing in Vietnam, for sure," Biff interjected.

"So, I've read in our CIA communications. It seems Saigon is on its third or fourth government by now."

"Fourth," Biff clarified. "It's their major form of conflict resolution."

"Bear with me while I wrap up this rundown up, okay? It gets a bit complicated, like that 'who's on first?' routine. You recall that old Abbott and Costello skit?"

"It's a classic!" Biff laughed.

"The major players break down into five groups: Laotian Rightists, Neutralists, and Royalists versus the Communist Pathet Lao and the North Vietnamese. Basically, a three-on-two confrontation."

"Over the years, the Vientiane government power structure has shifted between the Rightists and the Neutralists. Eisenhower backed the Rightist government of General Phoum Nosovan as his choice to fight international Communism. It's important to note that the Neutralists' leader, Souvanna Phuma, also received American support. But, at times, Phuma was suspected of collaborating with his half-brother, Prince Souphanouvong, who was Pathet Lao's titular leader, on the enemy's side. Not a good move. How complicated is that?"

"Very. Hedging his bets, I suppose."

"Exactly. Meanwhile, the North Vietnamese were calling most of the shots in the civil war up in northern Laos, conducted mostly in the Plain of Jars, and along the northern border of Vietnam. The Chinese also lent support to the Communist forces for political reasons, I might add."

Toby paused to see if he had lost Biff.

"I'm still with you, pal. Carry on." He hid his frustration well. He'd already been briefed and had studied this history. But, he remained polite, careful not to offend Toby.

"Bear with me. Those names are tough and the historical interaction a bit complicated. A major coup occurred in August 1960, led by a paratrooper officer, Kong Le. Following the coup, the Rightist government was replaced by Souvanna, a supposed Neutralist. But, on occasion, he was a Communist sympathizer if it suited his purpose ... a classic flip flopper. But, Souvanna could not defeat the Rightists' Royal Army, essentially checkmated."

"At this time of confusion, the North Vietnamese seized the opportunity to move the Ho Chi Minh Trail west into Laos for increased security reasons, away from American surveillance in Vietnam. The North Vietnamese committed a large number of combat troops in 1960 and 1961 to accomplish this purpose."

"In response, the U.S. then increased our commitment in Laos with additional Special Forces and CIA paramilitary personnel to monitor hostile activity. The U.S. enlisted and trained the fiercely independent, indigenous tribes of Meo and Hmong as a mercenary counter-insurgency force in northern Laos. A brilliant move, this amounted to over 30,000 troops. They were much like the Viet Cong in their guerilla lifestyle and tactics. Counterparts, you might say, but on our side."

Biff took a sip of his drink. "I recall that bit of history caused quite a stir in the company at the time, but worked out fine. We have a similar arrangement in the South Vietnam highlands with the Montagnards. Our Green Berets have nickname for the tribe, 'Yards.' They form a formable fighting force with the 'snake eaters,' believe me."

"Good analogy. Okay, just a couple of more points."

Biff grappled to keep all this information straight. He was on overload. Those Lao names threw him, how relevant was all this information to his mission? And, he thought South Vietnam was a mess! He turned his attention back to his associate.

"Meanwhile General Phoumi retook Vientiane. The Laos government returned to the Rightists, this time backed by the king. Nevertheless, the civil war goes on and on, without an end in sight. That's the complex political and military background as I see it today. Maybe that will help you understand what we are dealing with over here."

"Thanks, Crystal clear, Toby. Got it." He couldn't prevent the sardonic tone.

Toby let it go, inclined his head and furrowed his brow.

He recognized Biff's perplexed, frustrated reaction to so much complex history that had little to do with his task. So, he moved on to the main topic.

"Biff, your coded telex did not give me any details, but I understand your trip entails the evaluation of the illicit drug traffic in Laos."

"That's the primary purpose. Tell me what you know about that, and I'll tell you why I need your help. Your background information frames the Laos picture for me. Complex, but quite helpful." He tried to be tactful.

"Okay, here's the scoop on the drug scene. Our primary mission in Laos is to avert Communist takeover, just like Vietnam. So far, so good, for ten years we've held them at bay in the north. A good part of our currency with our tribal leaders and mercenary forces involves allowing them to grow opium, and traffic it. Essentially, we are doing what the French did, but only as a matter of practical expediency, rather than a profit motive. This is the key difference between the U.S. and the French intentions and practice."

"Alex briefed me regarding that feature." *Cut it short, man.*

"Then you know the French used drug profits to fund a significant proportion of their military operations in Vietnam, particularly through

1950 to 1954, until they were defeated at Diem Bien Phu. The French cleverly linked Laos poppy fields with Saigon's opium dens, a profitable undertaking."

"So Alex told me." Biff hoped to politely shorten the briefing and get on to other matters of importance. However, Toby was not deterred.

"After the French defeat in 1954, the CIA inherited all of these covert alliances in the opium trade, whether they wanted them or not. To my knowledge, the agency has never directly profited financially in narcotraffic. But, in all honesty, I'm the first to admit that opium profits have gone a long way to finance a tribal army of 30,000 mercenaries for over ten years in Laos without congressional oversight or military bureaucracy."

"Alex made the same point." *C'mon, Toby.*

"He understands the situation. There's no question in my mind or anyone else's here at the Embassy that these mercenaries are an indispensable fighting force. In fact, they hate the Communists. Let's face it, our CIA doctrine of covert action has married us to these tribal war lords. They are definitely a critical asset in this war against Communism. Without them, we lose Laos."

"I've heard that from other reliable sources, Toby." He hoped his growing impatience would not show.

"It's as simple as that, Biff. We rely on them. They grow poppy and sell opium, and fight like Banshees. That works for us. We just look the other way and move on while they support and accomplish our mission."

"Understand."

"Let me give you a cogent example. It would take a full U.S. battalion somewhere between 1000 and 1,500 men, to protect our radar installations in this country. Presently, this is accomplished very efficiently and effectively by several companies of Hmongs—between three or four hundred men, maximum. This all happens seamlessly at no financial cost to us. The drug traffic covers that. We made a pragmatic decision to go with that plan of action and it is working very well, so we don't intend to fix it based on some idealistic principle."

"Got it. Cost effective decision."

"Not only that, let me tell you, these tribal fighters are unrelenting. They perform hit-and-run ambushes on the Ho Chi Minh Trail. They rescue our downed pilots in the mountains and jungles. The CIA has an enormous asset we'd lose if we pontificate over what are decades-old established drug-trade practices. We have more-or-less chosen to tolerate their drug trafficking activities after a basic cost-benefit analysis.

"For example, we know that General Vang Pao, the Hmong Commander, transports opium and rice on Air America flights in Northern Laos. But, our pilots are not directly involved. It's handled discretely. It's a win-win situation. The tribes profit, we profit in a different fashion, quid pro quo. Laos is in the northeastern tip of the Golden Triangle. I wouldn't be surprised if they soon refine opium into heroin up there, just as they do in Bangkok labs."

Biff interjected, "They're already refining heroin, Toby."

"You're always one up on me, Biff. I better check out my assets." Toby smiled ruefully.

"The war is our overriding priority in Southeast Asia, Biff. That's the bottom line. All other issues take second place. I certainly would not deny it, it is reality. I don't think we can get too judgmental at this point in time and lose sight of our priority."

"I understand your line of reasoning."

"Smoking opium in Indochina has a long history. When the French ruled Laos it was a state monopoly designed to generate tax revenues. Now, the proceeds help fund our covert war efforts over here. It's a pragmatic solution to a complex problem. It's working, so we don't want to mess with it. Got it? We continue to focus on the big picture, defeating Communism."

"That's a good run down, Toby. You certainly have a firm grasp of the Laos situation." Toby had echoed his boss's concerns, and perspective. "But, here's our concern in Saigon. Troops on R&R are smoking pot in the Cholon bars and starting to experiment with opium in the dens. These troops are looking for bigger escapes from war's reality. Our fear is that the importation and widespread use of highly addictive heroin would be a military disaster. There is already a small outbreak of crude 'number 3 heroin' with addicts in Bangkok and Hong Kong. We don't need to add this problem in Saigon. We've got enough troubles."

Biff placed his empty tumbler on the end table and leaned forward to confide. "Just recently, a high-grade, potent number 4 heroin showed up in Cholon, exported from the Golden Triangle. It's a pure powder called 'Burma Gold.' It can be smoked in an ordinary cigarette without any trace odor—unlike marijuana with its distinctive smell. This heroin is highly addictive. But, it's also so potent that overdoses are not all that uncommon. The ramifications are frightening. If our G.I.s start buying these small plastic vials of ninety-seven percent pure heroin for only two or three dollars a vial, we'll soon have a stoned army addicted to heroin."

"Certainly a danger if it gets out of hand. They'll be unfit to fight."

"Precisely my point." On another matter, our intelligence assets indicate that General Ouan Ratikow is running a heroin lab right here in Laos. Do you know him?"

Toby's jaw dropped. "Yes. He's Chief of Staff of the Royal Lao Army. If that's true, that's an incredibly high level of corruption."

"Let me tell you, right under your nose, the general is producing a W-O Globe brand of Burma Gold. Our assets estimate his lab processes 100 kilograms of opium a day into heroin. The general is running a big-time operation, not a mom and pop shop."

"How'd we miss that?"

"Obviously, you were out of the loop about the local problem, not knowing the players and the extent of their enterprise. We tracked the source to your backyard from ours in Saigon. If Burma Gold spreads to the troops in Vietnam, it's just a matter of time before it becomes an enormous problem in the States. So, we've got to develop a strategy to avoid massive exportation out of here and other portals in the Golden Triangle. If we don't, it will come back to bite us in the ass."

"I grasp the big picture. I'm not trying to justify our actions or exercise a moral judgment. I'm just saying it's purely a matter of expediency for us when dealing with the tribes. As I said earlier, it's a pragmatic solution to our mission, so I'm not sure how to handle that source.

Regarding the general…" He paused and rubbed and hand across his forehead. Biff, we're good friends, going all the way back to Yale and our CIA training days on the Farm. I'll take your advice and try to nip that heroin exportation problem in the bud, okay? We'll get all over it. I'll assign a team to the project, knock him off if necessary. It's going to be a delicate situation for us to handle with care. It could blow up in our faces."

Biff inclined his head in agreement and leaned back on the sofa. "Okay. So, we're now on the same page regarding the big picture. That's a significant reason for my visit, but the main purpose in coming here is to enlist your aid in another problem. My boss refers to it as a 'sticky wicket.' Alex thinks there's an insider over here in Laos facilitating narcotraffic, a rogue field officer."

"Good Lord. What's that all about?"

"Remember Sammy Wong?"

"Yes. Asian-American, quiet, UCLA grad, gifted linguistic major. As I recall a very efficient operative, ten years our senior. Wong trained us at the Farm for a while. He left six months after we came into the program. Over here in Laos, he's been an outstanding field officer, been in the jungles eight, nine, maybe ten years, living with the Hmong tribes. Our other field operatives tell me he's as good as it gets. They say you can't tell him from the Hmongs. Sammy eats, sleeps, and fights with them, even has started to look like them. I have his file here in the office. He's established a distinguished record, if you want to look at it."

"Thanks, Toby, but I've already read it. I agree he's done a remarkable job in his covert capacity during the last nine years. By the way, when did you last hear or have any contact with Sammy?"

"Let me think. It's probably been well over a year or so, maybe two. Why?"

"My station manager, Alex Chamberlain, thinks Sammy's the rogue officer who's gone deep dark and is involved in major narcotrafficking from Laos to Saigon. He asked me to enlist your aid in exposing him, trapping him, or whatever it takes to bring him down. Right now, Sammy is a top priority with the boss. How should we proceed with this?"

The Embassy attache exhaled a long breath. "If this information is correct, I'll tell you, it isn't going to be easy. We're halfway around the world in a war-torn country, full of a myriad of combatants who speak vastly different languages and dialects. The tribes trust no one, and rarely stay in one place for very long. If Sammy has gone deep dark… with his range of nomadic and survivalist skills, we may never find him. Sammy Wong has six passports and aliases if he chooses to flee. He's fluent in at least eight languages and dialects. He's developed an ability to blend into any environment in Southeast Asia. Sammy's a virtual chameleon. No one in our entire field office in Southeast Asia has adapted to the boondocks the way he has. As I mentioned, the word is you cannot distinguish him from the Hmongs. My best guess is he'll remain in the wild with them and his family."

"I know it's not going to be an easy job. Just give it your best shot and keep me posted. Look, I've got to get back to Saigon. I have a lot of things going on, and I've got to get the ball rolling. Tell Ambassador Brown I'm sorry, but I've got to get back to the Embassy in Saigon. We'll have dinner another time, perhaps."

***

The Embassy limo dropped off Biff and his two pilot bodyguards at the Vientiane Airport secure parking area for small planes. As any experienced flyer does, the CIA pilot did a thorough walk-around inspection of his aircraft before taking off.

This routine paid off in big dividends in this instance.

He shouted, "Hey, Biff, come look at this!"

Biff went over to the spot where the pilot was looking up into the nose wheel well of their T-39. He peered in with the pilot at some white clay material with wires attached to what looked like a detonator charge.

"Holy shit!" Biff exclaimed. "Looks like C-4!"

The amazed pilot nodded agreement.

Biff returned to the hangar to contact the Embassy on a secure line. It connected immediately to Toby Collins.

"Toby, got a big problem over here at the airport. Someone has rigged up a bomb in our wheel well. We need a demolition man over here right away. He better be experienced, it looks like C-4."

"I've got just the guy for the job, Jesus Mendez, a former Special Forces Sergeant. He's our Embassy expert. We'll be right there, Biff."

Twenty minutes later, Toby, Jesus and two armed Marine guards showed up in an old Army jeep. They parked on the tarmac next to the plane.

Jesus jumped out and went right to work assessing the tenuous situation in the nose wheel well. After tinkering around for a few minutes, Jesus turned to them.

"Okay, amigos, pretty straight forward C-4 job ... with a twist."

"A twist?"

"Yes. This C-4 is attached to a detonator that is rigged to an altimeter, set to trigger an explosion at 10,000 feet. That explosion would blow you out of the sky without a trace, shortly after takeoff."

"Can you disarm it without killing yourself, or blowing up our plane?" Biff enquired.

"No problem, amigo. C-4 or RDX is a powerful plastic explosive, but it can be set off only by a shock wave from a detonator or extreme heat. Otherwise it is very stable and insensitive to most physical shocks. In other words, it can't be set off by a gunshot or dropping it on a hard surface. A detonator is required."

"Good to know," one pilot commented.

"It's not like nitroglycerin. That's a fragile explosive. If you drop it, NTG blows up everything. Look, see these wires stuck in the molded clay substance in the wheel well? Theyare attached to this little two-by-two-inch charge. This is the detonator. It is set up to be triggered by this other little gadget, which is an altimeter."

Everyone peered into the wheel well with fascination.

"This is a clever job, amigo. Good thing the pilot did a thorough walk-around. It will only take me a few minutes to disarm the device. I'm always amazed how well C-4 molds like clay. When pressed into cracks or gaps like this, it's inconspicuous. Only the detonator wires give it away."

Toby was impressed. "Good job, Jesus. You are at the top of your game."

"Gracias, amigos."

"Biff, sort of looks like someone has it in for you, big time."

"Got that right, Toby, maybe they ran out of hit men."

"How's that?"

"We've already taken out four would-be assassins between me and my bodyguards. I suspect either some Commie agents or some disgruntled ARVN secret service goon. Probably the Commies. They've got agents everywhere, a lot of assets to boot. I'm inclined to think they've infiltrated our Embassy and my diplomatic cover is blown. We've got to do some serious house cleaning at the Embassy for moles. Some spy is compromising our mission."

"This C-4 incident looks like a Special Forces job, very clever, requiring expertise. What do you think, Jesus?" Toby asked.

"I agree. Never seen C-4 hooked up to an altimeter. Pretty clever ploy, could have been a clean kill. No one would ever know what happened."

"We'll get on it, Biff, Toby interjected. We're sorry about this, buddy."

Biff, grinned and winked at Jesus. He replied in a friendly mocking Spanish accent, "*No problemo, amigo.*"

Both Jesus and Toby enjoyed a good laugh at Biff's joshing imitation.

Jesus shook his head, still snickering. *This American just missed getting killed, and he still has a sense of humor. Crazy* gringo*!*

Before departure, Biff placed a call to Cát at the U.S. Embassy in Saigon.

"Cát, Biff here. I'll be home early evening. Got a busy day tomorrow, I thought it would be nice to have dinner together at Le Bordeaux over in Binh Thanh district. I'll spend the night at the Villa. Alert the guards to check out the security system."

"They've got a new system to augment the electronic one."

"What's that?"

"Three beautiful Rhodesian Ridgebacks. Professionally trained guard dogs. They're trained to roam the riverbanks of the property. They are beautiful animals, two males, and one female. They're very friendly to me and Mama-san, but I bet they could get real mean with intruders. You'll love them. They keep me company while you are gone."

"I hope the Vietnamese guards don't eat them," Biff joked.

She ignored his rude remark. "You're awful! They're great dogs. You'll see."

"Okay. I'll take your word for it. I'll pick you up around 1900 hours."

"Would that be seven p.m.?"

"Yes, 1900 hundred hours is seven p.m., Cát. You are getting better."

"I hate military jargon."

"You'll get used to it. See you soon, love."

"I'm really looking forward to seeing you again, Biff," she cooed.

CHAPTER THIRTY-TWO
DINNER PLANS

Saigon, Vietnam That evening

Biff and his two bodyguards picked Cát up at the well-guarded Villa just before 1900 hours. They chatted amicably en route to Le Bordeaux, twenty minutes north of the Night Channel River.

The couple shared a house-specialty dinner of scallop ravioli and Norwegian salmon, accompanied by a fine bottle of Mersault. After dinner, Biff enjoyed a Cognac and his customary Cohiba cigar.

Meanwhile, the bodyguards occupied the bar in clear view of the couple. After picking up the bill, they escorted their charges back to their limo. They encountered very little traffic on their way back to the Villa. As the driver dropped them off inside the security gate, Biff heard loud barking down by the riverbank. The Ridgebacks were going nuts.

Biff looked in the direction of his bodyguards. "Better go check it out, fellas."

Anton and James rarely questioned Biff's judgment but, on this occasion, they did.

Anton replied, "The sentries will be on it in a flash, boss. Our job is to protect you. I get the feeling we should escort you inside while they sort it out."

Biff reflected on their good judgment.

"Alright, we'll go inside."

The sentries rushed to the shore area following the dog's loud barking at the property's edge, armed with semi-automatic rifles, .45 caliber pistols, and newly arrived rocket propelled grenades. The three Ridgebacks were jumping on the tall gate in the wall separating the property from the marsh, alerting the guards of intrusion in the shoreline reeds.

The sentries assumed the intruders were not coming to the villa to borrow a cup of sugar, so without announcing any verbal challenge, they acted preemptively. They launched a barrage of grenades in the general vicinity of the intruders approaching the gate, causing an explosive concussion that rocked the neighborhood.

After the assault, the sentries waded into the reeds with high-powered flashlights to assess the damage. They found three sappers, presumably VC, blown to bits in their black pajamas, armed to the teeth with AK-47s, grenades, and C-4 explosives.

They had landed their sampan in some reeds just south of the property and were hiking in when the Ridgebacks heard them and alerted the guards. Fortunately, this surprise sabotage—a major planned assault on the villa—was aborted by the dogs.

The sentries flashed an "all clear" to the villa after thoroughly checking the shoreline. The intruder's sampan was pulled to the dock for forensic inspection, clues or leads regarding the perpetrators of the aborted assault.

After receiving the all-clear signal at the villa, Biff and his two bodyguards came down to the dock to check out all the commotion, and assess the damage firsthand.

The Ridgebacks came up to him for a sniff, tails wagging, as if they sensed they had passed their first test with flying colors. The female was especially friendly to Biff. She kept rubbing up against his leg and licking his hand.

"Good dogs." Biff patted all three affectionately on their heads and backs. He agreed with Cát that they were beautiful dogs.

James walked up. "Pretty impressive performance by these dogs, Biff. They're a real asset to the perimeter electronic sensors. You just can't beat a good watch dog."

"Got that right, James. Be sure you and the sentries check everything out in case there is a second-wave attack, okay? Don't assume anything with these characters. They are getting real serious about killing me. I'm going to head up to the villa. Oh, by the way, make sure you get someone to trace that sampan. It might lead us to some more bad guys."

***

When he had undressed and about to jump in the shower, Biff shook his head, and lamented to Cát. "Someone has it out for me… Second time today someone tried to kill me. This is getting old."

"After your shower, climb into bed with me, Biff. I'll make you forget all your troubles."

The next morning, he arose with a headache, probably caused by the tension of two unsuccessful assassination attempts in one day, combined with last night's wine and Cognac.

As he shaved, Biff reflected on the odd coincidence that three sappers knew he'd be in the Villa last night. Who informed them?

Cát was the only one who knew, but she was above suspicion. Her sensitive position with the top-secret clearance at the Embassy required intense vetting. It occurred to Biff she may have innocently informed Mama-san of his forthcoming visit. Mama-san was scrambling eggs now for his American breakfast. Better check with Anton to inquire whether she was formally vetted or not.

Cát's family was driven out of Vietnam by the Viet Minh, so she hated them. Biff was absolutely certain she would never betray him, but Mama-san became the big unknown factor. He would ask Cát who had recommended the housekeeper.

After a soft knock on the bathroom door, it opened and Cat peeked in. "Biff, breakfast is almost ready."

She joined him in the bathroom, placing her arms around his waist as he completed shaving. "What else can I do for you, sir?" she asked playfully.

He smiled at her, but let it fade as he studied her reflection in the mirror. "Cát, who referred Mama-san to you?

"The Embassy mail room boy, Tran. Why?" she answered. She pulled away, puzzled as to where this was going.

"How long has he been at the Embassy?"

"At least two years."

"How well do you know him?"

"Not that well. He told me his aunt was an experienced housekeeper and was looking for a job."

"Was she vetted?"

"I assume so, but I really don't know for sure. Where is this leading? Have I done something wrong?"

This line of enquiry distressed her. She lived to please Biff. She loved him. She had never witnessed his stern, no-nonsense side. It made her stomach churn.

"Just trying to connect some dots, Cát. I'll explain later, okay? Not now."

Cát felt she had just been gently scolded. She hugged her arms defensively and turned to leave.

Biff knew he'd hurt her feelings and tried to make amends. "Please don't be upset, Cát. You'll understand this fully later on, okay? Trust me."

She turned and stared back with an earnest, sincere expression. "Okay, Biff. You know I'd never do anything to disappoint you."

"I do."

She smiled tentatively and suggested, "Why don't you have breakfast? Mama-san has it all prepared for you. I'm not hungry, really, and I need to shampoo my hair." She hated contention.

He hugged her for a long moment. "Sure, love. I'm not very hungry either. I have a bad headache. But, a bite will probably help me."

Biff was beginning to connect the dots. Intrigue and suspicion were inbred traits in the CIA mindset. Mama-san had to be the source for the tip-off of the assassins. It would be too much of a coincidence otherwise. He'd long suspected a spy in the Embassy. The mail-room boy was a highly suspect link to Mama-san, a mole. Both could monitor Biff's comings and goings and set him up for assassination attempts.

Biff's mind continued to churn as he sat down to his breakfast. Mama-san was cleaning up the house, out of sight. She had prepared him a huge plate of food, enough for two people. He took one bite of the scrambled eggs and that was enough. He just wasn't up for a big breakfast this morning. Two assassination attempts in one day made him tense. He was in a bad mood, and definitely not hungry.

He noticed a scratching noise at the door. The female Ridgeback was looking in at him, wagging her tail, begging.

Biff thought he'd reward her with his breakfast. She'd obviously taken a liking to him. Mama-san wouldn't know he'd given his breakfast to the dog. He went outside and scraped his food on the ground for the dog, who instantly gobbled it up, wagging her tail in approval of Biff's lavish gift.

He returned the plate to the kitchen table and wandered down to the boathouse to chat with Anton and James.

Anton sat on the dock talking on a secure line, presumably to James, who was not present.

"I'll call you back, James. The boss is here. I need to brief him, okay?" Anton hung up the phone.

"I've got some news for you."

"What's that, Anton?"

"We traced the sampan from last night to a boathouse area on the Ben Nghe Channel."

"Where's that?"

"About two miles southwest of the Majestic Hotel, off Duong Nam, up the channel a bit. Last night we staked the place out with a surveillance team down there, and guess what?"

Biff raised his eyebrows in question.

"We were suspicious about Mama-san and her possible connection to the ruckus last night, so James trailed her home. Guess where she lives?"

"From your presentation, I'd say somewhere in the vicinity of the boathouse that owned the sampan."

Biff was impressed with his CIA guards' detective work. These two guys were pretty sharp.

"Right, boss. Who else could have tipped off the VC about your presence here last night? You were in Vientiane all day."

"I'll go one step further, Anton. I doubt Mama-san was vetted. She's gotta be a VC spy. The mail-room boy, Tran, referred her to Cát at the

Embassy. So, he's also highly suspect. I think we should confront them both, don't you?"

"Absolutely, boss. Let's go up to the house now, okay?"

"In a minute, Anton, let me set up a surveillance and disinformation trap in downtown Saigon to confirm her connection to Tran. If they pan out to be the leakers, plan a covert op to take out the whole bunch at the boathouse. No questions asked. Not a word to ARVN Intelligence. Don't trust them. Just do a job on the VC spies, okay? Take 'em out."

"Got it, boss, consider it done."

As they returned to the villa, a thrashing dog on the grass near the kitchen attracted Biff's attention. The female Ridgeback lay on her side, convulsing in a pool of vomit.

Anton ran up to her. "What the hell's going on here?"

"This dog is dying! Get someone to take her over to the airbase vet clinic right now." Biff ordered.

Anton jumped to it on his field phone. That order taken care of, he stared at Biff.

"Boss, it looks like this dog has been poisoned. It doesn't look like she's going to make it."

"Oh, my God! I gave her my breakfast! I think we need to chat with Mama-san right now, Anton. Ask the vet to run a toxicology panel on the dog for poisons, drugs, or whatever, okay?"

"Got it, boss." Anton phoned, dispatching orders.

A sentry scurried up to collect the dog to take to the vet. The poor animal had stopped convulsing and was now comatose and breathing poorly. What a waste to see such a beautiful animal moribund.

The two men entered the kitchen to confront Mama-san, who was doing the dishes.

Biff sternly addressed her. "Mama-san, we have a problem to discuss with you."

She tensed at the menacing tone of his voice, and turned around warily, eyes wide, dish water dripping from her hands onto the tile floor.

"I'll come right to the point. You are associated somehow with last night's intruders. We've linked you to the sampan owner's quarters over in Duong Nam. We need to take you down to the Embassy for further questioning about your connections with the Viet Cong assassins, as well as the mail-room boy, Tran, who is supposedly your nephew. You also need to explain why the dog is dying after I gave him my breakfast. Did you try to poison me? You have a lot to explain, Mama-san!"

Biff's threatening tone and inference startled her. Mama-san's gaze flicked around the kitchen searching for an escape route. There was no way out. Trapped, her subversion discovered, her poison plot foiled, her game was up. These two Americans meant business. She had only one option left.

Despite slippery hands, she reached under her garment and pulled out a Chinese revolver concealed under her belt. She was determined to succeed where her comrades had failed. Cornered like a wild animal her instincts to fight kicked in since flight was not possible.

Anton and Biff instinctively recognized Mama-san's move. Before she could even raise her pistol, Anton became judge, jury, and executioner, shooting her twice in the chest. She gagged, gasped for air, coughed up bright red blood, and crashed face-first to the kitchen floor with a thud.

Cát screamed, hearing the gunshots. Hair still wet from shampooing, she rushed to the kitchen, wrapped only in a towel. She could not imagine what the commotion was all about. She feared someone had just shot Biff.

Instead, Mama-san lay dead on the kitchen floor, face down in a pool of bright red blood, a pistol next to her hand. Cát gasped in alarm. Her heart pounded inside her chest. Dizzy and speechless, her mind reeled trying to absorb the scene. She struggled not to feint.

Anton was holstering his semi-automatic. Biff was unharmed. Her emotions bounced between dismay and joy. She couldn't understand why Anton had shot Mama-san, but rejoiced that Biff appeared unharmed.

"What's going on?" Her voice came out shaky.

Biff quickly explained. "Cát, Mama-san was a VC spy and started to pull a gun on us. She tried to poison me with breakfast this morning. Unfortunately, I gave it to the dog who is probably dying on the way to the Air Force vet."

Cát's hands shook, shaken to her core. "Mama-san a VC spy? The dog poisoned? Oh, my God!" Distraught, she slumped into a chair, her hand covering her mouth, tears streaming.

Biff went over a put a consoling arm around her shoulder. "I'm afraid so. That's a Chinese pistol on the floor next to her. Only the VC and the NVA use them. It's conclusive evidence as far as I'm concerned. I'll go over all this with you in detail later. I know it' shocking, but that's the story of my life lately. Meanwhile, Anton and I have business to attend to, okay? Please finish getting dressed and we'll go over to the Embassy in about a half-hour."

Cát stood shakily, and left the room, overwhelmed. Though distressed, she trusted Biff knew what he was doing. She couldn't believe her judgment about Mama-san could have been so wrong. She realized she had endangered their lives by taking Tran's recommendation without checking him through proper Embassy vetting procedures. This was a lesson she would never forget.

Anton glanced at the dead servant. "We'll clean up and dispose of the body, boss."

"Where?"

"The Night Channel. We'll hook her up to an anchor."

"You're a tough customer, Anton."

"It just occurred to me, boss. Did you eat any of that breakfast?"

"Just one small bite, Anton. I feel okay."

"Better check in first thing this morning with the Embassy Doc just in case Mama-san actually did try to poison you, okay? We'll check the toxicology panel on the dog and have an answer for you this afternoon."

"Okay. Good idea. Except for a headache, I feel fine now. But, as the old story goes, an ounce of prevention is worth a pound of cure."

Biff was starting to really appreciate how good Anton was at his job. *He'll be up for promotion soon. I'll see that he's well taken care of in the process.*

"Better call on the Embassy, Anton, and have them take the mail boy, Tran, into custody for you to interrogate. He'll scoot if the word gets out about what happened here. See what information you can get out of him. Also, I'd mount that sampan downtown boathouse operation sooner rather than later. Take them down before they find out about Mama-san. If she doesn't show up after work, they'll flee."

"We'll take care of it, boss."

***

Biff and Cát were chauffeured to the U.S. Embassy. She was still visibly shaken by the early morning's events. She remained very quiet, while Biff started to experience some nausea and malaise. He also noticed some peculiar reddish splotches on his arms.

"Better see the Embassy doc right away," he muttered.

He let Cát remain in her withdrawn state. *She's tough. She'll get over it.*

The Marine Guards at the Embassy recognized them, saluted and waved them through the gates into the compound. Biff told Cát he'd check with her later and went directly to the Embassy dispensary.

On the way, a wave of nausea overwhelmed him. Biff knew that he wouldn't make it. He stopped at the nearest men's room, and vomited into the nearest toilet. He felt faint. Staggering, he managed to make it down the hall to the dispensary. The nurse recognized the signs of serious illness: pallor and cold sweats. She took his blood pressure and pulse. He was hypotensive with tachycardia, so she immediately rushed him into an examining room, inserted an IV for intravenous fluids, put him on a monitor, and called the doctor.

Doctor Edmund Jarvis was a long-time CIA physician who had handled many varieties of company cases, from minor gunshot wounds to the many sorts of illnesses associated with overseas postings. After a brief history and exam, he diagnosed immediately that Biff was suffering from either severe food poisoning, or just plain poisoning. He increased the rate of IV infusion, and inserted a nasal gastric tube to pump out Biff's stomach.

Biff objected to the unpleasant experience, but Doc Jarvis knew what he was doing.

"How long have the red blotches had been on your skin, Biff?"

"They appeared about a half hour ago, I noticed them on the ride to the Embassy."

It was uncomfortable for Biff to talk with the nasal gastric tube gagging his throat. Nevertheless, he told the doctor the entire story, including feeding his breakfast to the dog who convulsed and probably dying at the vet's office.

Doctor Jarvis had never seen a case of bacterial food poisoning this serious. Biff had to have been poisoned with some toxic chemical or substance. He racked his brain, considering possible etiologies in the differential diagnoses. In moments, it occurred to him what had made Biff so deathly ill.

Actually, it was a classical presentation for arsenic poisoning. The signs and symptoms offered the diagnostic clinical clues: nausea and vomiting, skin petechial, and hypotension.

Fortunately, Biff had only taken one small bite of the poisoned eggs, and fed the rest to the dog. He would send a sample of Biff's blood for toxicology screening. If it matched with the dog's test for arsenic, then his clinical diagnosis would be confirmed.

Doctor Jarvis explained his diagnosis and treatment to Biff, emphasizing how lucky he was not to have eaten the entire meal. Fortunately, he was exposed to a small, non-fatal dose.

"Arsenic is tasteless and odorless. As little as three grams can be fatal," he solemnly informed Biff. "Historically, it has been a favorite homicidal agent of death."

The doctor emphasized that he should recover fully without any complications.

Biff felt reassured, although he still felt pretty damned sick. They kept him overnight in the dispensary on IV fluids, the NG tube on suction, and with a nurse or medic monitoring his condition around the clock. A Marine guard stood watch outside the door. By the next morning, as the doctor predicted, he felt much better.

Doctor Jarvis came in on rounds early the next morning to check on his condition. He told Biff the prognosis for full recovery in the next twenty-four hours was very good.

"Oh, by the way, the lab reports on you and the dog confirmed arsenic poisoning."

***

Meanwhile, across town, the CIA paramilitary team was mopping up their take-down of six VC saboteurs and assassins at the Duong Nam boathouse complex. A surprise 0300 attack caught the culprits sleeping soundly. Three resisted and were summarily shot. Three were captured and hauled off to some undisclosed destination for intense interrogation. VC maps, literature, and communications were recovered in the raid. Ammo, mortars, AK-47s, and Chinese pistols were taken as evidence by the SAD commando team. It was a skillfully executed exercise, a textbook CIA operation by the staff.

Back at the Embassy, Tran was arrested by James, briefly questioned, and taken on a long ride out to the rubber plantation area northwest of Saigon. That's where the CIA maintained a "hospitality suite" for interrogation of spies. The interrogation of the boy's role in the assassination attempts on Biff's life would intensify upon arrival. James could be a hard-ass interrogator and would see that Tran spilled the beans.

Maybe Biff could rest a little easier after this episode. But, then again, who knows what the hell would happen next in the clandestine world of Saigon?

Biff spent the next two days recovering from his near-death experience. With Cát attending to his recovery at the villa, he progressed nicely. She doted on him. She'd calmed down considerably after his comprehensive explanation of the chain of events, but still harbored some guilt that she had inadvertently exposed him to danger. She didn't understand why, but thought Biff must really be important for so many people to continue to try to kill him.

Biff was important, but she'd never know just how important he was to the CIA in his Saigon role.

CHAPTER THIRTY-THREE
THE LECTURE

Langley Porter Institute, San Francisco May 1966

Murray Robeson's going-away party at Columbia University had been collegial and nostalgic, with his emotions torn between elation and sorrow. Elation in respect to having his own Department of Neuroscience with his own NIH grants at the new state-of-the-art Langley Porter Institute. Situated adjacent to the University of California hospital complex perched on Parnassus Heights, San Francisco, his top-floor office offered a panoramic view of the city and bay. It contrasted drastically to his present small office's view of the soot-covered building next door in Manhattan.

But, Murray also experienced the sorrow of leaving his friends and colleagues in New York City, and departing from the University that gave him his start in academic life.

Before leaving, he obtained a promise from his mentor, Dr. Eric Kantor, to visit him in San Francisco to address Murray's new staff. Eric could bring his staff up-to-date on the progress of research in neurobiology, in respect to memory restoration through cognitive enhancement. Murray envisioned this as an exciting new field of research in PTSD especially considering the increase of Vietnam war- related cases. It was becoming a hot topic and government grants were flowing.

Once settled in Parnassus Heights, Murray followed-up on the promise from Professor Kantor. Murray had dedicated his lifetime avocation to conducting research in memory restoration, employing ideas and techniques developed by Dr. Kantor and other researchers. He invited his professor to lecture on the subject, informing him he had a clinical case of PTSD to present on grand rounds. One of his first patients, Dr. Roe MacDonald, sustained brain injury during a mortar attack in Vietnam. The case would interest his mentor. The Vietnam vet suffered posttraumatic memory loss as a result of a severe concussion complicated by a subdural hematoma requiring neurosurgery. This condition posed a potential career-ending dilemma for Dr. MacDonald, whose early surgical career path prior to his service in Vietnam showed such great promise.

UCSF's Chief of Surgery Dr. Engels, had shown a strong personal interest in Dr. MacDonald's rehabilitation. The chief was a World War II vet and held a special affection for another surgeon who had served his country in wartime. The chief requested Dr. Robeson spare no cost on Dr. MacDonald's case. The University's insurance plan would pick up the tab not covered by the military or grants.

Murray explained to the chief that much of the diagnosis and treatment of this condition was largely experimental, but he planned to make Dr. MacDonald his major project. Dr. Engels, a pioneering surgeon, implored Dr. Robeson to probe the depths of emerging knowledge and to be aggressive in his therapy. If no progress was being made, he urged him to call in consultation for second opinions. Just give it his best shot.

Shortly after this conversation, Murray placed the call to New York City to Dr. Kantor's office. Murray told his mentor of his first big challenge at Langley Porter.

"Would you come out to consult on the case and deliver a lecture on memory? Kindly present the lecture as a status report to include the emerging strategies for therapy of stress-related memory impairment. The University will pay all your expenses and a handsome honorarium or a donation to your research lab."

Dr. Kantor didn't hesitate. "I would appreciate my expenses to be reimbursed, but prefer a donation to my laboratory research. No personal honorarium is necessary. I accept your invitation and agree to come to San Francisco next month. Just set up the dates, Murray. It will be good to see you again. I'm glad things are going well. It sounds like you have a very challenging case. I hope I can help you, seems there is a lot at stake in this man's career."

"Thank you, professor. I'll get a letter off this afternoon with all the details."

***

On the day of the lecture, the amphitheater was packed, standing room only. Murray had invited Dr. MacDonald to sit in, so he might gain some idea as to what was in store for him.

Doctor Kantor stood at the lectern, after the customary greeting and acknowledgements. "Neuroscience is entering a new and exciting era, based on five principles," he began.

"Think of the brain as a computer that can manage both simple and complex functions. The brain regulates emotions, thoughts, and sensory experiences, and commands our actions.

"The first principle is that the mind and brain are inseparable. The second principle is that neural circuits in different parts of the brain coordinate activity from the simplest reflex to the most creative acts. Third, the circuits all have in common the same basic signaling units, designated as nerve cells. Fourth, these cells communicate using specific signaling molecules. Fifth, throughout the biological evolution of man, these specific signaling molecules have been preserved generationally in our genetic coding. These five factors or principles govern how we perceive, learn, remember, feel, and act."

"Now, let's address memory loss. How do you explain it? Memory requires both cellular and molecular processes. In organic diseases, such as Alzheimer's dementia, structural damage in the brain exists, which is quite difficult to address therapeutically. Many anatomical deficits simply are irreversible, and do not respond to medications or emerging therapies.

"In contrast, however, in age-related and posttraumatic-induced memory loss, the defect is comparatively benign, much like a short-circuit or jamming of a control station, to use a simple analogy. It is a physiologic, rather than anatomic deficit. This physiologic condition is not associated with structural damage. Thus, it lends itself to emerging therapies for memory restoration, such as biofeedback and cognitive enhancers.

"At the present time, much of this work is largely experimental, but shows great promise as we gain knowledge of brain function and memory. It has been stated by researchers, particularly Dr. Steiner, that highly structured and selective images of the past influence our behavior. Recalling the past is a form of mental time travel, independent of time and space. Time travel allows us not to focus exclusively on the present, but to recall or reflect on past experiences. Time travel provides the ability to recall both pleasant and traumatic events, as well as to daydream and imagine the future. Time travel frees us from the constraints of the present reality."

He paused to consider his notes and to adjust his steel-rimmed glasses.

"The 1960s witnessed the merging of two disciplines in the biology of the mind—behavioral and cognitive psychology. The first is a study of simple behavior in experimental animals in response to certain stimuli. The second is a study of complex mental phenomena in humans, simply put, the science of the mind- memory.

"Let's talk about memory. It may not be rational or accurate, but memory persists, and gives us input in decision-making. Simply put, with intact memory, we are what we learn and remember."

"With impaired memory, time travel is fragmented, and the binding force of memory is splintered such that a comprehensive picture of the past is not constructed in our minds and relayed into our awareness. The thought process is jumbled, you might say, like in PTSD for example.

"Memory processes are unique in the aspect of recall. The mind has a natural tendency to remember positive events and suppress disappointing or traumatic events. In posttraumatic stress disorders or syndromes, however, unpleasant events may unpredictably emerge in consciousness, or subliminally persist. This experience is commonly known as 'flashbacks.' This may impair normal productive cognitive function and provoke sudden anxiety attacks."

"So, how do we reconstruct the memory process of recall? First, we must understand memory storage—long term and short term.

Doctor Kantor recapped what he'd covered about memory: short-term memory is mediated by proteins and molecules present at neuronal synapses—cyclic AMP and protein kinase enhance release of glutamate mediators from the terminals. He reminded the audience that such enhanced release is the key to promoting short-term memory formation, thus offered a potential for pharmacological therapies.

"But, what about long term memory? How does that happen?"

He scanned the room at many blank faces.

"Experiments have shown that long-term memory is dependent on synthesis of new proteins, involving the nucleus of the nerve cell where all genetic information lies. Just stop and think for a moment, how is intellectual information transmitted from one generation to the next? Life's key processes-storing and passing on genetic information-occurs through the expression of genes and the replication of chromosomes. Watson and Crick's discovery of DNA and messenger RNA in 1953 provides the basis for neuroscience's investigation of *memory genes.*"

While the professor paused for a sip of water, Roe tried to piece together what Dr. Kantor had said. He gave up when the doctor picked up his notecards again.

"Repeated sensory environmental stimuli reinforce nuclear encoding of response. The proteins involved, those filing the experiences directly into long-term memory banks, are yet to be defined. But, it is now evident that long-term memory requires repeated, spaced training with intervals of rest. This has huge clinical significance.

"For example, consider the benign process of age-related memory loss, early senescence or forgetfulness. This may simply represent an imbalance of specific regulatory proteins inside the brain cell responsible for consolidating long-term memory. Either a weakening of the activating regulator, or an overabundance of inhibitory regulators, could explain this particular aspect of memory impairment. It represents a physiologic deficit. It's apparent that a gene must be switched on to store memory, long term. Learning and environmental stimuli initiate this response, which determines predictable behavior appropriate to the stimuli. Experience is the best teacher." He paused to let that sink in.

"Memory persists through the growth and maintenance of new synaptic connections in response to experience. Changing environmental input results in constant modification of brain cells associated with memory. Old brain cells die and are replaced by new cells. Computational power is preserved and handed down through evolution in genetic coding, conferring the capacity to learn from one's environment, to adapt, and to respond.

"Once memory is properly stored in the neurocircuit, it can be recalled immediately. There are two forms of long term memory—implicit and explicit.

"Implicit memory is for routine functions, and doesn't require conscious effort. An example is riding a bicycle. More complex, explicit memory requires 'conscious recall' expressed in images or words associating people, places, and objects.

"Basically, we all possess a core memory. To recall all aspects of that specific memory requires creativity by the brain, which must reconstruct the episode it is requested to recall. This function of storage occurs in the hippocampus. This area of the brain is designated for specific memory of places, objects, and special relations which necessitate conscious attention. The hippocampus facilitates one's perception of the environment and represents and correlates multisensory experiences.

"Consider now a pharmacologic aspect of memory recall. We have noted the important role of attention or focus in conscious recall. Animal experiments strongly point to dopamine as a modulating agent in attention related phenomena. Dopamine is produced by midbrain cells and can activate receptor sites in both the prefrontal cortex and hippocampus. Dopamine mediates voluntary action and conscious recall. The importance of this observation is that the same regions of the brain that are involved in voluntary behavior are also recruited for attention processing. This observation reinforces the concept that selective attention is critical to the unitary nature of consciousness.

"Also implied is the potential role of dopamine in cases of memory impairment. While serotonin may mediate unconscious memory (implicit) by activating genes for long term storage, dopamine may play a similar role in conscious (explicit) memory storage. Dopamine acts as a modulator in the cerebral cortex, causing attention which, in turn, sends a voluntary signal to the hippocampus where long-term memory is stored and retrieved.

"This observation brings us to therapeutic considerations in memory impairment disorders. It addresses the issue of PTSD, why you all are gathered here today for my lecture. At this stage, the experience is mostly experimental. Post-traumatic stress syndrome is usually accompanied by depression. Most antidepressant drugs act through serotonin, a recognized neurotransmitter. If we could target receptor sites for serotonin and dopamine, we might design drugs appropriate to the neurologic disease or impairment-cognitive enhancers.

"Research such as this, opens a new field of molecular neuroscience employing cognitive enhancement drugs. Now, we're exclusively in an experimental stage, but I anticipate clinical applications will soon evolve."

I hope so, Roe thought, fidgeting in his chair.

"I've discussed the role of selective attention and memory, but the issue of memory impairment is more complex, involving different aspects such as seen in post-traumatic stress disorders.

"In organic diseases, the location of the defect in the brain defines the manifestations of the disease. For example, Parkinson's disease is a disorder of the substantia nigra—an anatomic location in the brain. But, it is important to note that in stress disorders there is no structural damage in a specific anatomic location. It is a physiologic defect. That fact is the 'take home' message from my lecture today.

"Post-traumatic stress disorder is usually manifested by recurrent episodes of fear, often triggered by a flashback, a reminder of the initial trauma. This represents a powerful emotional feature of 'learned fear,' the memory of which can be locked in the brain's unconscious memory storage for decades. It remains unconscious until a variety of stressful circumstances trigger the threat response. A flashback results in a sudden recall of an unpleasant memory that has been packed deeply away in the brain.

"Let me describe the two pathways of learned fear. One occurs through the cortex (conscience), the other through a direct bypass to the amydala (unconscious). This pathway relays information to the hypothalamus triggering the classic 'fight or flight' response. This response is clinically recognized by a racing heartbeat and pulse, tension, sweating, and a dry mouth.

"This scientific information could lead to a development of drugs to target and pharmacologically block the learned fear reaction. Certain drugs such as Librium, Valium, and other anti-anxiety agents show promise in decreasing anxiety. Newer drugs might approach the disorder from the positive side by instilling a feeling of security and self-confidence in the cerebral cortex which inhibit the reaction in the amydala. This positive enhancement therapy may well be the most productive approach in memory restoration in post-traumatic stress disorder. That's where we are headed."

The professor looked up and smiled at the audience who appeared to be intrigued by this promising therapeutic advancement.

"Working memory resides in the prefrontal cortex where complex mental processes occur. Cognitive deficits in this area can affect long-term planning and judgment as well as the planning and execution of complex behaviors. Depression associated with PTSD can adversely affect cognitive function. We know that depression is associated with decreased levels of serotonin. Anti-depressant drugs, such as monoamino oxidase inhibitors, increase serotonin levels which correlate with an elevation of a person's mood state. These medications promote feelings of well-being. Effective selective serotonin reuptake inhibitor drugs are now in clinical trials and offer great promise in the treatment of reversible cognitive impairment. We are pursuing all therapeutic avenues.

"In another remarkable discovery, anti-depressant drugs stimulate neuron production in the hippocampus. Perhaps the production of new nerve cells will counteract the memory compromise associated with depression in this critical memory storage area of the brain. Time will tell.

He adjusted his glasses. "Another doctrine to consider in PTSD is cognitive behavioral therapy. This approach in mild cases has been shown to be as efficacious as anti-depressants in controlled clinical trials. This would give us another therapeutic modality."

"In conclusion, most of our mental life is unconscious, becoming conscious only in our awareness, which is expressed in words and images. The future of neuroscience rests with our accurate assessments on a molecular, biological basis. As we discern the anatomical and physiological aspects of the brain at molecular level, we will be able to design medications targeting specific memory impairments. Herein lays the clue to memory restoration through cognitive enhancement."

The lecture received standing applause.

The following reception gave everyone a moment or two to share with the visiting professor. Murray personally escorted Roe to meet Professor Kantor.

As they left the lecture hall, Murray turned to his patient.

"What did you think of the lecture, Roe? Learn anything?"

"Elegant, as they say at Harvard. I'm a Penn man, but I predict the good professor is tracking a Nobel Prize. He's a brilliant scientist and a gifted teacher. He can relate a complex topic in a comprehensive fashion. I understood some of his lecture, though honestly, it was difficult for me to follow. The subject is far afield from my surgical discipline. It's a credit to him if he got all those complex points across to the audience."

Murray raised his eyebrows, wondering how Roe came up with such a detailed response. "Agree, it's a complex subject. It's understandable you had difficulty following the lecture. A year from now, you'll really appreciate his contribution to your basic problem and the process of memory restoration."

"I sure hope so, Murray."

CHAPTER THIRTY-FOUR
THE CLINICAL TRIAL

The following week Murray instituted intensive recall therapy sessions with Roe. After a month's treatment, he took Roe aside for a chat.

"We've gone through your childhood, both good and bad, mostly positive, I might add. With prompting and medications, we've released a lot of factual data, reorganized it, and stored it away in your updated memory bank. Now comes the most difficult part, to reassemble all the surgical information you banked in the few short years of formal training prior to your Vietnam duty as a flight surgeon."

"Here's my plan. We'll be using different combinations of cognitive enhancers. Your moods may vary, but under medication your moods will be mostly elevated. If I overshoot the dosage or the combination of drugs, you may even act silly or think you are hallucinating, losing it, or even going crazy. Don't worry, I'll correct the situation."

Roe frowned, but Murray put a consoling hand on his shoulder. "In your case, recall is a progressive project of restoration, consolidation, correlation, and organization. Those four factors are key to your recovery and will determine if you can return to your surgical profession. You are highly intelligent, and have compiled a huge databank of technical information. Our goal is to retrieve and put that databank into a functional framework. One that will allow you to return full-time to your surgical occupation. It's a huge process, but we'll get it accomplished."

Roe gave a smile of encouragement, trusting Murray would get the job done.

"Ready to get started?"

Roe took a deep breath. "Sure. Let's go. I'm ready to do whatever it takes."

Murray had Roe lie down on a clinical bed. An elderly RN, wearing an austere expression, started an IV drip to administer medications.

"So, let's start recalling episodes of your training with a touch of sodium pentothal to relax you. Then I'll administer a slow IV drip of cognitive enhancers. You won't be tripped out, like LSD, we'll try that later on. Okay, Roe, you are about to go on your first pharmacologically induced time travel. I'll give you cues and prompt you. Don't be hesitant to reply, just let it fly. At first, it may seem disjointed or jumbled, but just let it go, free flowing associations, back into your past."

Roe experienced an overwhelming sense of tranquility as the IV slowly infused the medications. He felt like he was on cloud nine. He'd never been so relaxed.

Murray spoke softly, "Let's go back to your days at Penn Medical School or surgical residency at Cal. What were some memorable experiences?"

Roe let his mind wander, chasing down the circuits of memory lane that had shorted out following his Vietnam head injury. Slowly, his mind searched for retrievable episodes, rifled past experiences to grasp images. Several flashed by briefly, disappeared, and were replaced by other fleeting images.

"Try to relax, let your mind flow. Then, try to capture a fleeting image. Focus your attention fully on it. Then reinforce it with a supporting cast of images, okay? Roe, no pressure, just let it flow into consciousness, don't try to force it."

Whether it was Murray's reassuring manner, the medications, or both, Roe started to put a couple of past episodes together.

"I'm a bit embarrassed, but one of the first and fondest memories is of an RN at the Mission ER. Her name was Natasha Marcocek. She and her family escaped from Prague before the Russian invasion. They came to Palo Alto in the fifties. Natasha was beautiful, one of the most sensuous women alive. We had a brief affair and I never saw her again."

Roe obviously did not recall that Natasha cared for him at Clark AFB after his injury. Completely forgot it. Murray quickly noted this memory deficit, but didn't correct him.

"Any remorse, any guilt feelings?"

"None, it was just one of those spontaneous things, a romp in the hay, as we used to say down home."

"Where's home?"

"Eastern Shore of Maryland, growing up. Now it's San Francisco."

"Are you married now?"

"Not yet. I've met a great gal, Ann Summerville, a brilliant woman and very attractive. A good buddy introduced us in Hawaii."

"Who's your buddy?"

"Biff Roberts."

"Biff?"

"Real name is Buford Cavendish Roberts V. Can you imagine that? Buford, who would name their kid that for five generations? No wonder he chose to go by the nickname, Biff."

"What's Biff do?"

"He's some kind of CIA operative, can't tell you much other than that. He was a prominent figure at the Saigon Embassy, undercover work, traveled back and forth a lot—Hawaii, San Francisco, Washington, D.C. I suspect he did some covert work in Laos. But he never tells me much. If he does, he says he'll have to kill me! He's always joking around. Actually, he's my best friend."

Murray knew Roe had no recollection of Biff recruiting him for the Baguio experience. No need to go there. One step at a time.

"I hope so. Let's keep delving into your past. What about med school?"

Roe, immediately responded, much to Murray's satisfaction. The drugs were working.

"Went to Penn. I lived off the main campus, near Wharton Business School. I lived in one of the medical fraternities, basically, an eating house right around the corner from Smoky Joe's café."

"Smoky Joe's?"

"A beer and peanut bar, a great hangout, famous in West Philly. Sort of a body shop. A lot of coeds and RN students hung out there along with the grad students, all looking to hook up with 'Mr. Perfect.' The only campus bar that could ever compete with Smoky Joe's was one in Baltimore called, 'And the Horse You Rode In On,' near the Hopkins campus. Both bars were colorful and attracted lively crowds."

"Hmm ... Tell me about med school. Penn has a great reputation."

"Let me think."

Murray patiently waited ... obviously recall was in progress.

Roe fought to focus. It was less than ten years ago. Slowly, flashes drifted back from somewhere deep down. He could envision Thomas Eaton's famous portrait of the Agnew Clinic hanging over the main entrance stairway to the granite Ivy League building, the country's oldest medical school. This painted image of the amphitheater further called up the memory of the lecture amphitheater where the seats were so hard and uncomfortable that no one ever fell asleep.

This image summoned up another, one of his favorite anatomy professor. "Old 'what's his name?' Can't remember ... sorry. God, I can see him now, hear his voice, I can recall his famous quote, though, 'It's a monument to misspent energy.' He used this gentle putdown in reference to students' overly descriptive bluebook essays, or to an overly meticulous cadaver dissection by some compulsive student."

"Sounds like an interesting professor. His name may come to you later. Don't get frustrated. Did the medical students interact with the undergrads on campus?"

"A lot in the bars, gyms, squash courts, and attending the Ivy League games at Franklin Field. But, mostly on Skimmer Day in May."

"Skimmer Day?"

"It's an annual rowing regatta on the Schuylkill River in the park. Competition not only between top Ivy League teams, but teams from California and Washington participate. It's a fun time in May with jazz bands, kegs of beer, and barbecues. It's quite a show. The weather is usually good."

"You're doing great, Roe. Remember any other medical school experiences?"

Roe is obviously thinking hard, quiet, pensive.

"It's all like a fog. Like studying, taking a test, go to another lab or lecture. I can't remember anything important right now, just some silly things."

"Like what?"

"Well, there were two fat guys, one short and one tall, who were sort of characters in my class. We called them the 'Greater and Lesser Omentum.' In retrospect, it was probably mean and unfair, but we joked a lot in med school. We had a weird sense of humor. We always kidded Don Martin about passing out while watching his first lumbar puncture, and Jan Ortung's comment to four guys at the next anatomy table. She was one great, tough gal. These guys had cut off their cadaver's penis and placed it in the vagina of Jan's cadaver. With savoir faire, she quipped the next morning, "One of you guys had to leave in a hurry last night, I see."

"She had remarkable command," Murray commented with a chuckle.

"Great gal, she married an upperclassman, Grant somebody-or-other, made a fine couple."

"Anatomy was my favorite subject, probably why I chose surgery."

"How did you remember all that anatomic detail?"

Roe surprised himself by responding quickly. "Acronyms, limericks, and rhymes."

Murray asked in a gently reassuring tone, "Any examples, Roe?"

Roe again surprised him at the speed and clarity of his recall on this subject as he gave examples interesting and meaningful only to students of anatomy and prospective surgeons. Maybe it was the medication kicking in.

"You'll love this one, Murray, pertaining to the twelve cranial nerves: On Old Olympus Towering Top, A Finn and German Viewed a Hop."

"And, that means ..."

"That was our way to remember the twelve cranial nerves. He quickly rattled them off, as if it was yesterday, and he was reproducing the information in a blue book exam. The twelve nerves are: Olfactory, Optic, Ocular motor, Trochlear, Trigeminal, Abducens, Facial, Acoustic, Glossopharyngeal, Vagus, Spinal Accessory, and Hypoglossal."

Murray was amazed at this tremendous exhibition of recall. "That's really great recall, Roe. Remarkable! This is how we are going to restore your memory. What's the most difficult thing you ever had to memorize?"

Roe, musing, hesitating, finally responded, "The Krebs Cycle for a biochem exam. It was a bluebook question in the final. I nailed it."

"What's the Krebs Cycle about?"

Responding quickly, as if his entire memory file on the Krebs Cycle had been recruited, "It's the molecular and biochemical basis of aerobic and anaerobic metabolism."

Murray was truly impressed. "That's fantastic recall. Would you be able to reproduce the diagram?"

"Some of it, maybe, but it would be quite difficult at this stage, to be honest."

"I understand. With time, we'll get it together. Recall any other memory prompts like the cranial nerves?"

Roe thought for a while. "I recall a couple. To remember the small bones in the hands we used: Never lower Tilly's pants. Grandma may come home."

"And that means?"

Roe recited the bones in order, "Navicular, Lunate, Triangular, Pissaform, Greater Multangular, Cunate and Hamate."

"Wow! I couldn't remember that, Roe. Good show. Any others?"

"In neck surgery, it is important to know the location of the laryngeal nerve, so we used this one. A bit rude, but effective: The laryngeal nerve took a curve around the hypoglossus, I'll be fucked, said Stenson's duct, the SOB double-crossed us."

Murray laughed and remarked. "That's quite humorous. I've never heard that one."

"There were more if I could just recall them."

"Okay, Roe, that's enough for this session. Next time, we'll focus on your residency training in surgery. It's okay to study your textbooks, notes, and old exams. Your knowledge is in there somewhere. We're going to recover it, organize it, and file it, so that it is easy to retrieve or recall in images and words, okay?"

"You've got it, Doc. Thanks a lot. See you tomorrow."

Murray was upbeat that Roe was starting to get it together.

"I'm encouraged, Roe. This is certainly a good start. I'm going to leave now. The nurse will come in and remove the IV. You should wait around for half hour or so. You might want to take a little nap, until the drugs wear off."

"Why? I feel super relaxed." He smiled from ear to ear, as a jolt of encouragement surged through him. "Been a long time since I felt this good, Murray."

CHAPTER THIRTY-FIVE
THE RAJAH

Interagency Conference, San Francisco July 1966

The bank stood majestically in downtown San Francisco. Its classic Greek arches looked out of place and time in the shadows of the modern skyscrapers of the financial district. Massive white stone columns with Doric flutes supported the vaulted stone roof. The plain capital letters on the façade simply identified the building as the U.S. Treasury.

This regional federal bank housed the U.S. Drug Enforcement Agency (DEA), headed by Photis Panagoupoulus. That day, the director was hosting a joint interagency meeting to coordinate efforts to counter an unusual epidemic of drug dealings emerging in the San Francisco Bay area. The situation was unusual in several ways.

A brand of high-grade heroin had set off the outbreak, appearing out of the blue. The narcotic's unexpected potency resulted in an unprecedented flood of overdoses, jamming the ERs. Odd in a city where heroin use was uncommon. Marijuana and LSD cornered the market during the sixties. Busting someone for cocaine occurred infrequently, and heroin overdoses were practically unheard of.

Unusual that the recent surge in trafficking involved a mysterious drug lord going by the name of "Rajah." The suspected kingpin was an elusive figure with no rap sheet, no physical description, and essentially no known identity allowing the DEA to track him. He existed as a specter with an unusual name circulating on the drug scene.

This dilemma presented an unusual challenge. In a city captivated by unusual capers and weird characters of the past such as the "Zodiac Killer," the latest crime outbreak provided a mystery with a twist right out of pulp fiction. "The Rajah" dominated conversation and the news in San Francisco. The public perversely thrived on crime mysteries powered by colorful villains. The latest bad guy intrigued them. They loved the drama of the hunt. The media hyped Rajah's reputation for eluding authorities, although they failed to report or record anyone ever sighting him, or even document he really existed.

Questions circulated: "Who is he? Where did he come from?" Mystery inspired the story lines: "Is he a mythical figure?"

The CIA and FBI had been called in for consultation. The DEA had only one clue to go on. CIA reports linked Rajah to an international operation, and possibly a concrete lead to the present location of his base of operations. Intel reports implicated a mysterious figure's involvement in the importation of a potent grade of heroin from the Golden Triangle of Burma, Thailand, and Laos into Southeast Asian cities. According to Saigon CIA sources, this kingpin, "Rajah," distributed heroin refined in the Golden Triangle from 97 percent pure opium, the same brand showing up on the streets in San Francisco. By association, it had to be the one and the same key player, not a coincidence.

Photis opened the meeting with introductory remarks, framing the pending discussion.

"The Vietnam War has introduced many returning young servicemen to hardcore drugs, particularly heroin. Recreational use of marijuana is prevalent in the Bay area, but is not usually a major problem associated with crime and prostitution. Addiction to heroin is an entirely different matter with a long track record of violent crimes. The DEA has dedicated most of its bureau's present activity to interdiction of this dangerous drug. Our police department has a special narc division dedicated to addressing the mounting problem. The purpose of this meeting is to organize an interagency program to interdict heroin trafficking." Photis emphasized this narcotic interdiction project would entail interagency coordination.

To those unfamiliar with him, the trim, sophisticated, middle-aged gentleman with prematurely gray hair combed neatly back appeared unapproachable in his demeanor. A man who did not bend with the breeze and went by the book. With his steel-rimmed granny glasses, tweed sports coat, pressed tan trousers, and paisley tie knotted tightly at the collar of a white oxford button down shirt, Photus could have easily passed himself off as a Princeton Distinguished Lecturer.

This first impression was shortly dismissed. He was anything but pretentious, or aloof. His pleasant manner and casual conversation belied his appearance, proving that first impressions often are misleading. A man of accomplishment, confident in his ability to coordinate the efforts of this interagency gathering, he announced he was anxious to hear everyone's opinions on the Rajah's role in the narcotics traffic from Indochina. Photis thrived on international intrigue and looked forward to the CIA's input, extending an invitation to Biff Roberts to shed some light on this menacing problem.

In fact, Photis and the DEA had predicted the drug epidemic in the Bay Area early in the sixties. Prevalence of low-cost, abusive drugs ranging from marijuana and LSD to cocaine made it possible. Photis viewed this as part of the "Cultural Revolution" and the disdaining of authority. His projects' objective was to head off addiction to illicit drugs that fostered prostitution and crime, namely, cocaine. The recent introduction of heroin escalated the problem.

The DEA agents had built up a lot of good will with young people in poor neighborhoods, who would gladly become his eyes and ears in the search for the Rajah. The DEA believed that capturing this elusive figure would cripple or topple the Bay Area drug network. That became their primary focus, recruiting youngsters as assets and informants.

Photis introduced everyone and presented the overview of the narcotic problem in Northern California, focusing on San Francisco. He viewed the problem in the social framework of the sixties—a complex interaction with the Cultural Revolution.

He noted the general loss of respect for authority bordered on anarchy, especially among some of the student activists. He cited the Students for Democratic Action (SDA), over in Berkeley and rabble rousers from SF State. Beatniks and other fringe groups all participated in the current revolutionary cause, but were less violent. They were more interested in smoking pot and getting laid than in promoting anti-war animosity.

Marijuana use was rampant, fanning the fires of societal breakdown, as kids sought to drop out, get stoned. Essentially, this practice was non-violent. However, Titus considered cannabis a gateway drug, the potential transition to hard core drugs worried him. He voiced his concerns.

"Our major focus is now 'Burma Gold,' a particularly potent form of heroin. It's plentiful, and cheap. It's a potential killer, overdoses are becoming commonplace. It must be stopped," he warned.

"That requires capturing Rajah, the ringleader in the heroin narcotraffic. Unfortunately, no one knows who he is, what he looks like, where he comes from, where he lives, or whether he resides in San Francisco or Southeast Asia. And, very little is known about the key players in his network. Easier said than done."

"Who are his accomplices, his sources, and how is his organization set up? Basically, the Rajah is an enigma, proliferating Burma Gold with impunity at this juncture, gentlemen. The SFPD has arrested some heroin street dealers, but they know no more about Rajah's identity than our department. No one has yet connected the dots to trace the elusive Rajah. I'm hopeful our CIA guest can shed some light on this drug lord."

The committee had invited Biff Roberts from the CIA's Saigon station to give his input on the Southeast Asian connection, specifically Rajah's involvement. Although he'd heard rumors of Rajah's involvement in Saigon, Biff shared their general puzzlement regarding the culprit's identity. DEA requested he present an overview of the Southeast Asian connection.

Biff took the lectern, grinned, acknowledged the audience, and launched right in, foregoing the usual gratuitous remarks.

"Here's the limited background as I know it. There're rumors in Saigon that Rajah has some connection to the Cholon opium dens. Cholon is the Chinese community on the southwest bank of the Saigon River. It lacks the relative upscale elegance of French Colonial Saigon on the north bank with its tree lined boulevards and parks. In contrast, Cholon has narrow, crowded streets lined by numerous bars, and marketplaces. It's a black-market haven, as well as a site for prostitution and drugs. The local traffic is congested with motorized rickshaws and scooters causing unimaginable jams. GI's congregate in Cholon because it is home to our Post Exchange (PX), which sells almost as many goods as the thriving, vibrant black market on the streets."

This remark elicited an outburst of laughter in the audience.

"Opium dens and bars are commonplace in Cholon and have been for over a century. GIs patronize these establishments to drink the local Ba Muoi Ba beer served by attractive young women whose services are also available. To a GI returning from duty in the jungles, or the 'boondocks' as they refer to it over there, Cholon provides an emotional release beyond their young imaginations. Many flock to the opium dens on a lark, but some unfortunately become hooked. Grass, pot, or weed, as marijuana is commonly known in Vietnam, is as available as the local beer without any stigma or control. It's not uncommon to see advertising posters stating, *'Rolled and Ready Reefers'* like those at Peggy Sue's bar."

The law enforcement audience chuckled at this remark. *If they thought North Beach was wild, Cholon would strike them as a den of inequity,* he reflected.

"We suspect Henry Wu may be the local heroin kingpin, Rajah the supplier. Henry runs two of the most popular GI bars: 'The Pink Taco' and 'Poontang' in Cholon."

That remark elicited some raucous "hoo-ha's" and a few snickers from the audience.

"Wu's right- hand man is Nguyen Tho, aka the 'Candy Man.' The CIA keeps both men under surveillance. The Rajah's name comes up periodically in Cholon, but he remains the mystery man behind the scenes. We don't have a handle on him as yet. Not a clue!"

"Let me present an overview to you on Cholon vice. Before the U.S. became involved in Vietnam, the Vinh Xuyen gang collaborated with some local Chinese to set up brothels, casinos, prostitution bars, and opium dens. This occurred during the French Colonial era, and thrived in the '40s and '50s."

"But, the French discouraged patronage of these shady establishments, and set up their own bordellos to travel with the French troops. This was referred to as BMC, 'Bordel Militauire de Capagne.'

"The Americans in Vietnam have no such reservations, or available traveling camps. Consequently, Cholon bars have flourished along with night clubs. Filipino bands play GI's favorite tunes. They sing along to 'We gotta get out of this place!' and other popular lyrics."

"This raucous scene has spilled over to Saigon, but not on such a grand scale. Massage parlors, bars, and nightclubs have proliferated around the Brinks BOQ area. They are nothing more than fronts for prostitution and drugs. Economics play a major role. The fact of the matter is that poor peasant girls can earn more in one week on the streets than their parents could earn in one *year* working in their rice paddies!"

This remark astounded the officers, who groaned at the dismal revelation.

"Not being too judgmental, this den of iniquity centralizes the narcotic traffic into opium dens and networks with the bars and clubs in Cholon. It has been a lucrative business for years and is still growing to this day. As narcotic traffic picks up, drug dealers are fronting for senior ARVN officers and government officials anxious to make a buck. Can you believe that? We know who they are, and we have them under surveillance, but politics restrain us from bringing them down. That gives you a glimpse of the level of corruption in Saigon."

More groans from the audience.

This practice represents nothing more than perpetuation of years of corruption at high levels in the South Vietnamese government. It's a way of life over there, fellows. This situation has been one of the factors resulting in several coups. Political jealousies and schemes thrive and become the order of the day. The U.S. has pumped so much unmonitored money and armaments into South Vietnam that a considerable amount never reaches its intended purpose to defeat the VC, and prevent the Communist takeover. It's pocketed."

The audience could not believe what they were hearing. They had no idea that much corruption existed in Vietnam.

"I'm here to tell you corruption is rampant in Vietnam and feeds on itself. We suspect that Vietnam' Airforce chief, Nguyen Cao Ky, and General Tran Thien Khiem are major opium players. Opium and heroin are readily available at bargain prices, tempting our troops to experiment.

These are highly addictive drugs, as you well know. Many GIs are simply seeking one night's escape from war's reality, but before they know it, end up with a lifetime of addictive misery."

Biff noted looks of disgust on the law enforcement officers in the audience.

"As I mentioned, we have two key players under surveillance. The Cholon boss, Henry Wu, receives Burma Gold through a Laos connection, presumably, Rajah. Wu also maintains a highly sophisticated network with the Hukawng Valley poppy growers in Kachn, Burma. They bribe the military to look the other way. The Burmese convert the poppy's opium into heroin and methamphetamine tablets, pack it into condoms to cross sensitive checkpoints within women's vaginas. These females are called 'mules.' Obviously, this is a small-volume operation to sensitive local markets. Larger supplies are ferried by trucks, planes, or ships. Most narcotics, however, are transported through the Golden Triangle by horse and donkey caravans through the mountains and jungles.

"For those of you not familiar with the Golden Triangle, it designated as the confluence of the Ruak and the Mekong Rivers, defining the borders of Burma, Thailand, Laos, and Vietnam. This is mountainous country with heavy jungle and rain forest which provides cover preventing detection of these convoys. To the north of the triangle is Yunnan Province of China, another illicit market we are monitoring. Let me continue my primer course to give you an idea of the magnitude of the problem."

Biff stood up from the table and walked along the perimeter of the room, meeting the gaze of each attendee as he walked by them. He knew they were eating up this foreign stuff.

"Most of the opium and morphine base produced in northeast Burma is refined into heroin along the Burma—Thailand border. Chinese and Burmese traffickers then ship the finished product to Bangkok, Saigon, and Hong Kong networks. The traffic is steadily increasing, on the verge of flooding the major Asian cities.

"In addition to the two bars I told you about, Henry Wu has at least a dozen other high-class opium dens with beautiful Asian hostesses dressed in the most fashionable ao dais soliciting our GIs. Unfortunately, Wu is untouchable. He's in tight with many higher-ups in the South

Vietnamese government and military. Their monetary involvement thwarts our attempts to interdict his network. We've actually tried with several covert ops, but the next thing you know, the word comes down through command channels to back off our operations.

"The corrupt Vietnamese government officials complain to Ambassador Lodge or some commander, forcing us to lay back. As we collect more HUMINT we've discovered these networks are starting to export narcotics to the States—creating your current problem—and are currently linking with Hong Kong Tongs.

"The second major Cholon narcotic link we're dealing with is Nguyen Tho, aka the 'Candy Man.' His source of opium comes from Laos, particularly up in the mountains of Vang Vieng and Muang Sing. He's built a strong relationship up there with the ethnic Hmong tribes who produce most of the opium in Laos. Here again, our hands are tied in this situation because the CIA pays thirty thousand Hmong tribesmen as mercenaries. They are an indispensable asset to us as they interrupt traffic on the Ho Chi Ming Trail, rescue downed pilots, and protect our radar installations."

He stopped pacing to assess their reaction. "This is classified material I expect you to keep private, gentlemen. Lips sealed."

The members in the audience nodded affirmation, but Biff noticed frowns and furrowed eyebrows on almost everyone. He knew he was overloading them with information that shocked and worried them. But, he was almost finished.

"Just as the French did in the Indochina War to finance their operations between 1945 and 1954 with drug profits, we pragmatically look the other way so the tribes can profit from their opium dealings. It has been rumored that they smuggle opium out of Laos on Air America flights, but I can assure you the CIA is not complicit. As the professionals you are, I expect you will not divulge a word of this classified detail outside this room. I relate this only because this elaborate background knowledge is essential to your understating the complicated situation over there. I'm sure it blows your minds."

"Got that right," someone commented from the back of the conference room.

Others laughed in acknowledgment.

"Another problem we have to deal with is very worrisome. We suspect a rogue CIA agent who has lived for nine or ten years with the Hmong tribes conducting covert paramilitary operations. We fear he is complicit and profiting in this narcotraffic. For all we know, dealing with Rajah. To date, we have not been able to pin this association down, but suspect his network is a huge supply line in the traffic. If we nab Rajah, we may unravel that connection. That, also, is classified, gentlemen."

Biff made his way back to his seat. So, in summary, we're stuck in three separate, difficult situations. Honestly, at this point, we're stymied in our efforts to interdict the narcotraffic at its source in Southeast Asia. That makes it imperative that we apprehend Rajah and bust his network in the process."

"The Vietnamese cannot help us because bribery and graft pervades and corrodes the Saigon government. The Vietnamese steal from our PX's, and warehouses, and then sell the goods on the street's black market right under our noses. Appalling, but true. If we get tough with them, they accuse us of neocolonialism, and compare us to the French. And, of course, MAVN fails to back us."

He leaned forward to confide. "Allow me to digress a moment to give you an idea of our Catch-22. The reality is that over there, we are instructed to be sensitive to all of this B.S.! We are told America's reputation and prestige are at stake. President Johnson wants this war over as soon as possible. We are told we must cooperate with the South Vietnamese. But, let's face it, it's now America's war to win or lose. On another front, the drug war is also ours to win or lose. But, we're restrained from eliminating the source."

He sat back, placing his hands flat on the conference table. "One of our CIA heroes, General Lansdale, who spent over three decades in China and Indochina, states a massive counter-insurgency—with no self-imposed sanctuaries for the enemy—is necessary to win the war. I agree. If we win the war, I assure you, we can shut off the narcotraffic sources in a very short time. But, until then, we lack proper authority to shut the drug traffic down. So, the problem is spilling over to the States and looks like it's impacting your job locally."

A glance told him his comment was well received. "To get back to the Rajah … You might wonder if he's connected to the shady characters' activities I've outlined for you here today? I have no doubts that somehow Rajah is shipping large amounts of heroin out of Vietnam to the West Coast. We haven't connected all the dots as yet, but I have some ideas to share with you."

That got Photus' attention. He sat up straight. "Please do."

Biff grinned. "I thought you'd be interested. I'll be glad to share what intelligence the CIA has gained so far regarding the trafficking. There's some preliminary evidence that heroin is coming into Travis AFB in Fairfield, California, hidden in body bags, Japanese electronic equipment, and hibachis purchased in the PX for returning GIs. Since returning GIs' B-4 bags are not routinely searched at Travis, that's another avenue for importation. Travis is just up I-80 from San Francisco, a cozy arrangement.

"The Rajah's network seems to have tentacles everywhere in Northern California. His extensive network has bought off a lot of accomplices. Travis is only about fifty miles from San Francisco, how convenient is that? You have to admire Rajah's ingenuity. His network requires precise execution and organization with sophisticated communications to coordinate sending and receiving of narcotic contraband. He's obviously bought off a lot of military air transport loadmasters at Danang, Tan Son Nhut, Bien Hoa in Vietnam, and developed dependable coconspirators at Travis AFB. Rajah must pay them handsomely for their high-risk duties, as they face court martial and serious jail time if caught. We are also investigating with the FBI the scenario of ships bringing in larger narcotic deliveries through San Francisco and Oakland ports. Stakeouts are in progress and the FBI is recruiting local informants.

"From the CIA's standpoint, we're just beginning to understand the complexity of Rajah's operation. We know some aspects, but others remain an enigma, as elusive as the Rajah himself.

"As I said earlier, Rajah's the number one mystery man at this point, the key to our puzzle. So, I conclude that interagency cooperation, exchanging and coordinating current information is crucial to closing the net around Rajah. I suggest we infiltrate some agents on the Travis

AFB flight line. There are three major air bases in Vietnam where we have CIA assets for surveillance. I suggest the FBI or DEA supervise the surveillance at Travis. I predict HUMINT will lead us to the Rajah. We also need to increase our coordinated surveillance of all regional ports of entry. In my career, I've found human resources to be the most reliable in these situations."

***

The DEA director, next conducted a Q and A session that demonstrated how difficult this joint operation would be. The Rajah's network demanded loyalty and secrecy with no toleration of rivals or snitches. The network adhered to a chain of command in which each lower level operative had only one contact person above him to carry out the operation, point to point. No doubt anyone failing to execute his duty or function would end up in the San Francisco Bay. Those performing according to plan would be duly rewarded. It would be difficult to penetrate such a well-run network, but that tasked the interagency mission.

Photis concluded that the two better options to pursue were: Winning the war in Vietnam and eliminating the Southeast Asia sources of narcotraffic. That option was the known formidable task, out of his hands, so forget it. But, finding the Rajah and destroying his local network, the known unknown, would be up to him. Maybe just as challenging as the Vietnam solution posed for the military.

CHAPTER THIRTY-SIX
THE TRIP

San Francisco August 1966

Roe was ready for the next major test in his memory restoration program. Murray had gone over his basic plan with Roe, using an analogy Roe understood as a surgeon. He emphasized the importance of natural biological checks and balances for every physiologic system. For every system "switched on," or activated, nature provides a "switch off," or deactivator, as a counter balance.

"For example, Roe, if you are bleeding, a clotting mechanism is activated to keep you from bleeding to death. This clotting mechanism, in turn, activates another system that prevents over-clotting, called the lysis system. If the clotting system is not regulated, counterbalanced, it becomes as dangerous as bleeding. The same check and balance phenomenon occurs in the nervous system.

"Due to your trauma, your memory recollection is fragmented, like scattered pieces of a jigsaw puzzle that must be collected, reassembled, and put back together to complete the full picture of recalling an event.

"I plan to take you on an LSD trip to see if we can elicit some locked-up memories related to your injury. LSD is a mind-altering drug whose proper name is Lysergic Acid Diethylamide. It causes visual hallucinations if given in large doses, but in smaller doses it has the positive clinical attribute of enhancing awareness of visual experiences with a greater sense of clarity. A side effect is that it may produce brightly colored images, just so you are aware. I need to know what you've got stored in your memory bank. What you've repressed in respect to your trauma in Vietnam. LSD will open the vault."

"You're not kidding me, Murray? You're taking me on a LSD trip?"

"Not kidding. Here's a little background to help you understand why. As you probably know, recreational LSD use was popular in the late fifties and is now widespread among the disciples of Timothy Leary. It binds to the same brain receptor site as serotonin, suggesting that LSD counteracts the serotonin effect in the brain. Some neurologists think normal mental physiology requires proper serotonin function to maintain sanity. Early studies suggested that LSD blocks this function in the visual cortex of the brain.

"I'm following you, it explains why trippers think they can fly and jump off buildings."

"In essence that's true, but this was an early hypothesis. Subsequent research seems to disprove this theory by demonstrating serotonin affects eighteen different brain receptors, while LSD only stimulates one receptor in the frontal lobe that produces hallucinations.

"We'll closely monitor this experiment on a small dose of LSD. You'll experience the feeling of escaping your mind control, and hopefully discover some past episodes more clearly."

"Sounds exciting, Murray. Don't let me jump out a window and try to fly like some tripped out LSD patients we've treated at SF General!"

Murray laughed, "I won't allow that to happen, Roe. I promise."

"LSD is just one of our therapeutic modalities, somewhat experimental. Our overall plan is to use multi-modalities and medications to restore your memory. We'll treat your subliminal depression with monoamine oxidase drugs. We'll use bio-feedback, psychotherapy, and different graduated trials of cognitive enhancers, including serotonin and dopamine activators and inhibitors. You will get the full boat of treatments."

"Give it your best shot, Murray. My surgical career is in jeopardy."

"I understand and assure you, I will do everything within reason to enhance your recall ability. Some of it experimental with your informed consent, of course."

"Really appreciate it. I worry…"

"Basically, we're attempting to increase your serotonin levels. We know there is a high suicide correlation in patients with low serotonin levels, not that we think you are a candidate for suicide, Roe. We plan to keep your serotonin level high."

"Good to know."

"Your therapy will be an intense relearning process. You'll recall past experiences and file them in an orderly fashion. I anticipate that in less than six months you will have complete confidence to return to full surgical practice with an intact memory."

"I sure hope so, Murray. I can't wait to get back to the OR."

"You're an exceptional case with a lot at stake. We'll leave no door unopened. You will work with my specialized staff in different disciplines when you are not working with me directly."

"Do you remember Professor Kantor's lecture regarding time travel? Roe, you are about to take the trip of your life."

"Bring it on, Murray."

He couldn't believe this was about to happen.

Roe found himself on a couch while the doctor administered a small IV dose of LSD.

"I want you to tell me everything you experience. It is important to unravel some distant memories. Just let it all flow out. We'll probably use this tactic only once. But, it's very important to tell me exactly what you are experiencing, no matter how weird it may seem to you. Recite your perceptions to me, okay?"

Roe noted an enhanced awareness of his visual perception that produced brightly colored images. With Murray's professional coaching, he flashed back to the Tan Son Nhut mortar attack six months ago. The alarming memory caused him to sweat and his heart to race, and his mouth became dry. Anxious, he gripped the sides of the couch.

Roe experienced reenactment of the surprise attack with great sense of clarity, accented with technicolor magnification so realistic it scared him. Frames projected in slow motion paraded across his recollection. He saw the mortars crashing around him in the flight line café, the injured pilot on the ground struggling to reach the bunker. Relived his instinct to rescue him.

Occasionally, the images flashed by vividly. He saw the perimeter fences with adjacent rice paddies. It was like watching a "slow mo" movie of himself in battle. He vividly recalled the explosions, the flashes, and smoke... even the smell of cordite. Roe recreated the moment the mortar fragment injured the pilot, visualized the collapsing Quonset hut. A bright image of the sandbag bunker with men frantically scrambling for shelter from the mortar bombardment appeared, then rushed across Roe's consciousness.

As the stunning scene projected across the screen of his mind, Roe actually recalled rescuing the wounded pilot. Reliving the moment, he heard the unmistakable whine of another incoming mortar. Roe realized he couldn't make it back to the bunker safely with the wounded pilot on his shoulder. The dramatic experience flashed into memory like a strange dream, shaking him to his core.

This altered state defined his past experience, but weirdly, as if he was looking on as a spectator from the outside rather than being directly involved as a participant. Roe experienced an eerie sense of detachment, an out of body experience. It was truly uncanny. Was he an apparition? Was this for real? Was this really happening to him? He had no control of the imaging. A mystical sense of his mind expanding came over him to the point of hallucination. This event could not be real. He felt disembodied.

Suddenly, it ended. The images vanished. No further memory was retrievable. His mind became blank, as if his cerebral computer had crashed.

Murray explained to Roe that this was at the point when an exploding mortar took out the Quonset hut, collapsing the roof on Roe and the pilot he was carrying to the safety of the sandbag bunker. Roe suffered a severe concussion at that point in time. His injury produced an unconscious state explaining why his mind's screen went black.

Murray commented to Roe that his heroic act earned him a Silver Star and a Purple Heart. Did he recall that? Roe had forgotten these awards on several prior occasions.

"It slipped my mind, but now I do vaguely recall the citation ceremony, Murray."

"Good, Roe. We are making progress."

As Roe came down off his trip, Murray assured him he'd retrieved the information that he sought- the frightening experience that triggered Roe's PTSD. By recalling the experience, Roe would learn to deal with it as he followed his cognitive enhancement program. Positive insight would be gained in that intensive program. Murray's staff would condition him to avoid flashbacks or manage them if triggered by an unexpected event.

Murray carefully explained that Roe's increased heart rate, dry mouth, and sweating were all part of his repressed fear. The threatening ordeal, the flashback, was over. Murray reassured him this information would guide further therapy of Roe's repressed memory and aid in his recovery.

***

Several weeks later, Murray took Roe aside. "You are tolerating your medications without significant side effects, and the bio-feedback and psychiatry sessions have shown progression."

He encouraged Roe to spend more time on his couch chatting about the past. He'd like to know Roe's thoughts, perceptions, and feelings about certain events. He urged him to continue his relearning program by studying his textbooks and lecture notes, to get plenty of rest, maintain an exercise program, and eat a good diet.

"It's been helpful that Miss Summerville visits you every day and has dinner with you in your suite. She inquired if she could move you into her Twin Peaks home close to the University, and have a therapist come by daily for treatment sessions. She thought the home environment might facilitate or accelerate your recovery. I agreed to this plan, and will organize home therapy sessions if you do well in your next session. You've progressed nicely, well ahead of schedule. I anticipate your return to the surgical staff next month. Doctor Engels will have a staff member scrub with you and help you care for patients for six months just to insure you have no memory lapses. You'll be off all medications. You'll be flying solo again, out of the Langley Porter nest."

At the good news, Roe experienced a great load lifted from his back. He smiled broadly in gratitude. "Thank you very much, Murray, for putting my life back together."

"You're welcome. You earned it. Look, it's not my business, but you might consider marrying Ms. Summerville. She's much more devoted than many of the wives who visit their husbands here. She strikes me as a very intelligent and caring person. She'd be a real asset to a busy surgeon, in my opinion."

"As soon as I am back on my feet and completely recovered, I plan to ask her to marry me" He met Murray's gaze.

"I sincerely appreciate the expert therapy you and the staff have given me. Everyone has been so considerate. I'm very grateful, Murray."

"You're welcome, Roe. I'm organizing the final exam on memory. I've read your file, as well as some of your spectacular cases. So, I'll mention a name or event to jar your memory, and you tell me what you recall. We've reconstructed your childhood, your education, and your war-time experiences. Now, let's see if you can be a productive surgeon again."

"I'll be ready, Murray. Things are so much clearer in my mind now. The circuits aren't jamming anymore, and I'm getting my sharpness back. My recollection and retention are almost back to normal. I don't have to rack my brain anymore to bring up factual data."

"The real test will be if you can maintain the same level of cognition while staying off medications like you are now. You can't conduct surgery on cognitive enhancers, you'd lose your license. Of course, I'm confident you'll do well. You've made a spectacular recovery. Our entire staff is quite optimistic about your future."

"I understand, Murray. I really do. Thank you."

He gave him a big hug and held him tightly for a moment, like a child rescued by his father from a life-threatening event. Their bond was tighter than words could express. Murray patted him gently on his back, understanding the genuine emotion conveyed by the gesture.

"I want you to always remember that you had no structural organic damage to your brain. You suffered severe physiologic dislocation of neuro-circuiting with your concussion and brain surgery for a subdural hematoma. Your white matter remains intact. You've recovered well from the anxiety, fear, and depression associated with what they used to call 'shell shock.' Your IQ is intact, and your memory bank restored. Your best days are ahead, Roe, I assure you."

Roe repressed a cry of joy until Murray departed. He was still emotionally labile, but knew complete recovery was right around the corner.

CHAPTER THIRTY-SEVEN
THE FINAL EXAM

San Francisco December 1966

Roe was excited, but a bit apprehensive. What if he didn't pass the final exam with Dr. Robeson at Langley Porter? Would he wash out of the UCSF surgery program?

He'd been under intensive treatment for ten months. He felt he was back to normal, but he couldn't help feeling a bit anxious. It was probably prior to his surgical boards that he last experienced butterflies like this. He had passed the boards with flying colors, so why not Murray's exam?

"Get a grip, Roe," he told himself.

Murray came in smiling, a large manila folder under his arm. He shook hands with Roe and patted him on the back. Actually, Murray was brimming with pride at his staff's awesome reconstruction of Roe's memory using cognitive enhancers to augment conventional techniques. He planned to present this case study at the next International Conference on Post Traumatic Stress Disorder associated with memory-related problems.

"Okay, Roe, ready to go? I'll say something to prompt you. When the memory kicks in, you recount your story. I have some of the more memorable cases of yours in these folders. You can do this. Ready to go?"

"I'm ready. Shoot."

"Okay. Tell me about the Golden Gate Bridge jumper."

Roe answered without hesitation, "Very interesting story. A twenty-year-old hippie on LSD hallucinated that a Russian sub was passing under the bridge with the intent to nuke San Francisco with a missile. He jumped off the bridge to intercept the sub and prevent the attack."

"How did you learn this?" Murray inquired.

"I asked him three days after surgery when he finally woke up from his coma in the ICU. He was only the sixth person to survive a jump off the Golden Gate Bridge. He came into Mission ER in shock, unconscious with a concussion, multiple rib fractures, bilateral pneumothorax, ruptured spleen, and a fractured liver with over 1500 cc of blood in his abdominal cavity. All four extremities were broken, plus both of his shoulders dislocated with torn rotator cuffs. We resuscitated him, put in bilateral chest tubes, and attached them to water seal and suction. We established an airway and took him to surgery to perform an exploratory laparotomy. He underwent a splenectomy, and liver fracture repair, followed by an extensive abdominal lavage. Then, our orthopedic surgeons took over to repair and stabilize his extremity fractures."

"Amazing case. How did he do post-op?"

"Great for three days. He woke up and told me what had happened, and actually thanked me for saving his life."

"Anything else unusual else happen?"

Roe, replied instantly. "Yes, as a matter of fact, it was tragic. That evening some hippie friends came in to visit him, saw the IV line and mainlined him with heroin."

"Mainlined?"

"Yes. They injected heroin directly into his IV line's portal. The patient was already getting small, interval IV doses of morphine sulfate, so they overdosed him. He arrested with a severe cardiac arrhythmia. We tried all resuscitative measures-defibrillation, narcan, and epinephrine, but he developed an irreversible, fatal arrhythmia and died. All that work for nothing."

"Tragic, indeed, A sorry episode, but you certainly demonstrated excellent recall on that case."

Murray quickly moved to another subject.

"Does the name Vincent Red Cloud ring any bells?"

Roe laughed. "What a case that was. Friday and Saturday nights in Mission ER are referred to as the Gun and Knife Club." He laughed.

"This case takes the cake. In the middle of the night, I get called by a Senior Resident who tells me he needs to take a full-blooded Cherokee Indian to the OR, stat. The patient is in shock with a hunting arrow stuck in his right buttock. Lines are in, IV fluids running wide open, blood's typed and crossed. The resident's working diagnosis is the arrow penetrated the iliac artery and vein posteriorly through his buttock."

"Tell me about it as you recall the case."

"I agreed with the diagnosis, but warned the resident not to pull out the arrow. Just cut it off at buttock skin level to avoid exacerbating the injury. Most hunting arrows are barbed and he'd make things worse."

"I arrived at OR number five at three in the morning. The patient was anesthetized and intubated. A nasal gastric tube and Foley catheter were in place. Large-bore IVs were running wide open. The patient's monitored blood pressure measured 80 with a pulse rate of 130, still hypotensive from internal bleeding.

"I asked the resident, 'What happened to cause this incident?' He said this guy and his buddy, another Cherokee, were drunk as skunks and got clowning around playing Indian games since no cowboys were available. His buddy nailed him in the buttock with an arrow. At first, he didn't think he had actually hit him. Both were pretty damn drunk. Fortunately, they called an ambulance when he realized what happened.

"I remember remarking, 'This is a first. Let's explore him and fix the problem.' At laparotomy we observed a huge right lower quadrant hematoma. The retroperitoneum was intact. Fortunately, it had tamponaded the hemorrhage. Otherwise, Vincent Red Cloud probably would have bled out. No other injuries were apparent. The hematoma was evacuated, and the right iliac artery and vein clamped after administering a dose of heparin. Both vessels had been nicked by the arrow, but not transected. Vascular reconstruction proceeded without problems. Type O blood was transfused in the OR. He returned to the recovery room in stable condition."

"That all?"

"Nope, one hour later the resident called to report the patient was becoming hypotensive again. We took him back to the OR thinking one of the vessel repairs had ruptured. But this was not the reason for the drop in blood pressure. The vascular repair was intact, dry as a bone.

We had removed the arrow in the first operation through the abdomen while the patient was still hypotensive and we didn't see any significant gluteal bleeding at that time. Much to our chagrin, when we turned the patient over this time, we discovered we'd missed a secondary diagnosis. He had an enormous hematoma in his right buttock where the arrow entered. Once his BP was restored with the vascular repair he bled into his buttock. We prepped him and explored the wound site deeply. At reoperation, with the patient on his side, we found the right gluteal artery severed and pumping. His collateral circulation was adequate, so we suture ligated the gluteal artery pumper. His vital signs soon returned to normal on the OR table. Vincent Red Cloud experienced no postoperative complications this time around. We discharged him five days later."

"End of story?"

"Nope, it gets better, Murray. Saturday mornings at the University we hold Death and Complication rounds for educational purposes. We call it D and C conference. We had to report this case because we missed the diagnosis of the gluteal artery injury during the first operation. That Saturday, Doctor Engels had a visiting surgeon from London sitting next to him. As I described the case, the visitor's eyes got bigger. He had the most astonished expression on his face. Dr. Engels laughed and nudged him, and said, 'It's still the Wild West out here.' Everyone had a great laugh."

"Anything else?"

"You won't believe the next coincidence with Red Cloud's case. Two years later, I was making rounds with students and residents, and we stopped in on a patient who was admitted the night before with acute pancreatitis. It was a good teaching case for the differential diagnosis of the acute abdomen. I recognized the patient immediately, but didn't let on to the students. The patient didn't recall that I had operated on him two years earlier. Red Cloud was almost in DTs, really out of it.

"I had emphasized to the junior staff the importance of taking a good history and performing a thorough physical. As I said, I didn't let on that I knew Vincent Red Cloud inside and out, literally and figuratively speaking. I wowed them with my history-taking, zeroing in on the old injury. They were really impressed."

"Did you ever tell them?"

"I confessed at lunch. We all had a good laugh over it."

Murray chuckled. "Let me present you with a hypothetical case that comes into the ER. Give me the probable diagnosis and take me through the management. A sixty-five-year-old male comes into the ER with a blood pressure of 60, pulse 140, skin moist, patient confused, complaining of severe back and abdominal pain. Your first impression is?"

"It's a classic presentation of a contained ruptured aortic aneurysm. An abdominal exam should reveal a pulsatile mass. If so, no x-rays or scans are necessary, they waste valuable time. The patient should be typed and crossed, including fresh frozen plasma, and platelets. A nasal gastric tube and Foley catheter should be put in place and two large IV catheters inserted. One is a central line, if possible, and fluids administered to raise his BP to 100 systolic.

"The patient should be taken to the OR stat. One of the most important factors in the management and survival is rapid aortic cross-clamping of the bleeding aorta to prevent continuing hemorrhage. At operation, the ruptured aneurysm is replaced by a prosthetic graft. Heparin monitoring should be maintained during the case and properly reversed. The common post-operative complications are coagulopathy, renal failure, and pulmonary insufficiency."

"Very good, Roe, a professorial synopsis. I'm calling Dr. Engels. You are good to go with proctorship for six months."

He shook Roe's hand enthusiastically. "By the way, Dr. Engels wants you to stop by his office on your way home."

"Okay, thank you, Murray, for getting me through this ordeal. I'll call on the chief."

"At the slightest hint of anxiety or relapse, call me right away. I don't anticipate any problems, but just in case, I'm always around. You've got my number."

"I can't thank you enough for all you've done for me, Murray. You're a good man." Roe gave another sincere hug to the man who'd saved his career.

***

Roe stopped by the Chief of Surgery's office. The old, white-haired chief was doing paperwork, his granny glasses down on the tip of his nose.

Dr. Engels had a ruddy Irish complexion and a jolly sense of humor. Although a man of great academic achievement, the professor never showed a sense of self-importance, his nature always kindly, never officious. The chief loved teaching and working in the OR with his surgery residents. He had done clinical research, but no one would ever accuse him of being a "rat doctor." The OR was his arena, teaching residents how to operate was his life's dedication. Many became professors of surgery later in their careers.

"Roe, my man. Good to see you again. Dr. Robeson called to tell me you knocked it out of the park on your final cognitive exam. He vouches for you. Says you are ready to resume your position at the University. I'll have experienced colleagues working with you during this early transition stage. They'll inform me when you are back in the saddle again and capable to resume normal duties. I anticipate it will be like riding a bike."

"I hope so, sir. I'm ready to get back to work."

"I had originally planned to put you on the Blue or Gold services at the University Hospital, but Blazer called. The SFGH Trauma Center just opened, one of six in the country. He has three faculty consultants out with the flu. He asked if I could loan you to him for a week or so. Christmas is coming up and he's short staffed. The General Hospital is operating up a storm with thirty or forty trauma cases a weekend. Right down your alley. What do you think, Roe? Give them a hand?"

"Sure. I like Blazer. He's been a mentor to me. He sure can operate. I hope he doesn't try to steal my cases."

The chief laughed, "Only if you start to screw up. I doubt that will happen, Roe, not after all the trauma you saw in Vietnam. I'll bring you back up to the University at the beginning of the New Year."

"That would be fine, sir."

"By the way, will you and Miss Summerville join me and Nancy for dinner tonight? I'll have some of your colleagues over."

"How'd you know about her, chief?"

"She practically lived at Langley Porter, waiting for you to come around. She's quite the lady. I understand she's a Fellow at the Hoover Institution down at Stanford."

"You don't miss a trick, do you, chief?"

"Goes with the territory, Roe."

***

Roe reported to San Francisco General Hospital the Saturday evening of Christmas weekend. The Chief of Surgery, known as the "Blazer" welcomed him back into the fold. He instructed Roe to call him at home if a tough case came up.

"Don't swim out too far. I don't want you to get in over your head until I check you out, okay?" His grin reminded Roe of Biff.

"Sure, no problem. I'll call you if I need you, chief."

The chief had just finished his Christmas Eve dinner at his home in St. Francis Woods when Roe called.

"Sorry to bother you at dinner, but some sociopath walked into a Market Street gun store and purchased a German Mauser rifle and ammunition. It's a huge gun used to hunt rhinos in Africa. He randomly opened fire on Christmas shoppers, killing two before wounding the two patients I have here in the ER."

"Fill me in, Roe." The chief said in a matter-of-fact manner. Nothing fazed or surprised him at this stage of his distinguished career, and he appeared not the least bit disturbed to have Christmas Eve interrupted.

"The gunman was shot dead by the police. The two wounded victims were driving in a VW bug crossing the intersection. The vehicle was struck by stray bullets that pierced the car door and shattered the driver's right femur, hitting his right femoral artery and vein. His lower extremity is ischemic with no Doppler signal. I don't think we need a preoperative arteriogram. We can perform one in the OR on the table, if necessary. I'm rushing him to the OR. Care to join me, Dr. B?"

"What about the other patient?"

"Oh. His wife just had a superficial injury in her arm as the bullet exited the other side of the car. She's being taken care of by the ER staff."

Blazer loved the OR, and he especially enjoyed operating with Roe MacDonald. Roe was one of his "hot shot" residents several years ago before he left for Vietnam. The chief could use that term sarcastically, or complimentary, as the situation demanded. In Roe's case, it indicated praise.

When Blazer arrived in the OR, Roe had already exposed the femoral artery and vein, and anticoagulated the patient with Heparin, after applying vascular clamps to stop the hemorrhage. Roe was harvesting a large segment of saphenous vein at the ankle with the resident. He was instructing the resident in careful dissection of the vein, which he intended to use as an interposition graft for the arterial-venous repair. The anesthesiologist was transfusing the patient.

Blazer thought, *He sure doesn't waste any time. Out of the OR for a year and he hasn't lost a step. He's certainly a gifted surgeon. Decisions are instinctive with him. The Vietnam experience stuck with him.*

"I'll scrub in, Roe, and give you a hand."

"Okay, chief. Thanks for coming by. I appreciate it."

The chief and his protégé debrided the traumatized artery and vein. The gunshot wound had severed them. Two segments of vein would be required. The next step Roe initiated really impressed the chief.

Roe passed a number three Fogarty catheter distally and retrieved clot that had embolized. Back bleeding was satisfactory, but Roe performed a quick arteriogram to make sure the patient had not trashed his trifurcation vessels below the knee with clot emboli. The angiogram was satisfactory, the patient's outflow tract intact.

"Good move, Roe," the chief commented.

Roe flushed the distal circulation with low molecular weight Dextran and heparin solution. The reverse vein was interposed and skillfully sewn in with 5/0 prolene. Arterial circulation was reconstituted indicated by a good Doppler signal and palpable posterior tibial pulse at the ankle. Both signs indicated a good operative result.

The venous repair went quite nicely also. Roe operated expediently… not rushing, but not wasting a minute.

The chief reflected, *He's sure smooth for a young surgeon.*

"Good to have you back, Roe. I'm sorry Dr. Engels is taking you back to the University Hospital. I sure could use you here."

Blazer rarely praised anyone, but in Roe's case, considering the circumstances, he said, "Very nice job, Roe. I'll head on home."

Roe, laughed. "Not my first rodeo, chief."

"Where'd you learn that phrase?"

"From you. I complimented you once when I was a resident assisting you in surgery, and that was your reply. I never forgot it. You were a good mentor to me. I always wanted to operate like you, JB, and Stoney. You three are surgical rock stars to the UC residents."

"I'll take that as a compliment, Roe," even though the chief wasn't sure about the rock star part.

"Ortho will be scrubbing in now to stabilize the patient's fracture. Make sure the resident stays around, so they won't ding our vascular repair, okay? By the way, how did the Mauser shooter get the money to pay for such an expensive hunting rifle?"

"He charged it on his American Express card. He never leaves home without it."

They both shared a good laugh at the dark humor common among some surgeons.

Roe checked on the gunshot wound victim in the recovery room before leaving the hospital. The patient was doing fine. Ortho had completed the case with internal fixation of the fracture of the femur. The patient's foot had recovered its color and was warm with a palpable pulse.

"Looking good," he commented to the resident with a wave of relief.

Roe had passed his first real life exam since his rehabilitation.

It was seven-thirty in the evening and he was hungry. He looked forward to Christmas Eve dinner, which Ann was holding in a warmer oven at home. It was a well-practiced exercise for her, as he was often late for dinner.

As he turned to leave, he noticed a lot of commotion in a nearby ER cubicle. Lying on a gurney, a handsome, middle-aged gentleman in a tailored business suit had a large briefcase handcuffed to his wrist. He had been rushed in Code 3 from the San Francisco International Airport, transported by Medivac from United Flight 708 from Dulles.

The patient was in shock, confused, and complaining of severe abdominal pain. He couldn't answer questions coherently. The ER Team was undressing him when Roe wandered over. Another resident he recognized was examining his belly, one nurse taking his blood pressure, others starting IVs.

Kelly, one of Roe's favorite chief residents said, "What do you think, Dr. Mac, ruptured aneurysm?"

"Let me examine him, Kelly."

Roe palpated the abdomen, checked for rebound, and listened intently with his stethoscope.

Kelly inquired, "Should we take him to the OR stat, Dr. Mac, or X-ray?"

"Neither, Kelly, at least not right now. Soon, but not immediately. Something doesn't quite fit here. I don't feel a pulsating mass indicating a ruptured aneurysm, but he does have a retroperitoneal mass. With his blood pressure of 70, I should feel some pulsation through his thin abdomen if he has a ruptured aneurysm. I think he's bleeding internally, but from what? Let's pry open that briefcase and check for meds or medical history, okay?"

An orderly cut off the handcuffs attached to the briefcase. He pried open the briefcase lock. Roe opened the briefcase and examined its contents.

Everyone was astonished to see it contained fifty million U.S. dollars in large denomination bills, CIA communication documents, and a first class ticket to Saigon. His special diplomat passport identified the patient as Jeremy Balfour from Chevy Chase, Maryland. A .9 millimeter Beretta and a clip lay inside a compartment pocket. In another compartment were some pills...

Roe quickly read the labels. "Dalmane 30 milligrams, a sleeping pill... Coumadin 5 milligrams, an oral anticoagulant."

He noted several other over-the-counter prescriptions for colds, all containing aspirin. They were half full.

He turned to Kelly. "Aspirin potentiates the anti-coagulant effect of Coumadin, therefore is a contraindication to take them when anticoagulated on Coumadin."

"We may have our answer, he's on Coumadin and his anti-coagulation is probably out of control because he's been taking cold medicines with aspirin. Get a stat pro time and order ten packs of fresh frozen plasma. Give him Vitamin K, IM stat. It may or might not help. My working diagnosis is he's bleeding out spontaneously into his retroperitoneum, not suffering from a ruptured triple A."

I better be correct in this diagnosis. If not...

He gave another nurse an unlisted 415 area code number to call with instructions to tell Mr. Roberts to get over here stat. The message: "We have a dying CIA purser in SFGH's ER by the name of Balfour and he's carrying a ton of cash."

The stunned RN ran off to place the call.

The fresh frozen plasma arrived and was rapidly infused to counteract the anticoagulant effect of Coumadin, which is a variant of Warfarin, a rat poison. The patient's pro time, a lab measure of anticoagulant activity, was off the scale, confirming Roe's clinical diagnosis of a retroperitoneal hemorrhage. Taking him to the OR would have been unproductive.

Packed red blood cells were also infused to maintain the patient's blood pressure and provide oxygen carrying capacity. Nevertheless, the prognosis was bleak if the patient continued to bleed uncontrollably into his peritoneum.

Kelly was really impressed. "Great diagnosis, Dr. Mac. I was about to take him to surgery."

"That would have been a mistake of no benefit to the patient. Just remember, Kelly, sometimes it is much more difficult not to operate than to operate. Learn from your near error in diagnosis, okay?"

The chief resident looked relieved that he hadn't rushed the patient to surgery. "I will."

"Good judgment comes from experience. Experience sometimes comes from bad judgment. That's a surgical axiom, Kelly."

"You bet. Thanks, Dr. Mac. I won't forget that."

"Kelly, one other adage, when you hear hoof beats in the hallway and you open the door you expect to see a horse, not a zebra. In this case, it was a zebra. That's what makes this profession so fascinating."

Glad I didn't rush him to the OR...

"Let's get the patient up to the ICU. I don't think he is going to make it, he's too far along. Mr. Roberts will contact his family, and notify the agency when he arrives. Make sure his briefcase is locked in our ER safe with a hospital guard standing by. No one is to discuss this case, got it? Mr. Balfour is CIA, therefore on some secret mission. Do not release any information to anyone. If the patient continues to bleed out despite our treatment, and dies, it's a coroner case, but only if Mr. Roberts okay's it.

Instruct the staff to keep it all 'hush, hush.' Remember, Kelly, 'loose lips sink ships.' Vietnam is still going on, we're at war."

Before leaving, Roe phoned Ann again to say this time he was really on his way home. It was now eight forty-five. He then phoned Blazer to give him a heads up on this high-profile case.

Blazer agreed it must be kept out of the newspapers. This was not information for the general public, especially the anti-war crowd. The CIA mission would remain classified. Blazer congratulated Roe on the case management, and called it a first-class job.

He agreed to let Mr. Roberts handle the delicate matters with the CIA, the patient's family, and the coroner.

"By the way, Roe. Have a Merry Christmas!"

CHAPTER THIRTY-EIGHT AQUARIUS: THE 11TH SIGN OF THE ZODIAC

San Francisco October 1967

Astrologists predicted ominous interplanetary activity and a total solar eclipse resulting in the end of the world in early February 1962. Fortunately, the celestial bodies did not collide, nor did the world come to an end. Everyone was still alive five years later in San Francisco, but not well. Civil society was turned upside down.

The world definitely changed in the sixties as cultures collided dramatically. The clash resonated across the nation. The reverberations would be felt for over a decade as the sum of attitudes, customs and beliefs that distinguished traditional America were challenged by the new worldviews in the Age of Aquarius.

Society underwent an extraordinary revolution and renaissance. The sixties' cultural discord triggered staggering changes in all phases of humanity – social, religious, political, economic, scientific, artistic, musical, educational, and behavioral attitudes.

The age spawned a whole new generation of young people, a counterculture referred to as "hippies." This hedonistic group embraced communal living, free love, free speech, psychedelic rock music, and marijuana. Many became acid disciples of Timothy Leary, preferring hallucinatory

LSD escapes from reality to dreamy, spaced out pot smoking. "Tripping out" became a popular pastime.

Hippies were an off-shoot of the beat generation, "beatniks." They congregated in the North Beach and Haight-Ashbury districts of San Francisco. From there, their credo spread from the west coast throughout the United States. The revolutionary lifestyle became national phenomena in an amazing short period of time.

Hippie dress, attitudes, and values radically changed an entire generation, exploring what many considered alternate-universe lifestyles. Adventurous, they delved into Eastern philosophy and spiritual concepts, shunning traditional values and mores. Young people migrated en masse to bohemian lifestyles. Some critics of the avant-garde movement suggested a herd instinct had captured their imagination and cautioned it would not end well. Others thought they'd simply flipped out on drugs. Many just looked on in fascination or amusement initially, but that perception soon soured. No one could deny the glacial change. It became apparent that the crusade was more than a fad, it was a revolutionary movement with permanent aftershocks like an earthquake shaking the Bay area.

When the hippies adopted an activist anti-war stance, sentiment quickly changed. As Vietnam became a cause for mass protests and civil disobedience a tsunami of negative public opinion followed that impacted the nation, dividing it into fragments of opposing opinions. Conventional society objected to this counter-culture group's unruly Vietnam protests. Benign, orderly protests at first, the demonstrations soon disintegrated into bitter, confrontational, and ugly civil discourse bordering on anarchy.

For the average American, that unacceptable behavior didn't fly. It came across as disrespectful to our troops, although the brunt of most protests was directed toward the LBJ administration, a distinction lost in the bitter fracas.

For a Vietnam vet returning home, it appeared the world had gone mad. A mind-boggling experience greeted him. Treated with disrespect and disdain, vets were confused. Who were these people? Were they disloyal, not patriotic? Were these pot heads communist sympathizers? Why did they view the world in such a weird way? Were they living in an alternate universe, or what?

In general, the veterans retreated into a comfortable shell of family and close friends rather than confront the opposition with firsthand experience, or to attempt to increase stateside understanding of Vietnam. They rarely discussed what it really was like in Vietnam, what actually transpired over there. The genie was out of the bottle, and it was too late to put it back.

The war wasn't the fighting man's fault. The vets adopted a cynical attitude that no one could convince this eccentric group of the complexity of the war's conduct, so why even try to lend some personal insight? The anti-war movement had gained too much momentum. There were too many of them, and too few vets willing to mollify their views. The anti-war activists' mindsets were set in stone as if they'd been brainwashed, so fuck it.

Less confusing was the rising popularity of American folk music and rock bands in the '60s such as the Grateful Dead and Jefferson Airplane. The rage for their style reflected the Age of Aquarius. Custom designed, the music became the sign of the times, so it naturally caught on and flourished. The beat and lyrics captivated a generation. Bands staged huge concerts in Golden Gate Park, the East Bay, and on the Peninsula south of San Francisco.

Janis Joplin of the Holding Company lived in the Haight-Ashbury off Golden Gate Park with other popular musicians and artists feeling at home in the iconoclastic community of hippies, mavericks, and nonconformists. Hippies flocked there in droves, fostering a cult following.

It was an unnerving time in San Francisco, an era of emotional disconnect. While our troops fought and died in Vietnam, the counter-culture partied and protested vigorously. Scott McKenzie's version of John Phillip's song, "San Francisco" became a sensational hit typifying the period.

"If you're going to San Francisco, be sure to wear flowers in your hair..."

It became a household lyric and a symbol of anti-war sentiment. It also represented an image of resentment for returning veterans who thought the world had flipped out. Part of society had, in fact … depending on your point of view.

The hippie credo flaunted traditional society and challenged authority with mottos such as "Tune In, Turn On, and Drop Out." The hippies espoused a permissive ethos that attracted disillusioned young people by the droves to San Francisco. Cynical about the war and established values, they rushed to embrace the counter culture in throngs as the revolution gained momentum. This generational mass migration puzzled many, its root cause confusing.

Some sociologists suggested that Dr. Benjamin Spock's pediatric textbook's advice on raising children contributed to this rebellious generation raised by parents who dared not to discipline. The problem arose by adopting a permissive attitude rather than establishing parental authority during the formative years. If they wouldn't obey their parents, who would they obey later in life? Many lacked disciplinary red lines growing up. Some became conditioned to challenge authority.

Spock fostered a concept of letting the child's self-expression come out. He championed empowering the child's self-esteem. His critics were quick to point out the consequences of the improper imbalance of permissiveness and discipline. Critics blamed the lack of proper childhood discipline as a root cause of the hippie generation.

A libertine generation was "acting out" in Haight-Ashbury around the clock, a case-in-point supporting that argument. Empowered and self-centered, they challenged authority without regard to the long-term societal consequences.

In simplistic terms, perhaps the hippie lifestyle of anti-work, anti-authority, pro-drug, and an indulgent, anything-goes lifestyle was a manifestation of parental shortcomings to instill childhood discipline. Others thought it was just hedonism run amok. Maybe it involved both propositions. The subject remains controversial.

One prominent trend of thought and feeling in the sixties was captured and magnified in the hippie Zeitgeist: searching for a new meaning in life, free from societal restrictions. San Francisco was the crucible for an era of profligate social philosophy and moral relativity, No one could argue otherwise with the grand social experiments taking place in the sixties, which caused lasting implications for future generations. What kind of children would they spawn? How would their children turn out? Were they sending the right message? How would history judge them? Have we reaped what we sowed? Think about those pithy implications.

As the social revolution escalated, Nambassa, hippie conceived festivals, lifestyle and dress caught on, as did Renaissance Faires with Victorian-style attire. Love ins, pot parties, and psychedelic rock music and art were all the rage. Long, unkempt hair, beards, jeans and sandals were "in" for men. Women went braless and barefoot with no makeup. Many wore bright-colored clothing, tie-dyed pullovers, bell-bottom pants, or long full skirts reflecting Native American, Asian, or African motifs. Scarves, headbands, beaded necklaces, and Native American jewelry really turned on the hippies. Most personal belongings were limited, carried in backpacks. A communal spirit thrived. All awaited the next Kumbaya moment of unity and closeness to celebrate.

The lyrics and melody of Kumbaya are thought to have originated with Creole slaves in the sea islands of Georgia and South Carolina around 1930. Musical versions by Joe Hickerson, Pete Seeger, and Joan Baez in the sixties rekindled the song's popularity among the hippies and later became the hallmark of the civil rights movement.

Straights, conservatives, and traditionalists all sarcastically branded the hippie generation as naive and pious in their narrow worldview, typified by their obsession with Kumbaya. Traditional society looked on in amazement and condemnation at the growing hippie trend. Some looked down their noses, regarding hippies as disingenuous or even a bit deranged.

***

This Helter-Skelter background was the general state of San Francisco society in the mid-to late sixties when Kelly, a senior UCSF Surgical Resident, invited his Consultant Surgeon, Dr. Roe MacDonald to attend a party in Haight-Ashbury.

How would a highly decorated Vietnam veteran handle it? Kelly wondered. He hoped it wouldn't blow his mind. He knew Roe's past history.

Kelly wanted Dr. Mac to meet two old friends of his from his Stanford undergrad days, Zack and Zoe. They planned to meet at the Blue Unicorn Coffee House near the Haight at eight in the evening. Following a drink at the colorful establishment, they'd go to the party in one car, since finding a parking space was a problem in the neighborhood, worse than downtown San Francisco.

Roe agreed to go with one stipulation. "No drugs." Dr. Engels would fire both of them if he found out, not that he had any interest.

Kelly agreed to the terms. He had a good relationship with Dr. Mac, and didn't want to jeopardize it. "No pot, just booze, okay?"

They met Zack and Zoe as planned at the Blue Unicorn. Kelly made the customary introductions. What followed was a revelation of the new-age generation to Roe, bordering on the mind-blowing experience Kelly feared as he watched Roe's reaction to his new-age friends.

Roe politely sized up Zack and Zoe with clinical observations and acumen, trying to remain unbiased.

Zack had an effete demeanor. He appeared anorexic, pale, and stood awkwardly, hunched over. His short, brown hair was parted in the middle, stuck up with gel. His darting black eyes avoided contact. His teeth were stained greenish-yellow probably from smoking pot. Zack reminded Roe of a Doonesbury comic strip character by Trudeau in the *Yale Daily News.*

Zack spoke with self- ordained, great authority in an educated, but vexing manner, which surprised Roe.

He's susceptible to superfluous discourse, Roe quickly observed. *A smart fellow, but dissembled. What does the attractive young coed, Zoe, see in this play-actor, Zack?*

The young man rambled on in rapidly changing discourse, skip jumping through topics, rarely with focus or depth. More like sound bites or slogans. The kind of guy who memorizes bumper stickers.

Zack busily started enumerating the political vices of the Washington D.C. political establishment, as if he were reciting a catechism by memory. No cue cards, no notes, no teleprompter, Zack had the preamble down pat. Roe hoped to avoid the postscript, but the proselytizer was just getting started.

Roe thought, *I've just met this fellow and he's already expounding on his egalitarian worldview, and clarifying the vagaries of the Vietnam War for me. Maybe he's sounding me out, trying to categorize me.*

Roe was a great observer of human nature and behavior. Zack could be a Grand Rounds' case study in eccentric behavior.

This should be an interesting evening, Roe reflected, *if this is for starters.*

Zack obviously was an avatar of the "save the 'whatever' generation." As in "save the whales, trees, earth, and planet"—whatever, just fucking save it. He was a born crusader, just give him a cause and he'd jump on it, run with it, and embody it.

He found Zack's prattle irritating, and eagerly awaited the drinks they'd ordered.

Christ Almighty! Why not save Jeremiah the Bullfrog while you are at it, pal! Roe thought sarcastically. *Probably shouldn't give him any more ideas, on second thought. He's already on overload.*

Roe wondered if Zack ever held a legitimate job. Or, if he was a trust baby? Educated at Stanford with plenty of time and money to indulge in the issues of the day? In the mid-sixties, there were plenty of causes, and Zack apparently indulged in most of them. It seemed the current campus rage.

It struck Roe that at least Zack was intellectually engaged, while a lot of the hippie crowds were just dropping out, "making love, not war," rarely a serious thought crossing their drug-crazed minds. Then again, Zack appeared to be more of a "wannabe hippie," but just couldn't let his causes go. He was too issue-oriented in an era with no shortage of issues to drop out entirely. Zack had an opinion on most matters, some of consequence, most he couldn't wait to share.

Roe's Chief of Surgery, Burt Engels, always said, "Beware of the surgeon who starts out an argument with, 'I had a case...' as that's anecdotal evidence, not objective."

In surgery, some anecdotal experience may influence decisions but, in the end, you must rely on tried-and-true substantiated, statistical data... evidence-based facts.

Zack had not progressed to this state of cognition and objectivity. Scientific observation and method eluded him, facts and fiction conflated.

A person devoted to gospel, not so much the truth loses the big picture when he mixes too many issues. Confused people like this drove Roe up the wall.

Roe continued his critical scrutiny of this odd young man who seemed inclined to keep bombarding him with his personal opinions. Roe maintained a polite listener's role, hoping to decipher Zack's mind-set. And, hoping Kelly would soon rescue him from his ensnarement.

For some reason, Kelly never intervened, despite Roe rolling his eyes, signaling "rescue me!" to no avail. Kelly failed to notice how uncomfortable Roe appeared, trapped in conversation with a zealot. So, Zack's monologue went on....

Zack seemed full of misinformation about Vietnam, only occasionally hitting upon actual facts. Like a lot of young people in the sixties, he was obviously obsessed with the Vietnam War. He wore a tie-dyed "Ban the Bomb" t-shirt, old Levis with the knees worn out, and looked every bit the part of the inveterate protester searching for the next march.

This guy had probably never talked with anyone who had actually served in Vietnam. Still, Roe chose not to go there. He chose not to challenge Zack's flawed concepts and misinformation. He did not want to run the risk of triggering a tantrum. Nor did he dare inform the young man that he'd served in Vietnam until seriously wounded. That would really set him off.

Plus, Roe had just completed his year of memory rehab at Langley Porter, and didn't want to relive that part of his life with this impulsive young man who was trying desperately to embrace the current avant-garde movement. Roe saw no reason to confuse him with any factual data regarding Vietnam.

Roe "Believed in God, but everyone else had to show him their data." He wouldn't indulge or confuse this young man with conflicting objective evidence, or relevant data. Not worth the effort. Roe had nothing in common with Zack other than inhabiting planet Earth. So, why bother?

What annoyed Roe the most about Zack was his use the word "nuance," whenever he possibly could, which came across as pretentious. Affectations obviously afflicted both Zack and Zoe. On the Eastern Shore of Maryland where Roe grew up, and in Vietnam, "nuance" was a code word for "bullshit." No one, but politicians talked like that.

Kelly finally did rescue him. *Thank God!*

Relieved of the ordeal, Roe engaged Zoe in a chat, anxious to see what she was like. Zack didn't seem to be a good fit for Zoe. What was that relationship all about?

Zoe was lovely, a poster child for the Cultural Revolution. Physically attractive, with coiffured dark hair, hazel eyes, and a splendid, tanned complexion, she presented an initial positive impression. She had a friendly smile, accented by perfect teeth. She wore a stylish dress, not overdone with jewelry. Her fashionable sandals matched her outfit perfectly showing off her polished, manicured nails. Her attire complimented her slender figure. Zoe came across quite well, until she opened her mouth. Unfortunately, Zoe had a tiny, squeaky voice, and spoke like a valley girl. Her colloquial dialect ended most sentences with the question, "You know?" Or, "like…"

That vernacular habit could get quite annoying, maybe even to Zack, "you know?"

On occasion, Zoe spoke somewhat intellectually, but used slang, or cute college phrases, not very reflective of her higher education at Stanford. She impressed Roe as more caught up in the "joi de vivre," rather than the hippie movement directed at the rejection of traditional values. Instead, her engaging personality was devoid of any activist agenda. Zoe obviously was into fun and games, not causes.

This could be a long evening, Roe thought after spending the last half-hour with these two characters. He started to wonder about Kelly's selection of Stanford friends. They definitely came across as a little flaky. Kelly must have been in the conservative control group down on the Farm, quite a contrast to Zack and Zoe. They possessed none of the refined qualities he associated with his Ivy League crowd at Penn at that stage of his life. And, far removed from the personalities of his comrades in Vietnam.

Roe had been away only two years, but the world had changed dramatically in that time span. Zack and Zoe might as well be aliens from another planet. Or, "like", maybe he'd arrived in another universe.

As a master of transactional analysis, Roe could quickly evaluate a situation and respond appropriately. Usually, his attitude didn't come across as judgmental, demeaning, or confrontational even in the most tedious situations. But, he recognized that these two young people had triggered a strong negative response. They turned him off. He realized he was indeed being very judgmental, hypercritical, in fact. But, he refrained from expressing his views and opinions, vowing to be polite out of respect for Kelly. That took considerable reserve. There was no escaping this uncomfortable social interaction. He resigned himself to endure, go with the flow.

Zack's opinions, and off-the-wall commentary rubbed Roe the wrong way. Zoe's prattle added to his annoyance. Roe was not that much older than these two chronologically. Maybe eight years, but in terms of maturity and life experiences more than a generation apart. Maybe more.

"Six degrees of separation? No way!" That theory did not hold water in this case. They might as well live in different universes.

Roe managed to remain a gentleman, engaging in polite conversation, but participated mostly as an intent listener and observer. But, he could not help being judgmental in his final evaluation of Kelly's friends.

Roe could picture Zoe being featured on the cover of the Stanford Alumni magazine dressed in traditional college attire, as a charming "Sophomore of the Year." Unfortunately, her persona sent conflicting signals.

Emotionally demonstrative, the content of her conversation led Roe to believe she tended towards the persona of a drama queen. She had a nervous habit of flicking her hair back, whether it was obstructing her vision, out of place, or not. Maybe it was an affectation. Whatever, it was almost as distracting as her unfortunate voice.

Roe finally decided that Zoe was a "hybrid hippie," somewhere between campy collegiate and hippie trendy. If only she'd taken an elocution class at Stanford, clearly, she'd be a ten on the Bo Derrick scale.

Zack, on the other hand, was a hopeless piece of work caught up in the cause agenda. He was obviously an empiricist. For him, subjective opinion and anecdotes would suffice. He certainly was very opinionated for a young man in his early twenties. He was also a peacenik, wanting to embrace the hippie movement, but he focused on antiestablishment aspects more than free love, pot, and the laid-back lifestyle of the bohemians.

He's a little too intense for the hippie crowd and, long-term, probably wouldn't fit in. I can imagine him leading a demonstration.

The young man's dynamic mind and convictions would ultimately lead him to being an antiwar demonstrator on some campus or in the streets. For Zack and countless other Bay area residents, the Vietnam War ignited a revolution, a cultural divide epitomized by the slogan "Make Love, Not War."

Glacial attitudinal shifts in worldviews occurred not only on the West Coast, but emerged even in conservative regions of America. The students' Vietnam outrage was not manufactured, it was genuine. And, it was escalating, catching on everywhere. Roe recognized the gathering storm and predicted it would not end well.

Despite his reservations, the conversation at the Blue Unicorn ended amicably, thanks to his extraordinary restraint and two rounds of drinks. The coffee chaser was outstanding, living up to the reputation of the famous hippie gathering spot off the eastern end of the Golden Gate Park.

Roe suggested they jump in his Mercury station wagon and head to the party in Haight-Ashbury. Kelly had really hyped the event. Roe was anxious to compare the encore with this engaging, but puzzling, encounter with Zoe and Zack.

CHAPTER THIRTY-NINE HAIGHT-ASHBURY HIPPIE PARTY

San Francisco October 1967

It was a beautiful late autumn evening in San Francisco, winding up the city's "summer," which weather-wise occurs late in September and October of each year. The traditional months of July and August are not considered summer because the weather is foggy, cold, and windy. It prompted Mark Twain to remark, "The coldest winter I ever spent was a summer in San Francisco."

They drove up an idyllic street lined with pastel Victorian homes. The iconic "Painted Ladies" were beautiful with their gingerbread cornices and flutes painted in coordinating tones. No trash or graffiti marred the neighborhood, which was extremely well maintained. Geraniums grew in pots and planters everywhere, lining and hanging from the porches, creating a warm and welcoming atmosphere.

They pulled into a cul-de-sac at the end of the street and were greeted by their first surprise of the night, a parking attendant.

Just like Trader Vic's, Roe thought. *Nice touch.*

Good thing. VW kombi's and bugs occupied all the parking spots. Kombi's were the signature transportation of the time among hippies who colorfully hand-painted them with psychedelic art and logos. Many brandished cannabis leaves, and Ban the Bomb logos. A beat up old yellow school bus painted with flowers and smiley faces took up the entire driveway.

As they approached the party, Roe observed several white Adirondack chairs spread over the mowed lawn. The freshly painted home was a classic three-story Victorian. The earth tones suggested restoration to its late nineteenth century grandeur.

Impressive! Showcase quality. Someone put big bucks into this venture. No ordinary hippie commune, Roe reflected. *All the fine touches of the architectural features defy any conservative notion of the hippie lifestyle. This home is an architect's delight, rivaling the mansions in the exclusive Sea Cliff area.*

Kelly pointed out Jerry Garcia, the lead guitarist of the Grateful Dead. "He lives just two streets over." The musician was talking on the lawn with an older man puffing on a large cigar.

Kelly seemed to know all the players. *Must come to a lot of parties here,* Roe thought.

Kelly followed up with the other man's identity. "That's Hal Kant with him. He's the rock band's lawyer.

The "Dead" was fast becoming America's quintessential band with a huge following of "deadheads" seeking spiritual inspiration from the classic beat of the hippie generation. Their Bay area concerts attracted throngs.

"This party is winding up 1967's summer of love," Kelly informed Roe enthusiastically.

"Summer of love?" That struck Roe as a misnomer, or oxymoron. It was a time of unrivaled controversy and adversity in San Francisco, in his opinion.

What ever happened to the perfect world I grew up in? Roe wondered. *Seems someone is out of touch with reality and I don't think it's me.*

The past August, twenty thousand hippies had gathered in Golden Gate Park for rock concerts and psychedelic art shows. Roe hoped to God that twenty thousand would not show up for this party. People were already stacking up on the front porch, drinking and puffing weed. Rock sounds were blaring from the large, surround-sound, Wharfedale speakers. The woofers were working overtime with earsplitting sound, more decibel noise than music.

Roe recognized the lyrics: "Rings on her fingers, bells on her shoes, the sky was yellow, the sun was blue…"

The music's beat welcomed the crowd. It was an appropriate tune for an LSD trip. Hippies enjoying hallucinatory states with a mystical sense of detachment had come to the right party.

Roe recalled his therapeutic LSD trip, monitored by Dr. Murray Robeson. These kids were not monitored, tripping out with reckless abandonment. Unintentional consequences were becoming the norm in San Francisco, resulting in the wild perception that one could fly off a balcony with impunity, ending with a trip to Mission Emergency.

Roe took it all in and laughed to himself at this "Alice in Wonderland" scene. It was a sociologic zoo of sorts, bordering on the bizarre for someone who'd just spent two years in Vietnam.

The crowd's attire was as wild as the psychedelic art on the VWs. It ranged from bleached jeans and tie-dyes to Renaissance Faire outfits. They wore flip flops, sandals, Birkenstocks, or just traipsed around barefooted. It seemed everyone tried to avoid conformity, yet, ironically, they conformed conventionally to one another. The incongruity escaped them.

Roe predicted that a lot of highs would be reached here tonight, hallmarked by Kumbaya moments. Some were already well on their way to tripping out or getting stoned.

Suddenly, out of context with the moment, Roe experienced a brief flashback to when he returned from Vietnam to San Francisco after his tour of duty. The societal and cultural changes were mind-boggling. He had attended a 49er game against the Minnesota Vikings at Kezar Stadium in Golden Gate Park, north across Parnassus from the University Hospital. One of the vaulted "Purple People Eaters" linemen, Jim Marshall, recovered a fumble and ran the wrong way. It was then Roe knew the whole world had gone bonkers.

Dr. Robeson had warned him about these sudden, crazy, disconnected flashbacks.

Roe quickly refocused on the Haight-Ashbury scene, but wondered why that memory popped into his mind.

Two mongrel dogs barked loudly from the top of the porch steps, tails wagging in anticipation of a kind pat from the visitors. In another sudden, weird flashback Roe recalled instances in Southeast Asia and Indochina where residents ate their dogs. He never quite figured out why or how they decided when to eat the family dog.

When it came to flashbacks, Roe had experienced some real doozies, like this last bizarre one. What set them off? He gently patted the dogs on their heads and entered the home, with Kelly, Zoe, and Zack chatting merrily.

Party time.

The interior of the home was professionally decorated, impressive with indirect lighting and fashionably placed faux Tiffany lamps. Roe thought again that some millionaire must live here. The interior architectural design and furnishings blended well with the polished hardwood floors and expensive area rugs, creating an aesthetic impression. It appeared no expense had been spared in the renovation of this classic San Francisco home. It was elegant, but not overdone, with emphasis on subtle ambience.

Fresh-cut flowers in art deco vases graced the living room, apropos to the Flower Children who bobbed and weaved to the beat of the Grateful Dead. Roe glanced across the room to an adjoining dining room, which emitted inviting aromas of food. A buffet with waiters and attendants in tuxedoes stood by a large, heavy, wooden rector's table covered with fine linen and china. A banquet fit for aristocracy adorned the table with food piled high.

Roe also caught a whiff of incense and marijuana emanating from the dimly lit dining room. Gregorian chants sifting from separate speakers in this room competed with the loud Dead Head music out by the front-door entrance. The oddness seemed to bother no one.

It was a very large living room with a spacious seating area. In a place of prominence above a large wrap-around leather couch hung a Van Gogh reproduction of "Starry Night." It was framed expensively and highlighted by arc lights.

It struck Roe as fitting, since this famous painting was completed by memory while Van Gogh was interned in an insane asylum in Provence, France. This party had a certain asylum atmosphere with everyone going out of their minds. The kaleidoscopic crowd of hippies, artists, musicians, drop outs, and wannabe's—most already stoned—defined the description of the Age of Aquarius. The muted lighting, marijuana smoke, and incense gave the room a surreal atmosphere accenting the dreamlike fantasy of the diverse crowd.

Surveying the scene, Roe reflected that in the novel *One Flew over the Cuckoo's Nest*, it was difficult to distinguish the inmates from the caretakers. Everyone here seemed to act out their proclivity without inhibition. Whatever they were inclined to do, they did with mutual affinity. No hang-ups here. Not on pot or LSD. Profligacy in its purest Hedonistic form prevailed in Haight-Ashbury.

As they entered the dining room, a tuxedo-clad waiter politely inquired, "Would anyone care for champagne or chardonnay?"

This elegant offer struck Roe as incompatible at a hippie party, especially since they were serving Dom Perignon champagne and an expensive Stags Leap Chardonnay.

Such an extravagancy, he reflected. *This is more like a Nob Hill event.*

It would be a false presumption that the party-goers knew each other. In fact, most did not. But it really didn't matter. They would party with abandon well into the wee hours, and then make love, or whatever. That was the program.

He had been to a couple of wild Dartmouth Winter Carnival toga parties, but nothing like this. More music—modern jazz—was coming from a back den. The polyrhythm in the three adjoining rooms was contrasting: Grateful Dead on the front porch leading into the living room, the Gregorian chants in the dining room, and Cal Tjader's progressive jazz emanating from the *den.*

The flashing disco lighting effect in the den and the blue illumination of the dining room created an eerie effect, like fantasy challenging reality. Roe thought for a minute he was entering *The Twilight Zone.* Much of San Francisco's alternate universe society had taken a quantum leap into illusion.

With clinical observance, Roe analyzed the crowds' makeup. For some reason, he had expected this party to be comprised predominately of hippies. Not the case, not even close. This crowd represented a cross section of San Francisco, a slice of urban life.

Roe noticed several scruffy Hells Angels bikers in their leathers and chains, dispersed throughout the home.

Probably a security measure, he thought. *They look menacing, but seem to be enjoying their Budweisers.*

Several other groupings attracted Roe's attention. In their orange robes with shaven heads, Hari Krishna's appeared to be in deep religious conversation across the room. They were out of place, he decided.

Other small groups of hippies were playfully laughing and groping each other, a form of not too subtle foreplay. These folks weren't the least bit bashful or reserved. Social conventions meant nothing to them. Roe couldn't imagine that type of behavior at a party in St. Francis Woods.

Another small group of cross-dressers and transvestites were playfully teasing each other. Probably about who would do what to whom later on, Roe reflected.

All this transpired within the first few minutes of their arrival. They had just barely made it out of the living room into the dining area into this menagerie of mankind, when another polite, somewhat obsequious waiter invited them to the "sumptuous buffet in the adjoining dining room."

Sumptuous? Probably part of the waiter's training, not pretension.

The buffet was indeed grandiose with a luxurious display of caviar, seafood, a side of beef, and every fresh fruit and vegetable imaginable. Hippies loved their veggies.

Roe didn't quite know if it was "sumptuous," but down home they would say it was "one hell of a buffet." This is certainly not a paper plate and plastic fork party, real china and authentic antique silver were the order of the day. However, at this point, the crowd seemed more interested in conversation, booze, and pot. The culinary delights were not attracting them yet.

Whoever owns this home is really laying it on. This is a top-drawer event! He couldn't get the thought out of his mind. *Nothing seems too good for this crowd. What's the story? Something's very odd.*

What was Roe missing? All this was going on about two miles from the University Hospital. It seemed improbable, but true. Who was the rainmaker footing the bill for this lavish party? It far exceeded his wildest expectations.

A cheer went up as the Gregorian chants in the dining room were replaced by the Dead's popular song "Fire on the Mountain." The crowd's involvement and animation increased several fold. They knew all the lyrics and sang along, laughing, and carrying on with each other in good fun. These were happy campers. Roe didn't know how much was drug induced, but he recognized happiness when he saw it. These kids were turned on, and very happy, not a care in the world.

That triggered a reflection on what must be going on in Vietnam right now. Platoons out on patrols, flight surgeons and medics evacuating the wounded from firefights. Certain that nothing had changed over there, he fought back the emotion and refocused on the party.

Kelly was right, Roe reflected. *This is a colorful crowd, in every sense of the word.*

Their devil-may-care disposition was interesting to observe. Their casual, laid-back approach to life was worlds apart from Roe's. Nonchalantly, they pursued life with a "whatever floats your boat" attitude. Their hedonistic indulgence was foreign to Parnassus Heights University, where academic rigors prevailed. This scene opened his eyes to another cosmos.

Leaving the "sumptuous" banquet room, Kelly and Roe wandered down a short hallway to a large den opening up to a back porch and another manicured lawn and garden area.

During the renovation, a wall must have been removed inside to create this much space, atypical for a hundred-year-old Victorian. The atmosphere in the den dramatically contrasted to the other rooms—dim, with disco psychedelic effects from special indirect strobe lighting. The unmistakable smell of cannabis whiffed through the air. A large ceiling fan, typical of those in Southeast Asia, slowly revolved. This attractive room was professionally arranged with an unmistakable Asian flair.

An eerie sensation suddenly struck Roe, almost blowing him away. This room looked like an upscale opium den in Cholon, Vietnam. In fact, almost an exact replica of the Pink Taco in the ethnic Chinese sector of Saigon that catered to GIs, offering high-class ladies of the night, booze, and, of course, the finest opium and heroin from the Golden Triangle. This room was not the vision of some high-end interior designer. Whoever designed this room had spent some considerable time in Cholon and committed the opium den's impression to exact memory.

Here I am half a world apart in an authentic opium den, reproduced right here in San Francisco. Close my eyes and I'm in Cholon. Unbelievable!

The music in this room set the mood. He enjoyed the Latin jazz of Cal Tjader, a musician very popular in North Beach in the sixties. The gifted musician had attracted crowds rivaling those of the Ramsey Lewis Trio located west down Broadway.

The atmosphere in the large den was more subdued, lacking the raucous activity of the two previous rooms.

Up 'til now Roe had witnessed a virtual menagerie of the '60s generation, a cross-section of the avant-garde of San Francisco, quite dissimilar to his social experiences in the '50s. The contrast was inescapable.

The Cal Tjader jazz subsided, replaced by a Kingston Trio version of Pete Seeger's, "Where have all the flowers gone?" It was a poignant reminder of Vietnam, something he was trying to forget, catching him off guard. This crowd embraced the hippie credo, "Make love, not war." So, they sang along with Pete's iconic tune.

Where have all the soldiers gone? Long time passing… Gone to graveyards, every one. When will they ever learn?"

Meanwhile Roe's heartstrings tugged with the memories of comrades he left behind in Vietnam, triggered by the song's word, "graveyards." A brief flashback recalled the carnage of his triage at Pleiku and Danang, causing a moment of remorse. He fought back anxiety and joined the present as his rehab had conditioned him to do in circumstances like this to avoid a panic attack. PTSD comes on without warning sometimes, he reminded himself. He regained his composure.

Scanning the room, Roe suddenly recognized someone out of his past. The man looked really different, but it had to be Cody. Yeah, it had to be him, reclining on a futon in a far corner. He looked much older, now sporting a Fu Manchu moustache. He had let his commando crew cut grow out, but instead of pulling his long black hair into a ponytail like he did in high school, he let it hang down, hippy style… long and scraggly.

Roe strolled over to greet him.

Cody looked like a disheveled homeless man, although it appeared that he obviously had a place to stay, and looked well-nourished judging from his pooch belly. His eyes were bloodshot and his pupils constricted. A hoop earring hung from his left earlobe, giving Roe pause to think, *Left is right, right is wrong.* That was a straight's way of determining if someone's earring indicated their homosexuality. Cody was certainly not homosexual by any stretch of one's imagination, he loved women.

Cody still hadn't recognized him yet. Roe continued to clinically evaluate him as he approached. His friend's body had changed as well, buffed out, pocked with multiple scars, and emblazoned with tattoos. He had a Ranger tattoo on his right biceps and a Ban the Bomb logo on the left, a contradiction in statements. He wore several bright-colored woven *brucero* bracelets from Guatemala, like those sold at all Grateful Dead concerts.

Beneath his baggy pants, he wore beat-up sandals on dirty feet. Cody's wrinkled tie-dyed t-shirt had small holes in it and bore a small cannabis leaf logo over the breast pocket. Cody never did get into fashion statements.

It appeared Cody was pretty stoned, but it wasn't from marijuana. The cigarette he was smoking lacked the distinct odor of pot. Roe suspected Cody's cigarette was laced with heroin, judging from his constricted pupils. This narcotic could be placed in a cigarette and smoked without any telltale odor. Cody tried to focus on him, but being pretty high and not expecting to meet him here, nothing registered yet. An out-of-time, out-of-space interaction in progress.

They just looked at each other a moment without speaking. Cody trying to focus, to pull up the connection with this man standing five feet away.

Cody's skin grafts had not completely healed yet, and part of his right ear was still missing from his Pleiku battle experience. Most troubling, though, he had a heavy, productive cough and kept tissues handy. The discarded tissues in the rattan trash basket next to his futon appeared slightly blood-tinged. Not a good clinical sign ... actually, worrisome.

Roe's mind quickly went to work. He suspected Cody had picked up tuberculosis in Vietnam during one of his tours. He would address that issue later when Cody was a little more coherent. His old high-school buddy needed a chest X-ray, plus an acid fast AFB stain of his sputum for diagnostic purposes. Roe never ceased being a clinician. He became convinced Cody had tuberculosis in less than two minutes, and decided to get him under proper treatment ASAP.

Next to Cody sat an attractive young woman, who, unfortunately, looked like she had been "ridden hard and put away wet," as they say in western vernacular. Her hair was unkempt, her long paisley patterned dress wrinkled and covered with wine stains—probably from the half-empty Napa Valley Cabernet Sauvignon bottle tipped over next to her.

Smoking a joint, this hippie had multiple rings on her fingers and wore multiple bright colored Indian bracelets. But, she had no bells on her toes, like the song lyrics. She was barefoot with small silver bracelets on her ankles. This young woman was dressed like most of the young women at the party, but this gal had taste, indulging in classy Napa Valley wines.

As Roe approached even closer to greet Cody, he recognized this young woman reclining on the futon. It was Natasha!

My God! What a transformation. She looks awful.

Although Cody and Natasha were stoned, both finally recognized Roe and greeted him warmly. They were effusive in their invitation to Roe to get high with them.

Natasha offered him a fresh joint of Mendocino's best cannabis.

"Join in the party, dude." Cody implored.

"Don't be a party pooper," Natasha insisted, "Come on, Roe. Why not get high with us?"

Roe replied, "I'd lose my medical license, Cody, and my job at the University. Can't risk it, man."

Roe looked around for Kelly to back him up, but he was out on the back porch hitting on a little blonde. Zack and Zoe had disappeared somewhere else. God knows where.

"How are you, dude? Haven't seen you since Pleiku in '65, well over two years ago. Heard you got banged up in a mortar attack at Tan Son Nhut sometime after." Cody sounded friendly, but his speech slurred and his eyes squinted.

"Just as soon pass on that subject, Cody. Looks like you are healing up from your reconstructive plastic surgery. By the way, I never had an opportunity to congratulate you on your Silver Star and two Purple Hearts. You deserved it. Sorry you took such a big hit."

"Shit happens, man. Not a big deal, dude, just doing my job over there killing gooks for God and my country." He laughed derisively. "At least I didn't buy the farm. Natasha told me you had brain surgery at Clark AFB."

Cody quickly switched topics, seeming coherent despite his drugged state. "How's that going? Coming back? You seem okay to me."

Cody pressed the issue, not realizing the topic was sensitive to Roe.

Roe relented, "I've essentially made a complete recovery, but still have some weird flashbacks. It was a slow process at first, but now I'm okay, Cody. I'm back to operating and teaching. Langley Porter was great to me. Good docs over there. They reconstructed my recall mechanisms. But enough of the war stories."

He turned to Natasha. "So, how are you, Natasha? It's been a long time since Mission ER."

"Five years ago, as a matter of fact. Bet you don't remember me from Clark AFB, do you?"

"Clark AFB? You were there?" Obviously, Roe still had some blank spots in his memory.

"Sure, I was there. Took care of you. Air evac C-130 brought you in from Vietnam, unconscious. You blew a pupil and underwent an emergency craniotomy for a subdural hematoma. I was your nurse and scrubbed on your case. You remained unconscious for several days after surgery. I attended you following surgery. I was transferred back to Travis AFB after you went to Baguio for rehab with your friend, Mr. Roberts. Sorry you went through so much, Roe. What a bummer! I'm out of the Air Force now, just kicking around the Haight. I may go back to nursing at SF General Hospital. I love the Mission."

"You're a great nurse. You should go back, Natasha. I never knew you were at Clark, much less involved in my case. What a twist of fate!"

He purposely avoided rehashing his Clark experience. Obviously, that episode was still safely tucked away, repressed in Murray's terms.

He looked again for Kelly, but he still wasn't in sight. "Would you excuse me for a moment, I want to check on my resident out there on the back porch. I'll come back in a moment, okay? It's getting late, and he has Grand Rounds early in the morning. I want to remind him not to stay too late, or get drunk."

As Roe turned to leave, Cody shouted to him, "Enjoy yourself, Roe. Nobody's going to frag you here, man. We got your six." He laughed at his own dark humor.

Roe knew what the war-time reference "frag" and "six" meant. The jargon sent a chill up his spine.

Natasha smiled at him mischievously, her seductive best, a sure invitation for him to return. "Come back now, you promise?"

"I'll be right back, Natasha."

Sexy even in her present state, how could he refuse?

Roe found Kelly and gave him five dollars for a taxi. He asked him not to tie one on, or stay out too late, and reminded him of Grand Rounds in the morning. It was a paternal instinct toward his favorite surgical resident. Zack and Zoe had vanished. He told Kelly he could round them up if he wanted to, but he doubted they would want to go home anytime soon.

When he returned to resume his conversation with his old friends, he noticed Cody had left his futon and was in deep conversation with a cabal of men in the far corner of the room. A private area, he supposed.

That's an interesting group, indeed, Roe thought, as he dissected this incongruous clique. *What are their associations with Cody?*

The odd mix of men appeared involved in some sort of intrigue, engaged in deep, serious conversation. The four closest to Cody caught his immediate attention. Two were well-dressed Hispanics. A scruffy Rastafarian in dreadlocks next to them seemed ridiculously out of place. Dressed hideously in mix-and-match clothing probably from some thrift store, he rolled a reefer. The fourth man was dressed in a conventional business suit, and certainly looked just as much out-of-place at this party.

The taller Hispanic attracted Roe's attention first. He wore a heavily starched white shirt open at the collar, revealing a heavy gold necklace. He had jet-black hair, combed back with a lot of hair spray. Not one hair could possibly move in a Cat One storm. The left side of his lip turned up in a permanent sneer or snarl.

Probably the result of Bell's Palsy, Roe thought. *Sinister looking character.*

Two other distinguishing features were his dark beady eyes and a pencil thin moustache. *Unforgettable features. Like a character out of a Marvel action comic book.*

This character appeared to dominate the conversation with Cody, gesturing with his hands in some sort of explanation.

Roe thought it was a bit unusual that this man wore a Mexican serape over his shoulders despite the warm evening. Well groomed, he wore freshly pressed tan trousers over polished, dark leather cowboy boots.

When not talking, a cigarette hung casually from the normal side of his mouth. His Mexican sidekick—a short, stout man in his mid-fifties with balding grey hair—interrupted him. Cody was intently gauging their reaction to what the fat man had to say.

The fat man appeared to be expanding on some topic, focused on Cody and the man with the sneer. The portly gentleman had a classy, aristocratic appearance, elegantly dressed in an expensive earth-toned Guyabara, a traditional Mexican wedding shirt worn without a tie. His shirttail hung out over his tailored white linen trousers The Guyabara almost hid his rotund abdomen, probably why he chose to wear it.

Standing somewhat apart, apparently totally disinterested in the conversation, was an ugly black man with dreadlocks, smoking a reefer he'd rolled to perfection. Eyes glazed, he was well on his way to being stoned. His face and arms were scarred with keloids, a sure sign of a serious mainlining habit, or lots of fights. He had obviously lived a rough life, and looked worse for the wear. He dressed atrociously, not one item matched another.

Roe continued to survey this group with overwhelming curiosity, evaluating their incongruous presence. For some reason, he made mental notes. These guys weren't hippies, no way. They were out-of-place here. And, something was coming down.

A few steps away stood a Sikh in a red turban and Middle Eastern Indian garb. The Sikh had a well-kept long beard with early signs of graying. He was trying to attract the attention of the stoned Rastafarian in the outrageous outfit. It wasn't going to happen.

Even in the dim flashing light of this room, the Rastafarian lit up the room. The man reminded Roe of a Bob Marley concert poster.

A few feet away stood several other characters who also appeared a bit odd, and just as out-of-place as the first group. They were either incognito or inconsequential party crashers. They simply didn't seem to fit in with this group or the party-goers ... or anyone else for that matter.

One was in a warm-up suit, looking like he had just returned from the gym to smoke pot or drink beer. His buddy was a dwarf, an absolute Toulouse Lautrec look alike, complete with a beret and limp.

Hilarious! Is Jose Ferrer still alive? This is unreal. Holy shit!

This party had everything. A virtual zoo. Almost like Hollywood staged it. Weirdo's with red frizzled hairdos, afros, tattoos galore, bells, bangles, and beads. But, this character topped them all. Talk about human diversity. Who could assimilate such a social collection in this Victorian mansion setting? The scene gave a new meaning to eccentric and eclectic.

The Sikh finally gave up trying to engage the Rastafarian in conversation and turned to an Asian man sitting nearby. The distinguished-looking Asian smoked with a silver cigarette holder in a practiced fashion, as if about to propose some deal. He puffed occasionally while he conversed with the intent Sikh, as if he was posing for a Camel advertisement.

In fact, this heavy-set, short Chinese man seemed to be quite interested in what the Sikh had to say. Natty, he wore a tropical tan poplin suit and silk tie. Next to him sat another Asian man wearing a stylist blue Brooks Brother sports jacket with a tasteful paisley bow tie and light-blue Oxford shirt. He wore tan loafers with tassels, completing his dignified, prosperous, Ivy League appearance. Roe surmised neither were American-born, but probably educated in the States, most likely the Ivies. They had that certain flair he recalled from Penn, channeling unmistakable Ivy League.

Roe noticed the two Asians had settled comfortably in two leather chairs separated by a small table, as if preparing for a long night. They were drinking red wine from a Napa Valley vintage bottle while perusing a manila folder, given to him by the Sikh containing several printed pages. They also appeared to be absorbed in some kind of business deal. Both were clean shaven and acted quite sophisticated in their manners. And affluent, wearing expensive Omega watches and gold signet rings. Nothing escaped Roe's clinical eye. He'd moved in close to better observe what was going down. No one cared to notice, he could be invisible for all intents and purposes.

Definitely educated in the United States, judging from their demeanor and behavior, Roe verified, eavesdropping on their conversation despite the loud music. Both appeared in their late forties or early fifties.

Looks like they are reviewing some spreadsheets given to them by the Sikh. What's going on here? This is no ordinary party.

Roe surveyed this group in the corner of the room. Like a searchlight scanning the bay, he took in everything, analyzing it, and committing it all to memory. His curiosity soon became a fascination. Something instinctively told him it would be very important to be able to replicate what he observed at this juncture of the party. He just could not put a finger on it. Something wasn't right. His premonitions usually panned out.

It didn't seem possible, but as the night went on, things progressed just one step short of pandemonium. The surreal effect of the sounds, the lights, and the juiced-up crowd was beyond belief for a guy who grew up on the Eastern Shore of Maryland. Southeast Asia was foreign, but this scene was alien in another sense.

He glanced around once more, to do a final study of the mysterious clique over in the corner. The well-dressed, distinguished looking Asians did not seem to fit with the others. Why didn't all this add up? Why were they here at this party?"

Roe began to expect the unexpected. Maybe Natasha could explain Cody's puzzling relationship to this diverse grouping that appeared to have nothing in common with his buddy, Cody, or each other, in fact.

Roe finally returned to visit Natasha who was still reclining seductively on the huge futon, posed like some kind of princess of cannabis.

"I thought you would never come back. I'd almost given up on you." She smiled mischievously at him, bringing back memories of her seduction five years ago. Even disheveled, she was one seductive woman.

She leaned over to whisper in his ear. He noticed she still didn't wear a bra. Her breasts were as beautiful as ever. She obviously remained attracted to Roe, as she gave him a come-on smile.

"Do you still believe in the Garden of Eden? Remember? If so, come up to see my room. You'll love it, I promise."

"Recall the Garden of Eden? How could I forget?" He laughed, returning Natasha's engaging smile. "Sure. Why not? I'm fascinated by gardens."

Natasha was surely one of the most sensuous women ever created. How could he resist? The memory of the last encounter aroused him.

She really turned him on, even in her present state. He wasn't married yet, so a toss in the hay not out of question, one last fling before tying the knot.

She took his hand and led him to her upstairs room on the third floor. It was decorated in a very feminine fashion. Everything was very tasteful, and neatly in place.

Her room is organized, even if her life is not, Roe quickly noted.

He didn't expect the fulfillment of their previous fantasy to be surpassed. Little did he know the effect of marijuana on her libido. He experienced one of the wildest nights of his life—unequivocally unforgettable and beyond imagination. They both fell asleep, exhausted.

During the night, Natasha's moaning and shaking chills awoke him. She was sweating profusely. She awoke momentarily when he nudged her.

Roe inquired about her condition. "Are you okay? What's with the shaking chills? How long has this been going on?"

"It happens every three or four nights since I returned from the Philippine Islands. I can't control it."

Roe astutely inquired, "Noticed any change in the color of your urine?"

This question really puzzled Natasha, "Lately, it has become dark, almost black. Why do you ask?"

Her answer clinched the diagnosis for Roe. Natasha had "Black Water Fever," a malignant form of malaria, fatal if untreated. No doubt she got it while on her tour of duty at Clark AFB.

"Get some sleep, Natasha. Tomorrow we'll go over to the University Hospital to get you treated for malaria."

"Malaria, are you kidding?"

"You should have recognized the symptoms, Natasha."

"Okay, Roe, got it, sure. Thank you very much."

And then she fell back fast asleep, obviously not understanding what Roe was talking about. She was still stoned, and in her blissful state of mind, blind to the malaria and its risks.

The next morning, when they awoke, she looked smiled at him. "Did you enjoy last night, Roe?"

"Sensational. But, most importantly, I need to arrange for you to get proper medical treatment for your malaria. That's why you get those shaking chills in the middle of the night. We should shower and go over to the University hospital as soon as possible."

Obviously, Natasha did not recall last night's conversation, so Roe explained it in detail again.

"Really? Malaria? That makes sense. I probably got it at Clark. There were tons of mosquitoes out there."

Natasha yawned and stretched. "Can't we just kick back here for a while before going to the hospital?" She still didn't grasp the seriousness of her condition, even though she was a nurse, and no longer stoned.

"We could, but that would be unwise. I'd like to have an infectious disease specialist see you as soon as possible."

He glanced around the room, his curiosity regarding the lavishness of last night's party overcame him.

"By the way, Natasha, who owns this place and pays for these lavish parties?"

"The Rajah."

"The Rajah! Holy shit!"

This was an unbelievable coincidence. Biff had told him of the drug runner's exploits.

"You're telling me I'm in Rajah's house?" Roe asked her, incredulous at the revelation.

Natasha nodded, unconcerned. "Yeah. Why's that a big deal?"

Roe recalled Biff describing the difficulty authorities experienced in tracking the elusive Rajah whose cartel controlled the drug scene in the San Francisco Bay Area. He decided to pursue that line of inquiry in a few moments. First, he wanted to know how she got in with this crowd, her relationship to Cody, and how much she was into drugs.

He was not enamored with Natasha, but he sincerely cared for her. He hoped he could give her some insight into her drug-abuse problem, as his surgical experience documented many sad outcomes associated with drug abuse. He didn't want Natasha to go down that dead-end street.

Obviously, Natasha wasn't ready to shower and go to the hospital. This frustrated Roe, so he got up and went to the bathroom. When he returned, she was smoking a cigarette, still naked with no hint of modesty.

She flashed him that little mischievous smile again, suggesting, "If you are still horny, bring it on."

Roe politely refused, only wanting to talk.

The conversation was enlightening. Natasha had no reservations or hang-ups. Cody was not a romantic interlude, just a platonic relationship. She considered Cody a party animal that looked out for her and her friends, providing them housing.

After her RN stint in the Air Force, Natasha wanted some time off to unwind. Her current circle of friends offered her an alternative lifestyle: fun, with no ties or obligations.

"Unconditional love, sex, and drugs, if you want them. If not, no big deal," she told him.

Roe gave her a brief lecture on the hazards of drugs. She was on marijuana now, but what next? LSD? Heroin?

"It's a dangerous pathway and I want you to know that, Natasha."

Natasha listened carefully and acknowledged, "You're right, Roe. I get it, but no sweat, I'm having a ball. Life is good in the Haight. You should try it, man."

She respected his advice, but said she simply enjoyed marijuana highs and had no interest in hard stuff. She had a nonchalant attitude toward drugs, typical in the Age of Aquarius. Roe felt frustrated with her attitude, but reluctant to preach to her, so he changed the subject.

"You say the Rajah owns this place? How does he afford it?"

"He has a really lucrative business enterprise." Natasha replied. "He sells pharmaceuticals."

Roe knew the Rajah was not selling baby aspirin. *What kind of business? Burma Gold, pot, LSD?* He mused.

"Do you know how many authorities are looking for the Rajah, Natasha?"

"No," she replied nonchalantly, as if she could care less.

"The CIA, DEA, FBI and the SF Police Department are after him, just to name a few."

"Wow! What's that all about?" She wasn't zeroing in.

"Rajah is the ringleader of a huge drug cartel. What does Cody have to do with the Rajah? What's the connection? Fill me in on this, Natasha, it's very puzzling."

A funny expression overtook her face. She looked at him like he was crazy.

"Cody gives me a place to live. I met him at Clark when he was air-lifted from Pleiku with severe shrapnel wounds. He is still spitting fragments. He just completed reconstructive plastic surgery. He's a good guy, very generous."

"I know all that, Natasha. Please answer my question. What's Cody's connection to the Rajah?"

No answer, just a blank stare from her.

"Natasha, are you and Cody both involved in this illicit operation?"

"Illicit? I've done nothing wrong. I just get a lot of free booze, pot, and a roof over my head. But, I'm far from being a junkie or addict. I don't sell drugs. I'm not a prostitute. Is that what you mean?"

"Let me ask you plainly, Natasha. Do you or Cody have any business involvement with drugs or prostitution?"

"Come on Roe, get serious." Was he kidding her?

"Just checking. Do you have any idea who the Rajah is?"

"Yes, I do, as a matter of fact. Why don't you?"

"You're freaking me out, Natasha, who the hell is the Rajah?"

She studied him for several moments with a strange expression on her face, obviously puzzled at Roe's line of inquiry. *Roe could not be serious. Was it a complication of his brain injury or what?*

"Are you kidding me, Roe? You've known him since high school. You air evac'ed him out of Pleiku, and you just spent half an hour talking with your old buddy last night."

Roe's jaw dropped at this astonishing revelation. A deep, sinking feeling filled the pit of his stomach. Had he heard her correctly? Roe didn't want to believe what she was telling him. The profound shock sickened him. He was in denial, it couldn't be true. No way, he had to sit down on the edge of the bed.

"What are you trying to say, Natasha?"

"I'm trying to tell you, Roe, that Cody is the Rajah. They are one and the same person. Can't you get it? 'Rajah' is his Ranger code name from Vietnam."

Roe remained speechless. The revelation overwhelmed and mortified him. He almost fell off the edge of the bed, put his head in his hands, and almost wept.

Eventually he raised his head, though his heart continued to thud loudly in his chest. "What's Cody's relationship with the odd group of men who were over in the corner of the den last night?"

"Those are his business associates, his network contacts."

She had no reservations telling him this. She did not see this line of enquiry as such a big deal. She lived in the age of moral relativity, the Age of Aquarius.

"Do you know them, Natasha?"

"Sure. They come to all the big parties, and hold a business meeting here every month."

"Any chance you can tell me their names?"

"Absolutely, I know them all."

Natasha saw nothing wrong with Cody's activities, nothing to hide or to protect. Her lifestyle was simply a matter of pursuing happiness. She couldn't understand why Roe even cared. She'd never seen Roe so inquisitive, so visibly upset. It had to be his head injury.

What's his problem? she thought.

Roe wanted to be very careful to memorize everything she told him. He knew it might be painful, but he must relay all of the information to Biff as soon as possible.

How ironic. Attending a simple party leads to this incredible discovery of Rajah's identity. My high school buddy went rogue. Unreal!

"Who's the Mexican with the sneer and pencil moustache?"

"That's Ricardo Sandoval, a bad actor from Tijuana. I really don't like him. He strikes me as mean. He's the Mexico marijuana connection, a kingpin heavily involved with the Mexican cartels."

"And, his Hispanic sidekick, the fat guy?"

"That's Jorge Gomez. He's the Mendocino pot connection and coordinates the Tijuana operation."

"And the Sikh?"

"That's Ram Gandhi. He's the Burma Gold coordinator and bookkeeper for Southeast Asia."

"And, who are the two prosperous-looking Chinese guys?"

"Henry Wu. He runs the biggest opium dens in Cholon and Saigon. You've probably heard of them: The Pink Taco and the Poon Tang. Cody met him during his tours in Vietnam, and talks about it a lot. He and Henry are close pals. Henry helped him design the party room."

"And the other Chinese fellow?"

"That's Ji Moon. He's out of Hong Kong and is one of the Sikh's go-betweens. Moon has his own Tong underground group."

Roe continued his gentle interrogation of Natasha, committing it all to memory.

"How do you know all this info?

"These parties have been going on for over two years. They all hang out here. It's pretty common knowledge."

"And, the Rastafarian, who is he?"

"That's Randy. No one really knows his last name, and he came from Bermuda, not Jamaica. He's a top San Francisco street dealer. He outsources drugs to the various districts in the Bay Area. I heard a local golf club member brought him to the United States to caddy at the San Francisco Club as a joke that turned sour."

"What about the dwarf? Who the hell is he?"

"You won't believe this. His nickname is 'Toulouse.' His last name is LeBain. He's an accountant with the guy who wears the track suits, whose name is 'Gym Rat' Bob Castle. They have an accounting office over in Chinatown."

"That leaves only two other guys, Natasha. One of them looked like a short Italian man in his early forties."

"Oh, that's Johnny Giovanni. He's a staff sergeant loadmaster up at Travis AFB."

"You really know all these guys?"

"Not really... not personally, that is. I know what they do, but I really don't know them like friends. Like I said, this has been going on for over two years. It's common knowledge among the regulars here. No one cares. The parties are fabulous."

"That leaves one other guy who looks like a Vietnamese. He sort of stands off from the crowd and doesn't seem to get involved."

"Oh, that must be Tho Nguyen. He's the Saigon coordinator for Burma Gold out of Laos. They have a good contact there. A former CIA guy who provides them high-quality heroin and opium from Laos tribes, I forget his name."

Roe was amazed that Natasha knew so many details of this elaborate organization, but she really didn't give a rat's ass!

Guess it goes with being spaced out and associating with this crowd of hippies. They obviously shun all authority. A conservative crowd would have immediately reported the goings-on here.

The thought of his friend at the center of it all tormented him. It was still extremely difficult for Roe to accept much less deal with the reality.

"You mean to tell me Cody Johansson is the Rajah, and he organized and put all this together?"

He couldn't let it go and refused to believe the circumstances. "Sure. Cody had two tours in Vietnam and saw it as a great business opportunity to pursue when he returned to the United States. All I know is that he's a very wealthy man, and a very generous one, I might add."

Roe just stared at her, at loss for words. *She just doesn't get it. Gotta be the drugs.*

"Why do you look so upset? You're supposed to be good buddies. What's that all about? Seriously, Roe, what's the big fucking deal?"

He ignored her questions, thinking ahead.

"Listen, Natasha. Please don't say anything to Cody about this conversation. We'll get him into a lot of trouble. It's important to keep this discussion private, just between us. Not a word to anyone? Okay?

"I frankly don't understand why you care so about Cody's business. Cody is a good guy!"

"He's one of my long-time friends. I just didn't know he was into this stuff." Roe inhaled deeply and let out a long breath. "Most importantly right now, though, we need to dress and get you over to the University for treatment of your malaria."

You're a good man, Roe. I really appreciate you showing so much interest in me, I really do."

"We'll get you well, Natasha, don't worry."

***

Roe skipped Grand Rounds that Saturday morning after the Haight-Ashbury party and took Natasha to the UC Infectious Disease Clinic for diagnosis and treatment of malaria. After he had gotten her under the care of one of the top docs, Roe drove to Half Moon Bay to contemplate this dilemma.

How should I handle this?

The drive allowed Roe to clear his head and reflect on this agonizing conflict. Cody was one of his best high school buddies. They had shared a lot of personal experiences. Cody was a war hero who'd gone bad on drugs. His exposure to opium in Vietnam had led to addiction, and a path of criminality.

As he guided his car around the ocean side of Devil's Slide, he started to regain his composure. He drove to the beach and sat for an hour watching huge waves crash against the boulder jetty. The cool morning chill allowed him to reflect on what Natasha had told him about the cartel.

After contemplation, he came to the conclusion that he had to do what was morally right: call Biff, and divulge Cody's role as the Rajah. It hurt him deeply to turn in a friend, but this was how he was raised and how he had conducted his life. No matter how agonizing, he just had to do what was right. It hurt to betray a friend.

Betrayal... That was a nasty deed. Not only involving Cody, but Ann. We're not married yet, but I was unfaithful to a woman who stood by me in my darkest moments. What was I thinking? God forgive me! A wave of guilt swept over him. *I'm better than that. Never again, dammit!*

Roe returned to San Francisco and called Biff. "Biff, you are not going to believe the uncanny twist of fate I happened upon today. Talk about irony..."

"Well, this sounds fascinating. What's up, Roe?"

"I've stumbled on to the identity of the Rajah, details about his cartel, the whole nine yards!"

"You've got to be kidding me. C'mon, this is not a joking matter."

"Nope, not putting you on. Can we meet at the Buena Vista off of Ghirardelli Square for coffee and a late breakfast in about an hour?"

"Sure. But can't you tell me a little bit over the phone?"

"Nope, I want to see your expression. Bring a note pad. I've committed everything to memory. Dr. Robeson would be proud of me. I want to get you this information while it is still fresh in my mind, okay?"

"You can bet your sweet ass I'll be there."

An hour later they met at the Buena Vista, exchanged warm greetings, and selected a private table in the small back room, which was empty of patrons at this hour. They ordered Irish coffees. Biff pulled out a large legal pad for notes, and they and got right down to business.

Biff was serious for once. No grinning, not even a hint. "So, what have you got to tell me, old buddy?"

Roe straightened his back and leaned rigidly forward. "The Rajah is none other than Cody Johansson!"

Biff sucked in a quick breath, and paused a beat as the idea registered. "No fucking way! You've got to be putting me on! This is not a joking matter, Roe."

He searched Roe's face, obviously trying to read his intention. When he saw only honesty, a look of disbelief swept over his face, followed by one of anguish.

"You wouldn't be kidding me about this, would you?"

"No. I certainly wouldn't joke about such a serious matter. It's the God's truth. Natasha told me the whole story early this morning."

"This is unreal. I can't believe it. Who is Natasha?"

"The nurse you met at Clark, an old friend who took care of me there postop."

"Oh yeah, the pretty woman from Prague."

"She told me everything, it's real, Biff. Remember, Cody had two tours in Vietnam. He didn't have to go back for the second one after his injuries at Pleiku, but he did. I suspect he had an ulterior motive. He was setting up his network of sources in Laos and Cholon. He saw it as a big business opportunity and took the risk involved. You'll be stunned at the elaborate and sophisticated cartel Cody has set up. The Rajah controls the entire San Francisco Bay area and much of Northern California.

Remember in high school we kidded Cody about 'still water runs deep" in our yearbook?' Well, he's deep into heroin and marijuana traffic with ten-to-one profit margins. Get out your pen and note pad, pal. You've got to write down all the details I discovered last night at a hippie party in Haight-Ashbury."

"What in the hell were you doing there? Don't tell me you are into pot and rock bands? Did you flip out?"

"You know I could lose my license if I did any of those things. I just went for the experience ... and it paid off, big time. Listen up, partner, this will blow you away!"

Roe proceeded to give Biff names, descriptions, and every meticulous detail he remembered about the cartel. He relayed even the finest points and descriptions with clinical precision, exercising his restored analytic mind with perfect clarity.

Roe thought he saw some amazement in Biff's widened eyes when he described the color of the bow tie worn by one of the Asians. He noted his buddy was clearly impressed with the remarkable memory recovery from his impairment. A huge improvement from his days in Baguio last year.

"Jesus Christ, Roe. Gotta say you've got your act back together, man. Terrific recall!"

Biff took copious notes and asked appropriate questions to ascertain that he recorded all of the information correctly. He didn't suffer through a moral dilemma as Roe had. He had no such reservations. While he was acutely disappointed and saddened by this news, he knew what he was compelled to do. This is what he did, his job. Cody went over the line. Way over.

Cody was not the same guy they grew up and played ball with in high school. War and drugs had screwed him up, big time. Now Cody was a threat to society and must be brought to justice along with his cartel.

It was a black-and-white decision in Biff's CIA world, no shades of grey. Cody was now just another unintended consequence of the Vietnam War, a victim of the collateral damage associated with heroin. Biff had only a brief pang of disappointment. He realized he was becoming a cynic, hardened by the realities of Vietnam.

"I can't thank you enough for this information, Roe. Now we can set up an interagency surveillance of these men and learn as much as we can about the cartel's operation before we bust them. The Rajah is elusive and really covers his tracks. Anyone who tries to compromise his cartel ends up in the bay. Dead men don't talk. We don't have any informants. They whack them before they talk to us."

"I find this sordid episode difficult to believe, Biff."

"Me, too, but gotta do what's right. Please keep this under your hat, okay? Also, is Natasha reliable? Any chance she'll tip off Cody?"

"I told her not to say anything, otherwise we would get Cody into a lot of trouble. She agreed to that. Cody's been good to her and her friends. He gave them a roof over their heads and a comfortable hippie lifestyle. Cody's been very generous to her, so I doubt she would do anything to harm him or tip him off."

"Okay, agreed. But don't you screw with him, even contact him. He'll take you out in a flash. He's a changed man. This will take some time, but we'll get him and his cartel."

He packed up his legal pad, and paid the bill for their drinks.

"By the way, Roe, how come Natasha didn't turn Cody in to the authorities for drug dealing? Isn't that strange?"

Biff, we now live in an age of moral relativity. Natasha and the hippies see absolutely nothing wrong with drugs. It's their lifestyle in the Age of Aquarius. Get with it, man."

That brought a wide grin and chuckle from Biff.

"Guess you got that right, pal. Times are changing, like Bob Dylan said. "See ya 'round, pal."

CHAPTER FORTY
PRESIDIO WEDDING/TAHOE HONEYMOON

Thanksgiving 1968

Remarkably, Roe returned to his surgical career having made a full recovery from his wartime trauma memory deficit. Chief of Surgery, Dr. Engels, promoted Roe to the position of Assistant Professor, where he worked seventy- to eighty-hour weeks teaching, operating, and caring for surgical patients. He loved every minute of it. His worst fears were over, he'd overcome a career-threatening injury. His peers admired his perseverance and everyone rejoiced in his extraordinary comeback.

Ann's career at the Hoover Institution in Palo Alto similarly prospered. Her talent and vast knowledge of political science stood out on the Stanford campus. Her Vietnam consulting experience served her well. Her opinions carried a certain gravitas. Her colleagues respected her viewpoints, and often sought her out for references and background information.

She and Roe lived a comfortable life together in their small home up on Corbett Avenue up in Twin Peaks. From their deck, they could see the University Hospital nearby. The deck also provided a 180-degree panoramic view of the city skyscrapers, San Francisco Bay, and its two bridges connecting Marin and East Bay to the city. In the evenings, they often enjoyed a cocktail and watched the Pacific fog bank roll in through the Golden Gate to meet the fog bank coming up the bay from San Bruno. The combined billows of mist dimmed the city lights from their terrace.

Their love affair in Hawaii had blossomed into a close, personal relationship. They shared a mutual trust and endearment. She stood by Roe during his darkest hours, and during his rehabilitation at Langley Porter. Roe knew Ann left a good position at Hickam AFB in Hawaii to shepherd his recovery. They weren't yet formally married, but in spirit they were inseparable, sharing genuine love and respect.

Roe thought they should make it official if they planned to raise children together. He wondered if marriage possibly might be an outdated traditional view in 1968 in San Francisco. Was he old-fashioned?

In the Age of Aquarius, the city seemed to promote free love in the communal spirit of the newly liberated generation. Anything seemed to go it seemed to Roe and fellow conservatives in the 1960s. Even with the traditional worldview turned upside down, the inversion of conventional values failed to confuse him. Roe had a strong moral compass, he felt compelled to marry Ann and start a family.

He finally proposed in the old fashion way.

"Of course, I'll marry you, Roe. I thought you'd never ask!"

He presented Ann with a diamond ring set in platinum. She faked a swoon and hugged him, laughing with joy.

He couldn't help a fleeting thought about whether he would have gotten a better deal from Jimmy in Bangkok than in San Francisco, but refrained from bringing that subject up.

Roe had four days off during the Thanksgiving holiday. He arranged for Biff and Beth to witness their private ceremony by the Chaplain at the Presidio chapel in San Francisco. Reverend Walter Thomason, a good friend of his at Letterman Hospital would perform the marriage.

Biff had married Beth at the Presidio chapel the previous year, soon after his return from Vietnam, two months before the fateful '68 Tet offensive.

"A great sense of timing," he joked with Roe. "I avoided that Charlie Foxtrot."

The Presidio was an impressive 18th Century military base. Roe and Ann were history buffs, frequently walking through the base's lovely pathways and lawns, framed by tall eucalyptus trees. The wide expanses of open space welcomed strollers and picnics. They always found a new path to amble through the woods and lawns to share their thoughts and discuss the future.

Their favorite walk was along the old Crissy Field beach. The views of the Golden Gate Bridge and the Bay were spectacular from this vista. Families ran their dogs freely on the beach. Old WWII fortifications still lay intact along the bluffs overlooking the Pacific Ocean on the eastern and western sides of the bridge. Huge waves rolled in from the Pacific to crash on the large boulder breakwaters, the majesty of their huge splashes unsurpassable.

The Presidio was originally a Spanish fort dating back to 1776, seized by the U.S. military in 1846. From then on it became the U.S. Army Headquarters, commanded by such famous generals as Pershing and Sherman. The base had a distinguished history chronicled in the base library.

At the turn of the twentieth century the Presidio was the assembly point for the invasion of the Philippine Islands and the Spanish American War. It was America's first military engagement in the Pacific. During World War II it was the western center for the Pacific defense. During the Korean and Vietnam conflicts, Letterman Hospital cared for the returning wounded.

The Presidio was special to Ann and Roe during their courtship and his recuperation at Langley Porter. They often dined there with friends at the Officers Club.

Roe had maintained a reserve status with the Air force at Travis AFB at the base general's special invitation. He drove one hour north to Fairfield every Friday to meet the air evac planes from Vietnam to supervise triage to determine who could go on to hospitals close to their home on the next flights. Others stayed at Travis for more care until well enough to go home on later aircraft. Triage was his expertise. Roe, a sincere patriot, felt obliged to continue to service his country's wounded. Although conflicted over the conduct of the war, he felt it was his duty to serve those who put it all on the line for their country.

After the small, informal mid-week wedding at the base chapel, they enjoyed a lunch together at the Officer's Club with the Roberts. Out of the blue, Biff's wife, Beth, generously offered her parents' ski chalet in Tahoe for their honeymoon.

Roe laughed. "We've been on a honeymoon for almost two years, Biff, but we'll take you up on your kind offer. Only on the condition that you and Beth come up and ski with us on Saturday and Sunday, okay?" he added.

"Sounds like a plan," Biff replied, grinning widely, as usual. "We'll barbecue some steaks, and I'll bring a couple bottles of special wine for the occasion."

"Don't forget the Cognac and cigars. It's a little difficult to get those contraband Cohibas in Tahoe."

"No problem. I have my sources." He winked.

"We're looking forward to the weekend with you guys. It should be a lot of fun."

As the two couples departed, Roe asked Ann. "How many people invite their best friends to join them on their honeymoon?"

"Not many. But, it didn't surprise me you suggested it."

Lake Tahoe is as close in character to Switzerland as any mile-high lake in the United States. A pristine lake surrounded by snow-covered mountains, Tahoe was the site of the 1960 winter Olympics at Squaw Valley. It had since grown in popularity with the Bay Area and Sacramento crowds, and Swiss-style chalets were being constructed at a booming pace. Beth's parents' chalet perched high on a hillside overlooking the Squaw Valley ski runs. The views featured spectacular mountain sunsets.

Roe and Ann enjoyed two leisurely days of skiing followed by intimate, evening fireside chats. They were enjoying the rest and privacy, but enthusiastically looked forward to Biff and Beth's weekend visit.

The couple arrived early Saturday morning. Ann prepared breakfast and mimosas. They set off for the slopes around ten in the morning. It was a beautiful early winter day. Biff wanted to ski KT22. The double black diamond slope had steep moguls requiring at least twenty-two kick turns to traverse down the mountain, hence the name. Roe convinced him that run was not a good idea in their present state of physical conditioning. He suggested they ski the Siberia Bowl, more of a cruising slope.

The last thing Roe wanted to do was "fall on his head," he stated emphatically.

"No way we're skiing KT22," Ann said on behalf of both ladies.

Biff reluctantly agreed Siberia was a better choice, so they spent their time on easy cruising slopes for the day. That put the issue to rest.

After a full day of skiing, the glow of the huge river-rock fireplace offered a delightful après ski setting for the two couples. The dinner that Ann and Beth prepared along with Biff's wines soothed their aches and pains. Everyone fell into a relaxed and reminiscent mood. Over Cognac, they started recounting the events of the past year. With America still caught up in the ongoing Vietnam struggle, the discussion of the war naturally came up. It was hard to get over.

"Not a banner year in American history," Ann remarked for starters. She brought up the surprise January '68 North Vietnamese Tet offensive that caught American and allied troops off guard, both in its magnitude and scope. There were huge attacks on Hue and Saigon, as well as smaller cities like Danang."

"I'm glad Biff returned home two months before Tet started." Beth exclaimed. "Thank God!"

"Timing's everything." Biff joked. His smile faded. "General Westmoreland incorrectly expected a major frontal assault across the DMZ in the northern Central Highlands. Khe Sahn had been under intense siege for months. Westmoreland had deployed more troops north to fortify the DMZ sector for the anticipated assault.

Ann asked Biff, "Was that a CIA intelligence failure?"

"Not entirely." He cringed slightly.

"What happened?" Putting Biff on the spot with a teasing smile.

"I suspect the CIA totally underestimated both the large number of NVA assembled, and the coordination of extensive frontal attacks in multiple providences and cities in South Vietnam. Allied with the Viet Cong, they were a formidable force. The enemy digressed from their usual hit-and-run asymmetric warfare by conducting conventional war tactics. The frontal attacks packed a big element of surprise, catching everyone off guard on the Chinese New Year. Basically, they changed their game plan."

"That's true," Ann added. "No one expected conventional warfare."

"As you well know from our Hickam conferences, our CIA intelligence estimates were right on the mark for years in Vietnam, but our recommendations went unheeded by LBJ's administration time after time. In late '67, the Saigon CIA staff underwent a big turnover after the boss and I returned to the States and missed the '68 Tet offensive. The new boys were just settling into their tasks and not quite up to snuff. But, I rather doubt the DC crowd and Westmoreland would have implemented our CIA advice anyway, even if they had gotten it right this time. That's my take on the agency's missed call on Tet, how it went down."

"No doubt," Ann conceded.

"I'm also concerned about the North Koreans capturing the Pueblo last January. We don't need two simultaneous wars in Southeast Asia. We already have over half a million troops tied up in Vietnam. Word has it that Westmoreland recently requested 200,000 more. In my opinion, it is about time to turn the war back over to South Vietnam, and let the chips fall where they may."

Ann found this candid admission by Biff astounding. *Biff used to be more of a hawk, but had a cynical side to him.*

Biff continued to render his opinion of the current situation in Vietnam as he stood and refilled everyone's brandy snifter. He longed for a Cohiba, but would have to go outside to smoke it and it was damn cold. Besides, he actually enjoyed revisiting the contentious topic. Someone had to parry Ann's remarks. He was getting into it.

"Tet's major offensive took us a month to defeat. We suffered over a thousand casualties in that brief period. The fighting continued sporadically for a year. We established an impressive kill ratio of the enemy, almost fifteen to one early on, but four thousand casualties over a year is still is a lot of American lives to be lost. It shocked the home front, so our favorable ratio became irrelevant. The fact the enemy lost so many more over the year never registered with the public. They focused on the negative."

"You bet it did. The newspapers couldn't print enough of the bad news coming out of Vietnam," Ann exclaimed. "It was a turning point, Biff."

"Politically, not militarily. The media ignored the fact that well over fifty-eight thousand Viet Cong and VNA enemy troops perished under our superior American firepower that year. But, you wouldn't know it from the selective press releases and the media."

"That number may be inaccurate, an exaggeration or fabrication by LBJ's administration, Biff."

"Possibly, but let me state for the record that not a single city or South Vietnam province was lost during Tet. While it was actually a huge American military victory on one hand, the war lost enormous public support on the other."

Roe chimed in. "I didn't know those military facts."

Ann acknowledged her husband's statement by raising thoughtful eyebrows. "That's astonishing. Biff, you never even mentioned those specifics to *me*."

"The press buried those numbers. Didn't fit their anti-war agenda."

"I agree with that statement. Subsequently, American public opinion fractured down the middle: war supporters vs. anti-war. The media still overwhelmingly supports the anti-war movement and continues calling for negotiations. Walter Cronkite is the leading voice in that movement."

Biff frowned, "Find it ironic, Ann? Just as you predicted in your last Joint Intelligence meeting in Hawaii two years ago, the first domino to fall was U.S. public opinion, not Vietnam. The public simply didn't buy into LBJ's policy. What did we get from our Vietnam involvement? How did that work out?" Biff shook his head in disgust before he answered his own question. "We got a state of anarchy. Riots erupting on campus and in the streets, draft card burning, and race riots in the cities. In my opinion, 1968 represented a general deterioration of societal norms in America."

He watched their reactions as they sat by the fireside. A log popped as if punctuating his statement and a flame shot up when the log shifted as it broke in half.

Ann inclined her head in agreement, while Roe and Beth remained silent and uncommitted. Their tilted heads showed their fascination with this intellectual exchange.

In Biff's view, America was undergoing a tectonic cultural revolution. He showed a rare glimpse of his frustrations and annoyance with the conduct of the war and its unintended consequences. His body language spoke volumes.

Roe had never seen Biff become so visibly upset. But, he was witnessing seven years of building frustration, dating from the '61 Bay of Pigs fiasco to the present. Biff was ventilating. Roe thought that reaction was healthy. Biff needed to get this off his chest and this was an opportune time among friends who understood where he was coming from.

After several moments, Roe gave his opinion, catching everyone by surprise. He'd been reserved up to this point.

"Perhaps Vietnam is the wrong war in the wrong place for the wrong reasons. With so many self-imposed restrictions, military victory will come at a great price, not only in casualties, but with a splintering of our domestic psyche. Look at the breakdown in traditional society occurring right before our very eyes. San Francisco is the poster child of the antiwar movement and on the verge of anarchy."

Everyone agreed.

Ann, knowing Roe's deep-seated opinions regarding Vietnam, didn't want him to get worked up. She went over and put a pillow behind his neck and gave him a hug... a message not to get too upset.

She turned back to Biff. "As I've said before, we can win the war militarily without question as you mentioned. But, we can lose it politically. We never really captured the hearts and minds of the peasantry in the countryside. They were never pacified. We never gained their commitment, their support. The South Vietnamese leadership went through five or six coups. I've lost count. In retrospect, the only leader with any chance of success, Diem, was assassinated in 1963. With our complicity, I might add."

Biff, laughed at the indirect dig at him and the CIA. "You couldn't resist that last comment, could you?"

"Nothing personal, Biff, but you'd agree, in hindsight, it was an ill-advised decision by JFK and his administration to allow Diem's assassination."

"Hindsight is always twenty-twenty, Ann."

Beth sat quietly, sipping her brandy. She never discussed religion or politics, even with close friends, but Biff was glad to see she appeared amused with Ann's and his friendly banter. He knew her well enough to know she was probably glad they were keeping such an emotional and divisive issue on an intellectual level. He grinned at his reserved wife.

Roe, reclining on the sofa, feet up on the hassock, leaned back on his pillow and glanced over to Beth and winked, indicating that this discussion may go on a while.

Biff joked that year seemed like the new Beatles' album, "The Magical Mystery Tour." Everyone laughed.

Ann changed the tone by giving an overview of everything that had happened during the year to bring them to this point.

She reminded them how the Tet offensive and the Pueblo capture had started off a turbulent year pivotal in dividing Americans into polarized camps, right and left—conservative vs. liberal, with rednecks and radical progressive activists at opposite fringes.

In March, Senator Gene McCarthy defeated President Johnson in the New Hampshire primary, supported by the anti-war student movement. This stunning defeat, the course of negative events in Vietnam, and the growing anti-war clamor prompted LBJ to announce two weeks later that he would not seek reelection. The sudden reversal took everyone by surprise.

The following week, April 4th, Martin Luther King Jr. was assassinated, igniting race riots throughout the country. Student riots and draft-card burning demonstrations escalated on campuses. Activist students took over five buildings at Columbia University in anti-war protests.

The turmoil in America continued into July with the senseless assassination of Andy Warhol, the famous artist, in New York City on the 3rd of July. The next day, a Palestinian immigrant, Sirhan Sirhan, shot Robert F Kennedy Jr. in Los Angeles at close range, mortally wounding him. The world was going mad!

On the international front, the Soviet Union occupied Czechoslovakia with tanks rolling into Prague streets, bringing "winter to springtime" twelve years after occupying Hungary in a similar military fashion.

The universal chaos and civil unrest extended into the summer Democratic convention in Chicago with anti-war demonstrators fighting pitched battles with the police. Tear gas subdued the violence. Among those arrested was Abby Hoffman, a founder of the "Youth International Party."

Ann recalled that the "Yippie" leader made headlines with his statement regarding revolution, a hallmark of the times. She quoted him verbatim: "Revolution is not something fixed in ideology, nor is it something fashioned to a particular decade. It is a perpetual process imbedded in the human spirit."

Biff, Roe, and Beth were all astonished at Ann's brilliant command of history, and her ability to pull up such esoteric quotes extemporaneously.

She went on to outline somewhat similar historical parallels between the mid-1960s civil conflicts in America with the "War of Roses" in England in 1453, a conflict that lasted three decades.

"That war was a series of dynastic civil conflicts fought between the landed aristocracy and feudal subjects…"

Ann saw a striking likeness to the present events occurring in the sixties in the U.S. The current revolt did not primarily focus on land and property; instead, it focused on ideology. She elaborated on this analogy.

"The cultural revolution of the sixties is a convergence of irreconcilable differences in society's attitudes and philosophies. Often, the divergence of political opinion and cultural mores reaches glacial dimensions culminating in a state of anarchy, like we are witnessing."

Ann explained that she saw a thin line between orderly, First Amendment democratic protest and violent rioting, as activists challenged authority for what they perceived as their government pursuing ignoble policies.

She gave as an example the Students for Democratic Action at Berkeley, a radical left-wing organization. Some viewed the SDA as a communist front, and most agreed they were prone to violence.

Biff could not let that go. "You know that a splinter group of the SDA, the 'Weather Underground' is definitely an anarchist organization, right? They were recently implicated in blowing up the Park Police Station in San Francisco, killing a Sergeant Sullivan. The FBI raided an apartment in the Mission District where they found Bill Ayres' fingerprints along with several Black Panther members' prints. They also found bomb paraphernalia and revolutionary literature. Ayres and his wife, Bernadette Dorhn—both possible suspects—fled to Chicago with some Black Panther leaders, Huey somebody or another. An ongoing investigation is underway."

Forced to agree with his assessment, Ann then redirected the conversation back to reflections on 1968 and the recent November presidential election.

"Earlier this month, Richard Nixon defeated Hubert Humphrey for the U.S. presidency. I was astounded that Alabama Governor Wallace, a white supremacist, received 13.5 percent of the vote! That vote made the presidential election close, 43.4 percent to 42.7 percent. Talk about polarization. Half the country went right, the other half left. Political and civic culture has been transformed. I predict it will continue to be difficult to resolve our future differences. This transformation will not end well."

"No argument there," Biff concurred.

"Supporting that viewpoint, last March the Kerner Commission Report proved prophetic. It stated what I've considered obvious for some time, that in 1968, America has two societies, 'separate and unequal.' The conservative side views America as fundamentally good, but always able to improve."

"That's the correct viewpoint," Roe chimed in. "America's fundamentally sound."

They all looked at Roe, who was definitely tuned in and voicing his viewpoint. Biff knew his friend's strong feelings on the topic and was glad he expressed them in context. He'd come a long way in his rehab, and was nearly back to his old self socially.

Ann acknowledged her husband's participation with an engaging smile.

"That's one school of thought, Roe. The opposing viewpoint, held by the left, is that our government is flawed and requires dramatic changes. To support their argument, they point to the student anti-Vietnam war rebellion and race riots. The United States no longer represents 'a shining city upon a hill' in their worldview. But, on the other side of the equation, the *right* views left wingers as political activists permeated by progressive radicals who are cynical, and even immoral. As in the 'War of Roses,' I predict this antithesis and rancor will last decades before being resolved. Unfortunately, the media will fan the fires of dissent, magnifying the differences."

She had their rapt attention.

"War of roses?" Roe asked. "Think that's a bit academic, dear?"

She politely ignored his friendly gibe, realizing perhaps she was a bit over the top with the analogy.

"Discourse will not be polite or civil. I was over on the Berkeley campus last week visiting friends, and made an interesting observation. Remember the banners that used to hang outside the dorm windows? Those painted sheets proclaiming 'Hey, hey LBJ. How many kids have you killed today?' They have come down now, but new banners reading 'Dick Nixon, before he dicks you!' have replaced them."

Everyone shared a good laugh at this college rip. Ann scanned each face in their small group, gauging their reaction to where all this was going. Sensing it was time to wrap it up.

"So, in conclusion, this demonstrates that the present turmoil reflects a conceptual, civic revolt, as much as political. There seems to be no end in sight to all this bitterness, no matter what political party is in office."

The conversation then went on to other matters, catching up with old friends and their activities. The men carefully avoided mention of Roe's last encounter with Cody at the Haight-Ashbury party in October. That was confidential information. Both choose to keep a lid on it while the surveillance operation proceeded.

Instead, Roe mentioned that Cody was undergoing another reconstructive plastic surgery at the University Hospital in San Francisco to repair the damage to his ear and to revise the ugly scars from the shrapnel wounds he suffered at Pleiku. The surgeons at Clark AFB did what was required under wartime conditions, debriding the wounds, and preventing infection. Cody had lost large portions of soft tissue, making cosmetic wound closure difficult. The Plastic Surgery Department at Cal was more than glad to take on the challenge as the Presidio Hospital was packed with wounded arrived from Clark for continued care.

Roe had visited Cody on several occasions and reported he was doing well, in general, though he seemed a little quieter than usual. "He was taking a lot of pain medication, more than required, it seemed. Guy was never really very talkative anyway, Cody seemed a little detached. Looks really different, almost didn't recognize him. He let his GI haircut grow out to shoulder length like a hippie, has a moustache, an earring, and a lot of tattoos. Nothing like the Green Beret I evac'ed out of Pleiku in '65. He told me that his old dog, Schooner, had died. Remember that great big Chesapeake Bay retriever, Biff? He was like a brother to Cody. Said his Dad died shortly thereafter, and his Mom is in a nursing home with Alzheimer's disease."

"Sorry to hear that bad news, Roe," Biff commented. "Cody's hit a rough patch."

"Agree, life doesn't seem to be going favorably for Cody. He expressed strong resentment directed to the anti-war crowds in San Francisco. He didn't like the disrespectful way they were treating returning troops."

"I can understand that," Biff commented. "It's disgraceful."

"Cody said they all thought our troops were napalming villages and killing kids, day and night. Asked me if, 'Can you fucking believe that?' Concluded they didn't have a clue about the war. He got real emotional, almost flipped out with anger. Really pissed."

"Anti-war propaganda drummed up by the media." Biff grumbled. "It's created a toxic atmosphere dividing the country into opposing camps."

"Everyone has so many misconceptions, I've lost count of them." Roe added.

"Cody said he finally gave up trying to explain what it was really like over there. He sensed there was no appreciation for the GIs serving in Vietnam, what they were up against, so no need to try to convince them otherwise. Said the concept of collateral damage was lost on them, and the anti-war crowd considered our troops were invading barbarians. That they hadn't even a remote idea what war was like. Basically, they lacked any sense of gratitude for our troops' sacrifices. So, he's adopted, 'Screw all them friggin' hippies' as his attitude."

Roe recounted Cody's bitter comment that they were, "All a bunch of frigging draft dodgers, not worth fragging!"

Biff said he had heard remarks like that from other vets and that there was a lot out anger out there among vets regarding their baneful reception upon returning home.

Roe went on to say he tried to explain that at least half the population was truly grateful for their service. He had tried to explain to Cody that it was a time of political upheaval and shifting societal attitudes, but his perspective failed to influence or calm down Cody.

Cody had listened politely, but replied with the old Eastern Shore saying, "Nothin' but a bunch of chicken shits!"

Biff rolled over laughing at that remark, "That's vintage Cody!"

And, for many returning servicemen from Vietnam, that statement sort of summed it up. That was their take on the cultural revolution.

Roe's recounting of Cody's views initiated another round of political discussions.

The group agreed that war had taken a great toll on American society, causing polarization of worldviews. All agreed that the far-left radicals were vociferous, activist, and even obnoxious in their protestations. Many exhibited unprecedented deplorable behavior. The protesters appeared to have the press on their side, fanning the fires of dissent sweeping the country. Civil discourse was becoming almost impossible. Emotions were replacing reason in a nation reeling with unbridled dissent.

On the right, it became the "Age of McCarthyism." A communist plot lurked or was suspected behind every left-wing movement. In McCarthy's view, they were "guilty until proven innocent," a total inversion of moral and legal values.

J. Edgar Hoover's investigations and exploits became legendary, further fanning the fires of dissent and accusations of fascism.

Roe expressed his opinion that, "While many on the left may be Socialists and anti-war, they are not avowed Communists. Perhaps a few were, but most were not."

When challenged by Biff, Roe conceded. "Okay, some are communist leaning, if not actually Marxists. For example, the SDA and the Weather Underground in the San Francisco Bay area."

According to Ann, the political and social polarization became more than philosophical. It became obsessive in some quarters, spilling over into violent street and campus protests. The Viet Cong and the North Vietnam National Army were not considered the enemy, D.C. was.

"Our government in Washington DC became the anti-war crowd's adversary because they got us into this mess during two Democratic administrations. These policymakers were viewed as the real culprits, especially LBJ." Ann stated.

"Quagmire" became the buzzword for Vietnam, she reminded them. All authority must be questioned. All government information and decrees must be closely examined for ulterior motives. The pervading mindset was that no one in government could be trusted. The mid and late sixties descended into political chaos, with public opinion splitting along extremely conservative and liberal lines.

They agreed with Ann that it would take decades to repair the damage, if ever.

The conversation then switched to a lighter tone on the subject of Colonel Al Ruey, now residing downstate at the Miramar Naval Air Station. He was setting up the "Top Gun" school for fighter pilots.

"Doing a great job," Biff related.

Roe and Biff went on to sum up the Air Force's current status and past history. Fighter pilots of the Marines and the United States Air Force were dismayed at the sparse number of MiG kills in Vietnam, Biff explained. Clearly, more expertise in air-to-air combat was called for, along with better missile technology.

Their high school buddy, Colonel Ruey, had been chosen to lead this challenge at Miramar. He did so with enthusiasm and authority.

Both Roe and Biff had spoken with Al recently, and were impressed by the concept and scope of the "Top Gun" school.

"Al is usually pretty reserved, but he appears to be really pumped up over this project," Biff said. "A-4 Skyhawks were our primary light bomber over Vietnam when we were there.

They provided close air support from carriers in the China Sea and Chu Lai Air Base on the central Vietnam coast."

The ladies were not particularly interested, but politely listened as the men appeared to be into the topic revering their old pal.

Biff explained the A-4 delta-winged aircraft was nimble, comparable to a MiG-17 in speed and maneuverability. The Air Force had developed a good system for air-to-air refueling. Colonel Ruey and other squadron commanders were now emphasizing air combat maneuvering training at the newly established Navy Fighter Weapons School to rectify Vietnam deficiencies. Biff noted that F-4s were taking over the A-4's roles, especially in target suppression. Though faster, they lacked the A-4 aircraft's maneuverability. He reminded Roe that the F-105s were heavy bombers flying missions over North Vietnam, not combat aircraft.

"Biff, I served in the Airforce. Know all that, but glad Al is refining our aerial combat capabilities."

"Sorry, slipped my mind. Let me tell you about DACT in case you're not up to speed. Al briefed me."

Colonel Ruey had explained to Biff that "Top Gun" introduced the concept of dissimilar air combat training (DACT) using A-4's striped "mongoose" configuration with fixed slats.

The plane's handling by a skilled pilot was ideal to teach fleet aviators the finest points of DACT, an enthusiastic Colonel Ruey had explained. He confided that the training program would clearly establish air superiority over MiG-17s and MiG-21s in Vietnam.

Biff went on and on…

The wives became bored with this discussion and retreated to the kitchen to clean up and run a load of dishes.

Biff leaned forward. "Roe, did you know that, in the early aerial fighting during 1965 to 1967 in Vietnam, the U.S. did not have the air superiority of earlier conflicts in Korea and World War II. Al told me Captain Frank Ault of the Naval Air Systems Command was instrumental in setting up his graduate-level school to insure a nucleus of fighter crews highly confident in air combat maneuvering.

"Yeah? And, did *you* know a new fighter jet, the Phantom F-4, will soon see action in Vietnam? They say weapons systems employment will be vastly upgraded to complement the advanced training of fighter pilots. That's what old Al told me."

Biff and Roe were proud of their old high-school classmate. Colonel Al Ruey was a literal embodiment of "Duty, Honor and Country—Semper Fidelis."

When they exhausted their conversation around three in the morning, they decided to sleep in, have breakfast, and hit the road early rather than ski, since a storm front was forecasted for the late afternoon. It was wise to avoid Sunday traffic on I-80 back to San Francisco during a storm. All agreed and went off to bed.

As he lay down and placed his head on the pillow, a wave of gratitude washed over Biff. In all of tonight's discussion, no one's feelings were hurt. True friends could agree to disagree ... even on the raging Vietnam controversy.

CHAPTER FORTY-ONE
MISSION DISTRICT SHOOTOUT

San Francisco June 1969

Biff received the call at three in the afternoon at the U.S. Consulate in San Francisco. The city's Chief of Police, Lucius Titus, was on the other end of the line.

"Our surveillance of Rajah's cartel places them on the fourth floor of a deserted bayside warehouse in the Mission District. Looks like some kind of deal's coming down. We're setting up a strike force for four-thirty. We've finally cornered them. Care to come over to observe?"

"Sure, absolutely. Few friendly suggestions, have a SWAT team loaded for bear, and notify the FBI for backup. Also, it's a good idea to arrange for DEA to confiscate the contraband drugs following the assault."

"FBI and DEA already notified, but you don't think we can handle the confrontation?"

"I wouldn't take any chances, Chief. We need to scramble all our assets on this. Go full bore, can't risk blowing it. It's been a year in gaining the opportunity. I'm sure they're heavily armed and won't go down without a fight. I've heard they're collaborating with the Black Panthers lately. Those hardcore East Bay guys are moving into drug trafficking. It's a smart move not to under-man your operation."

"Okay, good advice. I agree this could turn into a big-time shootout. We'll arm up, and double the number on the SWAT team."

***

The chief took Biff's advice seriously. At four-thirty sharp, the San Francisco police cordoned off the block and surrounded the warehouse. SWAT teams in two helicopters hovered overhead. The SFPD pulled up in ten squad cars with fifty uniformed men, all wearing flak jackets and helmets.

The chief and Sergeant Murphy hopped out of their car.

The sergeant lifted his binoculars to focus on the fourth floor of the abandoned warehouse. He saw a silver reflection, the glint of a rifle in one of the upstairs windows. Too late. That was the last thing he saw. A .223 caliber bullet, traveling at 3200 feet per second, hit him between the eyes, killing him instantly. The retort of the rifle shot arrived about two seconds later, traveling at 1200 feet per second.

"Holy shit!" Titus dove behind the squad car.

Police scattered frantically, ducking for cover between their cars. In rapid succession, three more shots rang from the upper-floor window, dropping three more police officers who didn't make it to cover.

"Good Lord! Who the hell is that shooter?" exclaimed the captain, astonished at losing four men in less than a minute.

"Not many men can shoot like that," Biff answered from behind his bulletproof CIA sedan. "Has to be Cody Johansson, the man's lethal with an M-16, a sniper-quality shooter."

"Cody who?"

"Johansson, aka the 'Rajah.' He's a decorated Vietnam Ranger, fearless and 'Nam battle-hardened. Better get that SWAT team on the roof right away. This is going to be one hell of a battle, Chief."

The chief radioed the two helicopters to land on the roof and conduct a full assault immediately. He warned them about the sharpshooter, the Rajah. One chopper landed on the roof, the other behind the four-story building, unloading fifteen SWAT team members. Many were former commandos with extensive battle experience in Vietnam.

The first team fast-roped out of the choppers and pried open the roof's rusty trapdoor. They swiftly descended on a toggle rope to attack the cartel holed up down the hallway. Meanwhile, the second SWAT team entered through the rear door of the building, which they blew off with a C-4 charge. They quickly ascended for a coordinated assault on the bad guys, cutting off their escape route.

In the streets, the police force and the drug cartel exchanged shots. Although superior in numbers, the police were clearly out-gunned, essentially pinned down from the cartel's vantage point. Fusillades of gunfire, volley after volley, were exchanged. Bullets ricocheted everywhere, creating a chaotic scene, hitting some squad car gas tanks causing fires and explosions. Captain Titus summoned the Fire Department, warning them of the danger.

***

Inside the warehouse, Cody had stored a huge cache of marijuana, opium, and 97 percent pure heroin recently delivered from Laos. The Golden Triangle produced the finest Burma Gold. The contraband was stacked high in cartons and wooden boxes. The Rajah was in the process of cutting his first big deal with three Black Panthers who'd come over from Oakland to finalize the transaction. He estimated the street value of the deal to be somewhere in the range of ten million U.S. dollars. Cody had obtained the contraband for about one million, including transportation and bribes. Not a bad mark-up for his cartel. That profit margin worked for him.

The three gunmen with him were good shooters armed with M-16 rifles. The three Black Panthers carried .9mm Springfield pistols. Fearing apprehension, they barricaded themselves in the upper-story room.

Cody was surprised at the magnitude of the assault. They far outnumbered his seven drug traffickers, and many of them fought like battle savvy commandos. Things didn't look good, but he would not surrender. He knew there was no way out, wondering who'd tipped off the police about this meeting. He'd eluded the police and the DEA for almost three years, thanks to his paranoia about security. Cody vowed he wouldn't go down without a fight. He had taken on greater odds in Vietnam. Surely his luck wouldn't run out now.

The SWAT team, armed with AR-15 assault rifles, blew open the heavy steel door with a charge of C-4 plastic explosive. They launched tear gas and smoke canisters into the room, waited a moment, and donned their masks. They yelled, "Drop your weapons! Hands up! Get over against the wall!" and entered the foggy room.

Cody knew the SWAT team would shoot first and ask questions later. Because they'd observed the police officers falling in the street below, they'd take no prisoners.

They huddled behind the boxes and cartons of drugs and paraphernalia, a poor defense, but the only one available.

One of the Black Panthers, coughing like mad, yelled in ghetto bravado through the haze, "Fuck you, Clancy! Bring it on!"

The SWAT leader told his men, "Forget about reading them their Miranda rights. Let's roll."

The team ducked through the doorway spraying the room with semiautomatic fire, quickly fanning out. Instantly, the room erupted into a mindboggling exchange of gunfire at close range. Initially for Cody, this was easier than shooting ducks on a pond. He dropped several of the early attackers coming through the door before the tear gas impaired his aim. Men started dropping like flies on both sides of the large room, yelling in pain amid hollered commands and warnings.

The SWAT team members continued ducking through the doorway, firing bursts from their semiautomatic weapons. Cody sensed for the first time that he might die—cornered, outgunned, and outnumbered. He dismissed the negative thought and engaged them, dropping one after another despite his compromised vision. Two of his men were down and the Panthers lacked accuracy and firefight skills. He knew this would not end well, but had no fear of dying. It would soon be over, though with no glory in this battle. He'd seen many men die gallantly in battle, and vowed he'd go down fighting like the Ranger company commander he once was.

The sudden volume of the exchange of gunfire was overwhelming, even by Vietnam standards. The barrage of bullets ripped through the cartons, sending millions of dollars' worth of Burma Gold flying through the air in white puffs, creating a dense haze in the room already filled with smoke and tear gas. The drug runners gagged and coughed, and tears ran down their faces. Their shots became wild on automatic cap bursts as their vision blurred.

It all ended in about three minutes of hellfire, but it seemed an eternity until his world finally went black.

***

Cody, his three sidekicks, and three Black Panthers all lay dead on the floor, or slumped over boxes, riddled by multiple gunshot wounds, bodies smattered in blood.

The scene reminded surviving SWAT team vets of the carnage in Vietnam.

One remarked, "That one guy with the scarred face could really shoot. Nailed a bunch of our guys."

Seven SWAT team members lay dead near the doorway with head shots, killed early on in the firefight. No doubt from Cody's marksmanship as they charged through the entry door. Their Kevlar vests and helmets provided no protection for a sharpshooter.

Arriving on the shootout scene, Biff and Chief Titus surveyed the appalling bloodshed.

"Nothing this devastating has ever occurred in San Francisco," Titus commented to Biff.

Sirens of approaching ambulances screamed outside the warehouse. Clouds of teargas, cordite, and opium still permeated the air in the room causing them to cough as they checked out the room. They had to retreat to the hallway momentarily.

As the air cleared, Biff went back inside the room to check Cody's body. *What a waste of a life!* he thought. A decorated Ranger/ Green Beret with two Purple Hearts and a Silver Star lay dead on the floor, body riddled. Biff thought it ironic that Cody was gunned down in a shoot-out with the S.F. police after surviving multiple skirmishes in Vietnam.

Such a sorry ending. Seems like it was just a few years ago we were playing football together.

He paused to reflect on how his high school buddy had arrived at this endpoint. It must have started for Cody in an opium den in Cholon, and probably escalated with heroin imported from Laos. His pal probably experimented on his second tour in the central highlands of Vietnam and set up his scheme to traffic narcotics. Biff wondered if Sammy Wong, the elusive rogue CIA agent in Laos, was involved in Cody's transactions. Probably. He made a mental note to trace that connection with Toby. It made good sense to follow up that trail.

A feeling of finality swept over Biff. Cody's elaborate scheme of drug smuggling had come to a regretful end.

Chief Titus walked up to him. "The DEA should be able to bust the rest of the cartel now that Rajah's gone."

Would they? Biff doubted it. Rajah had established an elaborate network with many untraceable sources. Vacuums in drug traffic didn't last long. The cartel had a deep bench of players. It would not take long to regroup the supply line.

Sammy Wong had gone deep dark in Laos, assimilated into Hmong tribal villages. Biff figured it would take considerable time and effort to bring down the clever CIA rogue agent. That supply line of Burma Gold, meanwhile, would remain intact, but enter the U.S. by different routes. The Rajah had constructed an extremely well-organized cartel. The head of one snake had been cut off, but like Medusa, other snakes would replace this one.

Biff recalled Roe's meticulous description of the cartel kingpins at the hippie party. There were lots of other snakes to go to wrap up this affair. This episode was just a starter. It was a long way from over, but he would not rain on Titus' parade. SFPD had pulled it off.

"You looked shocked, Biff. What's up?" Titus asked.

"This guy, Rajah, played football with me in high school, good friend back then. Knew him in Vietnam, decorated hero, two Purples and a Silver. Never suspected he'd end up like this. Sorta shakes you up how life turns out for some guys."

Titus patted him on the shoulder, "Sorry, man. Bummer. We'll get this mess cleared up. Wounded to ER, FBI and DEA forensics will manage the rest. He left to give Biff a few lone moments to get it together, reflect on their relationship.

Biff noticed the unmistakable Ranger logo tattooed on Cody's right biceps and the Ban the Bomb logo on his left.

Those tattoos represent contradictory statements. Cody was obviously conflicted. Biff reflected as he revisited Cody's body for one last glimpse of an old friend. *That sort of sums up San Francisco in 1969. War versus anti-war sentiment leading to conflict even affecting a seasoned vet.*

Cody's wartime scars were still quite evident despite his multiple plastic surgeries. His right ear still didn't look quite right, but his blood-stained long hair hid most of it from sight. The last time Biff saw Cody he had a GI crew cut and was dressed impressively in his Ranger camo's. Now he looked like an ordinary hippie out of Haight-Ashbury. But, Cody would remain anything but ordinary in Biff's memory.

He thought back to their high-school days on the Eastern Shore of Maryland. In retrospect, things were so calm and innocent then. That time of bliss and tranquility seemed like an eternity ago. Visions of Cody out hunting with Schooner crossed his mind. He could visualize Cody gracefully pulling in one of his TD passes, more than fourteen years ago. All fond memories, blown away in today's shootout.

So much had transpired in their lives since then. Vietnam changed it all. Things would never be the same, there was no going back. Mistakenly, many tried to relive their youth, an impossible dream. He wouldn't go there. It would be folly. Pipedreams don't hold up, they sweep away. They disappear like the sandcastles he built too close to an incoming tide as a kid in Ocean City. He had to move on even though Cody's twist of fate perplexed and deeply upset him.

Why did it have to end like this? he wondered as he stood over Cody's body. Biff fought a flood of mixed emotions, trying to understand the irony of it all. No one could have predicted this sorry ending back then in '54. Drugs made a mockery of a good man's life. It didn't seem fair, but he'd learned at an early age that life is not fair.

He thought back for a moment on Cody's experiences in Vietnam, first in the Mekong Delta, distinguishing himself with Colonel Vann's unit. His heroism on his second tour at Pleiku represented Cody's proudest accomplishment. The recognition and decorations he'd accepted with humility. He recalled Cody telling him he was just doing his job over there with thousands of other buddies in 'Nam. "Nothing special…" That was Cody's attitude. He served his country proudly until drugs intervened.

This episode represented a personal tragedy, rather than a triumph for Biff. A year before, Roe had given Biff the clue to Rajah's cartel. It had allowed Biff, the FBI, and DEA to track them through surveillance, figure out their operation, and eventually trap them. Biff felt he was an accomplice to Cody's take-down by the SWAT team. No, this was not a moment of triumph. It was a moment of sorrow and heartbreak, a good friend lost. Rationally, he realized it had to end this way. He resigned himself to that inescapable conclusion, patted Cody's shoulder and said, "Goodbye, old pal." He fought back tears as he departed. Cody's final image would never leave him.

***

The ambulances arrived at the Mission ER with eighteen men pronounced dead on arrival and at least a dozen other SWAT and policemen with serious wounds requiring emergency surgical care. Though it swamped the medical personnel, fortunately, most of the casualties were not life threatening.

Roe happened to be the attending surgeon for the triage of shootout victims. He and his surgical team triaged the seriously wounded, selecting those for surgery in the six ORs upstairs where operating teams awaited their arrival. They placed the walking wounded in a separate area of the ER to await treatment as soon as time and resources permitted. They concentrated on the seriously wounded.

Roe, sorted through the carnage. He pronounced a total of eighteen DOA: four policemen, seven SWAT team members, three Black Panthers, and four drug traffickers. He picked over another body—this one, a long-haired, tattooed hippie, remarkably buff compared to the other casualties. The corpse was riddled with multiple gunshot wounds to the head, neck, torso, and all four extremities.

Roe inhaled sharply, and gasped.

No, it can't be! His suspicions heightened when he noticed multiple frag scars and ear reconstruction scars. The Ranger tattoo on the right biceps, and "*Schooner*" tattooed across his heart with an image of a bird-dog in fading blue ink on his bloodstained chest, left no doubt of this man's identity.

My God! It's Cody in dreadlocks.

The unexpected discovery shocked even a seasoned veteran of war trauma like Roe. They'd played on a championship football team together, hunted birds, and double-dated at the Roundhouse burger joint. Just over three years ago, Roe had air evacuated this decorated hero out of Pleiku to Clark AFB in the Philippine Islands. Now an ugly ending cried out from a bullet- ridden body laying before him on a gurney before him.

Their conversation in Pleiku crossed Roe's mind. Cody had remarked how the IV morphine the nurse had given him for his painful wounds was better than the opium dens in Cholon. Cody had mentioned that he was "higher than a kite." He quickly ran the sequence of events through his mind.

That conversation was an ominous hint of events that would evolve in Cody's life, a foreshadowing. Drugs were more than a lucrative hobby for Cody. It became a capitalistic enterprise under his Ranger code name, Rajah. He organized an international cartel. One the DEA referred to as an unparalleled sophisticated operation in San Francisco. Natasha innocently identified Cody to Roe at a hippie party. Serendipity? Roe felt compelled to notify Biff and the wheels of justice swung into motion.

In the past year, Biff had discovered that Cody imported heroin through Travis AFB stowed in body bags, electronic equipment, and Japanese hibachis. Larger batches hidden on ships arrived from Asia into Bay area ports. Biff mentioned a deep dark source in Laos provided his operation with 97 percent pure "Burma Gold" at a handsome discount. No wonder Cody could afford a decorator showcase-quality Victorian in Haight-Ashbury. The Rajah could easily afford to throw lavish parties for his hippie friends. Rajah was rolling in money, filthy rich in both the literal and figurative sense.

Roe sighed heavily. The Age of Aquarius came crashing down to a cruel end for Cody. It all went wrong for him in Vietnam. Once hooked, there was no going back. He took the drug scene up in style, and lived life in the fast lane until the very end. Roe had witnessed so much death and tragedy in Vietnam that he was numb even to an old buddy's demise in a dramatic shootout. He not only felt sorry for Cody, but experienced a sense of emptiness. He offered a silent, contrite prayer for Cody's soul asking God to forgive this gallant warrior who wandered from the righteous path.

Remorsefully, he looked over Cody's dead body one final time, before resuming his duties in the packed ER. Roe never shed a tear. He'd seen the best and the worst of life, conditioning his analytical, detached response. And, he'd witnessed the hollow decisions people make that lead to tragedy. Actions have consequences and every man will be held accountable.

"Here's a good man corrupted by drugs. Will anyone ever tell this tragic, untold story of Vietnam's collateral damage?"

***

The following night, his chief resident phoned Roe at home. An attractive young lady in hippie attire had been brought in, code 2. The resident suspected she was an LSD jumper from her injuries, and incoherence—not an uncommon occurrence in San Francisco in 1969.

He'd seen the effects of hallucinatory acid trips that encouraged an epidemic of jumpers who literally thought they could fly. One- and two-story jumpers usually survived, but three-or-more-story jumpers were either dead on arrival or died later from severe head injuries. Dropping acid was not an innocuous pastime. Pot was a relatively safer diversion, but intense highs always presented a temptation. LSD provided this escape from reality sought by the new generation.

"Anyone experimenting with LSD must be emotionally distressed, or just plain reckless," Roe had told his staff on numerous occasions.

The resident went on to say the jumper was a former RN at the Mission. "She requested you, Dr. Mac."

Roe's heart sunk. He inquired regarding the extent of her injuries, uneasy about the request. *Could it be her?*

The resident replied, "Broken wrist, ankle, and ribs." I suspect a pneumothorax, and am obtaining a portable chest X-ray.

Roe responded that he would be right over, and instructed the resident to prepare a chest tube set up. It was a short drive to the ER without much traffic from his home in Twin Peaks to the Mission district. He made good time.

The head ER nurse greeted him and led him to the treatment cubicle. Roe drew back the curtain, and was stunned for a moment.

The jumper was Natasha. Now she's here in the same cubicle where we first met years ago in the Mission ER. The irony was inescapable. First Cody, now Natasha.

It struck Roe as paradoxical that he would meet Natasha here in such an improbable circumstance. The recurrent events were becoming uncanny. She kept popping back into his life. Periodic, strange occurrences, one after another.

He thought back to her initial seduction about five years before in this same Mission ER. Three years after that, she cared for him when he was at Clark AFB after his serious injuries in Tan Son Nhut. Then, just last year, he had met her unexpectedly at the Haight-Ashbury party They'd engaged in the second seduction, after which she revealed the identity of the Rajah as Cody, which led to his downfall in the Mission shootout earlier today.

He'd pronounced his high-school buddy DOA from multiple gunshot wounds just hours ago, thirty feet away in this very ER bed. Now almost a year following the revelation of Rajah's identity at the hippie party, Natasha had become a LSD jumper despite his warnings about drug abuse. He walked up beside her bed. "What happened, Natasha?"

"I just lost it, Roe. I never tried acid before, and I won't try it again, I assure you."

Her speech indicated she was coming down off a high, feeling little pain despite broken ribs and extremity bones. She had no difficulty breathing, a good sign she did not have a tension pneumothorax. Roe examined her and suspected the resident's diagnosis was correct. The collapsed lung was not life-threatening at this point, but she'd need a chest tube for re-expansion of the lung.

"I really thought I could fly, Roe. How silly is that? Now look at me. I'm messed up." A flush of embarrassment crept of her cheeks.

"Well, you're lucky you didn't land on your head, or break your damned fool neck, Natasha. You've broken your wrist and ankle, and suffered some fractured ribs. And, you also collapsed your lung."

"We'll get Ortho to cast you after I help the resident put the chest tube in to re-expand your lung."

"You'll have to spend a few days in the hospital. Then, I'm going to get you into a drug rehab program before you kill yourself. You're usually squared away, Natasha. Whatever possessed you to try LSD?"

"A combination of things. I've been depressed over Russia's occupation of my old homeland, Czechoslovakia for weeks. When I applied to return to nursing yesterday, I flunked the drug test. So, I have to wait awhile before they allow me to reapply. When I heard of Cody's death, I just tripped out."

"Were you doing any heavy stuff before this incident?"

"No, just smoking weed, nothing else until this acid trip.

"Not a smart choice, but Rehab can cure you, just stay away from the bad stuff, promise?"

"Okay," she meekly replied, chastised by a man she respected.

"We'll place the chest tube under the fold of your breast, so no one will notice the scar, okay?

"Thank you, Roe. I always sunbathe topless."

Natasha still had the body of Aphrodite. "I noticed your uniform tan."

Roe chatted to distract Natasha from the procedure, while his resident deftly placed the chest tube under local anesthesia. "Did you and Cody become lovers? None of my business, but just wondered."

"No," Natasha replied. "I told you before, just good friends. Some of us gals lived in his place for over two years and took care of the home. We kept it nice and neat, so it was always ready for his big parties. I met Janis Joplin who lived down the street, most of the Grateful Dead, and the members of Jefferson Airplane. Bill Hamm was a real character at the monthly parties. All of them lived in the Haight."

"Bill Hamm? The Red Dog Saloon and the Psychedelic Light Show guy?"

"Yeah, that guy. He's a hoot, quite a character."

Roe's resident completed the job, hooking the chest tube to water seal and suction to re-expand her lung. Natasha never winced. The local lidocaine anesthetic was effective.

Roe nodded to his resident. "Nice job. I'll take it from here . . . I know you've got a lot to do."

After he left, Roe turned back to his patient. "Ortho will be here soon to cast your fractures. Who will take care of you after you get out of the hospital and go home, Natasha?"

"I have some friends in the Haight who will pick me up and take me home. Will you come by for house calls?"

Roe recognized the open-ended invitation. "Better not. You are irresistible, Natasha. I got married last Thanksgiving. I've got to stick to my vows. Sorry."

"Oh. Congratulations, Roe. I'm happy for you. She's a lucky woman to have you."

"You'll find your man someday. Just stay off the drugs, okay? If you have any discomfort or pain, we'll leave orders for pain medication. Just don't get hooked on them"

***

Natasha made an uneventful recovery. Roe removed the chest tube on the second day and discharged her with a promise she would go into the drug rehab program he'd arranged for her. It was time for her to get her life together and move on.

Natasha took Roe's advice seriously this time around. She not only attended her classes, but became a patient advocate for drug rehabilitation. Her nursing license was reinstated. She then went on to become a drug rehab icon in San Francisco treating addicted hippies who wanted to beat the habit and go straight. Eventually, she became the director of the San Francisco Drug Abuse Program. Her first-hand experience with drugs gave her a certain insight into the problems encountered by the hippie generation in the sixties.

When he heard the good news. Roe was genuinely happy for Natasha. "Something good came from something bad."

CHAPTER FORTY-TWO
HILLSBOROUGH REUNION

September 1973

Although Biff and Roe had maintained contact through the years, their busy lives and professions left little time for recreation and dinners together with their wives.

It was early autumn on the peninsula, the best weather of the year. Ann suggested inviting the Roberts and their two young children, Buford VI and Caroline, to spend Sunday with them.

"Buford the Sixth?" Roe got a big kick out of that. Roe noted that the son went by the nickname, "Boo." Obviously, no one wanted to deal with a first name like "Buford." They planned doubles tennis in the afternoon at the Peninsula Tennis Club (PTC) in Burlingame, followed by dinner at their home in Hillsborough that evening. He knew the kids would be no problem, as their live-in Swedish au pair would look after the Roberts' children and their own two children, while they played. PTC featured a children's pool as well as an activity room. Everyone would be entertained. Roe thought it was a good idea and made all the arrangements with his old friend.

Biff said they would drive down from San Francisco after church and meet them sometime after noon.

"After church?" Roe asked.

"Yes, Beth has become a very religious Episcopalian," Biff replied.

"Really?"

"Yes, really, I'm not kidding. She drags me along."

"Sort of like Louie?" His comment referring to their high school prank of dragging their town drunk to a "Save the Sinner" evangelistic tent meeting.

Biff laughed. "Sort of, as I recall it changed Louie's life for the better. Maybe I'm next, Roe. Stranger things have happened, right?"

"You can say that again! Hey, we're looking forward to spending some time with you two. We haven't had a serious get-together since Tahoe."

"When was that?" Biff joked, testing his memory, still having some concerns for his pal's welfare. Their last visit demonstrated Roe's remarkable recovery.

Roe didn't even have to think about this. "November '68. Almost five years ago, Thanksgiving weekend. Recall, we went to Tahoe right after our marriage? It was a hoot. Best honeymoon I ever had!"

Biff laughed. "As I recall it was your only honeymoon, Roe."

"Looks like things are working out well for you and Ann."

"Couldn't have done any better. She's a good wife, and an even better mother to the little kids. With both of us working, we have a live-in au pair, a nice young lady from Stockholm. Her grandmother was a patient of mine when she visiting San Francisco several years ago. Now we have an endless supply of grand mom's relatives wanting to live in California for six months to a year. Sure works out nice for us. The kids love her. Her name is Helene."

"She's teaching them 'Twinkle, Twinkle Little Star' in Swedish. She's great with them. She'll look after all children while we play tennis. After that, we'll barbecue steaks at our home in Hillsborough and maybe play a game of HORSE basketball on the back patio. Are you up for that?"

"You've got it. See you Sunday, Roe. Can we bring anything?"

"Your Cohibas, I don't stock them. But, remember, you've got to smoke outside, otherwise Ann will flip out."

"Got it, partner."

Biff's Mercedes pulled up at 433 Chatham Road around noon. The good friends met on the PTC terrace behind Burlingame High School. Architecturally, the club's building wasn't the most impressive edifice, but many of the best tennis players on the peninsula belonged here.

As for local golf, you had to join Peninsula Golf and Country Club or The Burlingame Club. PTC was strictly tennis boasting a lot of nationally ranked players and former collegiate stars. The National Junior Hard Courts were held there for years. Its best feature was you could always find a game to match your level of play.

A small bar and sandwich shop was run by Lydia, who made the best tuna melts ever. The members were some of the nicest people you'd ever want to meet, successful in all walks of life.

On many occasions, Roe had encouraged Biff and Beth to join, so they'd see more of them. But, they were too tied up in the San Francisco social scene when Biff was in the country. He still traveled a lot, "spying on someone, somewhere," Roe joked.

***

They greeted each other with hugs and exchanged pleasantries. Roe informed them they were next up on court four. He was glad it wasn't court one in front of his friends. His game was rusty... too much time spent at the university hospital, not enough on the courts.

They played a tightly contested three-set match. Biff's big serve dominated them, but Roe's volley and Ann's lobs kept them in the contest. Beth returned nearly every shot. Not much pace, but always in play. She could wear you down. Biff and Beth won the match in a third set tie-breaker.

They checked on the children, who largely ignored them, fearing their parents would drag them away from the pool. The four kids really got along well and were having a lot of fun in the kiddie pool under Helene's supervision. The kids gave them the look that meant, "Just go away."

The couples enjoyed drinks by the poolside, watching them play. They engaged in small talk, catching up with their divergent lives.

Roe asked Biff if he'd heard from Al Ruey.

"Ruey is one of the 'Top Guns' at Miramar, still running the aerial combat school down there in the San Diego area, last I heard." He added that it looked like Ruey would make his star, a brigadier general. "How about that?" Biff grinned.

"That's great! Good for him."

Moments later, Roe noticed Biff's fixed gaze on the play on court one. A hot mixed doubles match was in progress between former collegiate players. They were really slamming the ball around, truly enjoying the vigorously contested match, laughing and congratulating each other on good shots.

Biff inquired, "Who's the young Asian couple, Roe?"

"That's Guy and Eva Lau, who played at Cal and USC. Terrific players, especially Eva. Guy's a bit unorthodox, but she's textbook perfect. Got a lot of talent. Watch 'em. The other couple is from Palo Alto. Both played at Stanford. They come up on some Sundays to play the Lau's. I can't recall their names, good players and nice people."

"Guy and Eva Lau? It couldn't be. I met them when they were kids playing at Cercle Sportif in Saigon. Their families were about to move to Paris: the Hsu's and the Lau's. Guy was a skinny little kid then. After their match, I'd like to say 'hi' to them. Wonder how much they recall from that period of their lives?"

"I doubt they'd forget playing at Cercle Sportif. I recall it was a posh, private club in Saigon where we had dinner once."

After the match concluded, Biff went over to introduce himself to Guy and Eva. Immediately, both recalled the Saigon connection at Cercle Sportif with their folks, just about nine or ten years ago. They all enjoyed a good laugh at the coincidence of meeting here at PTC. Biff asked them to join Roe and their wives for a round of drinks and conversation to catch up on the last few years.

Guy recounted that after the Lycee´ in Paris, and a short time at the Sorbonne, their families moved to San Mateo, California. Guy attended the University of California in Berkeley, Eva USC. After college, they married and moved to the peninsula near their parents, planning to raise their family there. They maintained their tennis skills and really enjoyed PTC, describing the membership as "so unpretentious."

After drinks and a pleasant conversation, Guy explained they were meeting the grandparents for dinner and must leave. "Nice to see you again."

"Small world!" Biff said after they departed.

Roe agreed. Amazing how coincidences pop up. Maybe there was something to the "Six Degrees of Separation" theory.

Later that afternoon, they rounded up the kids for the short drive home. Hillsborough was a leafy, affluent, hillside community three and a half miles west. Roe and Ann's home on San Raymundo Road was an attractive Spanish Mediterranean white stucco beauty with an orange-tiled roof. It was designed in 1926 by a famous Scottish architect, Angus McSweeney. It faced southwest on a two-third acre lot The property was lined with fruit and palm trees, azaleas, and ten-foot high rhododendrons. A four-foot-high old brick adobe wall surrounded the property. A manicured lawn provided play space in the front and sides for the children's games. Front and back patios provided space for the adult games. It was an ideal place to live and raise children.

Roe challenged Biff to a game of HORSE and went on to rip him. Roe had the home-court advantage, as the rim was springy and he knew you needed a lot of arch to sink a shot. Furthermore, he practiced a lot. It was an outlet for him after work.

Ann took Beth aside and asked her to consider staying overnight. They had plenty of room. By staying over, they would avoid the Sunday evening traffic into San Francisco. That would allow more time to chat, and enjoy a leisurely dinner and wine. Ann even suggested Cognac on the front patio after dinner, so Biff could smoke his Cuban cigar—a major concession for her.

Beth laughed. She agreed it was a good idea.

Done.

When Roe was in London on a cardiovascular fellowship at Great Ormond Street, Ann attended advanced cooking course, a follow-up to the introductory course on her junior year abroad. When she had time, she could prepare a feast. Tonight, it was leg of lamb. She knew Roe had suggested barbecued steak to Biff, but she'd trumped his offer, and did her own thing in style.

It was a great meal accompanied by some fine wines Biff selected from Roe's basement cellar. The authentic cellar maintained fifty-five degrees year 'round in this old Spanish Mediterranean home with thick insulating walls.

Biff selected a '64 Mouton Rothschild and a Cheval Blanc from the same year for comparison. Two of the best ever ... Biff had a good nose for wine, a true connoisseur, while Roe was still on his learner's permit.

Helene put the little ones to bed early, as they were exhausted, and helped Ann and Beth clean up.

Dessert would be served on the front patio. It was a warm evening, quite comfortable to sit outside and chat. Without hesitation, Biff lit up his Cohiba, while they all sipped a Hennessey Cognac. Helene served *crème brûlée* with a caramelized crust, a perfect end to a great meal and fun day.

After catching up on family and professional activities, the conversation turned to Vietnam, a sort of recap for them. The last time they got involved in such a discussion it continued into the wee hours at Tahoe. They all agreed to not let that happen this time.

Just as they were starting to get deeply involved in conversation, six helicopters suddenly came roaring over, flying low at tree-top level, spraying for fruit flies. The choppers' intrusion appeared suddenly, out of nowhere, without warning.

Their loud distinctive rotary sound frightened Roe, sending a shock wave of alarm through him. He experienced a sudden flashback to the Tan Son Nhut firefight. He broke into a cold sweat, panicked, and dove under the patio table, yelling frantically, "Take cover! Take cover!"

Biff, Beth, and Ann had never seen Roe act like this. They were witnessing an acute anxiety attack associated with post-traumatic stress syndrome, triggered by the low-flying helicopters.

Biff tamped out his and crawled under the table to console Roe, telling him they were spraying for fruit flies to stem an impending epidemic threatening the peninsula, not attacking his Hillsborough home.

"Get a grip, pal. It's okay. No threat. No danger."

Ann ran to the medicine cabinet to fetch a bottle of Librium Dr. Robeson had given her for an incident like this. Actually, this was Roe's first panic attack since his treatment after Vietnam. Dr. Robeson had prepared Ann for such an episode. She knew what to do.

She also crawled under the table to console Roe and give him the tranquilizer to calm him down. She would call Dr. Robeson in the morning, choosing not bother him on a Sunday night. After ten or fifteen minutes, Roe started to regain his composure. Shaken, embarrassed, he tried to pull it together as he crawled out from under the table.

"Sorry, guys. I lost it." He smiled sheepishly, brushing off his clothes. "Brought back an unpleasant memory."

The choppers were gone. No strafing occurred, no rockets launched, no firefight. He was safe.

Roe apologized profusely for his erratic behavior, ashamed at his uncontrollable reaction. Of course, everyone understood in their own way what Roe had been through in Vietnam, but had no real conception of Roe's frightening flashback experience triggered by the helicopters leading to his uncontrollable behavior. Only he could relate to that.

No one knew quite how to react, sincerely trying to be empathetic and reassuring.

"Thank God they don't fly choppers in my OR." he attempted to joke, eliciting nervous laughter. Roe tried to make light of this episode, but he knew that some dark, unpleasant memories still lurked somewhere, suppressed deep in his mind. It was a disturbing, scary thought.

What if this episode really had happened up at the University Hospital? Better talk to Murray and get some input on this situation, he thought.

The medication soon took effect, potentiated by the brandy. A relaxing wave of security and tranquility sweep over him, chasing away his anxiety. Almost magically, Roe resumed normal conversation and behavior, and again apologized to his close friends.

"No apology necessary, pal," Biff insisted. "We understand."

"Thank God."

"The choppers caught you by surprise and brought up your tragic experience at Tan Son Nhut. You couldn't help it, Roe. Dr. Robeson warned you about flashbacks. It's a reflex reaction. The sudden flyby triggered a flashback, you couldn't help that. You're among friends, okay? Relax and enjoy the rest of the evening. It's so good to get together again."

Once Roe calmed down, the four became intensely involved in dissecting the failing Vietnam War policy, recapping and reflecting on the Southeast Asia conflict.

It was amazing how Ann, once politics became the subject, could render an extemporaneous thumbnail sketch of major events with timelines and all pertinent factual data. She had encyclopedic knowledge of political science and history.

With a total command, she recited the key events since they last discussed Vietnam in Tahoe, almost five years ago.

"The first major event was LBJ's decision not to run for re-election in 1968. His popularity dwindled after losing the New Hampshire primary. The second major event was our military victory during the Tet in '68. Although we won the Vietnam battles, we lost the war at home. Our political defeat at home was characterized by anti-war protests, draft card burning, and student riots that reached their zenith late that year. Race riots occurred in big cities. Recall all that turmoil? Not a good year by any metric."

"The next major event came with Nixon's election... Nixon and Kissinger saw the handwriting on the wall. Despite 540,000 troops in South Vietnam, there was no end in sight. On Guam in 1969, Nixon pronounced his 'Doctrine' declaring that the U.S. expected its Asian allies to manage their own military defense in the future. Nixon then stepped up withdrawal of U.S. combat troops from South Vietnam, but increased the bombing of North Vietnam and Cambodia.

"This action admitted we were no longer seeking a military solution in Vietnam, but a political solution. That's my take on the no-win strategy. Meanwhile, Kissinger initiated behind-the-scenes negotiations to end the war in secret Paris talks with Le Duc Tho."

Ann was on a roll and had their rapt attention.

"The end of 1969 and early 1970 marked two other major events fueling the public fires of protest: the Mai Lai massacre by Lt. Calley's platoon, which actually had occurred the year before, but was only revealed publicly a year later."

"They couldn't bury it," Biff interjected.

"Right you are. Then, in May 1970, the Ohio National Guard killed four Kent State students while quelling an anti-war riot. You recall that America was on the verge of anarchy as a result of that unprecedented action."

They looked grimly at one another, recalling the incident.

"By the end of 1970, American combat troops had been drawn down by fifty percent to 240,000. By the end of 1971, Nixon further decreased the level to 140,000 as his doctrine accelerated troop withdrawal from Vietnam. The troop drawdowns coincided with the increased Vietnamese responsibility for conducting the war, Nixon's intent. In other words, U.S. policy reverted to the 1963 strategy where it all started! We essentially became advisors again. The South Vietnamese had to fight their own war. Over ten years later, we came full circle."

Roe thumbed the edge of his glass. "What a waste."

Ann shook her head. "No argument there. If that wasn't enough to deal with, do you remember when *The New York Times* rocked the public with the publication of the Pentagon Papers? They had the audacity to print classified information exposed by Daniel Ellsberg's report! That blockbuster development exposed years of policy flaws through JFK's, LBJ's and Nixon's administrations in their conduct of the Vietnam War. Ellsberg's report exposed and highlighted LBJ's deceit in deluding Congress and the American public."

"I could have told you that long before Ellsberg," Biff added.

"Bet you could have, Biff. Last year, in early 1972, the North Vietnamese Army crossed the DMZ to invade the South. We responded by increasing the bombing of North Vietnam, including Hanoi and Haiphong Harbor. But, the U.S. did not send combat troops into action that time to seal the deal. We were well on our way out of Vietnam, seeking political negotiations."

"Too little, too late, once again," Biff noted.

Ann held out her glass and Beth poured in more brandy. She sat slightly forward.

"The next major event occurred in June 1972, with the 'Watergate Affair' which brought about Nixon's downfall. Who could forget that fiasco?"

"No one." Biff said emphatically. "Dumb move."

"Seems it was. Meanwhile, Henry Kissinger continued to press for negotiations to end the war, including a secret meeting with Brezhnev in Moscow and Le Duc Tho again in Paris. Finally, in January of 1973, they reached an accord for a cease-fire agreement. American POWs were released from the Hanoi Hilton, including John McCain and Everett Alvarez, Navy fighter bomber pilots who had been in captivity for six to eight years after being shot down over North Vietnam."

"Sad commentary," Roe said with conviction.

"What most people would like to forget are the unintended consequences of our withdrawal from Southeast Asia. Over the next two years, after we pulled out, hundreds of thousands died, mostly in Cambodia at the hands of the vicious Khmer Rouge. Many Vietnamese who failed to escape, also perished. That's it in a nutshell. A capsule summary of a mismanaged, illogical war that we'll be discussing for years to come," Ann concluded.

Biff had listened intently. He loved Ann's systematic analysis. "What about the Domino Theory? What's your final impression?"

"Good point, it seems to me it might have been a flawed concept."

"How's that?' Biff pressed.

"My three key observations are: First, South Vietnam didn't start to fall until 1973, four years after the Nixon Doctrine put the war back in the hands of the Vietnamese. That doesn't fit the theory. Southeast Asia didn't collapse either after we left Vietnam. Second, the war in Laos lasted twice as long and ended in a coalition government. No domino effect happened there. Not to discount the tragedy, but Cambodia's genocide by the Khmer Rouge hardly fits the Domino Theory. Third, all the other SEATO countries remained intact after South Vietnam fell into communist hands."

Biff pursed his lips in thought. "How do you explain that? Shouldn't we totally disregard the Domino Theory? When Vietnam fell, all of Southeast Asia did not topple like dominoes as predicted as you pointed out."

"It's not that simple, Biff," Ann quickly countered. "That proposition takes out of consideration several major world events occurring in the ten-year interval between 1965 and 1975 that greatly influenced the outcome in Indochina. It could be argued that our involvement in Vietnam bought time for the world to transform in a positive direction geopolitically, all changes favoring U.S. interests."

"Interesting concept. Please elaborate on that."

"My thinking is influenced by two prominent historians: Mark Moyar and H. R. McMaster. I essentially agree with their assessment. It's not revisionist history. It's good deductive reasoning on their part, in my view."

"So, what is your interpretation of the situation and the events?"

"The key argument against the Domino Theory is that the Eisenhower and JFK administrations were wrong in their basic assumption. The contrarians maintain that the dominoes were not in danger of toppling in the early 1960s because the dominoes didn't fall in 1975 when the South Vietnamese government fell to the communists of North Vietnam. But, this may be fuzzy thinking on their part... Despite flawed policies, the U.S. attained its objective of containing communism's spread in Southeast Asia with its intervention in Vietnam, not so much by the effectiveness of our policies, but mostly by buying important time for other significant changes to occur elsewhere. These interval changes significantly influenced the outcome in Southeast Asia's containment of communism."

"Interesting point. Any pertinent examples?" Biff asked politely, knowing Ann never made claims she could not back up.

"Several, in fact. One of the most important events was the cultural Chinese revolution diminishing China's threat to the region. The overthrow of Sukarno in Indonesia represented another contributing factor. Third, Britain prevailed in its Malaysian conflict, another key factor in thwarting communism's spread in Southeast Asia."

"Convincing argument." Biff conceded. Biff reflected on her valuable contributions to their joint intelligence conferences years ago. *She hasn't lost a step, still sharp as a tack!*

Ann smiled. In her element, she enjoyed every minute of the intellectual stimulus and debate over a contentious topic.

Ann continued with zest. "The Sino-Soviet rift was very material in modifying the Russian and Chinese outlook on Southeast Asia. Another important influence was Nixon's détente with USSR and China. All of these represent seminal historic events impacting the outcome in the region.

She asked if they recalled how the wars in Vietnam, Laos, and Cambodia went on for over ten years without affecting Thailand, Singapore, the Philippine Islands and other major SEATO nations' democratic forms of government. After that long period of war, the Southeast Asian countries were certainly more capable of protecting themselves from the spread of communism. More importantly, they possessed the commitment and determination, as well as the will power to do so. On the other side, by 1975 China and the Soviets were disinclined to pursue their original goal of the early sixties, which was communist domination in Southeast Asia. Times change, perspectives and objectives change. Simple as that, Biff."

"That's a good way to look at it. Very compelling, hard to argue against your comprehensive overview. Great summation."

Biff glanced over to Roe, who remained very quiet. "How are you doing over there, Roe old buddy?"

Roe had calmed down and recovered. He was enjoying the discussion, quietly sitting with Beth. Still slightly embarrassed about his reaction to the helicopters, he realized it was a flashback reflex that he had no control over.

"I'm fine, Biff. Sorry I got so spooked. Glad I was among close friends."

"Please stop apologizing, Roe. We all understand your situation. Dr. Robeson said it's a process. You'll get over it. It'll just take some time, pal."

"I certainly hope so," Roe replied. "Please continue the discussion. I find it very interesting to try to understand our role in Vietnam."

"Okay. Where were we, Ann?"

"Well, just to wrap this up. In retrospect, JFK and Eisenhower got us involved, but LBJ got us mired over there. Mired, as in 'quagmire,' an apt description coined by Clark Clifford."

"No argument there," Biff said.

"LBJ based his decisions on Maxwell Taylor's graduated pressure strategy, which some authorities brand as a lack of strategy. McNamara's rosy interpretations and system analysis programs gave LBJ false assurance that things were going well over in Vietnam. Late in the war, Westmoreland 'saw the light at the end of the tunnel,' but it was an oncoming train."

Everyone laughed at her humor, especially since she rarely joked.

"Westmoreland was a famous general accustomed to conventional warfare, not guerrilla conflicts. Vietnam ill-suited his military experience. The outcomes speak for themselves."

"Ouch!" Biff exclaimed.

Ann just smiled "Link his shortcoming up with the South Vietnamese government's ineptitude, and add five coups d' etats ... what expectations do you have? With each successive Saigon leader as ineffectual as the other, you have a grand recipe for disaster. It's debatable that we may or may not have avoided the dismal outcome with a sound strategy, but it's all a matter of opinion. Time will tell."

She sipped the last of her Cognac. "LBJ falsely believed he could control the level of U.S. involvement in Vietnam. He was wrong, very wrong. This concept represented his fatal flaw. The unfolding events in Vietnam controlled him, always placing him in a reactionary position. He practiced self-imposed restraints throughout the entire war, never taking the initiative with full commitment. He mastered half measures."

Biff raised both hands above his head. "Hear, hear."

Ann leaned forward for emphasis. "LBJ compounded his policy errors by disregarding the advice of the Joint Chiefs of Staff, the National Security Council, and the Joint Intelligence Services time after time. LBJ ignored the experts, those with real-time war experience. Why? Because he simply disregarded advice he did not want to hear. Advice that might interfere with his personal domestic programs and political fortunes. Frankly, LBJ was disingenuous with the American public at best, a deceitful liar at the worst."

"Pretty strong words for a lady, Ann," Biff jested, though he agreed entirely.

"The truth hurts. The war was not lost on Vietnam battlefields, or in the media, or in the street protests. Not even by college campus riots, as many thought, including me. Earlier, I took that viewpoint. Vietnam was lost in two places, worlds apart."

She paused.

"The war was lost at the hamlet and village level in Vietnam, and in Washington DC. As a result of stubborn inaction, one bad decision after another, the inability to correctly analyze, and properly action intelligence data, the administration failed. But, most importantly, the war was lost because of human frailty, arrogance, selfishness, and failure to uphold the top office's prime responsibility—to protect the best interests of the American people."

"Wow! Well spoken, Ann," Biff complimented.

Roe inclined his head, and smiled widely at his wife. "Very impressive analysis."

Ann tilted her head and shrugged slightly. "This is what we do at Hoover, Biff. Think it out. Logic is our template. Reason prevails."

The four good friends had one more nightcap of Cognac. Biff slipped outside and lit another cigar, out on the terrace, of course. They turned in at ten o'clock. The kids had already been asleep for two hours. Helene had left the kitchen and dining room spotless.

***

Times indeed had changed. They were family people now with children to raise and jobs to do. The strong bond between them would last forever, most of it unspoken.

It was interesting that after that night's lengthy discussion, the painful subject of Vietnam rarely came up again, and if it did, only in a passing comment or two. It seems they finally got the confusing and confounding topic of Vietnam out of their systems. That allowed them to pursue other goals in life, spend time on more fruitful family and professional life pursuits. It had been a long journey, but they reached their destination.

For others, however, particularly the progressive political faction, the Vietnam War psyche lingered on for decades. Some, psychologically scarred, never got over it. Many remained conflicted to this day.

The "Vietnam syndrome" still affects American politics, society, culture, and life in general more than five decades later. Whoever said "time heals all wounds" did not consider Vietnam.

EPILOGUE

The Vietnam War's aftermath led to ingrained mindsets and perpetuated confused perceptions lasting decades and into the present. It's difficult to unravel the complex issues, determine what's relative, what's credible in the fog of a war with so many conflicting versions and opinions preserved in the archives and historical literature. Authored by war hawks and anti-war doves, both sides advocate divergent worldviews. Attitudes die hard and reflect the way people behave after perceiving the same event and reaching a different interpretation. Often contradictory viewpoints clash despite authors striving for objectivity. I'm certain to be accused of bias. Naturally, my experience and research influenced my opinions. I offer no apologies. Everyone is entitled to their opinion, but not their facts. I've carefully checked mine and will stand by them.

There are "Lies, damn lies, and statistics." This quote popularized by Mark Twain, is attributed to British Prime Minister Benjamin Disraeli's allusion to the persuasive power of numbers.

Pick your choice, take any number, and stand in the long opinion line. Find a number that fits your perspective from the broad range of choices. The Vietnam era offers three categories of lies: deception, disinformation, and shameless prevarication. Many are supported by numbers to mask their lack of veracity. Don't be misled. Do some critical thinking before making your selection. It's difficult to get comfortable with three shades of lies, but politicians seem not to have any trouble managing all three categories.

Fortunately, the truth eventually comes out despite the cover-up, which is often worse than the original transgression.

The most egregious example of LBJ's ignominious behavior and duplicity came to light in 1980 almost twenty years after the bombing of North Vietnam commenced. War correspondent, Peter Arnett of CBS interviewed LBJ's former Secretary of State Dean Rusk in a Canadian documentary, *The Ten Thousand Day War.*

Rusk confessed that he and Defense Secretary Robert McNamara provided the North Vietnam government the list of targets the U.S. planned to bomb the next day. Our detailed aerial attack plans were relayed through the Swiss Embassy in DC to their Swiss Embassy in Hanoi. Rusk attempted to justify this policy by saying the National Security Council wanted to demonstrate to North Vietnam that America could strike at will, but wanted to avoid killing innocent people causing collateral damage. A utopian goal on paper, but untenable, impractical, and not well thought-through for real life solutions. Typical of DC's naïve and fuzzy thinking.

There are no noble wars, just noble warriors. LBJ's administration's flawed policy vainly attempted to conduct a "noble" war, one at great risk of putting our pilots in harm's way. The reckless nature of telegraphing of our bombing raids ignored the peril to our flyers, the "noble warriors." LBJ once bragged our air force could not bomb an outhouse without his approval. On another occasion, he stated wars were too important to leave decisions with generals. That is the essence of astounding conceit and arrogance.

Those pompous statements should leave no doubt LBJ was onboard with this contemptible "tip off" policy instituted by Rusk and McNamara. Many principled critics would consider it an act of treason. If not, they should. Where was the outrage? MIA? Like the fate many pilots suffered as a consequence of this deceitful policy?

Our pilots soon suspected the enemy had foreknowledge of their objectives, facing heavily fortified ground fire upon arrival at their classified missions' targets in North Vietnam. Not without reason, the enemy possessed inside information. It was not an uncanny coincidence. North Vietnamese intelligence was not that good.

The telegraphing of proposed classified bombing missions represented a reprehensible betrayal of our military by LBJ's administration, an irresponsible, despicable perfidy, if not treason.

There is no final reckoning of how much this outrageous folly contributed to our loss of aircraft and crews. Or, how many POWs or MIAs resulted from the cause/effect of the betrayal of classified information. Or, how much the LBJ administration's deceit contributed to the following statistics. Documents verify that ten percent of Vietnam War mortalities were associated with aircraft fatalities.

1961–1973: USAF/USN/USMC

Fixed wing aircraft losses – 3,222
Pilot/crew fatality – 3,365
POWs – 497
MIA – Statistical and accounting discrepancies exist, but MIAs are estimated as high as 1,800
Helicopter / Rotary aircraft loss – 5,086
Pilot and crew member fatality – 2,251 / 2,275
POW – 766 (114 died in captivity)
Helicopter MIAs – 2,338
Summary: 44,000 air crews served in Vietnam with a mortality of 0.4/1,000 sorties.

Many pilots were shot down by heavily defended targets, including former Navy pilot/ Senator John McCain who spent almost six years in the "Hanoi Hilton," Ho Lo prison. Medal of Honor Admiral Jim Stockdale, captured in '65, endured torture for more than seven years. Everett Alvarez, the first pilot captured, endured more than eight years of captivity. LBJ's administration policy to remain mum regarding the abysmal treatment of our POWs added insult to their injury.

Dean Rusk attempted to pass off this misguided policy as a morally honorable cause. It was most certainly not. Collateral damage is part and parcel of war. PC is not. War is Hell, remember? Security of our pilots and air crews should have been the moral imperative, the top priority. Rhetorically, did Geneva conventions prevail in NVN where torture of POW pilots was a rampant practice?

Signaling the enemy our proposed targets twenty-four hours in advance is inexcusable. A crime that put our military at great hazard.

Rusk's shameful confession remained buried for years. Where was the public outrage? Why did our free press fail to expose this policy's treachery? Policy's exposure by our free press? The silence of the fourth estate of democracy was deafening.

Those elite pundits who exposed Nixon's misadventures at Watergate were MIA, never publishing accounts of the LBJ administration's crime. Never condemned this appalling circumstance a decade earlier. How did such contemptible, irresponsible behavior by our country's leadership escape public exposure for so long? Nixon's crimes at Watergate and the cover-up pale in comparison. The contrast in duplicity is earthshaking, the disparity mindboggling. The punishment didn't fit the crime. There is no moral equivalent between treason and a petty political crime and cover-up. No one died as a consequence of Watergate.

Nixon had his flaws, but after he unleashed the "dogs of war" in December 1972 with heavy bombing of previously restricted targets in North Vietnam, the massive damage to infrastructure in Hanoi and Haiphong forced the resumption of negotiations to end the war within ten days.

Operation "Linebacker II" was not "too little," but "too late." But, it gave a glimpse of the efficacy of bombing strategic targets previously "off limits" for years under LBJ's policy. This operation offered a reflection of what might have been if that tactic was instituted early on in the war, as the CIA and many senior military officers advised.

JFK and LBJ's administrations too often disregarded the normal chain of command in conducting the war. In Vietnam, MACV and CINCPAC referred military recommendations based on conditions in the field to the JCS, who sent it up the chain to the NSC, who advised POTUS and his staff. CIA Intelligence estimates were often shelved, which further limited military options. JFK had his Whiz Kids, "the best and the brightest." LBJ had his "system analysis" experts. They ran the war, called the plays while the generals and admirals were relegated to the sidelines. For better or worse, Nixon cleaned up the mess.

Lesson learned: politicians should not attempt to micromanage wars. Leave strategies and tactics to professions trained for that job.

By the early '70s, public opinion dictated it was time to end the war. Nixon did so without telegraphing the targets like LBJ's administration did. To his credit, he forced the "unwinnable war" to wind down in a short period of time.

Hindsight is always 20/20, but it's never too late to assess our decision-making process in matters of vital national concern. Societies disinclined to learn the lessons of history are condemned to repeat the same mistakes over generations ... almost as if their leaders suffered some sort of learning disability, a historical blind spot. Experience often proves to be the best teacher. Why not learn from it?

Declassified CIA intelligence reports regarding Vietnam reveal an elemental understanding of this observation that has been around for some time. Santayana pointed out this tragic pitfall of human nature in the Spanish philosopher's *Life of Reason* in 1905. Seems this common sense logic didn't sink in during the Vietnam strategy sessions. Our leaders failed the nation and our military, who paid the ultimate price of misguided policy.

False assumptions and nebulous reasoning lead to poor outcomes in both war and peace. Case in point, Vietnam is a classic study of teachable moments and unintended consequences resulting from inept action or inaction. History has established some basic fundamentals. Those lacking appreciation of history's axioms will not heed them and will eventually pay a price for ignoring their empirical value. Leaders incapable of rational deliberation of the inherent value of past experience will suffer the consequences of poor judgment, as will the nation.

Good judgment comes from experience, but much of it is derived from bad experience. Unfortunately, that is rarely the optimum way to learn and achieve positive outcomes. You could argue Vietnam was a bad experience. Did we learn anything of value? Does Iraq or Afghanistan come to mind?

We fought the VN war with a WWII, strategic, frontal-war mentality, with many generals fighting the last war, not the next. General Westmorland and others suffered that mindset. VN was an asymmetrical conflict, a guerrilla war. General Abrams realized that, but arrived too late to alter the course. The die was cast, the Rubicon crossed, no going back.

Case in point, it's tempting to see Vietnam as a parallel with our wars in the Middle East, Iraq, and Afghanistan. They share similarities. When will we learn that wars require a well-defined cause, not a pretext to become involved? Maintain a strong national interest and will to prevail? Employ precise strategies to attain a swift and lasting victory?

America has proven it has no patience for protracted wars of attrition. The enemy is well aware of that fact. They are not stupid, they are willing to wait us out. They think in terms of decades and centuries. That's why our objectives must be clear. Victory must be defined in terms everyone can understand. Why can't we seem to comprehend these fundamental tenets? Learn from them? And, put them to judicious and productive use?

The public malaise following the Vietnam War resulted in a severe ideological polarization that has smoldered for generations up to the present in some respects. Take a look at the political fabric of America today. We are a country seriously divided, civility in tatters, longing for proper leadership to define us as a nation.

The passion following Vietnam never entirely flamed out. It continues to simmer. The war's aftermath seemed to scar America's psyche, resulting in a national PTSD of sorts. We still suffer a psychological condition characterized by recurrent antagonistic themes, obviously difficult for the nation to resolve, get over, and move on. Vietnam was not a proud or sanguine period in our history. Few positives came out of the conflict. Two nations were damaged. The era still remains controversial, still ignites arguments and triggers resentments. Have we lost sight of our guiding principles?

What happened to our moral compass? Our leadership? America was betrayed by non-productive rhetoric and ill-conceived ideas.

In the real-world, policy counts more than ideas, actions speak louder than words, and results matter more than intentions.

"Victory has a thousand fathers, but defeat is an orphan." A JFK quote following the "Bay of Pigs" fiasco in Cuba, 1961.

War is a weapon, use it wisely. Historian Bernard Lewis observed a decade ago regarding the Middle East conflicts, "In 1940, we knew who we were, we knew who the enemy was, we knew the dangers and the issues… It is different today. We don't know who we are, we don't know the issues, and we still do not understand the nature of the enemy."

That well-spoken statement could be relevant and appropriate to our Vietnam involvement more than a half a century ago.

CREDITS AND DEDICATIONS

High school football buddies:

Brigadier General Al Huey, Marine Corps A-4 and F-4 Fighter pilot (Deceased)

Major Frank Pettyjohn, Army, Nha Trang Special Ops CTZ III (Deceased)

Medical/Surgical Colleagues:

Dr. Mark Congress - Army Captain, MC, CTZ IV, wounded in action (WIA)

Dr. John Baldwin - Army Lt. Col, MC, CTZ II

Dr. Jim Morrison - Army Captain, MC, CTZ II (Deceased)

Tennis Buddies:

Lt. Eric Schmidt - Army platoon leader CTZ III, (WIA) near Parrot's Beak, Cambodian border, Tay Ninh Province

Lt. Col. Bob Stirm - USAF F-105 fighter pilot, Udorn AFB Thailand. POW. [He was pictured in a famous *Life* magazine cover, showing his family rushing across Travis AFB tarmac to greet him after his release from Hanoi Hilton - POW camp—a snapshot capturing the joy of a returning Vietnam vet.]

Golf Buddies:

Lt. Col. Dennis Grose - Marine A-4 Fighter pilot, Chu Lai CTZ I

Master Sergeant Roy Hall - Army MC, Chu Lai CTZ I Medic, (WIA)

ACKNOWLEDGMENT

Book Shepherd Ann N. Videan – my editor, who was a taskmaster in editing this long fictional historical narrative. The military jargon and acronyms drove her to the edge, but she persevered in taking on my long-term project of describing my characters' immersion in the Vietnam experience and the aftermath in 1960s San Francisco. I truly appreciate her quality effort in helping me put the story into a perspective. It will enable readers to learn a great deal about that period of history, while following the characters' compelling journey through this turbulent time of American history.

OTHER PUBLICATIONS BY R. LAWSON

Cabo Caper
Killing Time
Retribution
Existential Threats
The Carrington Prophecy

For more information, please visit www.RLawsonAuthor.com.

Made in the USA
Columbia, SC
31 October 2017